KILLING

ELLIOT FINER

Published 2020

PROLOGUE

THURSDAY 29 SEPTEMBER

The young man in Utilities Section 3 stood up, stretched and looked across the open-plan office, which had the dimensions of a low-ceilinged sports hall. He gazed at the satisfyingly complex pattern formed by the dozens of blue privacy screens. The hum of computers, the clicking of keyboards and the murmured exchanges of other officers made him feel calm and secure.

He settled back to work, but suddenly jerked upright and listened intently. He pressed a few keys and listened again. He whipped off his headphones and strode round to Utilities Section 2, where his colleague was absorbed in her screen. He tapped her on the shoulder.

She turned to him. 'Sorry,' she said, 'I was…'

'No worries. Can I borrow you a moment?'

'Sure. What for?'

'I'd like you to listen to something, if that's ok. I want to check I haven't misunderstood.'

He led the way back to his cubicle. She sat at his desk, donned the headphones and nodded to him. He pressed a key.

'You didn't tell me it was in French,' she said. She concentrated, and then her eyes widened. 'Bloody hell!'

'Well?'

'He said that this would cause the worst dispute with England since Napoleon.'

MONDAY 10 OCTOBER

Mark Redstone swung open the laboratory door and lurched in, panting heavily. The benches were covered with electronic equipment and glassware, shining in the bright light from the plate glass windows.

'Morning!' said David Pepper cheerfully, looking up from a microscope. 'Ran up the stairs again?'

'Yes,' Redstone gasped.

'Must be – er – a hundred and twelve steps. Well done!'

'No, it's a hundred and eighteen. You assumed each flight's sixteen steps, but the ground floor's ceiling is higher than the rest.' He took a deep breath. 'Poor data. Bad science. You're fired.'

'You can't fire me – I don't work here. You fired me last Friday for saying that I preferred opera to jazz.'

'Oh, ok. You're rehired, with a ten per cent rise.'

'Great. That makes it 11p an hour.'

Redstone smiled and weaved through the lab. Two young women mumbled greetings and carried on staring at their computers. A small group of men and women were huddled around an array of grey boxes and coloured wires and tubes, in deep conversation, and didn't notice him.

He entered his PA's airy, untidy office. Joanne, a cheerful woman with greying hair, wearing a loose black jumper and a white multi-stranded necklace, was leafing through a pile of papers. They exchanged greetings, and he walked through into his own office, settled at his PC and started going through his emails. Joanne came in bearing a mug of tea.

'Thanks, just the job,' he said. 'Have a good weekend? How did the celebration go?'

'Very well, thanks. We had a great time. The grandchildren loved it. How about you?'

'Er… Fine, thanks.'

She rolled her eyes and gave a theatrical sigh. 'I take it you didn't…' The phone rang in her office. 'I'd better answer it,' she said, hurrying out.

She buzzed Redstone's phone. 'A woman called Jill Totteridge wants to speak to you. She says she's the cabinet secretary's personal assistant. I'll put her through.'

'Just a min… oh, ok.'

His phone clicked. 'Morning, Dr Redstone. My name's Jill, and I work for Sir Dominic Malvern, the cabinet secretary.'

'Yes, I know him.'

'Of course. I'm phoning on his behalf. He asks if you could come to see him urgently, here at 70 Whitehall.'

'What about?'

'He asked me to tell you it's a matter of utmost importance, but he can't say more outside the Cabinet Office building. Are you free to come round at noon today?'

'Afraid not. Please tell him I've got another engagement.'

'Oh. Can you make any other time this afternoon?'

'No, sorry. I'm really busy. Please thank him for the invitation. Bye.' He put the phone down.

Joanne bustled in. 'That was a bit abrupt. Why did you refuse to see him?'

'I just didn't want to.'

'Come on. You can do better than that.'

'He's…'

Joanne's phone rang. 'Sorry,' she said, rushing out.

Redstone's phone buzzed. 'It's Sir Dominic Malvern himself this time!' She switched him through.

'Hello, Mark. How are you?'

'Fine, thanks, but frankly, I'm surprised you're phoning me.'

'Well, I…' Malvern cleared his throat. 'Something's come up, and the government needs your help. It's extremely important, and obviously I wouldn't bother you otherwise. Could you come in to discuss it?'

'What's it about?'

'It's extremely sensitive, and I can't go into it on the phone. It's of national importance. Can you please come round?'

'I'm afraid I'm busy.'

'Look, you haven't heard what I'll be able to tell you if you come here.'

'True, but that doesn't stop me being busy.'

'Mark, I know you must… please think carefully about this. You can't refuse just like that.'

'Oh?'

'You know I wouldn't be bothering you unless it really mattered. Don't just dismiss this out of hand, just because of the past.'

'But the past is hardly something I can dismiss, is it? You can hardly expect me to agree to help you, given what…'

'Are you saying you refuse to help the government, without knowing what the problem is, and even though I've told you it's a major issue?'

'No doubt you remember that I used to try to help the government every day, till you suddenly gave me the boot.'

'Look, I'm… let's not go there. This is a unique problem. At least come round and listen to what I can tell you if you're here in person.'

'I don't see why…'

'Let's be clear. Are you rejecting my request?'

Redstone felt this was a surprisingly formal thing to say in this context, and had a flash of insight. 'Are you recording this?'

'I never record my phone calls.'

'Oh, of course – your PA's listening and making notes. Hi, Jill!'

'Please stop playing games. For the last time, will you come here, or are you saying no?'

Redstone hesitated. 'How about you coming here? I'm near University College.'

'Sorry, the security aspects mean I can discuss this issue only in the Cabinet Office.'

Redstone sighed. 'Oh, ok. I'll be there at noon.'

'Right. Er… good. See you then.'

Redstone replaced the phone as Joanne walked back in. 'Shall I order you a taxi?' she said. 'Or will you now be travelling in a fleet of limousines with motorcycle outriders, given your new circumstances?'

'Tempting, but I'll go by tube. Today, anyway.'

*

Redstone came out of Leicester Square tube station and trudged down Charing Cross Road, weaving through groups of people standing outside the theatres and tacky souvenir shops. He made his way across the Trafalgar Square crossings amongst a throng of pedestrians and walked slowly down Whitehall. The grand stone edifices and elegant brick buildings for once failed to inspire him. The road was full of slow-moving red buses. He entered 70 Whitehall through a pair of unprepossessing black doors and checked in at the reception desk.

He went to a group of chairs and sat down, gripping the chair arms and feeling the edges of the wood pressing into his palms. He looked around the lobby. Why was he putting himself through what he knew was going to be a highly unpleasant experience? He couldn't see any advantage. Malvern's wishes were of no significance to him anymore. He decided to make some excuse to the receptionist and return to London Bio.

As he stood up, a young woman, exuding energy, pushed into the reception area through a narrow revolving glass door and walked over. 'Hi – I'm Jill,' she said, shaking his hand. 'Please follow me – put this badge on the reader and then squeeze through the security door.' Before he had time to respond, she had gone back through the door. He followed.

They walked down a nondescript office corridor and up some stone stairs, where the corridor suddenly became a tastefully restored Tudor passage with exposed red brickwork, windows overlooking a garden, and a flagstone floor.

'I've always loved this part of the building,' he said.

'Yes, me too. I suppose you came here now and then when you were a civil servant.'

'I did.' He cleared his throat. 'Jill, I owe you an apology. I was pretty rude on the phone. Sorry.'

She looked surprised. 'I don't recall your being rude – but it's kind of you to apologise anyway.'

They entered a dingy room with a narrow, incongruously modern steel lift door in the corner. She called the lift and gestured Redstone inside. It creaked up slowly. Her perfume scented the air, and the forced intimacy created an awkward atmosphere. Neither spoke. The door opened, and they stepped out into a scruffy waiting area, furnished with assorted battered dining chairs upholstered in sagging brown cracked leather.

'Please take a seat. I'll tell Sir Dominic you're here.' She disappeared through one of three doors.

Redstone hadn't been in this part of the Cabinet Office before, though he had attended several meetings in this building when he was a Department of Energy official. He thought of the cabinet secretary as the spider at the centre of the gigantic complex web which was the government machine. Except that Malvern didn't eat lesser civil servants who got stuck in the web. Or maybe it was a good metaphor – look what Malvern had done to him, admittedly before becoming cabinet secretary. Redstone half-smiled – he had escaped from the web, injured but not eaten, and had recovered and thrived in the freedom of life outside the web. Well, except for... but that was nothing to do with the job.

He'd enjoyed the complex challenges of civil service work, but it was a huge relief that he could now make decisions and get things done without having to stick to bookshelves of rules and consult hundreds of other people. And he felt so comfortable amongst his London Bio colleagues. They were like family.

And then there had been the difficulty of the dual hierarchy – serving ministers, with their political agendas, while at the same time reporting up the civil service management chain, with their career-focused priorities. He thought he'd done better at the former than the latter. Ninety-nine per cent of issues were non-political, so his own opinions rarely, if ever, got in the way, and he always respected that ministers had stood for election, which he would never have the guts to do. Ministers liked the fact that he had outside experience and that he understood technical issues.

On the other hand, some senior civil servants had felt his background was unsuitable for a senior policy official. He supposed he'd been too dismissive of the subtleties he would have acquired had he studied classics or history or literature rather than chemistry. And a few of the top officials had pursued agendas which seemed to him personal and disloyal, which had caused tensions. All behind him now, thank goodness.

How long would he have to wait before Malvern called him in? The last time he'd waited to see Malvern, six years ago, the meeting had turned out to be his deeply humiliating and completely unexpected sacking. But this was different. He wasn't now in Malvern's power. And it seemed that Malvern needed him, though God knew what for. So why was he so nervous?

He took out his phone and tried to browse through his emails but found it difficult to concentrate. Squaring his shoulders, he took several deep breaths. He returned to his emails.

After some time, he looked at his watch. He'd never been kept waiting like this when he was a civil servant – people might have been long-winded and occasionally inefficient, but they were also courteous and thoughtful. He stood up and wandered around. He counted the different styles of chairs. He calculated the volume of the room. He tried to estimate the weight of rain falling on the building in a year.

He knew there was a door somewhere near here which allowed the cabinet secretary direct personal access to Number 10, which backed onto the Cabinet Office. Was it that one in the corner? He recalled the route he'd taken to get to this room, figured out exactly where he was and concluded that door might well be the one.

He looked at his watch again, grunted and stood up. He went to a different door, the one through which Jill had disappeared, and opened it to find himself faced with a cluttered office containing Jill and three other people at desks, crammed together.

'Hi. My appointment was at noon, and it's now half past. What's going on?'

Jill stood up. 'Sorry, I did tell Sir Dominic you're here. He's a busy man. I'll remind him.'

'Jill, I know the delay isn't your fault, but I can't just hang around here. Perhaps I shouldn't have… well, I'll wait another couple of minutes, but then I've got to go.' He walked out and sat down again. He searched for something to occupy his mind, and tried to remember what it was like walking in the Alps with Kate.

Five long minutes later, he checked his watch and breathed a sigh of relief. He got up, made his way back to the reception area and walked out into the bright noisy street. He should never have agreed to the meeting, and felt as though a weight had been lifted off his head. He started to stride up Whitehall.

After only a few seconds, he heard his name being called. He turned and saw Jill running towards him.

'Please come back!' she panted. 'Sir Dominic won't keep you waiting any longer. You've come all this way.' She struggled to catch her breath.

Redstone hesitated. 'Look,' he said. 'I came only because Dominic made it sound particularly important, but now it seems that it wasn't important enough to figure high in his priorities. That's fair enough, and I understand that he's probably got bigger fish to fry, but I do have to get back to work.'

'Please! I do understand, but I'll be in trouble if you don't go back.'

'Oh… ok. But if there's any further delay, I will have to return to my lab.'

They retraced their steps back to the anteroom, but this time Jill ushered him through a door which opened to a second, inner door, leading into the cabinet secretary's office. The room was panelled in light oak, and two of the walls were lined with bookshelves in the same wood. An old-fashioned desk straddled a corner next to a window, and an ugly group of two boxy grey armchairs and a sofa occupied the centre of the room. Redstone supposed that Malvern had better things to do than put effort into making his office a pleasant place. Like managing the whole government machine.

Malvern stood up and walked from behind the desk. Something about his thin face and round glasses made him look as though he had been transported from a century ago. Redstone resisted the temptation to look for a bowler hat hanging somewhere.

Malvern looked at Redstone expressionlessly. 'Thanks for coming. Sorry for the delay. You know what it's like.'

'Er – no, I don't know what it's like, actually.'

'I do apologise. I had to deal with some urgent cabinet business. About EU farm policy. The Commission has… well, never mind. Please have a seat and help yourself to coffee.'

They sat in awkward silence for a moment. Malvern cleared his throat. 'I understand you've come into a bit of money recently.'

'You make it sound as though I came into an inheritance. That's not what happened.'

Malvern fiddled with the folder in his hands but said nothing.

'Some colleagues and I formed a company and invested in developing an idea,' said Redstone. 'It paid off.'

'That's excellent. Um – I understand your work is something to do with injections.'

Redstone knew that Malvern would have been fully briefed. What was he up to? This wasn't the subtle, assured man he remembered. 'Our invention is a way to deliver drugs through the skin without using a needle. Have you ever had an injection in the roof of your mouth at the dentist's?'

Malvern grimaced and looked down at his folder. He lifted the corner and glanced at a typewritten page. Redstone glimpsed '*Top Secret*' at the top.

'Can we please get down to business?' asked Redstone. 'Why did you want to see me?'

Malvern clutched his hands together. 'A particularly important job has come up. It's thought you'd do it well.'

Redstone waited for Malvern to say more.

'The job requires some specific talents and expertise, which you apparently have. It would be a limited-term appointment.'

'What does that mean? How long?'

'At present, we're not sure.'

'You can't expect me to take on something open-ended. I've got a company to run.'

'I'm afraid you wouldn't be able to do that while you were working for us. But you'd have the satisfaction of knowing you're doing the country a great service.'

'How many days a week, then?'

'I can't say.'

'I'm being silly. Why are we talking about how much time it would take when you haven't told me what the job is?'

'It's highly sensitive, and I'll need you to agree to take it on and sign some special confidentiality agreements before we can go further.'

'You won't even give me a clue?'

'We'd like you to help investigate a hugely important issue which is so sensitive that even the possibility of its existence can't be revealed. You'd be working with two government departments. The issue may turn out to be a non-issue, but if it's real, it'll need... well, I can't say any more at this stage. What's more, what I've just said is covered by the Official Secrets Act, so please don't reveal it to anyone else.'

Redstone smiled. 'You realise what you just said sounded like a scene from an episode of *Yes Minister*?'

'The reason *Yes Minister* was such a successful series was that it was based on real life.'

'Yes, but it was still satire. Actually, this whole thing sounds more like the bastard child of *Yes Minister* and *Catch Twenty-Two*.'

Malvern flushed. Redstone realised that the cabinet secretary was unused to being challenged, let alone hearing someone poke fun at his words. The whole conversation was unusual; Malvern would never normally spout such rubbish. Unexpectedly, Redstone felt he had the upper hand. Why was Malvern behaving like this?

'Sorry if I offended you,' Redstone said. 'Is everything ok? I sense there's something...'

'Yes, everything's fine,' Malvern snapped. 'Let's stick to the subject. Will you do the job?'

'Who would I be reporting to? You?'

'Yes.' He held Redstone's stare.

Redstone leaned forward. 'How much would you pay me?'

'I'm afraid we couldn't pay you anything. You decided to take redundancy when you left the civil service, with the result that we can't re-employ you. In any case, what we might have been able to pay wouldn't matter to you, given your new financial circumstances.'

'When you suddenly sacked me, you said my experience and skills weren't what the civil service needed. Right?'

'I… let's not revisit the past. Anyway, things evidently turned out well for you.'

'That's not the point. You're now saying the civil service needs me. What's changed?'

'Let's concentrate on this job. Will you take it?'

'Are you joking? You won't pay me. I have to stop running London Bio, which I love and which is bringing real benefits to lots of people. And you want me to agree to this job of yours without my knowing what it is. Or how long it would take.'

'You know how things work here,' said Malvern. 'I'm constrained by the system.'

'I thought the cabinet secretary was in charge of the system.'

'Look, Mark, the government needs this job to be done. As I said, you're thought to be the ideal person to do it. I must press you to put the greater good above your own wishes.'

'But you haven't told me what this greater good is!'

'I'm afraid I have to repeat that the security issues mean I can't reveal anything at this stage.'

'In that case, I'm sorry, Dominic, but the answer's no. I don't suppose that surprises you.' Redstone stood up.

'Well, I'm disappointed you won't consider taking on this task. I hope you'll go back and reconsider. Time's pressing, so if you do change your mind, please get in touch immediately.' Malvern walked to the door.

Don't hold your breath, Redstone thought, but said, 'Thanks for the coffee,' as he opened the inner door. Jill simultaneously opened the outer door.

'I'll escort you out,' she said.

They waited for the lift. 'Amazing how you happened to open the door just as I was leaving,' said Redstone. 'Anyone would believe you listen to what's happening in the cabinet secretary's office.'

'What an interesting thought,' she said.

Redstone exited the Cabinet Office with a spring in his step. He decided to return via Piccadilly Circus. He pushed through the crowds in Horse Guards and strode along the edge of St James's Park, past bright flower beds to the Duke of York steps, enjoying the stretching of the muscles in his legs. He weaved through the small groups of tourists who were sitting on the steps, eating, talking and consulting their phones. His mind churned over the meeting: why the hell would one of the country's most powerful people go through that charade? Redstone was sure that Malvern had been relieved when he had declined the job. What was going on? What was the 'hugely important issue'? Oh well, he'd probably never know. He could live with that.

He walked briskly up to the tube station, the weak sunshine warm on his back, and went down to the Piccadilly line. At the bottom of the escalators, a plump young woman, wearing jeans and a sparkly black top, was standing in the busker's spot, singing a blues song. Redstone normally walked past the buskers, but this time he was drawn to step over and stand in the small group of onlookers by her as she alternately sang and played the harmonica. The timbre of her voice, the way she bent the notes and played with the timing, combined with the lyrics and the plaintive tune to choke his throat and tug at his soul. She seemed to be singing just for him, as she mourned the death of her lover. Tears trickled down his cheeks. As she finished, he took out all the notes in his wallet and carefully placed them in her hat on the tiled floor. The singer gasped and asked him if he was sure. He nodded wordlessly, turned away and stood with head bowed, recovering his composure.

Another member of the small audience asked him if he was ok. He looked up and saw an attractive chestnut-haired woman with smiling eyes, wearing a scarf loosely knotted over a tailored black jacket.

He cleared his throat. 'Yes, thanks. Or I will be once I've gone to a cash machine.' She looked into his eyes and gave a half-smile.

He made his way through the crowded tunnel to the platform. A packed train arrived, and he pushed his way into the space next to the double sliding doors. Other passengers forced themselves in, including the woman in the smart black jacket, who was with another, younger woman, perhaps her daughter. Both were laden with several shopping bags. They stood close to him, the older one looking extremely uncomfortable as other passengers pressed against her. She glanced around nervously and noticed Redstone looking at her. He smiled, he hoped reassuringly. The train jerked away and accelerated with a loud rising whine which was augmented by banging, creaking and rattling as it roared through the tunnel.

'Excuse me – this train is the right one for Russell Square, isn't it?' the older woman asked, her voice raised above the racket. Her English was slightly accented – Redstone guessed she was Scandinavian.

'Yes – it's just four stops. I'm getting out there myself.'

'Thanks.' She exchanged a few words with her companion in another language. The train jolted, and she lurched against Redstone. A shopping bag banged against his leg.

'Oh, I'm terribly sorry. I…'

'Don't worry about it. Is this the first time you've been caught in a crowded tube train?'

'Is it that obvious? Yes, this is my first time in London. Though my daughter's been here before.' The daughter smiled at Redstone.

The train jerked along for a few minutes, and Redstone and several other people, including the women, got out at Russell Square. They jostled their way to the lift. As they squeezed in, the mother dropped two of her bags. Redstone bent down and picked them up.

'Glad to see you're helping the London economy,' he said, smiling at her. 'Shall I hold these bags for you till we're safely out of the station?'

She returned his smile. 'Yes, we have done rather a lot of shopping. It's truly kind of you to help.'

'She means *she's* done a lot of shopping,' said the daughter with a grin.

The passengers stood in awkward silence, packed together, as the lift rose smoothly. Redstone could see over everyone's heads, but he knew he'd feel claustrophobic if he were shorter and wondered how the mother and daughter were coping.

The doors opened, and everyone piled out. The mother breathed a visible sigh of relief and turned to Redstone for the bags.

'Which way are you headed?' he asked. 'Maybe I could help you further with these?'

'Oh, yes please. I'm ashamed of how much we bought. We're staying at the Benet Hotel. Do you know it?'

'Yes, I work nearby. Happy to carry the bags there for you. No need to be ashamed about buying things if you needed them.'

'I'm not sure that "need" is the right word, but thanks anyway.' She gave a guilty smile.

As they walked along, the younger woman said something to her mother in the foreign language. The mother took a deep breath, nodded and turned to Redstone. She swallowed nervously.

'You said you worked nearby. May I ask what sort of work you do?'

'Of course. I'm a chemist.' His instinct was not to tell a stranger his full role, though he didn't know why. 'How about you?'

'I'm a consultant analyst. Ingrid has just finished her university studies.'

Redstone did not know what 'consultant analyst' meant but ignored it. 'Are you enjoying your time in London?' he asked. 'Apart from the crowds, of course.'

'Yes, thank you, but you're right about the crowds. We come from a small Norwegian town, and I'm finding this big city a bit overwhelming.'

They carried on chatting. She told him her name was Christina and described her home town. They arrived at the hotel, and Redstone walked into the lobby with the women and put the bags on the floor. Ingrid spoke a few words in Norwegian to her mother, turned to Redstone and said goodbye with a mysterious smile on her face.

'I… er… Ingrid's going to meet some friends,' said Christina. 'I… that is… it was so kind of you to bring the bags here. I should, erm…' she paused.

'It was nothing. And thanks for being kind when we were listening to the busker.' He stood there awkwardly, wondering whether he should just go, or seize the opportunity of chatting to her for a while longer. Joanne would tell him off if he reported that he'd just walked away, and so would Sophie, his daughter. But Christina might just want to get rid of him. Maybe she was tired or had another engagement. But if she did want him to go, surely she'd find a way of saying so without humiliating him. He ought to ask her if she would like a drink or something.

He swallowed. 'I wonder if…'

Simultaneously, she said, 'Would you…'

They laughed. 'I need some lunch,' he said. 'A sandwich. I expect I could get something in the bar. Would you like to join me?'

'I'd love to. Let's go straight there.' She asked the receptionist to take care of the shopping and took Redstone's arm. He enjoyed the light pressure of her hand and mused that this was the first time a woman had touched him for months. They walked through the small, low-ceilinged lobby into a cosy bar.

*

Two hours later, Redstone walked into Joanne's office.

'So, it was a long meeting. And successful, judging by the smile on your face.'

'As it happens, it was a short meeting and totally unsuccessful,' he said.

'But?'

'I was picked up by a beautiful woman and had lunch with her!'

'Are you serious?'

'Yes! A Norwegian woman called Christina got chatting to me on the tube. Or maybe I got chatting to her.'

'I bet she made the first move.'

'She's in London with her daughter.'

'Hmm. A daughter. Is she – this Christina, I mean – available?'

'Oh, for goodness' sake. She's divorced.'

'What's she like? Is she tall, slim and blonde? I'm jealous already.'

'No, she's curvy with wavy dark hair. Anyway, if you're jealous, why won't you marry me?'

'Roy might be irritated. Tell me more about this Christina.'

'How is Roy?'

'He's fine. Thinking about retiring and playing even more golf now that…'

Redstone's brow furrowed. 'Would you…'

'I haven't changed my mind. It's fun here, and I wouldn't know what to do with myself. I don't know the difference between a birdie and a bogie. Stop doing that!'

Redstone took his finger out of his nose and collapsed with laughter. Joanne started laughing too. 'I'm laughing because you're laughing, not because of your childish joke,' she said.

'Yes, Kate said that I had a puerile sense of humour. Often. I told her I'd no intention of growing up.'

'Well, you've kept your word.'

Redstone gave her a warm smile. 'Thanks again for staying on. It's great that the three of you decided against packing it in and living off your well-gotten gains. And I deeply appreciate how you look after me.'

'Someone's got to do it. And we love it here. Anyway, stop changing the subject. Tell me about your new girlfriend.'

'You don't let up, do you? Well, she doesn't normally stray far from her home town, but her daughter persuaded her that they should come here to celebrate her graduation.' He sighed. 'At least Kate got to celebrate our twins' graduations before… it was the last time we all…' He cleared his throat.

'I know,' Joanne said. She paused. 'Anyway, back to Christina. How did she collar you?'

'I was helping carry her shopping to the Benet. The daughter told Christina to invite me in for a drink, which became my having a sandwich and a long chat.'

'She sounds like a woman who recognises a good catch when she sees one. Are you going to see her again?'

‘Please, Joanne, not everyone is like you, blinded by desire for my… maybe I’d better not continue this stupid joke. She asked for advice on where to visit while they’re here, and I offered to help her, over lunch tomorrow.’ He suddenly stopped smiling, and looked down. He frowned and sighed.

‘Is everything all right?’ Joanne asked.

‘It’s just that I suddenly remembered happy lunches with Kate.’

‘You can’t keep leading a hermit’s life forever. It’s only a lunch. It’ll do you good.’

‘Hardly a hermit. I’m here, aren’t I, with you? And everyone else in the company.’

‘But that’s all you do, isn’t it? You never go anywhere else.’

‘A bit of an exaggeration. Anyway, that’s not the point. This lunch… I don’t know… somehow it doesn’t seem right. I think I’ll cancel. Would you do me a favour and phone the hotel?’

‘Oh, Mark. Kate wouldn’t have wanted you to live the rest of your life not socialising.’

‘I suppose not. But I haven’t got over… I won’t make a good lunch companion.’

‘You’re just making excuses not to go outside your comfort zone.’

‘What’s wrong with wanting to stay comfortable? Oh, ok, I’ll think about it.’

‘While you’re doing that, what happened at the Cabinet Office?’

*

The hall sprang into brightness as Redstone turned on the light. The rug was straight, and there were no shoes or bags dumped on the floor, no coats draped over the chair, no books piled on the chest of drawers. He went into the sitting room; the cushions were neatly aligned and plumped up, the carpet was spotless. Elena, the

Bulgarian cleaner, had cried every visit for many weeks after Kate's death.

The house was silent – no sounds of the twins squabbling upstairs or music playing or pots banging in the kitchen or phones ringing. Elena still called Kate 'my lovely lady'. There was no smell of cooking, just the scent of furniture polish.

There was no one to give him a welcoming kiss.

Once again, the loss hit him hard. It was so cruel and untimely. He and Kate should have been helping each other enjoy the twins growing up and leaving home. They should have been enjoying going on holidays, socialising together… all taken away. He was alone. He felt again the acid anger which gnawed at his brain, intruded into his thoughts and woke him at night. He needed justice with every fibre of his being.

Thank God for his colleagues at London Bio and for the twins' support. His throat ached, and his eyes prickled. The cat strolled up to him. He picked her up and clutched her warm body to his chest.

He wouldn't be a fit companion for Christina tomorrow. He'd cancel the lunch.

TUESDAY 11 OCTOBER

Redstone sat opposite Christina in a booth against the wall of a small Turkish restaurant. The sides of the booth were topped by intricately carved wooden screens, and the table was illuminated by a pendant lantern with elaborately patterned glass. Christina studied him anxiously as he hunched over the menu.

He gave a start as his phone buzzed on the table. It was Joanne. 'You'll want to hear this straight away,' she said. 'The prime minister's office rang – you're invited to lunch with him tomorrow! I accepted.'

'Is it a big do where he meets industrialists or scientists or something like that? I don't like that sort of thing.'

'No, I asked. It's just you!'

'Good God! Just me? It must have something to do with yesterday's fiasco with Dominic Malvern. Did they say what it's about?'

'No, except that it's confidential, but you'd learn more tomorrow.'

'Thanks, Joanne. I need to digest this.' He rang off and stared into space.

Christina looked at him. 'You seem distracted. Don't feel we have to stay for lunch if there's a problem you have to deal with.'

Redstone suddenly realised how rude he must be appearing to Christina. He'd hardly spoken since they'd arrived, and now he'd taken a phone call which she must have seen was important but without saying a word to her about it. She must be thinking he was a terrible boor. He was indeed being a terrible boor. Why on earth had he been behaving like that? There was no reason at all why he shouldn't be enjoying lunch with this good-looking, interesting woman. He'd been self-indulgently wallowing in his sorrow at Kate's loss, almost enjoying a sort of martyrdom. As Joanne had repeated when she persuaded him to come, Kate herself wouldn't have wanted him to stop socialising for ever.

He realised that Christina was preparing to leave and launched into a fulsome apology for his behaviour. She quickly agreed to stay when he explained that he was struggling with a personal matter.

'Oh, I see,' she said. 'If it'd help, feel free to talk to me about it. Sometimes it's easier to discuss things with strangers.' She wrinkled her brow. 'Not that I'm an expert in solving personal problems.'

'That's a kind offer, but I don't want to burden you with my problems. I've been enough of a pain already. Let's order lunch.'

They chatted about London and its contrast with Oslo, Redstone interrupting himself with more apologies about his earlier behaviour. She assured him he was forgiven. As they started to eat, he told her about the invitation to lunch at Downing Street.

'Sounds interesting. Are you famous here?'

'Absolutely not.'

'The prime minister must want to use your expertise in some way. What are you expert in?'

'Nothing. The combination of jobs I've had is unusual, but I can't see why that would make me of interest to him. It's truly mysterious.'

'Well, you'll find out tomorrow. I'd love to know what it is he wants!'

'Me too. I'm a bit nervous, to be honest. I like to be prepared when I go to meetings, especially with senior people, but I just don't know how to prepare for this one.'

'I'm sure you'll be fine. Just remember – the prime minister wipes his bottom like everyone else!'

Redstone snorted with laughter. Other diners looked round and smiled. 'Is that a Norwegian saying?' he asked.

'No, it's something I made up for myself. I get nervous about meeting anyone. In fact, I'd never have invited you for a drink yesterday if Ingrid hadn't told me to. But I'm really pleased I did.'

'I bet you weren't pleased half an hour ago. Again, I truly am sorry for… anyway, I'm so pleased you did what Ingrid said.'

They carried on eating. 'You said you've had an unusual combination of jobs,' she said. 'May I ask what they were?'

'My first job was in a cosmetics company, mostly in France. But I don't think the prime minister would be interested in my knowledge of skin chemistry.'

'So, you lived in France for some time?'

'Yes, five years in Lyon. Great food!'

'This food in this restaurant is exceptionally good. Though not English, of course.'

They finished the main course and ordered puddings – Turkish ice cream for her and a quince-based dessert for him. He told her that he preferred Turkish puddings even to French desserts.

'I suppose you speak French fluently?' she asked.

'I'm not a natural linguist. But I did learn to speak French pretty well, as a result of living there, though my accent isn't great.'

'What did you do after that job in Lyon?'

'We came back to the UK, and I changed direction and joined the Department of Energy. Well, it was the Business and Energy Department then, but the new prime minister thought energy was too important to be lost in a big department and split it off.'

Christina leaned forward. 'I'm sure he was right. Your work there must have been interesting. What was your role?'

Redstone told her he'd worked in three areas over the years he'd been there – nuclear power, the electricity industry and North Sea oil. He explained that they were policy jobs: he'd left science behind. ‘Basically, I’m now a jack of all trades and master of none.’

‘Interesting expression! I think I understand it.’

‘Sorry – I keep forgetting that English isn’t your first language. You speak it so well. Unlike me, you must have a gift for languages.’

‘I don’t know about that, but thanks. We’re all taught it from an early age, and then there’s TV, songs, books, films and, of course, the internet… Anyway, carry on about your civil service career.’

‘Nothing more to say. The point is I haven’t any special expertise that would make the PM want to see me.’

She became more intense. ‘Well, you must have some expertise or experience he wants. Think carefully – what might it be?’

Redstone smiled. ‘You said yesterday you were a consultant analyst, and to be frank, I didn’t know what that meant. Does it mean you help people analyse their strengths and weaknesses, or something like that?’

She blushed. ‘Oh, sorry, nothing like that at all. I got carried away. Your situation sounds so interesting.’

‘So, what is your job?’

’I analyse complex policy issues, especially if there are engineering aspects. I trained as an engineer.’

‘What sort of engineer?’

‘We covered the whole discipline. I didn’t pursue my studies to the point where I had to specialise.’

‘Tell me more about your job. What was your most recent project?’

She looked down. ‘I… I’m afraid I can’t say any more because my work’s always confidential. I’m sorry.’

'That's ok,' said Redstone. 'I was used to keeping quiet about what I was doing when I was a civil servant. Let's talk about other things. Do you read English novels?'

They discussed books they'd read recently, and Redstone was pleased to find there were several they'd both found interesting. He was thoroughly enjoying her company.

'You didn't finish telling me about your career,' she said. 'Obviously, you left the Department of Energy – what happened then?'

'I started London Bio. That was six years ago. We've been quite successful.'

'So, six years of hard and happy work?'

Redstone's face darkened. 'The work itself has been… well, four years ago my wife was murdered. The killer's never been caught. I'm afraid it's hardly been six happy years.'

'Oh, Mark, I'm so sorry. I had no idea. It must have been awful for you.' She put her hand on his.

'I didn't mean to make you feel bad for what you said. You weren't to know.'

She looked into his eyes. 'Is that why you were unhappy earlier?'

'Yes. It still colours my… the killer's still free and unpunished… well, you can…'

'Of course.' There was an awkward silence. Redstone thought he'd now spoilt the atmosphere and resigned himself to saying goodbye to this attractive and interesting woman. They carried on eating to the chattering of other diners and the clatter of cutlery.

Christina looked up. 'I must say, this food's been excellent. Can you recommend anywhere I might go tomorrow?'

'Um… you might like to go to Hampstead. It used to be a village, but it's now part of London. It's got some beautiful old buildings, and there are lots of good restaurants. It's next to a huge green space called Hampstead Heath. Very hilly, good views.'

'I might be imposing on you, but Ingrid will be spending the day with her friends – would you be able to find the time to go there with me? My treat, of course.' She touched her hair.

'Oh! I'd love to, but as you know, I've got a lunch appointment already!'

'How stupid of me. How about dinner?'

*

Redstone stood outside the restaurant watching Christina turn the corner and disappear. He felt excited by the day's events – almost elated – but at the same time, nervous at being so far out of his comfort zone. So many new things were happening.

WEDNESDAY 12 OCTOBER

Redstone walked into Joanne's office. She looked up, scanned him appraisingly and smiled.

'You still look very relaxed, for someone who's going to have a mysterious meeting with the prime minister and who doesn't like leaving the lab.'

'Oh, for goodness' sake. Have you arranged to see the financial adviser yet?'

'Well…'

'Joanne, you must take this seriously. You've now got a lot of money, and it's not doing you any good if it lies in the bank. I'd be happy to help if you like.'

'No, Roy and I'll sort it out, thanks.'

'Ok. But I'll keep pestering you. Could you please ask David to come in?' David Pepper was a biochemist who'd worked as a section head for a big pharmaceutical company in Essex. His wife was a primary school teacher, and David himself gave the impression of being a kindly and slightly unworldly teacher.

David and Redstone were discussing the latest results of the company's research programme when Joanne entered the room to remind Redstone that he needed to get ready for his meeting at Number 10.

'Sit down, Joanne,' he said, 'and let's the three of us talk through what this might be about. Maybe you can help me prepare.'

'Everyone's fascinated,' said David. 'Most of the staff think it's more likely to do with you personally than with London Bio.'

'My guess is it's something to do with energy,' said Joanne.

'I can't see why they'd need me for energy-related stuff. There's a whole Department of Energy in the government, and it seems to have managed perfectly well without me for the last six years. Anyway, what aspect of energy? There aren't any big new North Sea oil or gas developments. And our nuclear power stations are working fine.'

'I thought we were close to running out of electricity,' she said. 'The papers were full of it.'

'That was a couple of years ago. Fortunately, the reactors now produce a lot more power. France Nucléaire were able to modify them.'

'Pity our nuclear power stations are run by the French,' David said. 'All those profits going abroad.'

'Yes, in a different world, British governments would have gone with British designs operated by British companies. But in this world, they didn't.'

'As long as they're safe,' said Joanne. 'So, are you saying that your energy background can't be the reason the PM wants to see you?'

'I can't see how it can be.'

'It must be the science, then. That's good, isn't it? Good for you and good for the company. Ah well, you'll find out soon. Time you got ready.'

*

'Well,' Redstone muttered, 'how about this?' He wondered what Kate would have said about his being invited to lunch with the prime minister. He walked past the two mounted soldiers on duty outside Horse Guards – their helmets gleamed in the autumn sunshine, and the vivid red of their capes stood out boldly against the dull clothing of the tourists gathered around them. One of the horses snorted.

He arrived at the gates of the entrance to Downing Street. A police officer looked at him suspiciously. He introduced himself and said with some pride that he had an appointment with the prime minister. The officer looked at a list, nodded, examined Redstone's driving licence and signalled to his heavily armed colleague, who opened a gate. 'Please come through, sir. Walk down to Number 10 and show your ID to the officer outside. He'll let you in.' He spoke into his lapel radio.

Redstone walked down the famous street, which was empty of people except for the police officers. The much-photographed door opened, and a man beckoned him inside.

'Welcome, Dr Redstone. May I take your coat? And if you have a mobile phone on you, please deposit it in the rack to your left.'

The inside of the building looked much bigger than the outside suggested. A corridor stretched ahead, and another led to the left. He walked a few paces down the left corridor and found a wooden rack containing several mobile phones. With some trepidation, he left his in a vacant slot. Leaving it there brought back feelings of being a small cog in a big machine, of not being in control of his working life – feelings he hadn't realised he had till he'd shed them on leaving the civil service.

As he walked back, a young man came down the staircase on the right of the entrance hall.

'Hi. My name's Tony. I'm one of the prime minister's assistant private secretaries. You're having lunch on the first floor. May I show you the way?'

They walked up the staircase. The left wall was lined with pictures of previous prime ministers.

'The prime minister's wife, Anne, will also be joining you for the lunch.'

Redstone was surprised. Anne Jones was not a public figure, though the media would have liked otherwise. She was reputed to keep strictly out of government affairs. 'Very nice, but why will she be…?'

'Oh, the PM often asks her to join him when he lunches with people he thinks she'll find interesting. He finds it creates a better atmosphere. More relaxing. You'll see why – you'll like her. She probably won't stay for the whole meeting – she normally leaves when the PM gets onto policy matters.'

Tony ushered Redstone into an airy dining room which looked as though it belonged in a posh house in a TV drama. There were sash windows on two sides, and pastel green walls on which hung a few paintings. The table in the centre of the room was laid for three, and a fragrant buffet lunch was arranged on a sideboard. The Number 10 caterers had excelled – Redstone peered at little labels reading '*Halloumi Fries*', '*Coronation Chicken Scones*', '*Vodka-Baked Salmon*' and turned away because he found his mouth watering uncomfortably.

'The prime minister and Mrs Jones will be along shortly,' said Tony. 'Meanwhile, you might like to look at the paintings. They're on loan from the Tate. I rather like them.' He left the room. Redstone walked around, admiring the pictures. He thought he recognised a Turner seascape but not the others. One was slightly crooked, and he straightened it.

The prime minister walked in. He had long, wavy, greying fair hair, swept back, and was quite narrow-shouldered. 'Hello, Dr Redstone – I'm Michael Jones. Many thanks for coming here at such short notice – and for straightening that painting!'

'Hello, Prime Minister.' He gestured at the painting. 'Sorry about that. I'm honoured, though I don't know why I'm here!'

'If it's ok with you, I suggest we use first names when we're in private like this. Call me Michael. May I call you Mark?'

'Of course, and I'll try to call you Michael, Prime Minister. Er… joke, of course.'

'I may be a politician, but I still have a sense of humour. If truth be told, some would say that the only way to survive as the leader of my party is to have a strong sense of humour. Would you like a drink? Anne will be down in a minute.'

Redstone felt he could use a whisky to calm his nerves, but asked for a lime juice and soda. Anne Jones walked in. She was wearing a taupe trouser suit over a blue open-necked silk shirt, with a silver pendant at her throat. The prime minister made the introductions and invited Redstone to help himself from the buffet.

They sat at the table. 'I wanted to have lunch with you to get to know you,' said the PM, 'and over lunch, I'll tell you about why we'd greatly appreciate your help. Anne will then leave, and we'll be joined by a senior official, who'll brief you in more detail. Just to remove some of the mystery, it's about our nuclear reactor programme.'

'But… I suppose you know I haven't dealt with energy matters for years?'

'Yes, of course. All will become clear!'

'And I suppose you know about my abortive meeting with the cabinet secretary. Will he be the person who joins us later?'

The prime minister cleared his throat. 'Yes, I do know about that meeting. It was why I decided to try myself to persuade you to help us. Dominic won't be joining us.'

'Why did he want me to refuse the job?'

'Well, maybe he had someone else in mind. Anyway, I'm sure you're the person we need, as we'll explain shortly.'

'Michael thinks Dominic Malvern's an excellent cabinet secretary,' said Anne in a pronounced Welsh lilt. 'He's a master of strategy and tactics.' She stopped and said no more, in a way which suggested she had reservations about Malvern.

'I don't think anyone could be a good top civil servant without those skills,' Redstone said. 'Maybe Dominic was right to get rid of me. I suppose you know about that.'

'I do, but I gather that leaving has worked out well for you,' said the PM. 'Tell us how you built up your company.'

'After I left the Department, I spent a few months developing an idea I'd had years before, when I was working as a scientist. My late wife and I then decided we should spend my redundancy payoff to rent some lab space so I could develop the idea further. University College London was extremely helpful.'

The PM nodded. 'Good university.'

'I advertised for another scientist, and I also needed a part-time finance expert and a PA. I asked for people who were prepared to invest some money to build up the company. In the hope of rewards later, of course.'

'I bet that caused a long delay,' said Anne.

'No, it was surprisingly easy. The three who started the company with me all had some new redundancy money they were prepared to invest. They were wonderful. With that sum in the bank, we could raise further funds, and as our research started to look promising, we managed to raise even more. We gelled beautifully as a team. We were determined to make it a success.'

'How many staff have you got now?' asked Anne.

'Forty-three.'

'And how did you generate profits?'

'We've only just got there. We were living off our loans and shareholders' capital till a couple of weeks ago. To cut a long story short, we've now licensed our invention to Star Boston Pharmaceuticals.'

Anne clapped. 'I work in venture capital. That's exactly the sort of success we try to produce. Michael, you ought to use Mark as a role model.'

'Interesting thought,' said the PM. 'I do agree that Mark's story is impressive.'

'I'd like to hear about the science you've been pursuing,' said Anne, 'and I'm sure Michael would too – as long as you don't make it too technical.'

Redstone launched into a description of his work, and gained confidence as he proceeded. He liked talking about the science and enjoyed the challenge of explaining it to non-scientists. He could see they followed him with interest.

‘Excellent,’ said the PM. ‘It’s good to learn something outside the normal run of what I have to deal with.’

‘Yes,’ said Anne. ‘I can see you love your science, don’t you?’

‘I do,’ said Redstone. ‘I find it stimulating and, well, fun.’

‘I hope you don’t mind my mentioning it, but I know your wife was murdered four years ago. It must have been awful for you and your children. I, er… I guess your work’s been a way of coping with the grief. Sometimes companies grow because… Sorry, that was very insensitive.’

Redstone paled. ‘Grief and anger,’ he said. ‘You can’t escape. But getting heavily involved in something else does help.’

‘I understand, of course.’

‘You’re right, though. I did throw myself into developing London Bio. It wasn’t just the science – it was the company of my colleagues. You feel so lonely when your partner suddenly dies.’

There was an awkward silence. The prime minister cleared his throat. ‘Time marches on,’ he said. ‘Let’s switch subjects and talk about our nuclear programme.’

‘Do you need me to leave now?’ asked Anne.

‘No, it’s fine for you to stay a bit longer. What I’m about to tell Mark is only mildly confidential. I’ll say when we’re about to get onto the stuff where I’d have to kill you if you remained in the room.’

‘In that case, I’m going to take some fruit. Mark, do help yourself.’

They walked over to the buffet. ‘I assume you’re up to speed on our nuclear reactor programme,’ said the PM.

In the late seventies, the UK had decided to major on nuclear, partly to weaken the power of the coal miners. The government had invited France Nucléaire to construct and operate the reactors because of the success of the nuclear programme in France. The early UK reactors were now coming to the end of their lives, so France Nucléaire had been commissioned to build a second wave.

'I think so,' said Redstone. 'The first new reactors are due to start up soon.'

'That's right. As it turns out, we're going to need the new wave even more keenly than we expected, especially in the winter. Our renewables won't fill the gap. Anyway, I've been invited to open the first new one in a few weeks' time. We should be just about ok for electricity this coming winter.'

'That's what I understood,' said Redstone. 'What's the catch?'

'This is where it starts to get sensitive. We picked up information suggesting that France Nucléaire will delay the start-up of the new reactors. Or worse – maybe even cancel them. We don't know why. They deny it, but we think they're lying.'

'Christ. That would be disastrous.'

'Exactly. So we'd like you to investigate.'

'I can see you need someone to look into this, but I'm sure you've got the wrong man. What about MI5? I'm years out of date on nuclear stuff, as I said before.'

'There are several reasons why we need you – to work with MI5, as it happens. I'll tell you some of them, and the others will become clear during the next part of the briefing.' Anne looked on with an interested expression. 'First,' said the PM, extending his thumb, 'we need someone senior who can command the respect of the French officials who are running the show.' He extended his forefinger. 'Second, we need someone who understands spoken technical French.' The middle finger came out. 'Third, our chosen person must have enough of a feel for technical issues to tell if the French are trying to pull the wool over our eyes.' The fourth finger. 'And fourth, you do have a good background in nuclear reactor issues, even if it is out of date. We could quickly bring you up to speed with some intensive briefing.'

‘I still think there must be people better qualified than me.’

‘As I mentioned, there’s more to come,’ the PM said. ‘You’ll see why it’s you. Anne, I’m afraid this is where I have to ask you to leave.’

‘Of course.’ She stood and shook Redstone’s hand. ‘A real pleasure to meet you, Mark. I look forward to the next time. See you later, Michael.’ She walked out.

Redstone sat down again, and the PM continued. ‘The first signs of a problem came from material intercepted by our security services. They’re now heavily involved. A further reason why you’re our best candidate for this job is that you have very high-security clearance because of the work you did in the Department of Energy. And we’ve brought it up to date, I’m told.’

‘Really? I’d no idea my security clearance was very high, and I certainly didn’t know the spooks have been looking into me recently.’

‘I suppose that shows they do their job well. Anyway, you can see how the focus is narrowing onto you. But there’s more to come.’ He looked Redstone in the eye. ‘Before I go any further, can I take it you’re inclined to accept this investigative role? To put it another way, if you say now that you rule it out, we can leave it there, and I won’t continue. Though, in any case, you must keep quiet about what I’ve told you. It would be disastrous if people thought we might lose a lot of our electricity supply. Loss of investment, devaluation of the pound, panic buying… you name it.’

‘Understood.’

‘So, inclined to accept?’

Redstone thought quickly. He was fascinated by the story and wanted to find out more. But he was nervous at the thought of leaving the routine of his life working at London Bio. ‘How long would this take?’ he asked.

'I don't see it taking more than about a month. Oh, I must mention something I know you discussed with Dominic – remuneration. Forget what he said. We'll pay you properly. Your company won't suffer financially from your absence.'

'Thanks,' said Redstone. 'I certainly don't rule out doing this job for you, but I can't commit till I've heard the whole story.'

'I fully understand. Then this is where I bring in the official I mentioned earlier.' He walked to the door, spoke to an aide outside and returned. Almost immediately, another man entered. Redstone at first thought how unremarkable the man looked – he was average in every way – but then saw the air of authority and a certain hardness.

'You probably haven't met Gavin McKay. He's head of MI5.' They shook hands. 'Gavin – I've briefed Mark on the background, so now it's over to you.'

'Before we go any further,' said McKay, 'we need to discuss confidentiality and Mark's cover story, if he agrees to accept the challenge. May I pursue that, Prime Minister?'

'Of course.'

'The first thing is to clarify the boundaries of who you can and can't tell what you've heard and what you're about to hear.'

'Ok,' said Redstone.

'You can't talk about the involvement of the security services to anyone except me, the prime minister, one of his aides and some of my staff. I'll introduce them to you later. You can't mention us to other civil servants or ministers, special advisers, your family, your colleagues or your friends. Including your new friend.'

'New friend?'

'Your Norwegian acquaintance.'

Redstone reddened. 'Christ. Michael, they've been monitoring my new friendship with a woman. I don't like this at all. If this job means I have no privacy, I quit now. Or rather, I refuse to start.' He started to get up.

'Look,' said McKay, 'I'm just being honest. We haven't been monitoring you. We investigated various things only so we could bring your security clearance up to date. I assure you we won't be monitoring your private life.'

Redstone doubted whether to take this at face value but couldn't see a way of challenging it. He settled back, feeling that he'd missed an opportunity to bow out without loss of face. 'Well, I've yet to decide whether to take it.' He gazed out of the window. 'Given what you've said, I couldn't work on this project from my own office. Would I be based in the Cabinet Office?'

'Certainly not,' said McKay, and at the same time, the PM said, 'No. You'd be based here, in Number 10.'

Redstone assumed this was so that MI5 could more easily keep an eye on him. Presumably they didn't trust him, despite the vetting.

The PM continued, 'Your cover story would be that I asked you to look into progress with the new wave of reactors before I give my speech at the opening ceremony. It has the advantage of being close to the truth.' McKay nodded.

'I can see some holes in that,' said Redstone. 'Why would you ask me rather than, say the Energy permanent secretary or one of her staff? I've got a slightly different suggestion, if you don't mind?'

'Oh yes?' said McKay sceptically.

'Yes. You, Michael, asked me in for lunch because someone – perhaps Anne? – had suggested I have the right background to draft your speech. You want to cover energy, of course, but also science and business. All areas I know about. It would be a major policy speech. And I'd need to get chapter and verse on what's happening with the nuclear reactors, to help me do the drafting.'

‘That’s great!’ said the PM. He looked at McKay, who nodded. ‘What’s more, I think it should be more than a cover story – let’s make it real. I’ll get my staff to tell relevant government departments to cooperate.’

‘Oh,’ said Redstone. ‘I didn’t mean… oh well, why not? Could be interesting. I used to enjoy that sort of thing when I was a civil servant.’ He got up and walked to the window. ‘And what about Malvern? What’s his role in all this?’

‘He knows we’ve spotted a threat to the nuclear programme,’ said McKay. ‘I told him we need help from someone with a technical background who understands the nuclear industry, speaks French, has been highly vetted, can work with MI5 and is senior enough to command respect. And can look at it all with a fresh eye. As I suppose the PM has already told you. And we’d identified you.’

The PM continued, ‘Malvern was keen to take on the task of recruiting you to the job, which makes it all the more interesting that he seems to have done his best to put you off.’ McKay said nothing.

‘Anyway,’ the PM continued, ‘we’ll simply tell him that you will indeed be doing the investigation and also writing the speech, which is why you’ll be reporting directly to me.’

‘There will be some people who know what happened yesterday,’ said Redstone.

‘If it comes up, we’ll say he tried to recruit you to do the job, but his heart wasn’t in it because of the history between you two.’

‘And what about the special advisers? They’d normally be heavily involved in producing a major speech.’

‘True, but the security aspects mean this will be an exception. I’ll tell them that, without saying what the security implications are, of course.’

'Ok,' said Redstone. 'But I still don't understand why you don't get someone from the Department of Energy to do the real job.'

'You'd be surprised how unusually well qualified you are for this,' said McKay. 'But there's another reason, as well.' He looked at the prime minister, who nodded. 'We believe someone in the Department of Energy is leaking information to France Nucléaire.'

'Ok,' said Redstone, further intrigued. 'Tell me more.'

'Right,' said McKay. 'We picked up indications of a serious problem with the reactor programme. Then there were some high-level meetings within the London office of France Nucléaire, and following that, their top engineer resigned, and his deputy went on extended sick leave.'

'Surely that could have been a coincidence?'

'Then the UK CEO, a Frenchman – one of their administrative élite – started moving his family back to France. That itself was odd because he and his wife were playing a leading role amongst French expatriates in London and hugely enjoying it, apparently.'

'Well, but…'

'Then we intercepted part of a discussion where the CEO said that "this" could cause the worst relations between France and the UK since the Napoleonic wars.'

'Ah.'

'Unfortunately, he didn't specify what he was talking about. So we put more resources into trying to find out, but suddenly everything went silent. We're fairly sure the French got wind of our interest from the leak I mentioned. They've now put top-level security in place.'

'What does that involve?'

'For example, we think they now hold all their sensitive meetings in a special screened room.'

'So, you can see,' said the PM, 'we do need to find out what is happening. If the new nuclear reactor programme doesn't go ahead, we'll be revisiting the three-day week problems of the 1970s.'

'But it would be much worse now, because of the electrification of the economy,' mused Redstone. 'Christ, the more I think about it… lucky it's just the new reactors. But even so, we're now so dependent on electricity for lighting, heating, communications, industry—'

'Quite. We've got to sort this out before the winter. Furthermore, I can't risk opening the new plant in a few weeks if the reactor and its sisters then fail to produce electricity, the country's economy collapses, and people die from the cold. I'd be mocked in the history books as the powerless PM, or worse.'

'I understand all that,' said Redstone, 'but how can I succeed where professional spies have failed?'

'We don't call ourselves spies,' said McKay. 'Anyway, that brings us to the final part of the plan. I warn you – prepare to be astonished!'

'It's not exactly been a normal day so far,' said Redstone. 'If you can surprise me even more, that will be something to tell my children,' – McKay started to protest – 'except I'm not allowed to.' He smiled. 'Go ahead.'

'Ok. What do you know about string theory?'

'You've already surprised me! I know it's an attempt to explain why the fundamental particles which make up the universe are what they are. And that its concept is that every particle is a minute string, which vibrates in different ways to produce the different particles.'

'More than I knew,' said the PM. 'And I still don't understand how a vibrating string can be a particle. Or different particles.'

'They're not really strings,' said McKay. 'It's just a way of trying to visualise what the maths says. I'm afraid that's true of a lot of modern physics.'

'I'm trying to think of a clever and witty analogy with the opposition's policies,' said the PM, 'but I can't. Carry on!'

'Well, the theory gets even more peculiar, doesn't it, Mark?'

'Erm… the vibrations have to happen in about eleven dimensions for the theory to work?'

'Yes. And the reason we can't see most of those dimensions is because they're curled up minutely.'

'Let me see if I've got a grip on this,' said the PM. 'We live in a three-dimensional world. Even I know that. Or I thought I did, but according to you scientists, there are actually eleven dimensions, and it seems like three because eight of them are curled up tightly.'

'Exactly.'

The PM walked to a window and stared out.

McKay turned back to Redstone. 'I was a physicist working at GCHQ before I found my way into MI5,' he said. 'Some years ago, I wondered whether it would be possible to access the extra dimensions. If they are minutely curled up, there'd be no point, but suppose that one or more of them is on a human scale.'

'Yes, I can see why MI5'd like that,' said Redstone. 'One of your spies,' – McKay winced – 'could disappear into that dimension, do the spying and then reappear in our three-dimensional world. It would be like a two-dimensional world where everyone lived flat, sliding around like on a sheet of paper – and then someone found how to get off the paper, look at what's happening on it and then get back on.'

The PM sighed.

'And seem invisible while they were off the paper.'

The PM walked to the sideboard and poured a coffee. 'Do help yourselves,' he said.

'May I try another analogy, Michael?' said Redstone. 'A very rough one. Suppose your whole world was the Palace of Westminster. You believed there was no world outside.'

‘Sounds realistic,’ said the PM.

‘And you and all the other parliamentarians were totally unaware of the windows and the external doors. Everything you all knew or could conceive of was in that building. But suddenly you, and you alone, found you could go outside, move around outside and go back in through different doors. Or stay outside but look in through the windows you hadn’t known were there. Think how powerful you’d be!’

‘Brilliant!’ said the PM. McKay, looking irritated, said nothing.

Redstone turned back to McKay. ‘You’d need to explain why we couldn’t see the extra dimension if it did exist as you describe.’

‘We discovered a variant of the theory, which turns out to work rather well. One of the extra dimensions grows and shrinks periodically, with a period of a few centuries between maximum and minimum. Its size varies as a wave. We’re currently at a stage where the size of this “wavy dimension” is about three metres, which is its maximum.’

‘When you say it works rather well, what do you mean? I thought nobody had managed to produce any evidence at all for string theory.’

‘It’s true that there’s no published evidence. But you must understand that MI5 doesn’t publish its work. Indeed, the only people outside MI5 who know what I’ve just told you are the prime minister and you.’

‘And only one of those understands it,’ said the PM. ‘Guess which one.’

‘I find this astonishing, I must say,’ said Redstone.

‘Not as much as I do,’ said the PM. ‘Tell him about the evidence.’

‘One of our staff has actually moved into the wavy dimension!’

Redstone looked at the PM to check that they were not engaged in some bizarre trick. The PM nodded and shrugged.

'Let me guess. You want me to find out what the French are up to by spying on them from this wavy dimension,' Redstone said sarcastically.

'As it happens, that's right. Though I wouldn't have put it in quite those terms,' said the PM.

Redstone stared at them. 'But I come back to my earlier question. Why can't we all move into this wavy dimension?'

McKay answered. 'We haven't evolved to do it naturally. The wavy dimension grows and shrinks, as I said, and the time when it would be useful, when the size is sort of human scale, is very much shorter than the timescale for evolution.'

'Then how did your colleague access it?'

'To cut a long story short, we can access it if we use our brains in a certain way.'

'Go on then,' said Redstone. 'Do it.'

'The problem is that most people's brains don't have the capacity to do it.'

'Why not?'

'There are a few regions of the brain which need to be highly developed. They're associated with certain abilities. You know about London cab drivers – one area of their brain becomes more developed by their training and job?'

'The part responsible for spatial memory. I recall that brain scans show it's unusually big.'

'That's right. Well, it's the same idea for shifting dimensions. In a nutshell, the person must have a brain which makes them highly mathematical, practical and able to think laterally. So, they must have had years of appropriate training and experience – in addition to some innate abilities. We've found that nearly everyone like that is an inventive physical scientist or engineer. Maybe there are others who'd fit the bill, but we had to narrow the field for the purpose of screening. So we concentrated on successful technical people.'

'That's why I'm off the hook,' the PM said.

'But you're very much on the hook, Mark,' said McKay. 'We looked at test results and career information for all members of the armed forces, civil servants and ex-civil servants. We found that when we included security ratings, the ability to understand spoken technical French and background knowledge of nuclear reactor policy, you were top of the list. I recommended you to the prime minister, who agreed.'

The PM nodded.

'Surely there are other candidates at least as well qualified as me?' said Redstone.

'Think it through,' said McKay. 'How many reasonably senior soldiers, civil servants or ex-civil servants do you think could understand the details of a conversation between a couple of nuclear industry people about technical aspects of their reactor programme?'

Redstone thought. There would be Department of Energy people, Nuclear Safety Inspectorate experts, and a few people in other departments. And people who worked on nuclear submarines and nuclear weapons. 'Maybe two hundred?' he offered.

'And if the conversation was in French?'

'Ah. Maybe ten?'

'And how many of those ten would be people who had a record as a successful inventive physical scientist or engineer?'

'Well, probably quite a few. Maybe half.'

'And what would be the probability that they would have been thoroughly vetted and have a high-security rating?'

'Pretty high, I'd think. Given the subject. Maybe three of them?'

'Pretty good guesswork. As a matter of fact, there were four on our list. But when we scored them, you came out top. By a long way.'

'That's why we need you,' said the PM.

Redstone felt embarrassed and under pressure. 'This is beginning to sound like a Marvel comic. Do you want me to dress up in blue tights and a close-fitting red shirt with a logo on the chest saying "*spy*"?'

'Certainly not,' said the PM. 'It'd have to be yellow, not red.'

They all laughed.

'So, if I've got the right sort of brain, why can't I just disappear in front of your eyes right now?' asked Redstone.

'Because your brain needs help in making the right connections. We have some equipment which does that. As I said, it worked on one of our team, a scientist who was instrumental in developing this process. Unfortunately, he doesn't have the other qualifications you have. But if the worst comes to the worst, we'll use him. By which I mean if you decide not to accept the job.'

'Are you saying that you want to modify my brain?'

'Yes – to make it even more powerful.'

'Let me get this clear. How many people have you tried this on?'

'Just the one, so far. The scientist who developed it, as I said.'

'So, it's unproven, possibly dangerous, and you want me to be a guinea pig?'

'No. It's not dangerous, and we know it works, with the right people. If it doesn't work with you, you won't be any worse off.'

'This seems like a hugely important discovery. No, not seems like – it is. We're talking Nobel Prize material. The most important physics advance in our lifetimes. Aren't you going to publish it? The science community needs to know about it, to investigate it, to develop it. The general public would find it amazing – you'd be media stars. It's fantastic! You're not going to keep it secret, are you?'

'Yes, we are going to keep it secret, and that includes you. I accept what you say about its scientific importance, but its only practical uses are for intelligence gathering and military purposes. We believe we have an advantage over every other country, and we aren't going to give it away.'

The PM nodded. Redstone saw he had no hope of persuading them. Keeping this astonishing advance secret went against his instincts, but he couldn't think of a counterargument.

'Even so,' he said, 'surely you've got more important uses for it than looking into a nebulous issue about the electricity supply?'

'Like what?'

'I don't know. Terrorists? Russia?'

'I'm not saying we're not going to use it for other purposes. Of course we are. But it's new, and this issue has just come up. There's no reason not to use it now, just because we could also use it elsewhere, as soon as…' Redstone noted the qualification, but decided not to ask what the "as soon as" referred to. Not yet, anyway.

The PM intervened. 'And don't underestimate the importance of the electricity issue.'

'Well,' said Redstone, 'obviously I know a reliable supply is fundamental. But you've only got a vague suspicion that there's a threat.'

'No,' said McKay. 'That's not how these things work. We piece together lots of what you call vague suspicions and do a proper analysis of the risk. There's a big risk.'

Redstone was sceptical. Fine-sounding words, but such analyses were carried out by flawed human beings. 'Like weapons of mass destruction in Iraq?' he said.

McKay flushed and clenched his jaw. 'Oh, for Christ's sake, don't pretend you're some unworldly boffin with no knowledge of current affairs.'

The PM cleared his throat noisily.

McKay crossed his legs. 'Look, you've got enough sense to know the politicians didn't reflect what the intelligence community had concluded. We didn't get it wrong.'

'Wasn't me, of course,' said the PM.

'No, of course not,' said McKay. He turned to Redstone. 'Just think. What would happen if we lost half our electricity in the depths of winter? If a terrorist could achieve that, they'd regard it as a stupendous triumph.'

'Yes,' said the PM. 'The economy would collapse. So would the NHS. Lots of people would die.' Redstone shuffled uncomfortably, and the PM continued, 'If I ignored the possibility, indeed if I didn't devote every effort to looking into it, I'd go down as the worst prime minister in recent history. And rightly.'

'It doesn't matter what you think about our priorities,' said McKay. 'What matters is whether you'll help us.'

Redstone swallowed. Assailed on both sides. 'What are the side-effects?' he asked McKay.

'We haven't discovered anything negative. Indeed, we think the procedure would enhance your cognitive abilities. In fact, the only problem is that the effects seem to wear off after a couple of weeks.'

'I can't believe that anything which altered someone's brain wouldn't affect their personality and maybe other things. And why should it all turn out to be advantageous? Seems against the odds.' He frowned. 'Anyway, what is the procedure?'

'It involves using a modified MRI scanner – the imaging equipment used in hospitals. But it would be best if you came to Thames House to learn more from our expert. Can you come tomorrow morning?'

Redstone fiddled with his coffee cup. His scientific curiosity made him want to pursue this amazing possibility, and he did feel a sense of duty to the country. But he was nervous about such a major new venture. What's more, the procedure must be risky, whatever McKay said. He shifted uneasily in his chair.

He was on the verge of ducking out when he suddenly realised that he could use the technique for his own purposes. He could get into Enfield police station undetected, and …

'Oh, bugger it. I've got to admit I'm keen to learn more, so I will go. But… but I'm definitely not committing myself, except to maintaining confidentiality.'

The PM leant over and grasped his shoulder.

'Understood,' said McKay. 'Ok, let's talk logistics. We don't want anyone to see you entering Thames House, so I'll send a vehicle to pick you up at King's Cross station tomorrow morning at nine thirty. If you wait in the taxi queue, one of my staff will find you and lead you to the vehicle.'

'How will I recognise him?'

'Her. You won't need to. She'll recognise you.'

'Just remember to wear your yellow shorts and blue tights to help her, though perhaps you'd better omit the word "*spy*",' said the PM. 'And with that statesman-like advice, I've got to call this meeting to a close. Mark, I do hope you'll agree to take on this task. I look forward to hearing the outcome of tomorrow's session.'

The PM shook Redstone's hand and walked out. An aide escorted Redstone to the front door. 'Don't forget your phone,' he said.

*

Back in his office, he sat down with David, Joanne and Colin the accountant and told them the cover story, feeling guilty about not telling them the whole truth.

‘I’m not sure I want to do it’ he said. ‘I’ve got so much to do here.’

All three colleagues groaned. ‘You’ve spent enough time doing nothing but work here,’ said Joanne. ‘You’re ready for a new challenge, outside London Bio. Time to spread your wings.’

‘I agree,’ said Colin, a big, shy man of few words who had joined London Bio from an insurance company in the City. ‘You need it. It’ll do you good. The company can run perfectly well without you for a few weeks. In any case, we’ll be able to reach you if necessary.’

‘Go for it,’ said David. ‘You really should. Not only for your own… well, this speech, or rather the policies you cook up, could make a significant contribution to the UK.’ Colin nodded.

‘You’ll regret it if you don’t,’ Joanne added. ‘You need a change. This’ll be quite different from anything you’ve done before. Well, for a long time – I guess it’s not that different from what you used to do when you were a civil servant.’

If only you knew, Redstone thought. ‘Ok, I suppose I ought to do it,’ he said. ‘I’m genuinely grateful to you for… well, for caring. And being so supportive. If you hadn’t said… well, I wouldn’t…’ He tailed off, blushing.

‘We do care,’ said David.

‘Yes,’ said Colin.

‘Speak for yourselves,’ said Joanne. They all laughed.

‘Well,’ said Redstone, ‘one of you has to be in charge while I’m away. Obviously, Joanne will really run the show, like when I’m here – stop smirking, Joanne – so I mean, nominally in charge.’

‘Not me,’ said Colin. ‘I’m the epitome of a backroom boy. Not my forte at all.’

‘That leaves you, then, David,’ said Redstone. ‘You did run a section in your last job.’

‘Yes, but that’s not the same as… oh, ok. As Colin said, we can reach you if we need to.’

Later in the afternoon, he phoned his children, gave them the cover story and got the same reactions. For once, Graham and Sophie agreed. He put the phone down and paced up and down the office. He didn’t like the idea of his brain being messed with, but if he was just being put in an MRI scanner, it should be ok.

And it would be worth it if it helped him get justice for Kate.

*

Redstone sat opposite Christina at a window table in a busy, bright, noisy restaurant, high in a City skyscraper. They looked out at the extensive views of twilit London, with trains worming into London Bridge station and the curve of the river contrasting with the straight lines of the streets and buildings.

‘Great view isn’t it?’ he said. ‘Very different from Hampstead. I’m sorry I couldn’t take you there. Did you go by yourself?’

‘No, I couldn’t… That is, I thought it wouldn’t be easy without someone to show me where to go. I went shopping again – London has fantastic shops!’

‘You do look very smart,’ he said, gesturing to her patterned black silk shirt.

‘Oh, thanks. I bought this today. But that’s boring – are you able to tell me about your meeting with the prime minister?’

As they ate, he told her about his lunch with the PM and Anne Jones and that his little talk about his company and his work had gone down well. She asked him to give her the same talk, and as he did so, she frequently interrupted with intelligent and thoughtful questions, about the science but also about his interactions with his colleagues and his feelings as the work had developed.

‘That’s so interesting!’ she said. ‘You have a gift for explaining technical issues. And you’ve done so well with your company!’

He liked the way her eyes crinkled when she smiled. ‘You’re very kind. I never know how much to attribute to luck.’

‘I’m sure you worked hard for your success. Anyway, what happened after you told them about your company? Am I allowed to know?’

‘Well, the PM asked me to put together a major policy speech. He’ll deliver it at the opening of the first of the next wave of nuclear power stations.’

‘Ah! That’s very interesting. I assume it’s because of your experience in the Department of Energy.’

‘That helps, but it’s also because of my work with London Bio.’ He took a swallow of wine, again feeling uncomfortable about not telling the whole truth. ‘Now, tell me more about yourself. How did you get into consulting work?’

‘Oh, through people I met in Oslo and a friend from Kristiansheim. I was asked to do one job, and it grew from there.’

‘I suppose it means quite a lot of travelling.’

‘Not at all,’ she said with surprising vehemence. ‘I do nearly all my work at home, using the internet.’

‘Did I say something wrong?’

‘Oh, no, sorry. Not at all. It’s just – it’s just that I don’t like travelling.’

‘I can understand that,’ Redstone said. ‘I don’t mind it, though I haven’t done much at all since… over the last four years. You must have found coming to London even more difficult than I first thought.’

‘Well, it is a bit overwhelming, I must admit.’

‘Er… don’t hesitate to say no, but would you like to visit a smaller city, like Cambridge? I’d be happy to take you and Ingrid there for the day if you like.’

'Oh! That's kind. Er… could I discuss it with Ingrid? I don't know all her plans.'

'Of course. Don't feel you're under any obligation… I mean I'd like to take you, but I realise you might not want to go. Or have the time.'

'No, I'd love to. But when would it be? I'm going back home on Sunday.'

'That just leaves Saturday.'

'Tell you what – I'll phone Ingrid now.' She picked up her phone, and within a moment was chatting in Norwegian.

'I'm afraid Ingrid can't make it on Saturday,' she said sadly.

'Pity.' He chewed on a mouthful of food. 'Er… I wonder… I don't want to seem pushy, but perhaps you'd like to go with me anyway? Just you and me?'

She beamed at him. 'Yes, I'd love to.'

'Great! Shall we meet at King's Cross station on Saturday at ten a.m.? Would that be ok?'

'Of course. I'm looking forward to it already!'

'Me too. Er… look, I've enjoyed this evening very much indeed.'

'Me too.'

'So, if, that is, I mean, how would you feel about meeting again before Saturday? Could you make dinner tomorrow evening? Please don't hesitate to say if you've got other plans, or…'

'That would be lovely!

*

Redstone entered his house. Treacle ran into the hall, looked into his face and opened her mouth wide to meow. As always, Redstone was amused at the contrast between the pink tongue and the black fur.

'Hello to you too,' he said. He picked her up and stroked her. She purred loudly.

He reflected that Christina had said that she didn't like travel, and he'd then idiotically offered her even more travel, namely to Cambridge. 'But she seemed pleased, so I must have got it right. For a change.'

THURSDAY 13 OCTOBER

The car was accelerating down a steep hill, but Redstone was unable to reach the brakes because he was sitting in the back, behind the driver's seat, stretching forwards and only just managing to grasp the steering wheel. He started to panic.

And then he was awake, sweating and filled with dread. The room was illuminated by the green glow of the bedside clock, which read 3:30. He quickly got out of bed and stumbled to the bathroom. The fan started humming. He washed his face with cold water and sat on the closed toilet seat with his head in his hands.

His life was getting out of control. Until recently, he'd been in charge of his own day-to-day routine, enjoying his research and the familiar companionship of his London Bio colleagues. But everything had changed. Almost overnight he had become wealthy, which had of course brought security and opportunities, but also new pressures. And now he was faced with this nuclear project. Working at such a high level – personally interacting with the prime minister – would be nerve-racking. He'd be away from London Bio. The prospect of dimension-hopping was scary. Maybe he should back out while he could – though that would mean losing the chance of pursuing his plan to get revenge for Kate.

And then there was Christina. He was becoming attracted to her, but the relationship clearly couldn't last, and besides, he was still mourning Kate. Perhaps he'd better cool it.

Kate had often reminded him that problems seemed more difficult at this time of night. He wouldn't make any decisions now. He drank some water and went back to bed.

*

He walked out into the spacious forecourt of King's Cross station, in front of the yellow brick façade with its huge arched windows.

He joined the taxi queue and almost immediately felt a tap on his shoulder. He turned to find himself facing a fair-haired, fit-looking woman in her thirties, wearing a gold gilet over a black polo-necked jumper. She had the air of a recently retired ruthless tennis champion. She said, 'Follow me,' and strode up towards the left of the station. As they reached Pancras Road, a black cab, with its taxi sign unlit, pulled up next to them, and they got in.

'I'm Laura Smith,' she said, 'and our driver's Lewis. Next stop, Thames House, but Lewis will take a roundabout route to check we're not being followed.'

'I suppose I don't need to introduce myself,' said Redstone. 'Indeed, you probably know more about me than I do.' Smith smiled. 'I see you don't deny it. Are you genuinely concerned that we might be followed? Isn't this cloak-and-dagger stuff a bit over the top?'

'The French are trying to find out what we're doing to investigate the reactor issue. They know we're looking into it.'

'How'd they find out?'

'Presumably the leak Gavin told you about yesterday.'

'When you say the French, who exactly?'

'We don't know whether the French government's involved, or if it's just France Nucléaire. Or, if it is just France Nucléaire, whether it's only the UK arm or the Paris headquarters too.'

'God, there's a lot to find out, isn't there?'

'Yes, there is. Incidentally, Lewis isn't privy to what you're going to be briefed on at Thames House, so please let's not speak about it till we're there.'

As the cab drove through back streets on its way south, Redstone sat back, feeling as though he was in a movie and that reality would soon intervene. 'I take it this isn't an ordinary cab. Has it got an ejector seat? Hidden machine guns? Rotating false number plates?'

'No,' said Smith, 'not even a ray gun. We bought it second hand, under the guise of being a taxi company. Lewis even has a licence from Transport for London. Well, it appears to be from them.'

'Yes,' said Lewis from the front. 'And I've taught myself how to spout eccentric right-wing political views.'

'At least tell me you have a gun in your handbag,' Redstone said to Smith.

'Certainly not,' she replied. 'Although I could, of course, kill you with my bare hands if you offended me.'

Something about her manner made Redstone wonder whether this was totally a joke. 'Have you always worked for MI5?' he asked.

'No, they don't employ children.'

'Ho, ho. I take it you're not going to tell me the story of your life, then.'

'No.'

'That just reinforces the feeling I've been getting, that I'm an actor in a spy movie.'

'Don't worry,' Smith said. 'You'll be surprised at how quickly everything becomes normal. Before you know it, we'll have you ordering Martinis which are shaken, not stirred.'

They alighted from the taxi in a quiet street at the back of Thames House – a huge neoclassical building with grey stone walls and recessed multi-paned windows – and walked up a few steps to an inconspicuous door which opened smoothly as they reached it. A uniformed guard examined Smith's pass, and she led the way along a corridor to an impressive marble staircase. They descended two flights. She keyed a code on a pad by a metal door, which swung open to reveal a cavernous area lit by strip lights. To the right were rooms of various sizes, formed by partitions with glass panels. Some people were sitting in offices and others were working in laboratories. There was a low hum of air conditioning.

Ahead and on the left were various pieces of large equipment. Redstone followed Smith to one of these at the far end; next to it was a short, stout man with a friendly, beaming face, who introduced himself as Jim Clothier.

'Let me show you my baby,' Clothier said. He pointed to the machine. 'This is our MRI scanner, which we've modified a bit. You've been told what it can do. I'm the person who acted as the guinea pig.'

Redstone examined the machine. He knew that it could produce pictures of the tissues in different parts of the body, and was the only way to study living brains. The main element was a huge squat white cylinder, on its side, containing a powerful electromagnet. A platform bed was connected to the surprisingly narrow tunnel in the centre of the cylinder.

'You must be using this in a different way from normal if you're affecting how the brain works.'

'Yes. We can target specific parts of the brain and enhance their efficiency. I've been given permission to let you see the report I wrote on this work. You can't take it out of the building, or even out of my office, but would you like to read it?'

'Yes, please,' said Redstone. The scientist in him was getting very intrigued.

Clothier led the way into his office. 'Here it is. Help yourself to coffee. I'll come back in about twenty minutes.'

Redstone read the report carefully. Clothier returned.

'A couple of questions,' said Redstone. 'First, you didn't mention that you have to inject this compound,' – he waved the report – 'to make the neurones respond to the radio waves. What about other effects of the injection?'

'There aren't any that we've found.'

'And second, if it worked on you, can you now demonstrate moving into the wavy dimension?'

‘Unfortunately, no. It seems that the effect wears off after a couple of weeks or so. Well, it was a couple of weeks in my case.’

‘So, how do you get into the wavy dimension? I mean, what do you actually do?’

‘Let me ask you – how do you move within the normal three dimensions? Like going to the left?’

‘Obviously, I use the appropriate muscles, mainly in my legs.’

‘Yes, but what does your brain do? How do you convert a wish into movement?’

‘Ah, I see,’ said Redstone. ‘Well, it’s a built-in instinct. Various nerves fire, without my conscious control. But that can’t be true for your dimension.’

‘No, it isn’t, until we do our treatment. In a sense, that’s what the treatment is for.’

‘Yes, but for moving left, I know what it means. I can see it. I can point to it.’

‘You could move left in the pitch dark. You don’t need input from your senses.’

Redstone found himself moving his left leg. He stopped. ‘So, are you saying that I just think about moving into the wavy dimension and it happens?’

‘Yes, more or less. I found that I twisted mentally, without moving any muscles, and it worked. Try that. After you’ve been treated, of course.’

‘Ok. What was it like in the wavy dimension?’

‘At first, I was overwhelmed with nausea. My brain was struggling to make sense of what my eyes were seeing.’

‘Oh, that’s not good. Sounds a bit like seasickness. Which I get.’

‘I suppose it is. Anyway, eventually, that wore off. When I looked around, it was like being in a corridor which was semi-transparent but made of mirrors. If I looked forward, I could see my own back a few yards ahead! If I looked down and ignored the floor, I could see the top of my head. If I looked sideways, I could see myself again, but between me and my image, I could see what was happening in the normal world.'

'Sounds scary but fascinating,' said Redstone. 'What was it like for people observing you?'

'I can answer that,' said Smith. 'One minute, he was there, then he made a slight twisting motion with his head, and he disappeared with a little pop.'

'Presumably, that was the air filling the space I left,' said Clothier.

'We couldn't see him at all,' Smith continued. 'And then he appeared in a different part of the room. Frankly, it was like magic!'

'Yes, people have said that lots of modern technology would seem magical to stone-age men – even to Victorian people, I suppose,' Clothier said.

'I know,' said Redstone. 'Think what Queen Victoria would have made of my asking Google a question on my mobile and hearing the answer spoken by a virtual assistant.' He leaned forward. 'Another question – what travels with you when you go into the wavy dimension? I assume your clothes stay on your body, since Laura didn't say that there was a pile of clothes left on the floor.'

'Yes, everything you're wearing or holding goes with you. It's the same as when you move in one of the normal dimensions, say to cross the room.'

'Good.'

'So, now, it's crunch time, Mark,' said Clothier. 'Are you in or out?'

'Are you sure that there are no adverse side effects? Did you feel different? Happier? Moodier? Did your family notice any changes?'

'Only one thing – I found that every morning, I was completing the crossword more quickly than before. It could have been a coincidence, but it is in line with what we would have expected. My family didn't make any comments suggesting they'd noticed anything different in my personality. Well – what's your decision?'

Redstone hesitated. He walked to the bookcase and stared at the books without seeing them. He visualised finding out what the police actually knew about Kate's murder, and then… Straightening his back, he turned to Clothier, 'I'm in. When do we start?'

'How about now? The procedure itself takes a few hours, and my experience is that your brain won't have finished processing the changes till a couple of weeks have passed.'

'Ok. Let's do it.'

'Before we start the procedure itself, we need to scan your brain to identify the exact positions of the parts we're going to strengthen. I suggest we do that this morning. The computer can then work on exactly where to target the radio waves, and we'll be ready to go tomorrow morning.'

'Fine,' said Redstone. 'Er… I'm surprised you can target very small parts of the brain with radio waves, since their wavelength is at least several centimetres.'

'I do enjoy interacting with a scientist!' replied Clothier with a grin. 'Solving that problem was one of our challenges. I can give you another report on how we do it if you like.'

'Yes please – but maybe some other time. Let's get my brain scanned.'

'I'll disappear for now,' said Smith. 'Using conventional means! See you later.' She walked out.

Clothier led the way into a small room where Redstone changed into a gown. 'We'll be asking you to visualise various things,' said Clothier, 'and after that, we'll show you a number of cards and monitor your brain's response.'

They walked back to the machine, and Redstone lay on its narrow, hard bed. Clothier disappeared into a room with a big window looking onto the scanner. His voice came through loudspeakers close to Redstone's head. 'Are you ready?'

'Yes,' said Redstone, his mouth dry. The bed moved back so that his head was inside the magnet – effectively inside a tunnel. He felt somewhat claustrophobic but reminded himself that he could easily slide down and out of the machine if he wished. The machine was very noisy, but Redstone could hear Clothier clearly asking him to visualise walking through his house, looking at a bird in the sky, driving, and unscrewing a joint on a waste pipe. Clothier then switched to showing Redstone cards, using a remotely controlled device. The cards showed mathematical equations, chemical formulae, geometrical diagrams and various word and number puzzles.

After a couple of hours, Redstone was tired, and he was glad when Clothier announced that the session was finished. He went into the changing room. Smith was sitting waiting for him when he came out.

'How was it?'

'Not too bad. Well, it was quite stressful.'

'I suggest we have some lunch nearby, and then I take you to our new office in Number 10. There's a small Italian restaurant up Victoria Street. Nothing fancy but very pleasant. Shall we go there?'

The restaurant had a narrow, unpretentious frontage but was surprisingly deep. The walls were decorated with paintings of Tuscan scenes.

'The service is good,' said Redstone, 'but have you noticed that the waiters' station seems to be a dating agency? Some of the staff can hardly keep their hands off each other. Good luck to them. I can just about remember being that young.'

'Yes, nice to see youngsters enjoying their workplace. I think they're all from the same part of Italy. Maybe they choose to work here knowing they might find a partner.'

Smith asked Redstone about his background, and he was happy to chat. She was less communicative about her past but told him she'd recently married a high-flying police officer. She was quite senior in MI5. She explained that her cover story would be that she had been seconded from the Home Office to help Redstone with his work for the prime minister. She would pretend to be more junior than she was.

'Before we leave,' she said, 'let me give you this.' She handed him a security pass with a complex design and a rather good photo of him. 'It'll let you into Number 10, through the staff entrance at the back, off Horse Guards Road.'

'I don't recall seeing this picture of myself before,' he said. She smiled.

They left the restaurant and walked down Victoria Street.

'Oh, look,' said Redstone. 'I hate these people.' Ahead was a group of young men dressed in bright blue t-shirts over their outer clothes. The shirts were printed with a logo for '*World Animals*'. The young men were stopping passers-by and hassling them for donations.

'Me too,' said Smith. 'I've seen them here before, several times, wearing different t-shirts. They get a rake-off from the money they collect.'

As Smith and Redstone approached the group, one young man stepped to block Redstone's path and said, 'You look a kind man. Can I interest you in…'

'No, thank you,' interrupted Redstone and walked ahead without deviating. The young man clearly judged that he would come off worse in a collision with Redstone, who was much bigger, and moved aside to block Smith's path. 'You look a kind woman. Would you donate…'

'No, thank you,' said Smith and stepped to her left. The young man stepped to his right to continue blocking her path. She moved again, but he moved back again to continue blocking her and reached out to hold her shoulder. She stood still and stared at him, expressionless.

'Take your fucking hand off me.'

He snatched his hand away as if her shoulder were red hot. 'Sorry, sorry,' he said and backed away.

Redstone mused over the incident as they crossed the road and walked by the hulking side of the Queen Elizabeth II conference centre. There was something scary about Smith, but he couldn't put his finger on it. They made their way to the back of Downing Street where a police officer opened a tall gate to let them through.

Smith led Redstone into Number 10 through the back entrance, and they climbed several flights of stairs to the top floor. She took him through a warren of small, low-ceilinged rooms to a beige office, furnished with two desks facing each other, a couple of office chairs and a dented grey filing cabinet with a locking bar down the front. The worn, ribbed grey carpet had a coffee stain near the door. He felt a surge of excitement to be working for the government again, indeed in a more central role than when he had been a civil servant.

'Home for the next few weeks,' she said. 'It's not the luxury you private-sector types are used to, but we'll be spending a fair amount of time out of the office anyway.'

'Certainly not luxurious!' he replied, sitting at one of the desks. 'I'm amused at the contrast with the posh rooms downstairs. Anyway, let's work out a plan of action. It seems to me that our priority should be to arrange to see the UK Chief Executive of France Nucléaire. As soon as possible. Do you agree?'

'Yes, I do. We might pick up some useful information, though I wouldn't bank on it.' She took out her mobile phone and consulted it. 'The CEO's name is Albert Lesage. I'll call now.'

She was on the phone for several minutes, and Redstone could see that she was getting more and more impatient. 'They've now put me on hold,' she said. 'I'm… ah—' she listened. 'Would you like me to tell the prime minister that Mr Lesage won't see Dr Redstone for another month?' She listened further. 'Excellent. Tuesday at ten a.m. in your office.'

'Well done,' said Redstone. 'I'd also like to meet the chief nuclear inspector. He or she should know as much as anyone outside France Nucléaire about the details of the reactor programme.'

She nodded. 'It's a him.'

'I'd also like to understand how the new reactors will differ from the existing ones. It would be helpful if we could meet on Monday so that I'm briefed before we see Lesage.'

'It's arranged!' she said. 'I thought you'd accept the job. I set up the meeting this morning while you were in the MRI machine. We're to meet in his office in Victoria Street on Monday morning.'

'Blimey, you are efficient! What's his name?'

'Alan Cunningham. He's an engineer with a long history of working in the nuclear industry. He joined the Nuclear Inspectorate about three years ago.'

'Great. Will you come with me?'

'If you want me to. I do think it might be helpful. I'll play the junior assistant, there to take notes.'

Redstone left Downing Street and travelled to the Benet Hotel. The receptionist recognised him and phoned Christina who appeared almost immediately and embraced Redstone.

'If it's ok with you,' he said, 'I thought we could go out to Docklands. It's a quick ride on the tube. The new buildings are exciting, and I know a good tapas restaurant there.'

'Lovely!'

*

Over dinner, Christina asked about Redstone's work for his speech. He described the office in Number 10 and told her about Laura Smith, whom he described as his assistant. She then asked him about his time in the Department of Energy. He was impressed by how well informed she was about energy policy.

Redstone paid the bill. 'I thought the food was ok, but not as tasty as it looked,' he said. 'But the atmosphere and service are good, aren't they?'

'Yes, they are, but I enjoyed the food as well. We don't have any tapas restaurants in Kristiansheim. And Docklands is amazing! The scale of the buildings and the variety of styles! I didn't realise that London is so varied.'

'Does that mean you'll miss it when you go back?'

She smiled and looked into his eyes. 'Are you fishing, if that's the right expression in English?'

He grinned. 'Maybe you should have been a *psycho*analyst. Well, I'll certainly miss your company.'

'I'm not gone yet. But to answer your fishing question, yes, I've truly enjoyed these meals together. As for London, I'll be pleased to have been here. You've made it a marvellous stay. I'm so grateful.' She stood up, walked around the table and kissed his cheek.

'If I take you to dinner again tomorrow, can I have two kisses?'

'You can have two now.' She kissed him again.

On his way home, he checked his phone. There was a text from Sophie. '*Hi. How's things? Love Sophie xxx.*' He texted back. '*Not too bad. Looking up, as it happens. Tell you more when we speak. Love Dad xxx.*'

Bizarrely, he wished that Kate could have met Christina. She would have liked her, he was sure.

FRIDAY 14 OCTOBER

Redstone lay on the bed of the scanner. The drip in the back of his hand contained a sedative as well as the chemical needed to make the procedure successful. He dozed off.

He was woken by the sound and motion of the bed sliding out of the magnet.

'Wake up!' said Clothier. 'It's finished.'

'How long have I been in the machine?' asked Redstone groggily.

'Two hours. Fancy a coffee?'

They walked to Clothier's office.

'How will I know when my brain's adjusted enough that I can move into the wavy dimension?' asked Redstone, sitting down in an easy chair.

'In my case, I just suddenly realised I could do it, and how to do it seemed obvious. So, I tried it, and it worked. I felt an unpleasant pressure in my head, but it quickly went, and there I was.'

'And when you're in the wavy dimension, can you see and hear clearly what's happening in normal dimensions?'

'Well, the distortions I mentioned yesterday can make it tricky. Things are clear, but there are lots of competing images. And the same happens with the sound, so I found it a bit difficult to make out what people were saying.'

'You said the effect wears off. Is there a danger that I might be trapped in the wavy dimension if it wears off while I'm out of the normal world?'

Clothier shifted in his chair. 'I worried a lot about that. As a result, I stopped going into the wavy dimension as soon as I found doing it a bit difficult, even though I'd only done it four times by then. My strong advice is that you do the same.'

‘Ok.’ Redstone sat back and thought. ‘Can you tell me again what it’ll be like?’

‘It’s as though you’re in a very odd corridor, constructed from half-silvered glass and distorting mirrors. Like in a hall of mirrors at a fairground.’

‘I’m looking forward to experiencing it myself. It’s a fantastic scientific advance. I still find it difficult to accept it’s not being published.’

‘Well, you know why we’re not publishing it. And to be honest, you won’t find it a pleasant experience. The scientist in you will be extremely interested, to put it mildly, but it is extremely stressful. Well, that’s what I found. It might be different for you.’

‘More stressful than watching England get bowled out in the Ashes?’

‘A close-run thing. Oh, a couple more issues, before you go,’ said Clothier. ‘I’ve been asked to tell you that you shouldn’t use the new ability for any purpose other than those agreed with us. Of course, there’s no way we can control your use, but there it is – I’ve delivered the instruction.’ He looked straight at Redstone, who looked straight back and said he understood.

‘And the other thing is that we’ll need to monitor you, to make sure you’re ok. I suggest you come in every Monday morning. But sooner if there’s anything you think we should discuss.’

Redstone said that sounded sensible, but secretly wondered how much of the monitoring was to keep an eye on his activity rather than his health. He left the building looking forward to enjoying a total change of scene and company that evening.

*

He sat with Christina in a recess in an upmarket French restaurant near Covent Garden. She was wearing a cerise dress which left one shoulder bare, and Redstone thought she looked stunning.

Jazz played softly in the background, and the air smelt faintly of garlic. A candle flickered on the red-and-white chequered tablecloth. Redstone held his wine glass to the candlelight and admired the clear ruby colour. Christina raised her glass to him.

'I think you've got me a bit drunk,' she said, 'but I'm not complaining. This has been a lovely evening. So different from anything I've done for years.'

'Me too,' he replied. 'I wish you weren't going home so soon.' He leaned forward, picked up her hand and kissed it. She giggled.

'I can't believe I just did that!' he said.

'Nor can I. It was pathetic, compared with this.' She pulled him round to sit next to her on the banquette and kissed him on the mouth. Her lips were warm and soft, and he felt a wave of love. He put his arm around her and returned the kiss.

Back at her hotel, Christina told Redstone that he looked tired.

'I think you ought to go home now and get a good night's sleep.'

They embraced. She smiled at him but looked strained. 'Tomorrow's my last day here,' she said.

'I know, only too well. Let's talk about it while we're in Cambridge.'

SATURDAY 15 OCTOBER

Redstone leaned on a wall in King's Cross station, next to the platform for trains to Cambridge, feeling detached from the crowds milling about under the soaring lattice roof and staring anxiously at the departure screens.

After a few minutes, he spotted Christina looking around uncertainly. She was dressed in an elegant grey coat. Redstone himself was dressed in a casual jacket and jeans, and he wondered if he'd misled her about the nature of the outing. He called out to her, and she waved and walked briskly towards him. They embraced.

'You look extremely smart,' he said. 'You know we're just going to wander through the colleges and then have a bit of lunch?'

'Oh, I hope I'm not embarrassing you,' she said. 'I just wanted to look nice.'

'Of course not, you look lovely.'

They sat quietly, looking out of the window, as the train sped through the Hertfordshire countryside. The only noise was a low whine from the motors and distant chatter from a group of pensioners further down the carriage. The green-and-brown landscape was dotted with copses. Patches of sunlit field shone in the rays beaming through breaks in a heavy grey cloud. Redstone felt at ease, looking forward to the day, but then sensed something was bothering Christina.

'Is everything ok?' he asked. 'You look a bit worried.'

'Oh, I'm sorry,' she replied. 'Yes, everything's more than ok. I'll be fine.' She seemed almost to shake herself, and smiled at him.

They took a taxi from Cambridge station, through bustling streets that were thick with cyclists, mostly students but occasionally smartly dressed older people. At Magdalene Street, Redstone paid the taxi driver and took Christina along the crowded pavement, past the castle-like entrance of St John's College. They turned into a large cloistered court in Trinity College, enjoying the sudden quiet, and went through to emerge on a narrow bridge over the Cam.

For Redstone, Christina stood out in three vivid dimensions against the calm environment. He enjoyed standing close to her as they stopped to admire the view of the river curving past the lawns and stone buildings.

'You must have thoroughly enjoyed your time here as a student,' she said. 'It's so beautiful.'

'I did enjoy parts of it, but there was a lot of stress and pressure. Students here have to work extremely hard.'

'Did you play any sport? That's a good way to reduce stress.'

'Yes, some cricket, and also I took up archery.'

'Sorry, I know about cricket, but I don't know what "archery" means.'

Redstone mimed drawing a bow and letting fly an arrow, with exaggerated actions and sound effects. She laughed. 'Ah, now I understand. Do you still do it?'

'No, though I still have all the gear. In my loft at home.'

'I suppose that means you'd have a lot of difficulty finding it if your loft's like mine.'

'Not really. I'm a very organised person. Some people find that quite annoying. I hope you don't!'

'No, not at all. Anyway, I'm afraid we have bigger differences than that. Like where we live.'

'Yes. Let's not spoil the morning – let's discuss it over lunch.'

They wandered through the peaceful meadows and trees of the Backs, returned over the Cam and made their way through a couple of narrow, slightly eerie streets like canyons between honey-coloured stone college buildings, to the back entrance of King's College chapel.

'This is literally awe-inspiring, even for those of us who've been here many times before,' Redstone said, as they waited in a short queue for admittance. 'It's superb from the outside, but wait till you get in there!'

Christina smiled, but as they entered the chapel, she gasped in wonder. They sat on a pew and gazed up at the soaring walls and windows and the intricate stonework of the roof. They wandered further down and exchanged superlatives about the complex beauty of the carved woodwork.

'Do you mind if we just sit and contemplate for a while?' asked Redstone.

'Not at all – I'd like to do that,' said Christina in her precisely pronounced English.

Redstone sat and wondered what he was doing there with this lovely woman who wasn't Kate. Joanne had advised him, in effect, just to live for the day, but he wasn't that sort of man. He was falling for Christina. He knew she'd have some flaws – he almost hoped she did – but he hadn't yet spotted them. Her command of English was outstanding. She was sympathetic and understanding about Kate's death and the effect it had had on him.

But she was rooted in Norway, and he was rooted a thousand miles away in London. Could a relationship between them have any future? He knew this was an issue which faced hundreds of thousands of people nowadays, but he couldn't figure a way through it. Maybe he should end the relationship before it went any further. It wouldn't be hard, because Christina was going back home tomorrow. Maybe he was being ridiculous – he'd met her only a few days ago.

He looked at her and saw that she had tears in her eyes. She smiled.

'This isn't like me at all,' she said, clearing her throat. 'It's the combination of this breath-taking building, being so far from home and... and being with someone new. It's as though I'm someone else. To tell the truth, it's rather liberating.' She stood up. 'Is it ok if I just walk down there and collect myself?'

'Of course,' he said. Christina walked away slowly. He watched her go and bent his head and closed his eyes. The way she was acting made her even more attractive. He sat and agonised. If he did continue with Christina, what would his children think? He didn't want to hurt them – they'd suffered enough already. Sophie had urged him to look for a new relationship, but he suspected that she'd have mixed feelings if he told her he'd found someone. He suspected Graham would rationalise the situation but in reality be upset.

'What shall I do, Treacle?' he muttered.

'Pardon?' Christina said, having returned without his realising it.

'Oh, sorry – I have this habit of talking to my cat when I'm alone, and I was so lost in my thoughts...'

'What did you say his name was?'

'Treacle. It's a her. Kate and I got her when she was a kitten. She's now about ten years old. I have deep and meaningful conversations with her, and she's totally non-judgmental. Especially when she's not present, like now. Talking to her helps me clear my mind. Or just register thoughts.'

'Does "treacle" mean something in English?'

'Yes, it's a sticky dark syrup. It's made from sugar cane. We called her that because she's so sweet.'

'Ah, syrup. I understand,' Christina said. 'Do you find those conversations a comfort?'

'Well, it's undeniably not the same as having a human being to talk to, but it's better than nothing. I suppose you went through something similar when you got divorced? Sorry if I'm being intrusive.'

'No, of course you're not being intrusive. After my divorce, I found myself desperate to talk to someone about everyday problems. And bigger problems, too. I couldn't burden Ingrid with them – she was too young at the time. I was lucky to have some close friends I could talk to. Friends from childhood.'

'When I went out with male friends,' Redstone said, 'Kate often used to ask me what we'd discussed. She was always surprised when I told her it was politics, technology, sport, but not personal issues. More than surprised – critical. I do discuss some personal stuff with my oldest friend, but we don't meet very often. He lives in Manchester.'

'Do you use Facebook? People keep in touch on social media, though I admit I don't.'

'Nor do I. I tried it, but it wasn't for me. And there was all that fuss about personal data being misused. But the twins are heavy users.'

'Ingrid too. Anyway,' she said, putting her hand on his, 'did Treacle help you with your problem?'

'Frankly, no. I think you know what my problem is. Shall we go to lunch now? I've reserved a table in a bistro near the chemistry labs. It'll take us about twenty minutes to walk there.'

'Lovely.'

They left the chapel and walked out of the college onto King's Parade. Redstone took Christina's arm as they crossed the road. They continued walking away from the college area when suddenly she pulled him into a narrow alley and led him to a cottage with two steps leading up to its front door. She let go of his arm, mounted the steps and turned to face him. She held his shoulders, pulled him towards her and kissed him on the lips. He kissed her back. She smiled, descended from the steps, and without a word walked back to the main road. For a moment

Redstone stood still, engulfed in a happiness he hadn't felt for years. Pulling himself together he strode after her, and as he caught up, he thought how lucky he was that this attractive, sophisticated woman could also be so spontaneously affectionate. To him.

They walked into the bistro and were seated at the back of the restaurant.

'This is lovely!' said Christina, looking around at the low, uneven white walls, the pristine cloths and the dark beams.

'Yes, and the food's imaginative and particularly good. You'll see.'

As they waited for their starters, Christina raised her glass. 'Thanks for a lovely morning. I don't want it to end.'

'I feel the same. I don't know what this morning has meant to you, but for me, it's been wonderful. I've loved your company. It's been the best day I've had for years.'

She smiled and leaned across the table and put her hand on his. 'Me too.'

'Which brings me to what I wanted to raise with you, I suppose,' he said.

'I guess it's the same as what I wanted to raise with you,' Christina responded, looking embarrassed. 'You go first.'

Redstone blushed and cleared his throat. 'I… I'd really like to develop our relationship, but I don't know what to do about the fact that we live a thousand miles apart…'

'Exactly,' she interrupted. 'I'm sure I don't want to say goodbye forever when I fly home tomorrow.' She squeezed his hand.

'We're like a couple of teenagers,' he said.

'Except that it would be easier if we were. We wouldn't have all the ties that bind us to our home towns.'

'Or if we did, we wouldn't recognise them. Or wouldn't care.'

'What would teenagers do in our situation?'

'If they had the money we have, I guess they'd fly backwards and forwards between London and…'

'Kristiansheim,' she supplied.

'…sorry – Kristiansheim as often as they could.'

'Sounds like the least bad solution,' she said. 'It might not be ideal, but I'd want to give it a try.'

'Yes, let's do that.'

'But I'm also worried about something else,' she said. 'My town could hardly be more different from London. It's tiny and quiet. It's a long way from anywhere. I'm afraid you'd get fed up with it very quickly.'

'How do you feel about London? Do you find it too busy? Too big?'

'Yes, I'm afraid I do,' she said quickly.

The first course arrived, and they started eating. He looked across the table and felt a wave of tenderness. He sensed a fragility in her, an internal conflict, and wanted to take her in his arms and protect her. She glanced up and saw the way he was looking at her. She seemed to read his expression and gave him a smile which melted his heart. He quickly looked down and carried on eating.

'Will this speech-writing task allow you enough time to visit me in Norway?' she asked.

'That's up to me, and I've already decided! How about two weekends from now?'

'Marvellous! It'll take you most of a day to get to my house from yours, so it would be good if you could travel out on Friday morning and back on Monday morning.'

'Fine,' said Redstone. 'I'll put it in the diary and ask Joanne to organise travel.'

'Maybe it will be easier if I get the travel arranged from the Norway end. If you leave it with me, I'll get my secretary to sort it out. She'll liaise with Joanne.'

They carried on eating and chatting. He suddenly realised that they were the only customers left in the restaurant. He paid the bill.

'Maybe I could see you once more before you go home. Would it be helpful if I took you and Ingrid to the airport tomorrow?'

'That's kind, but I've got a car arranged, and it'll be very early. Anyway, I'd like to avoid an emotional farewell at the airport. Let's do that back at the hotel.'

*

At home, he phoned Sophie in Brussels and told her how his relationship with Christina was developing. He said he was worried that she might find it hurtful, but she was enthusiastic. Feeling encouraged, he phoned Graham, who was much more cautious.

'Think it through, Dad. Be careful.'

'What do you mean?'

'How's it going to end? I don't want you to get all fucked up again.'

Redstone worried that this was code – Graham was still traumatised by Kate's death and didn't want her replaced in his father's emotions. But Graham read his mind: 'And it's not about me,' he said. 'I'm ok with you finding a new… partner. More than ok, indeed – to be honest, I'd feel less obliged to worry about you. I just think you're setting yourself up for problems.'

'But I really like her…'

'I know, but look where you're coming from. It's great that you're having a good time with her, but…'

'Ok, ok. Sophie was much…'

'Yes, she would be. Just take care.'

MONDAY 17 OCTOBER

Redstone and Smith walked up Victoria Street.

'I'm quite nervous about this visit,' said Redstone. 'I haven't been to the Department since Malvern sacked me six years ago.'

'Did you enjoy your time there?'

'Yes, but the ending was a shock. I was lucky to have Kate to help me through it.'

The Department of Energy was in a modern glass-and-stone building with a large glass entrance lobby stuck on the front. They walked to the linear reception desk that ran parallel to the back wall of the lobby.

'Hello, Dr Redstone,' said the receptionist. 'How nice to see you again! How are you?'

Redstone immediately recognised the woman he'd greeted every morning for several years when he'd worked there. 'Hello, Elsie! I'm fine. How are you?'

'Mustn't grumble,' she said with a smile. She looked at her screen. 'I have your appointment. Please take a seat over there, and someone will be down to collect you. Here are your security passes.'

They walked across the marble floor to a group of low, boxy armchairs. Redstone sat and looked out at the street, feeling exposed and uncomfortable.

'I'm surprised that the chief nuclear inspector is in this building,' he said.

'Why's that?'

'He should be independent of the Department of Energy. His work should be determined only by safety stuff. Policy needs should be irrelevant to him.'

A woman in a blue uniform came up to them. 'Dr Redstone and Ms Smith?' she asked. 'Please come with me – I'll take you up.'

The escort took them up in a lift and into an office containing four people working at desks. Redstone suddenly realised that it was the permanent secretary's outer office. The escort announced, 'Dr Redstone and Ms Smith for Mrs Hitchcock.'

'There's been a mistake,' he told the young man who walked over to them. 'We aren't here to see the permanent secretary. Our appointment's with the chief nuclear inspector.'

'Yes, I know that was what you asked for, but Mrs Hitchcock felt it would be helpful if you met her and Mr Cunningham together. Please come this way.'

A grimace – almost of disgust – crossed Smith's face. Redstone wondered what that was about, but decided to go along with the new arrangement and see what happened.

They walked into the permanent secretary's spacious office. The only personalisation was an arrangement of group photos on one wall. Valerie Hitchcock rose from behind her wide desk. She was tall and imposing, wearing a charcoal trouser suit with a large brooch on the lapel. Her face was tanned, and her nose reddened.

'It's been a long time,' said Redstone. 'You look well. Just returned from holiday?'

'Yes, I have, as it happens,' Hitchcock said.

Redstone looked at her jet-black hair, blacker than he remembered, thought, *Life's a beach and then you dye*, and whipped out a handkerchief to smother a laugh, which he turned into a coughing fit. 'Sorry,' he spluttered, as Smith looked at him with a raised eyebrow and Hitchcock stared.

She gestured to a thin, balding man with an anxious demeanour. 'This is Alan Cunningham.' She ignored the young man who had taken them in, who Redstone assumed was her private secretary, and paid no attention to Smith. 'Let's get started.'

They sat down at a plain bare conference table. Redstone suddenly remembered sitting in the same place when Malvern had told him he was being made redundant. A cold wave passed through his body.

'Right,' Hitchcock said. 'I understand that you've got yourself a job writing a speech for the prime minister.'

'Well, I…'

'And a lot of it will be about energy policy,' she continued.

'Well, some of it.'

'And you'll be looking into rumours about the new wave of reactors not being ready in time. Which is highly confidential, of course.' She scanned the group to ensure everyone understood that and then looked at Redstone with a cold, challenging expression.

'Your description of what I'm going to do is correct,' he said. 'That's why I thought it would be useful to talk to Alan here. I didn't want to bother you.'

'Well, given the strong policy content of what you'll be doing and the complete overlap with my responsibilities, I feel it would be best if you work closely with me. You need top-level oversight since you're working for the PM.'

'Very considerate of you to offer your time like that. Of course I'd be happy to hear your views on the policy issues, but at the moment I want to get input from Alan about engineering aspects of the reactor programme. Not policy stuff. So I'd rather just talk to him. I know you're not an engineer. Anyway, I'm not a civil servant anymore, so oversight from you won't be necessary.'

'Who's managing your contract? Patently it's not the PM himself.'

Smith coughed. Redstone glanced at her and replied, 'I'm afraid I can't tell you that.'

Hitchcock flushed. 'In that case I can't allow Cunningham to give you any information which might be classified. You no doubt remember the rules about talking to contractors with no security clearance.'

'Look, Valerie, let's…'

'He's got the highest security clearance,' said Smith. She stared at Hitchcock. 'And I mean the very highest. If you like, phone the PM's private secretary. He'll confirm it.'

Hitchcock's surprised glance at Smith was followed by a fleeting scowl. Redstone surmised that Smith was implying she knew Hitchcock's security clearance to be less than the highest. If that were true, it would be unusual for a permanent secretary.

Hitchcock turned back to Redstone. 'Even so, I still need to be in control of all this. It goes to the heart of my responsibilities.'

'Are you saying Alan reports to you?'

'I don't think that our management reporting lines fall into your remit, do you? Let's stick to the issues you've been tasked with.'

Smith addressed Hitchcock again. 'Just so I can get things clear, Alan's the chief nuclear inspector?'

'I thought you'd know that.' She turned back to Redstone. 'As I was…'

'A senior, experienced, specialist engineer in charge of a large group of trained professionals?' said Smith.

Hitchcock stared at her. 'He…'

'I think that's accurate,' said Cunningham.

'And he's responsible for the safety of hundreds of thousands of us?'

'Look,' said Hitchcock, 'I don't…'

'Possibly millions, if you add it all up,' said Cunningham.

'And he earns more than you.'

'What!'

‘I just wondered why he should report to you, rather than the other way round.’ The private secretary gave a muffled snort, and Redstone looked at Smith with astonishment. Cunningham studiously looked away.

‘Who do you think you’re talking to? Who exactly are you, Ms…? I didn’t catch your name.’

Smith stared expressionlessly at Hitchcock and said nothing.

Hitchcock paled, and Redstone thought she’d just realised something about Smith, as if Smith had some power Hitchcock couldn’t match. Smith calmly squared her notebook on the table, picked up her pen and waited.

Hitchcock stood up. ‘I’m going to get a drink. I’ll be back in a minute.’ She marched out, her head held high, avoiding any eye contact. The others remained seated. Nobody said a word. Redstone fiddled with his phone, conscious that the private secretary and Cunningham would be fearing problems with Hitchcock in the future as a result of having witnessed her humiliating exchange with Smith. He put his phone down and studied the photos on the wall, realising that each featured Hitchcock among a group of notables. He resisted a strong temptation to get up and straighten one photo, which was askew.

Hitchcock returned and sat down. ‘Let’s get on with the meeting.’

Redstone cleared his throat. ‘Tomorrow, I’m meeting Albert Lesage, the UK chief executive of France Nucléaire.’

‘I know very well who he is,’ snapped Hitchcock. ‘I have regular meetings with him.’

‘Excellent. Where are those meetings?’

‘Why on earth do you need to know that?’

‘Are some of them in France?’

‘As it happens, yes.’

‘Right. Please tell me all you can about him. Not his professional self, but rather his personality.’

'Our relationship's been strictly professional, so all I can tell you is he's a highly competent manager. He's one of France's top people. It's under his leadership that France Nucléaire has increased electricity supplies from the current power stations.'

'How did they do that?'

'As you observed, I'm not an engineer.'

'But Alan is. Alan, your people and your staff must have monitored these power stations as they increased output.'

'Well,' said Cunningham, 'we monitored all the safety indicators.'

'I detect a "but". What is it?'

'We haven't been monitoring the stations physically for nearly three years – we just examine the data they send us.'

'Why on earth not?' asked Redstone. 'Surely it's an integral part of your job?'

'Our job changed after we were absorbed into the Department of Energy. Valerie's the best person to explain the policy change.' He turned to Hitchcock, who was studiously avoiding looking at Smith.

'I reached an agreement with France Nucléaire that the physical inspections were a waste of my budget and their time,' Hitchcock said. 'They do their own regular inspections, and as Alan says, they send us all the data. It was pointless for our inspectors to waste time visiting remote areas just to read data off screens and second-guess professionals.'

'You agree with that?' asked Redstone of Cunningham.

'My job's to implement the policy set by others,' he said, looking at Hitchcock for confirmation. She nodded.

'And have you visited the new plants, the stations under construction?' asked Redstone.

'Yes. I'm satisfied they're being built to the required standards.'

‘What remains to be completed before the first one starts generating electricity?’

‘That’s Dymbury. All the civil works, like buildings and access roads, are complete. So’s the electrical side – the turbines, the generators and so on. France Nucléaire still has to load the nuclear fuel and start the final live testing.’

‘Do you know of any reason why the start-up might be delayed?’

‘That’s an interesting question,’ said Cunningham. ‘I’ve been wondering…’

He was interrupted by Hitchcock. ‘It’s not Alan’s role to speculate about the nuclear timetable. His job is to ensure nuclear safety.’

‘But it is your job, Valerie, to tell ministers if there’s likely to be a delay,’ said Redstone. ‘Do you know of any reason why the start-up might be delayed?’

Hitchcock flushed. ‘I don’t need lessons from you about how to do my job. If I knew there was going to be a delay, I would have told ministers. I don’t, so I haven’t. This meeting’s now at an end.’

She stood up, walked to the door and held it open. ‘Goodbye.’

Cunningham stood up. ‘Goodbye, Dr Redstone, goodbye, Ms Smith,’ he said awkwardly.

Once Redstone and Smith had left the building, Redstone said, ‘What the hell was that about? You, having a go at Valerie?’

‘I have my reasons.’

‘So, you’re not going to tell me. But we were trying to get some information from her.’

‘Do you think we would have got more if I hadn’t riled her?’

Redstone thought. ‘Probably not.’

‘No. People who are upset are less in control. Anyway, she was manifestly angry with you. What was all that aggression about?’

'I'll tell you when we get back.'

They crossed the road and walked in front of Methodist Central Hall, an unsympathetic, dominant, domed and pillared edifice. They made their way back to the office in Number 10.

'Right,' said Redstone. 'The spat with Valerie. It dates back to when we were both in the Department of Energy. Our secretary of state asked me to do a quick review of budgets and spending across the Department.'

'Why you, and why did he ask that?'

'*She* asked it,' – Smith smiled wryly at being caught out – 'because Malvern was constantly telling her that she couldn't do things she wanted to do, as we didn't have the money. She wanted someone other than the financial management people to do it, and she knew me well because of my work on North Sea oil policy. I guess she also assumed that I was pretty numerate, given my scientific background.'

'It sounds as though she trusted you, too.'

'Probably. We got on well. Anyway, I wasn't keen, but I had no choice, so I did the review. I found some budgets which their holders agreed could be cut, and there wasn't the bad feeling I'd feared. But then I realised that Valerie had been spending money improperly.'

'Meaning?'

'She spent a lot of money on an expensive consultancy without declaring that it was owned by her brother-in-law. Her sister's husband.'

'How did you know he owned it?'

'Kate and I had spent some time chatting to him at a Departmental Christmas party, while Valerie was off smarming with Malvern. Valerie had taken her brother-in-law as her guest. I don't know why she didn't take her husband.'

'Maybe the brother-in-law's consultancy made the best bid for the work.'

'Even if they did, Valerie should have declared an interest and let someone else decide which consultants to employ.'

'Yes, of course. Are you saying she got a rake-off?'

'I don't know. But she reacted violently when I asked her about it.'

'And?'

'I spent a week thinking about it and then Malvern suddenly sacked me. That gave me bigger fish to fry.'

'You didn't report it?'

'No. I didn't tell anyone. But she evidently took it badly that I found out. She was the only colleague who didn't send condolences when Kate was killed. I got the impression that she resented me not only because I found out, but also because I kept it to myself. It's bizarre. I still don't understand it.'

'It's because what you knew gave you a hold over her.' Smith sat still for a moment. 'It all fits together. I'm going to tell you something in the very strictest confidence. Have you registered that last bit?'

'Yes, of course.'

'Malvern and Hitchcock are lovers. What you've just told me makes me think it goes back longer than we'd realised.'

Redstone was stunned. 'Bloody hell! I know he's not married, but she is. Well, she was.'

'She isn't the first person to have an extra-marital affair,' said Smith tartly.

'But… well, she can be charming. And she's very impressive. But I still can't quite believe it!'

'I think you've lived a sheltered life,' said Smith. 'These things happen all the time.'

'Not in my circles.'

'Maybe there are fewer affairs amongst scientists than amongst normal people. Because you're all cold-hearted calculating machines with no passions except for your work.'

'Ho, ho, ho.'

'I may be joking, but you do think a lot before you get involved, don't you? Or even when you are involved.'

'Yes, that's true,' he admitted. 'But returning to the Grand Affair, are you saying she told him of my findings and persuaded him to get rid of me to save her bacon?'

'Exactly, except that the word "persuaded" might be a bit weak. I'll ask my colleagues if there's any evidence of the affair going back that far.'

'Shit. Shit, shit, shit. So that's why I was sacked. All this time I'd been thinking it was due to my own incompetence, and now it seems it wasn't. That bloody woman's manoeuvrings turned my entire life upside down. Though to be honest, I suspect I wouldn't have got much further in the civil service anyway – I'm not political enough. But still – all that agonising for nothing. I don't know whether to be delighted or furious.'

'You're allowed to be both, you know.'

'Thanks.' He got up and paced about the cramped room. 'So, coming back to the present, is that bloody woman's affair why McKay and the PM didn't want Malvern involved in our work? Because they feared he'd tell Hitchcock? Anyway, why would it matter?'

'Yes, it is why Malvern couldn't be involved. The reason it would matter is we suspect that Hitchcock is too close to France Nucléaire. We think she's the leak. She's a traitor, to use plain English. In fact, given what you've told me, a corrupt, manipulative traitor. I don't like traitors. I despise them.'

'Bloody hell! Well, that would fit with what she said about meeting Lesage in France. And it explains why Malvern deliberately tried to put me off doing the job.'

'Yes. She got him to act like that. You might have found out things she doesn't want revealed. After all, you've done it before.'

'Do you think Malvern knows she leaks secrets to Lesage?'

'Your guess is as good as mine. Well, maybe not quite as good.'

'Do you think Malvern got her promoted to permanent secretary?'

'Interesting thought. I'll look into it,' said Smith.

'What about the fact that the Nuclear Inspectorate was moved under Hitchcock's wing?'

'Yes. It looks as though Hitchcock got that to happen. It could have been just to acquire more power. Or she could have done it at Lesage's request.'

'Or to enable her to meet Lesage's request, if it was his idea to stop the visits. By the way, is it true she earns less than Cunningham?'

'She didn't deny it, did she? I guessed, on the basis that specialists in short supply can earn more than top policy people.'

'And so they should!' said Redstone. 'How much are you paying me for this job?'

'What you're worth. No, more. Going back to the skulduggery, it should be much easier for us to get evidence once you're able to go into the wavy dimension. Any signs your brain's adjusting so you can do that?'

'No, none. I keep looking out for it, but I'm not sure what it'll feel like. Anyway, it's early days yet, if it takes about two weeks, which is what Jim Clothier said. I suppose it'll be obvious when it happens.'

'How do you feel about it?'

'Nervous, but there's so much else on my mind that I'm not as excited as I should be.'

'Why? What else is happening?'

'Er… well, it's stuff in my personal life.'

'Do you want to talk about it? Don't if you don't want to.'

Redstone looked down and clenched his fists. 'It's about my wife. My late wife. Kate.'

‘I know she was murdered. It must have left an awful scar.’

He nodded.

‘I know that bereavement… creates a horrible wake of emotion,’ she said. ‘Even the death of a colleague, let alone a wife.’ She gazed at the floor, her brow furrowed.

‘Sorry if I’m bringing back bad memories,’ said Redstone.

‘Don’t worry about it.’ She straightened her shoulders.

He straightened his too. ‘I wonder if you feel angry, like I do. If you want justice. Revenge.’

‘Some of that. But a death in… the line of duty is different from when a loved one’s murdered.’

‘It’s that the killer’s still at large. I imagine him bragging to his friends, enjoying his life – while Kate lies dead, and my life and my kids’ lives are damaged forever. I’d like to… I wish I had your toughness.’

‘You wouldn’t wish it if you knew how I acquired it.’

They sat in silence for a few moments.

‘Right,’ said Redstone, ‘back to the job. Alan Cunningham. We need to find a way of talking to him on his own without Hitchcock being present. Or even knowing about it.’

‘Yes, I agree. I imagine a man in his position does a fair amount of travelling for his job, so maybe we could meet him while he’s away from London somewhere.’

‘Good idea. How should we arrange that?’

‘My view,’ she said, ‘is we’d get more out of him if he wasn’t able to prepare for the meeting and worry about it beforehand. I’ll get hold of his diary and see if there’s a way we can arrange to bump into him somewhere, as it were.’

Redstone grinned. ‘I like your expression “get hold of his diary”. Anyone would think you were a professional spy!’

‘I can assure you that I won’t need to break into his office, if that’s what you’re thinking. I’d be amazed if a man like that doesn’t keep his diary electronically, and if that’s the case, our pals in Cheltenham will have no difficulty in accessing it. In some ways, modern technology makes our life easier.'

*

Back home, Redstone sat in his comfortable armchair, using his tablet for a Skype conversation with Christina.

'Can you please show me some of your house?' she asked. 'I've been wondering what it's like.'

'Of course. It's nothing special – just a typical London suburban house, built in the 1930s when the tube line was extended as far as here.' He walked from room to room, showing her the way he and Kate had furnished and decorated it over the years. 'What do you think?'

'I didn't know what to expect, because I've never been in an English house like yours. I can see that it must be comfortable to live in. And it's very light.'

'Yes, that's the style – big bay windows. Not particularly good for retaining heat though.'

'But good for all your houseplants, I suppose.'

'Yes, they do seem happy.'

'And you're very tidy.'

'I'm not sure if that's a compliment, but I'll take it as one!'

'Oh, it is. But your house is so different from mine.'

'Your turn, then – now show me your house!' he said.

She looked awkward. 'Of course, but you must remember that we have quite different backgrounds and lifestyles here, so don't be too surprised at what you see.' She walked around, and he saw an old building with large rooms, dark antique furniture, lots of paintings, wooden floors with rugs, and a huge kitchen with modern fittings and appliances.

'Looks like a stately home,' said Redstone. 'How long have you lived there?'

'All my life,' she said, a touch defensively. 'It's been the family home for generations.'

'Christina,' he said, 'you look worried. Please don't be. I worked out a long time ago that you can't blame people for being born rich or posh.'

'Oh, thanks for saying that. I'm relieved. It's bad enough that we have other differences.'

'Well, what I've seen of your home is very impressive,' Redstone said. 'Especially the kitchen. Do you do a lot of cooking?'

She looked embarrassed. 'No, I hardly use it. We have a cook.' She turned away and then looked back into the camera. 'And I need to tell you that I haven't shown you the whole house. There are many rooms. Are you sure you're not upset?'

'No, I'm intrigued. I'm looking forward to seeing it when I visit you.'

'I'm looking forward to seeing you. When you come here, I'd like to host a dinner for a few friends to meet you. Would that be ok?'

'Of course!'

'Our group tend to dress up for dinner, so you'll feel more comfortable if you bring a suit.'

'Oh, ok, I'll do that. Now tell me what you've been doing today. If it's not too confidential for me to know!'

TUESDAY 18 OCTOBER

The leaves on the trees in St James's Park whispered in the chilly wind. The sun's low rays still had warmth, the air was clear, and Redstone felt he could see for miles. He felt energised. Waterfowl splashed on the lake, and the paths were crowded with tourists.

Smith briefed Redstone as they dodged the selfie-takers in front of Buckingham Palace. Lesage was a member of the French elite – a graduate of France's prestigious ENA, the school for France's top officials. He lived in Kensington, he and his wife entertaining lavishly as the doyens of French society in London. MI5's assessment was that his self-confidence was matched only by his love of status.

They strode through the back streets to France Nucléaire's UK head office, which was in a wedge-shaped glass-faced building at the Victoria end of Victoria Street.

A receptionist showed them to Lesage's spacious corner office, furnished in a traditional style, its windows overlooking the brick-built cathedral. Lesage was of medium height and had an aristocratic air. Redstone noted wryly that the Frenchman was much better dressed than him, in an expensive-looking suit, white shirt and blue-and-red silk tie. Lesage spoke in good English, albeit with an unmistakable French accent. He seemed tense.

'So, how can I help?'

'You know about the speech,' said Redstone. 'I'm doing some background research and wondered if you would talk to me about the nuclear programme in the UK.'

'Of course. What specifically?'

'Well, its history, its future and how the collaboration has affected the relations between our two countries.'

'Happy to do that,' said Lesage, leaning back and interlacing his fingers. 'Shall I start with the history?' He spoke at length about the early days of nuclear electricity, how France had installed a fleet of reactors to reduce their dependence on oil, how the British government had decided to invite France Nucléaire to construct a fleet of the same reactors in the UK and how wise a decision that had proved to be over the years. Now they were about to commission another fleet.

'And how are the new reactors different from their predecessors?' asked Redstone.

'Hardly at all. We decided we wouldn't complicate matters by having to seek new permits for changes from the existing reactors.'

'Has the construction of the new reactors gone smoothly?'

'Yes, to time and budget. A rarity for large projects, isn't it!'

'The prime minister's due to open the Dymbury reactor on November twenty-ninth. Is that date firm?'

'Of course,' said Lesage.

'I understand that you still have to load the fuel and start the live testing. Isn't the timetable a bit tight to do all that in six weeks?'

Lesage leaned forwards. 'Not at all. We can… there is a small problem… with the fuel, but nothing that we can't overcome.'

'What is the problem?' asked Redstone.

'That's a commercial matter on which I can't comment,' said Lesage smoothly. 'As you may know, the contract we have with your government specifies outcomes, not how we achieve them. Subject to safety, of course.'

'I see. On safety, now you mention it, how do you feel about the fact that the Nuclear Inspectorate doesn't visit your existing sites?'

'We give the Inspectorate all the data they need and ask for.'

'Don't you think you'd benefit from outsiders looking at what you're doing?'

'Physical visits take time away from our staff and the Inspectorate's. The arrangement was your government's decision, and we're fully content with it.'

'Do you have a good relationship with the Department of Energy's policy staff?'

'I expect you know that we have a particularly good relationship with the Department, including with their excellent permanent secretary, Mrs Hitchcock. Do you know her?'

'Yes, I do,' said Redstone.

'Do you, Miss Smith?'

'*Ms* Smith. I have had one enjoyable meeting with her,' said Smith enthusiastically. Lesage struggled to maintain an expressionless face.

After further discussion, Redstone drew the meeting to a close. 'Before we go,' he said, 'may I look out of your window? You have an excellent view.'

'Of course,' said Lesage, visibly relaxing. They walked over to the window together.

'How many floors do you have in this building?' asked Redstone.

'Just three,' said Lesage. 'Our meeting rooms are on this floor, and we have two floors of open-plan offices below. The lower floors are occupied by other companies.'

Redstone admired the view and then turned to leave.

'Ms Smith, if you aren't busy this evening, I wonder if you'd like to join me for a French dinner?' said Lesage. 'I've a table in an excellent restaurant.'

'That's truly kind. Sounds great. And I assume you're inviting my husband too?'

'Ah, er… I'm afraid the table's only for two.'

'Oh, well.'

They said their goodbyes, and Redstone and Smith walked back towards the park.

'Smarmy git,' said Smith.

'I nearly burst out laughing. You weren't tempted by his Gallic charm, then?'

'I just about managed to resist.'

'Let's wait till we get back before we dissect the meeting.'

'Ok. Any signs of being able to dimension-hop yet?'

'No. I try several times a day, but nothing.'

'It's still early days, I suppose.' She lifted her face to the sunshine. 'Nice, isn't it? Raises the spirits. Are you feeling ok? You were a bit down yesterday.'

'Yes, I am feeling better, thanks. I had a good chat with Christina last night.'

'Good. I hope that everything's going well for you.'

'Why is it that every woman I know wants me to have a love affair with another woman?'

'It's because we're all caring people who want other people to be happy. Unlike men.'

They walked on in silence, and then she said, 'Do you feel able to tell me more about your wife's murder?'

'I'd like to talk about it. Kate was a social worker who specialised in supporting the elderly. One afternoon, she was visiting a housebound client in a nice block of flats in Winchmore Hill. Do you know that area?'

'No. I don't know London very well.'

'Sorry. It's a middle-class suburb. Anyway, according to the old lady, Kate made her visit, checked the flat, chatted and then left. The next thing anyone knew was that a neighbour had found Kate dead on the walkway, a few doors down from where the old lady lived.' Redstone swallowed and walked on. 'She'd been stabbed and robbed.'

'That's terrible. What did the police say?'

'What they said was they couldn't find any evidence to determine who killed her.'

'Are you implying that they did know?'

'I'm fairly sure they know. But they didn't admit it.'

'And so nobody was charged?'

'That's right.'

'How awful for you. Because of the crime and, as you said yesterday, because nobody was brought to justice.'

'Yes. The crime had a huge effect on me and our children, of course, and on all the people who knew Kate – she was very caring. It may be why the kids both chose to go abroad for a few years.'

'Have the police been in touch subsequently?'

'They kept in touch for a few months, but of course they had to move on. We don't have contact anymore.'

'Would you mind if I speak to my husband about the case, to see if he knows anything?'

'Not at all – I'd be delighted.'

'It won't do any harm to ask, but don't get too hopeful. I'll let you know what he says.'

Back in their office, Smith opened her notebook.

'Well, the first thing we got from the meeting was an assurance that there won't be a delay.'

'I don't trust that at all – do you?'

'Certainly not. Lesage then went on to say – accidentally, I thought – that there was a small problem with the fuel, but refused to elaborate.'

'Yes,' said Redstone. 'We must find a way of talking to Alan Cunningham about that. He may have some ideas about what's going on. It seems very odd, since the new reactors are essentially the same as the old ones. You'd think that the fuel assemblies would be identical to those used in the existing reactors, for the good reason that Lesage gave – if you don't change the design, you won't have hold-ups for certification of new designs.'

'I've got some news and a proposal about talking to Mr Cunningham – can we come back to it later?'

'Of course. The next thing which struck me was it was obvious that Valerie had briefed him about our meeting with her.'

'Yes. The evidence against her is piling up.'

'And then my masterstroke, which I hope you admired – finding out which floor we expect their shielded conference room to be on.'

'Outstandingly brilliant. Well, mildly satisfactory,' Smith said. 'Yes, it's on the top floor.'

'And I assume it will be somewhere in the middle, rather than having an outside wall. Can you get a plan of that floor?'

'Yes, I'll get my colleagues on it as soon as we've finished talking.'

Redstone leaned back and put his hands behind his head. 'Not a bad morning's work. Now, what about talking to Alan Cunningham?'

'As I suspected, he often makes visits outside London. This evening, he's driving to Sheffield for a meeting tomorrow morning. It's quite a long way, so he's bound to be making service station stops. We can arrange things so that we join him on his homeward-bound comfort break.'

'How can you know where he will stop, and when?'

'We've put a tracking device in his car. Lewis will drive us up to Cunningham's first likely stop, which is Peterborough service station, and we'll wait to see if he pulls in. If he chooses to go further south before he stops, we'll follow him and pull in when he does. Don't worry – Lewis is good at this sort of thing.'

'A bit different from what I'm used to! I wonder whether it might be less intimidating for Alan Cunningham if I meet him alone, rather than the pair of us?'

Smith thought. 'Yes, I think you're right. I'll stay in the car. By the way, it won't be the taxi this time – it'll be a suitable car for a senior executive to be driven in for a long journey. In case you're spotted.'

*

'Hi Joanne,' Redstone said as he entered her office. 'Any news?'

'Hello! Yes, I need to show you the travel plans Mrs Nissen's secretary has sent me.'

'Who? Oh yes, Christina. Let's have a look.'

'Here you are. You see you'll be travelling by private plane from Oslo to Kristiansheim.'

'Good heavens! How much is that going to cost?'

'Nothing – at least not to you! They're paying.'

'I'm starting to realise that I've got myself involved with a woman from a rather higher social group than mine,' said Redstone. 'I suppose it shouldn't matter, though. As Christina said to me in a different context, we all wipe our bottoms!'

'Maybe they don't – maybe they have servants to do it for them!' said Joanne.

'Joanne, I'm constantly surprised at how a religious woman like you can be so deliciously coarse.'

'The gods know all about our bodies,' said Joanne mysteriously. 'Anyway, her social group isn't higher – it's simply different.'

'Yes, but will I find that difference difficult to handle?'

'No more than they'll find you difficult to handle – or possibly even less. Though I'm sure Mrs Nissen will handle you just fine.'

'Are you being coarse again?'

Joanne laughed. 'Coarseness is in the mind of the listener,' she said. 'Anyway, are you happy with the travel plan?'

Redstone studied it. 'Yes, it seems fine. Please thank Christina's secretary.'

'I will.'

'Now to some science. Could you please ask as many of the staff as can make it to go down to the meeting room? I want to bounce some ideas off them.'

Thirty minutes later, a couple of dozen of London Bio's scientists were sitting in blue plastic chairs in the crowded meeting room, looking expectantly at Redstone.

'I've had some ideas for a new project,' he said, 'and I wanted your reactions. Don't be shy – tell me if what I'm about to describe is total rubbish. It wouldn't be the first time.'

He walked to the whiteboard and started sketching diagrams. 'This is about a cream which would help the body's immune system cure some early-stage skin cancers, where the cancer was caused by exposure to the sun.'

'Good lord!' said David. 'That would be an amazing advance!'

Redstone pointed to a diagram. 'Our skin has a balance of good and bad bacteria on the surface.'

'Yes,' said Saira, a slim, confident woman in her forties, wearing an embroidered white jumper and designer jeans. 'And some skin diseases may be caused by an imbalance between the two types.'

'And there are viruses which can alter or kill bacteria.'

'Yes, that's right.'

'And some good bacteria can help the skin to heal itself.'

'Up to a point,' said another scientist.

'And some cancerous cells are naturally killed by the body's immune system, and more would be if the immune system could recognise the cells with mutated DNA.' Several people nodded.

'And viruses can be used to alter DNA.'

'Yes.'

'And some treatments for other diseases use chemicals which are activated by light.' He pointed to a different diagram.

'That's right,' said a grey-haired man enthusiastically.

‘And our company knows how to get chemicals beneath the outer layers of the skin.’

‘Of course,’ said David.

‘So, if we can design something which we can apply to the skin which does this…’ he scribbled some formulae. ‘And if we look at how nanoparticles are used in catalysis…’ he scribbled further, ‘and how viruses…’ he stopped talking and carried on writing for a few minutes.

‘So, what do you think of that?’

‘Well,’ said Saira. ‘I can see one reason why it wouldn’t work. Look—’ she walked up to the whiteboard. ‘This here will interact with these cells to…’ she scribbled on the board. ‘So the immune system would destroy this…’

‘Oh,’ said Redstone, crestfallen. ‘You’re right, of course. Oh well, it was worth…’

‘Don’t give up that easily!’ Saira said. ‘Look. If instead, we do this…’ she scribbled, ‘…and this, that problem might be overcome.’

‘It’s certainly worth trying,’ said David. Several others voiced agreement, and then there was a heated discussion, with ideas being tossed around amongst the staff.

‘A great advantage of this approach,’ said a young woman, ‘is that it uses only medicines which are already licensed. We know their safe limits.’

‘Yes, though things can change when the chemicals are combined in one treatment,’ said Saira. ‘And there’s also the effects of activating the treatment with the blue light. Still, you’re right – we should be able to try this out very quickly.’

‘Except that we need to acquire the blue-light equipment,’ said Redstone.

‘No, we don’t,’ said a voice from the back. ‘I got it a few months ago, for…’

‘Oh, of course! Excellent!’

Discussion continued.

'Ok,' said Redstone. 'The consensus is that it's worth pursuing this. David and Saira – can you take the lead?'

As they milled out, David collared Redstone. 'Mark, that was great. The way you've brought in ideas from other fields and synthesised them. Something's happened to your brain – have you been eating lots of fish?'

Redstone stared at him. Maybe the MI5 irradiation had improved his cognitive abilities. McKay had said it might. 'Are you serious that it's a big step forward?'

'Of course it is.'

'It would have been nothing without Saira's idea.'

'True, but that's how teams work. And this company is a team.'

Saira joined them. 'Thanks again for your input,' Redstone said. 'You saved the day!'

'Don't be silly,' she replied. 'You can take all the credit because you hired such a brilliant scientist. Me.' They all laughed. 'Anyway,' she continued, 'I'm familiar with the scientific literature in this general area, and I've seen nothing like this. And I haven't picked up anything like it from my contacts in other pharma companies.'

'Between you you've come up with some truly inventive thinking,' said David. 'Saira and I'll take the ideas away and see if we can work them up into something practical, but I'm very optimistic.'

'I'm itching to get to work on them!' said Saira.

'I'm now truly enthused,' said Redstone. 'Please keep me informed of how it progresses, even when I'm stuck over at Number 10.'

After the two scientists had left his office, Redstone sat back in his chair and reflected on the meeting. He felt guilty for getting praise when it wasn't the real him who had produced the idea – it was a modified version of him. He was sure that the treatment he'd received at Thames House had improved his inventiveness. He didn't deserve the credit – it wasn't as if he'd worked hard to get the idea.

Anyway, his brain was responding as predicted, so he should soon be able to move into the wavy dimension. He tried to move into it there and then, but nothing happened.

He texted the twins and told them about the idea without going into the science. Both replied immediately – Sophie with an enthusiastic good luck message and Graham wanting to know more. Redstone phoned him and explained, and was gratified by Graham's thoughtful encouragement.

WEDNESDAY 19 OCTOBER

Redstone climbed the back stairs at Number 10, wondering if his personality had been changed by the irradiation. He couldn't himself detect any effect, apart from the anti-cancer idea. But he'd probably be the last person to know, and there was no one he could ask without breaching the Official Secrets Act. Perhaps it didn't matter, as long as the effect wasn't extreme.

Smith was already in the attic office, working at her desk.

'News,' she said. 'I've looked into whether Malvern promoted Hitchcock while the two were having an affair.'

'And?'

'Malvern was on the appointments committee. I'd say his fingerprints are all over it.'

'Oh dear. But nothing provable, I suppose?

'No. I also said I'd find out whether Valerie and Malvern were having it off before you were sacked. The answer is yes. I guess we were right about why you were given the boot.'

'Christ. She's plainly got him wrapped round her little finger. I wonder how? Oh well, it's worked out ok. Maybe more than ok. My sacking, I mean.'

'Moving on, we couldn't find a legitimate reason why Valerie neutered the Nuclear Inspectorate. It must have been to please Lesage.'

'So, he didn't want the Inspectorate visiting the plants. Interesting.'

'We should see if Alan Cunningham can throw any light on what Lesage might be hiding.'

'Yes. It could be important, but I can't see how, since we know the existing plants are fine. Maybe it was just a control thing – he wanted to be totally in charge.'

‘We’ll see. Now to what you’re being paid for – here are plans of France Nucléaire’s offices.’ She passed over some diagrams. ‘This is the most likely place for the screened room.’ She pointed.

Redstone studied the plans while Smith looked over his shoulder.

‘The other rooms all have outside walls, except this one,’ she said, pointing at another part of the plan. ‘But that looks tiny. It’s probably just used for storage. So, my money is on the large room.’

‘It’s all a bit academic at the moment,’ said Redstone, ‘because I still haven’t been able to move into the wavy dimension. I keep trying. I wonder if I’m doing something wrong. I suppose I’m being silly – it’s still early days, according to what Jim said.’

‘Have you felt any signs that the treatment’s had an effect on your brain?’

Redstone steepled his fingers. ‘Well, I have come up with a scientific idea which my colleagues say shows some good thinking. But one example proves nothing. It could have been the sort of brainwave we all get from time to time.’

‘Yes, I get them constantly,’ said Smith. ‘Like “those shoes would look great with this outfit!”’

‘I’m afraid my brainwaves aren’t that sophisticated,’ said Redstone. ‘As you can see.’ They both looked at his shoes and burst out laughing.

‘If nothing happens in the next few days, we’ll see what Jim Clothier has to say,’ she said, staring at her own shoes.

‘Ok. So, assuming I can eventually go into the wavy dimension, how should I eavesdrop on the meetings we want to listen to? How will it work? I can’t stay there all the time just waiting for someone to pop into the room for a chat.’

‘No, of course you can’t. My colleagues will monitor when Lesage is meeting people likely to be in the know of whatever is going on. That'll include the chief engineer and maybe any high-level visitors from Paris.'

'And then what?'

'We'll deliver you to the back of the building, and you'll go into the wavy dimension and use the stairs to get to the meeting room floor. And then you'll find your way into the meeting room itself.'

'You make it sound easy. I doubt whether it'll be as smooth as that. We'll have to wait and see.'

Smith's phone rang. 'Ok,' she said. She turned back to Redstone. 'That was Lewis. Alan Cunningham's showing signs of leaving his meeting. Time for us to get moving.'

Lewis was waiting at the back of Downing Street in a polished black Jaguar. He got out and opened the rear doors for them. He was wearing a grey suit, white shirt and navy tie.

'You look very smart, Lewis,' said Redstone as he settled back in the cream leather upholstery. 'Anyone would think you were a professional chauffeur.' The car door closed with a pleasing thunk and the outside noise disappeared.

'Thank you, sir,' Lewis replied. 'Where can I take you this morning? A nice intelligence-gathering operation?'

'Yes, let's have an exciting day out. I've always wanted to go to Peterborough motorway service station.'

They drew away. Lewis told them that Alan Cunningham had given a presentation at a meeting on engineering safety in Sheffield. MI5 expected him to use the A1 to return south, because his home was in Welwyn, just off the A1 in Hertfordshire. 'It's a gamble as to whether he'll stop at the Peterborough services, but that seems the most logical place. If he stops further north, we're probably stymied. But if he doesn't stop at the Peterborough services, we could get on the road and follow him south. It's very unlikely that he'd drive all the way from Sheffield to Welwyn without a break.'

They drove through Swiss Cottage and West Hampstead, crossed the North Circular Road, and joined the A1 motorway. The scenery changed from built-up suburbs to open, wooded hills and fields.

The car was quiet and smooth. Redstone looked at Smith. 'You look relaxed,' he said.

'Why shouldn't I be? It's a nice day out. We're being driven by an expert driver in a luxury car. I don't have any work ahead because you're going to do it all. Lewis's going to buy us a slap-up meal in the drive-through McDonald's, on expenses, while you're chatting to your nuclear friend. What more could a woman ask?' She stretched back and smiled.

Redstone watched the scenery go by. 'I've been thinking about what Lesage said, about there being a small problem with the fuel. The more I ponder it, the more puzzled I am. How could there be a problem with the new reactors but not the old ones, which clearly work well? Maybe they did change the design and Lesage was lying to us. I'm interested in what Alan Cunningham will have to say on that.'

'It's lucky that you know something about nuclear reactors,' said Smith. 'I know very little.'

'May I switch into teaching mode?' asked Redstone. 'It'll help me get my ideas clear, even if it doesn't help you!'

'Sure.'

'Well, the purpose of the nuclear reactor is to produce heat, which boils water to produce steam. The steam is under pressure. It blows through turbines, making them rotate, and the turbines are connected to electrical generators. Loads of lovely electricity's produced and shoved into the national grid.'

'Isn't that the same as, say, coal-fired power stations?'

'Yes. The big difference is that coal-fired stations use huge quantities of coal, whereas nuclear stations use relatively minute quantities of uranium.'

'So why isn't nuclear electricity really cheap?'

'Good question. When it was invented, people thought it would be so cheap that it wouldn't be worth charging for. But all the safety features make building the reactor very expensive, and those initial costs have to be recovered by selling the electricity.'

'Interesting. I know that the heat is produced by uranium, but my knowledge ends there.'

'Yes, what happens is that uranium atoms naturally fall to bits, giving off heat as they do so. In a reactor, the bits thrown out by one atom hit other uranium atoms and make them fall to bits, giving out more heat and more bits. And some of those bits make further atoms fall to bits, etcetera. You get a chain reaction and lots of heat.'

'I suppose "bits" is the technical term you erudite scientists use to confuse laypeople like me!'

'Sorry. They're normally called particles. The type of particles that stimulate the nuclear reaction are neutrons.'

'Surely the process must be more complicated than that, otherwise naturally occurring uranium, in mines, would be melting or something!'

'Well spotted. The main reason it barely happens naturally is that natural uranium is a mixture of two types – one that's good for reactors and one that's useless. There's a lot more of the useless type, and we have to take some of it out to make the fuel rods that go into the reactor.'

'Thanks,' she said. 'That's clear. Oh look – I love it when I see a road sign that says, "*The North*". I feel I'm escaping.'

'I guess from your accent that you come from Leeds, or thereabouts.'

'I haven't got an accent. It's you London lot, who can't pronounce the letters "a" or "l", that ruin a good language.' She thought a minute. 'Or most of the other vowels. Or the letter "t".'

'I fink thass baws,' said Redstone.

A few minutes later, Smith said, 'Back to reactors. How d'you control the reaction, once the water's added? Why doesn't the system get so hot that it melts or explodes or something?'

'By putting in some control rods which are made of a substance which absorbs neutrons. Pulling them partly out increases the reaction, and so the quantity of heat produced. And pushing them in decreases it.'

'So, if the control rods are taken out fully, the nuclear reaction goes bananas? Does the reactor explode?'

'No, there are lots of safety systems. Anyway, the worst that could theoretically happen, if all the safety systems failed, is a meltdown, not a nuclear explosion. Making a nuclear bomb requires different technology.'

'So where's the scope for France Nucléaire to have discovered a problem with the fuel rods for the new reactors?'

'It must be some engineering issue, I suppose, like the rods being a bit too fat or too thin or something. That's where my knowledge runs out and where we need Alan Cunningham's views.'

'We'll be at the service station in about half an hour,' said Lewis from the front. 'You need to decide how you're going to play it – how you're going to arrange the "accidental" meeting and so on.'

'Simple,' said Redstone. 'I'll sit nursing a cup of tea till he comes in. Then I'll join him and play it by ear.'

'He's no fool,' said Smith. 'You'll have to have a cover story about why you're there.'

'I think the best approach is to be truthful, up to a point. I'll tell him we knew he was giving the presentation and gambled on him stopping at Peterborough because I wanted to chat to him in an environment where he could speak his mind.'

'Good luck!' said Smith.

*

Redstone sat in the sparsely occupied barn-like eating area in the service station. There were food and drink outlets around the edges of the complex, but only the one area where Cunningham could sit and drink or eat. 'That's assuming he does come here, Treacle,' he muttered. 'What's more, he's highly likely to go to the loo first. We don't all go and dig a hole in flower beds.' A woman at the next table looked at him suspiciously. He gave her what he hoped was a reassuring smile. She looked away.

Redstone's phone rang. 'He's here,' said Smith. 'Just getting out of his car.'

Redstone pretended to study his phone while watching the entrance. Cunningham came in and walked straight through to the toilets. After a couple of minutes, he returned and went to a coffee outlet. He bought a drink, turned to search for somewhere to sit and immediately spotted Redstone.

He walked over to Redstone's table. Redstone put away his phone and stood up to greet him.

'Let me guess,' said Cunningham sarcastically, 'it's a pure accident that you're sitting here just as I come in. You aren't following me. You aren't trying to get me alone so that you can find out more about what France Nucléaire is up to. You aren't trying to go behind Valerie Hitchcock's back.'

'Please sit down, Alan, and I'll explain,' said Redstone nervously. Cunningham sat down opposite him.

'Frankly, almost everything you guessed is true. The only exception being that I'm not following you. We knew you were giving the presentation this morning and estimated that you'd stop here on the way home.'

'My first reaction is that was a pretty clever bit of estimating, but on reflection, the probability was quite high. Anyway, where's your bodyguard?'

'Bodyguard? What do you mean?'

'Isn't that Laura Smith's real job? She certainly didn't act like a junior note-taker, and I found out that she belongs to the Home Office, which probably means MI5 or some similar agency, in reality.'

'God, you are on the ball, aren't you? I'm so pleased I could meet you here. I do hope you'll talk to me off the record. But Laura isn't a bodyguard! Why on earth would I need a bodyguard?'

'If you say so,' said Cunningham.

'Anyway, as you worked out, I'm here in the hope that you can throw some light on what's happening with the new reactors. And Laura's outside in the car, but I suggest you and I talk alone, if you're willing.'

'To be honest,' said Cunningham, 'it's a relief to be able to talk it through with someone who wants to know what's going on. So I'm happy to talk. But you're going to be disappointed, because I don't know very much.'

'I'm sure you know more than I do,' said Redstone.

'Possibly. But why do you need to know what's going on there? I deduce your role is rather more than you let on when we met in Valerie's office.'

'I can see that each of us is going to have to trust the other with some highly confidential information. I'm happy to tell you what I know, on the understanding that it won't go any further.'

'Agreed,' said Cunningham.

'Good. I'll now tell you why the prime minister's concerned about whether the next group of reactors is really going to go ahead as planned.' Redstone told Cunningham of MI5's findings. 'Laura and I met Lesage yesterday, and I asked him outright if the opening of the first new reactor would be on schedule. He assured me that it would be, though he did admit that there was a problem with the fuel. He refused to explain what that was.'

‘That ties in with my own concerns. I told you that everything’s finished except for loading the fuel assemblies and carrying out final testing.’

‘His excuse for not telling us more was that the company’s contract with us specifies outcomes, not how they achieve them, but he admitted that this was subject to safety. That seems to give you a basis for finding out more.’

‘You’d think so, wouldn’t you,’ said Cunningham. ‘But at the moment, I haven’t got any reason to demand more information. They’ve told us that the fuel and control system will be the same as currently used in the existing reactor fleet, and we know that those reactors work very well and with full safety.’

‘What’s your overall impression of France Nucléaire?’

‘Their engineers are very clever, and their design of the core has proved itself again and again. It’s unique – their reactors can be refuelled far more quickly than other designs. And they demonstrated their ingenuity with their recent modifications. They can now pack in more fuel without producing excessive temperatures or neutron fluxes. They also efficiently modified the non-nuclear side of the power stations to deal with the extra heat. So they’re generating even more electricity.’

‘I take it you’re happy with the modifications?’

‘Yes. To be honest, I initially had my doubts, but the data speak for themselves – the reactors are working fine.’

‘Will you be carrying out any more physical inspections of Dymbury before it starts up?’

‘We’ll examine the fuel system when it’s installed. But it’s not our role to query delays, which are what you’re worried about.’

‘How could there be delays for the new reactors but none for refuelling the existing fleet?’

‘I can’t think of any reason.’

'You're absolutely confident about the safety of the existing fleet?'

'No safety inspector will tell you that he's absolutely confident about anything. I'm quite confident, based on the data we get regularly from the company.'

'Would you be more confident if you inspected the reactors yourselves, rather than relying on data sent by the French?'

'Frankly, yes. But, as you know, that's not possible because of the government's agreement with France Nucléaire.'

'I do find that agreement rather odd,' said Redstone. 'I would have thought that Valerie would be happier if you were looking at the reactors. She's a bit exposed if something goes wrong.'

'Yes, but you may underestimate how close she's got to France Nucléaire. She's been working with them for ages. She claims it was her efforts which led to the contract to build the new fleet of reactors. Maybe the light-touch inspection arrangements were part of the deal she did to get the French to invest.'

'Why would the French not want you to inspect in person, do you think?'

'God knows. Maybe it is just to save the hassle, as Valerie says. Since we get all the data anyway, I suppose it's not anything to worry about.'

'Anyway, France Nucléaire must be laughing all the way to the bank with the extra money they're making, now they've increased the quantity of electricity the current reactors produce.'

'True,' said Cunningham. 'They're raking in hundreds of millions of pounds extra a year. You'd think that would make anyone want to invest, without any extra persuasion.'

Redstone stood up, stretched, looked around and sat down again. 'If you didn't know any background and someone said to you there was a problem with the supply of nuclear fuel, what thoughts would pop into your head?'

'Well, the first one would be worry about diversion of fuel into terrorist hands. The technology to convert reactor fuel into a nuclear bomb is almost certainly beyond ordinary terrorists, but there's the real risk of just spreading radioactivity, say in a city, using stolen fuel rods.'

'I'd subconsciously assumed that was impossible here. Do you have any reason to believe it is possible?'

'Nothing like that is impossible, but I'd be surprised if it were true. The fuel's audited all the way from its manufacture to being loaded into the reactors, and we check the audit figures.'

'Those are figures supplied by France Nucléaire?'

'Yes, like all the other data we check.'

'I hope you don't mind if I alert MI5 to the possibility of fuel going missing, if they haven't considered it already.'

'No, go ahead. I assume you mean that you'll tell the formidable Laura Smith!'

Redstone smiled. 'I don't deny that Laura works for the Home Office or one of its agencies. Back to the issue. What other thoughts might you harbour?'

'Much more mundane ones, such as machining problems, meaning the fuel rods don't fit properly, or the control rods don't move in and out smoothly. Very unlikely in this case, since they're the same specifications as are already being used in the old reactors.'

'Could there simply be a shortage of some essential component?'

'I don't know of any supply problems of that type, but I'll look into it. I'll let you know if anything crops up.'

'Many thanks, Alan.' Redstone leaned forwards. 'Why do you think Valerie wouldn't allow us to have this conversation in her office? And why did she insist on being present?'

Cunningham looked embarrassed. 'Maybe you should be asking me why I didn't insist on having the conversation alone with you. Well, the answer to that is I can't risk losing my job, unfortunately.' He looked down. 'My family relies on my income. I just need a steady salary, I'm afraid. My wife's… well, never mind.' He swallowed. 'Valerie has a record of getting rid of people who don't toe her line.'

'I wasn't getting at you at all,' said Redstone. 'I was wondering about Valerie's attitude.'

'I suppose it stems from her long-standing relationship with France Nucléaire,' said Cunningham. 'I've given up trying to understand it, let alone challenge it – I just live with it, like other colleagues in the Department of Energy. She's a tough woman. Though her behaviour towards you on Monday was even more confrontational than usual.'

'Yes, I'm afraid we have a piece of shared history which has affected her attitude towards me. Though I thought there might be more to it than that. Anyway, back to the main issue – we seem to be left with a puzzle. If you had a free hand, how would you approach solving it?'

Cunningham didn't hesitate. 'I'd physically inspect everything I could.'

'That must be right,' said Redstone. 'I think I need to apply pressure at the very top to get us access.'

'Us?' said Cunningham. 'With respect, do you know the difference between a fuel rod and a banana?'

'Yes,' said Redstone. 'The banana contains more potassium.'

Cunningham roared with laughter. People at other tables turned and smiled. 'Spoken like a true chemist! Which reminds me – you'll like this. Last April Fool's Day, I sent Valerie a memo explaining that a result of the Second Law of Thermodynamics is that a lot of the energy used by power stations goes into waste heat; so, could she use her influence to get the Second Law repealed?'

'Let me guess,' said Redstone. 'She didn't laugh.'

'Clearly you do know her,' said Cunningham ruefully.

'Seriously,' said Redstone, 'back to an inspection, would you mind if I accompanied you? I certainly don't know anything about the engineering, but two heads are always better than one, and I might be able to pick up hints that we're being told porkies if that happens.'

'No, that'd be fine, if you can arrange it. I'd enjoy having you along.'

'Excellent.' Redstone leaned over and shook Cunningham's hand. 'It's been a real pleasure talking to you like this, as well as having been extremely useful. Next time, we must find somewhere a little more luxurious and convenient!' He stood up.

'I'll stay here and finish my coffee,' said Cunningham, 'and wait to hear further from you. Of course, you'll respect my… my problems in the Department, when you do contact me.'

'Of course,' said Redstone. He gave a half-wave and walked out.

*

Back in the car, as they were driving back to London, Redstone debriefed Smith. 'So we need to get Alan and his staff, and me as a hanger-on, into the relevant nuclear plants. And you need to talk to your colleagues about the terrorism possibility.'

'I think we could link the two issues,' said Smith. 'We could tell the French we've heard a rumour about diversion of fuel, and so we need to get inspectors in there – wherever "there" is – in person. They could hardly refuse.'

'Good idea. Can you pursue it with your MI5 colleagues?'

'Yes, I'll do that when we get back.'

'Once you have an answer, someone ought to tell the prime minister what we're up to.'

'I think it should be you,' said Smith. 'The only alternative would be Gavin McKay. That'd be fine, but I'm sure the PM would welcome another meeting with you in person.'

‘I can’t get used to the idea of moving in such circles,’ said Redstone. ‘But I guess you’re right. I’ll have a word with the PM’s office.’

THURSDAY 20 OCTOBER

Laura Smith walked into the Downing Street office.

'Hi,' Redstone said, looking up from the phone, 'I'm trying to arrange to see the prime minister…' he held up his hand and spoke into the phone. 'Eleven a.m.? Ok, I'll be there.'

He put the phone down. 'I can't believe it. He's going to see me in…' he looked at his watch, '…sixty minutes!'

'In that case, I'd better brief you quickly on what I've learned since we came back from Peterborough,' said Smith. 'I spoke to our anti-terrorism specialists. Of course they were aware of the possibility of terrorists stealing nuclear material and making a dirty bomb, but they think it unlikely that it's happened. Their opposite numbers in France are confident that no material has gone missing between its manufacture in France and delivery to the UK fuel assembly plant.'

'Where's that?'

'Next to the West Avon power station – it's part of the same complex.'

'That's on the coast, isn't it?'

'Yes, on the estuary. Anyway, my colleagues think it's a good idea to use the possibility of terrorist activity as an excuse to get inside the facility.'

'In that case, I'll mention it to the prime minister. Maybe he can drop a word in the French president's ear, to ensure there's no diplomatic problem.'

'Yes, that would ensure that Lesage couldn't raise objections. You'd better get your thoughts together for the meeting with the PM.'

Redstone made some notes and then went downstairs to the plusher part of Number 10. He walked into a crowded office. A young man greeted him.

'The prime minister will see you in the Cabinet Room.' Redstone looked surprised. 'Don't worry – it'll be just you and him. He likes to hold meetings there.'

They walked into the Cabinet Room, which was dominated by the famous boat-shaped table, covered with a green baize cloth. 'The PM'll be along in a minute,' said the aide. 'Take a seat.' He left the room.

Redstone looked around. The room was traditionally decorated and furnished. Sash windows on one wall made it feel light and airy. Three brass chandeliers hung from the high ceiling. The table was surrounded by carved chairs, but only one had arms – the one in the middle of the long side of the table, with its back to the fireplace. He assumed that was the prime minister's seat. 'I'm going to sit in it, Treacle, just because I can,' he muttered. As he approached it, Michael Jones walked into the room.

'Hello, Mark! Were you about to sit in my chair?'

Redstone flushed. 'Yes – I had a momentary flash of idiocy, Prime Minister.'

The PM laughed. 'Go on – sit there. You'll find it's no more comfortable than the other chairs. And you can tell your grandchildren, when you get some, that you did sit in it!'

Redstone sat down awkwardly. 'You're right about the lack of comfort, Prime Minister…'

'You mean "Michael",' said the PM, sitting down next to him and swivelling his chair so that they faced each other.

'Oh, yes. I was thinking that maybe the designers were instructed to make the chairs uncomfortable to ensure that cabinet meetings didn't drag on.'

'No, I think it's just that prime ministers tend not to have been as tall as you. Anyway, has MI5's procedure taken effect yet? Can you disappear at will?'

'No, not yet,' said Redstone. 'I'm getting a bit anxious, but they say it's still early days. But we have made some progress on the reactor issue, and I'm here to ask for your help.' He outlined why they'd like to use the possibility of diversion of nuclear material as a ruse to gain access to the West Avon site, and how the agreement of the French president would overcome any opposition.

'Wait a minute,' said the PM. 'Why do we need a ruse for the Inspectorate to go in?'

Redstone explained the arrangement with the Department of Energy that the inspectors would keep away.

'I find that very odd,' said the PM, 'don't you?'

'I do, and surprising. And so do others, including the chief nuclear inspector, who strikes me as very sensible and intelligent.'

'And why did the Department of Energy get involved anyway? Isn't the Inspectorate a free-standing, independent body?'

'It was, Michael, but it isn't now. I think it should still be. Your instincts are right.'

'I'm annoyed I wasn't told about this before. I've a good mind to call in the cabinet secretary and tell him to give the Inspectorate back its full independence and scrap the agreement that they won't inspect the sites.' He leaned back. 'But I suppose I ought to talk to the Secretary of State for Energy first.'

'I bet they've avoided telling her too,' said Redstone. 'But I wonder whether it would be a good idea to change the arrangements at this stage. We don't know what apple carts would be upset. I suggest you wait till I've got to the bottom of what's going on.'

'I suppose you're right. Wise advice. Fancy a job as my special adviser?'

Redstone assumed that the PM was joking but was unsure what to say. He thought of a way out. 'But you don't know my politics. At least, I hope you don't!'

'Is that a coded way of telling me that you wouldn't touch the job with a bargepole? Because if it is, that makes me respect you all the more. Ah well, politics' loss is science's gain, I suppose.'

Redstone smiled weakly.

'Seriously, it's a pity that politicians like me are surrounded by political groupies. It's lucky I have Anne to keep me sane. Incidentally, she was extremely interested in what you told us about your work the other day. You must come here again for lunch. Or perhaps you'd like to go out to Chequers one weekend?'

Redstone looked at him and decided this was a serious offer. 'That's truly kind. I'd be delighted.'

'Is there anyone you'd like to bring along – as a social partner?'

'Oh. May I think about that?'

'Of course. I'll arrange for you to get a proper invitation.' He leaned forwards. 'Let's get back to the nuclear problem. So, what you want me to do is ensure there's no opposition to your visiting the West Avon nuclear site?'

'Yes, although I wouldn't be leading the visit – that would be Alan Cunningham, the chief nuclear inspector. But I'd accompany him and his team.'

'Ok. I'm due to go to an EU Council meeting next week, and I'll have a word with the President of France in the margins of the meeting. My private secretary will set it up.'

'Many thanks. Of course, I'll keep you informed of any further developments.'

Redstone made his way back upstairs. 'Now I've got another problem,' he muttered. 'Who shall I take to Chequers?'

He told Smith about the meeting. 'Excellent,' she said. 'I'll make sure the PM's private secretary knows the background. Now I've got something to tell you.'

'You look serious. Go on.'

'It's about the murder of your wife. I talked to my husband about it. He already knew a bit, but he made some more enquiries.'

Redstone paled. His mouth went dry, and his heart started to race. 'What did he find out?'

'As you know, there was no physical evidence to give clues to the identity of the murderer. That strongly suggests it was unlikely to have been a random attack by a normal mugger. It must have been someone more sophisticated.'

'I sense a "but".'

'Not a "but", rather a "however". The police suspect a man called Paul Kemp, who lives a few doors away from the lady your wife was visiting.'

Redstone felt breathless. He stood up and paced around the office. 'Why do they think it was him?'

'Right. Sit down. I'm going to tell you what I've learnt about the Kemps.'

'Kemps, plural?'

'Yes.' She explained that there were two brothers – Paul, the older, and Terry. They were educated and clever – and violent, Paul in a cold, calculating way and Terry more unpredictably. Paul had an accountancy qualification. They ran a large drugs supply network using skilled management, brutality and terror. For cover, they also managed a modest business importing antique furniture, with a showroom in a back street in Westminster. They owned two flats, side by side, along from the woman Kate had visited.

The police had been watching them for years but without acquiring enough evidence to mount a prosecution, not least because potential witnesses had been killed or intimidated into silence. Kate's killer had to have been Paul because Terry had been in Belgium at the time. The police were surprised that Paul, the cool-headed one, had murdered Kate on his own doorstep, since the brothers had so far succeeded in keeping their illegal activities away from their homes. Kate must have overheard or seen something seriously threatening to the drugs operation, and so Kemp's evil logic meant she had to be silenced there and then.

Redstone sat back, frozen, fists clenched, breathing rapidly.

'Are you ok?' asked Smith.

He found his voice. 'I don't know why I feel so shocked. It's not as if I didn't know Kate was murdered.'

'I suppose what happened now feels more real to you. Now you know who probably did it.'

'Yes. That's good. Now I don't need to… I can…' He gripped the edge of the desk. 'I'm going to go and visit the block of flats to… er, well, to understand it all better. I've never been there before. It was too horrible, but now… I want to see where…'

Smith looked at him carefully. 'I'll go with you. These are extremely dangerous men, and I don't want you to do something stupid while you're there.'

'Are you employed as my bodyguard?' Redstone asked. 'Alan Cunningham thought you were.'

Smith stood up. 'Look at me!' She turned around and back again. 'What do you see?'

Redstone was nonplussed. What should he say? 'I see a, umm, good-looking young woman, fit, slim, wearing a navy jumper and black slacks.'

'Do you see a gun? D'you think I could be carrying a gun?'

'No. But I suppose there could be one in your handbag.'

'No bodyguard carries a gun in a handbag. It'd take too long to get to it in an emergency. If I were a real bodyguard, I'd be wearing a gun in a shoulder holster or in a holster on my waist.'

'So Alan Cunningham was wrong. I'm relieved in a way.'

'I have several responsibilities,' Smith said, 'and ensuring your safety is one of them. To put it another way, if something bad happened to you, I'd get it in the neck. Your well-being's highly important to the country.'

'And I suppose the country's invested a lot of money in me,' said Redstone cynically.

'You've no idea!' said Smith. 'That chemical which was injected into you – you're a chemist – did you consider how difficult it was to make?'

'Not really. I did see that it was an extraordinarily complex molecule.'

'Jim Clothier can tell you more, but I reckon you'll be amazed.'

'All this doesn't make me feel any better. I'm sorry I asked.'

'Don't worry about it. I'll accompany you and won't interfere.'

'Actually,' said Redstone, 'I'd welcome your going with me. Thanks for offering. I'm now itching to go.' He looked at his watch. 'It's too late to set off now. Are you free to go with me tomorrow?'

'Sure. Shall we aim to get there at about noon?'

'Yes,' said Redstone. 'The best way would be for me to go from home, since I live not too far from Winchmore Hill.'

'We need to travel in an inconspicuous way. Is it easy to get there from your house by public transport?'

'Yes. We can take a bus from Southgate tube station, which is about fifteen minutes' walk from my home. You could either come to my house first or I could meet you at the tube station.'

'Probably best if I'm not seen at your home,' said Smith. 'Shall we meet at Southgate tube at eleven thirty?'

'Excellent. I'll work from home till I meet you. I need to get some thoughts together about the speech.'

A messenger came in and handed him an envelope.

'Oh, look!' said Redstone as the messenger walked out. 'A real letter! In a posh envelope! Just like the good old days, before emails!'

'Well, open it, old man,' said Smith.

He opened it – it was a formal invitation to Chequers, for Saturday fortnight. He showed it to Smith. 'Enjoy,' she said.

FRIDAY 21 OCTOBER

Redstone dressed in a casual jacket, woollen hat, jeans and trainers. It was a dull day with drops of rain in the air. The wind chilled his face as he walked to Southgate tube station, a circular Art Deco building like a concrete flying saucer, next to a noisy roundabout. Exhaust fumes bit at the back of his palate. The bus terminus was separated from the station by cracked paving stones and an ugly bare packed-earth raised bed.

Redstone found Smith looking in the window of an estate agent at the edge of the station entrance hall. She was wearing a blue zipped quilted jacket.

'Thinking of moving out here?'

'Not at these prices,' she said. 'I don't know the area, but from what I've seen outside, I can't understand why anyone would pay so much to live here.'

'Places round a station are always more sordid than the wider area. You'll see.'

Their bus arrived quickly. 'It'll take about ten minutes,' said Redstone. 'Then another ten minutes' walk once we get off.'

'That's good, from the security angle.'

The scenery outside the bus quickly changed. Soon, they were travelling down a tree-lined road of sizeable Edwardian houses, and then along an avenue of mansions set well back from the road.

'Just for millionaires,' said Redstone. 'I'd have thought a drugs baron would live here instead of a nondescript flat.'

'That's the problem with being a drugs baron,' Smith said. 'You can't flaunt your wealth. At least, not in this country. Maybe this road is more suited to biotechnology company millionaires?'

'Can you see me living in one of these monstrosities?' asked Redstone. 'I assume you meant me.' Smith smiled and nodded. 'I have thought about moving,' Redstone continued, 'but I don't see the point. I'm perfectly comfortable where I am.'

'People don't spend their money just for comfort. They also want to impress others, and make a statement.'

'You're right, of course. I'm sure you know I once worked for a cosmetics company. Their skin products were based on good science, but some were priced ridiculously high, just for the reasons you said.'

'Are you telling me I should buy cheap cosmetics?'

'The mid-range ones are likely to be the best value. Unless you want to impress people with your wealth and status, of course.'

'I don't think my wealth and status are very impressive. Anyway, thanks for the advice. You see, it was worth coming with you today!'

They got off the bus and walked through quiet back streets lined with identical pre-war semi-detached houses with neat front gardens, some with professional-looking displays of dahlias, others with summer flowers fading in the late autumn. Nobody was about, even at the several sites where lofts were being extended under huge scaffolded canopies.

'It all feels a bit eerie, don't you think?' said Redstone.

'Yes. Very quiet. The weather doesn't help. And you're here to visit the site of a horrible event.'

They saw a break in the line of houses. A stand of tall gloomy conifers shielded a wide block of flats, set back from the road, with cars parked between the trees and the flats. They looked up at the building, three stories high, brick built.

'Your wife's client lives on the top floor. Number thirty-eight.' Smith pointed. Each flat had an entrance door facing the road, opening onto a walkway protected by a waist-high wall. Neighbouring doors were separated by two substantial windows, most of which were lined with net curtains.

'I'd like to go up to where Kate was found,' said Redstone.

They walked to an open entrance at the end of the block. Inside was a sheltered flight of concrete stairs, punctuated by landings. They climbed to the top.

Redstone paused and looked down the length of the walkway. Nobody was around. He walked slowly past the row of doors and windows, until he was outside flat thirty-eight. A cracked dead leaf lay on the bare concrete floor. Tears sprang to his eyes.

'Her hand was always warm,' he said, his voice breaking. He bent forwards, sobbing.

Smith put her hand gently on his arm but said nothing. They stood there for a while.

'Sorry about that,' Redstone said, straightening and wiping his eyes.

'Don't be ridiculous,' said Smith.

They walked back towards the lobby at the head of the stairs. 'Where do the Kemp brothers live?' Redstone asked.

'In these two flats we're passing now, numbers thirty-one and thirty-two. Don't…'

Redstone paused and stared at the curtained windows. 'I was going to say don't show obvious interest,' said Smith. 'Too late. Let's go.'

They went back down the staircase and walked away from the grounds.

'Why do you think Kemp didn't move Kate's… Kate somewhere away from the flats after the murder?' asked Redstone. 'It would have lessened suspicion of him.'

'Who knows? Moving a body is quite difficult, and he didn't have his brother there to help. And maybe he didn't have time before someone spotted her. And he would have had to clean the walkway to get rid of… the forensic signs, which would have aroused suspicion.'

'Oh.'

They walked on. 'I know a nice old pub not far from here,' said Redstone. 'I'm not very hungry, but I suppose I should eat something, and we can get out of this wind. Fancy a spot of lunch?'

'Excellent idea.'

Redstone led the way to an older part of the suburb, containing a few shops and restaurants, and a ramshackle pub right on the edge of the road. They went in, Redstone automatically ducking to avoid banging his head on the low beams. They ordered food and took their drinks to a table.

'You said Kate was probably killed because she saw or heard something the Kemps wanted to keep secret.'

'Yes. It was just a guess.'

'I've an idea. I suppose the Kemps are careful not to keep anything incriminating in their flats?'

'Yes, that's what my husband said.'

'But they must keep incriminating stuff somewhere where they know they can easily get hold of it?'

'I suppose so. Like cash, for example.'

'My thought is that they might store stuff in the neighbour's flat – Kate's client's – and Kate saw it there. Do you think the police looked into that possibility?'

'I don't know. I'll ask Doug – that's my husband. It's a fair idea – the Kemps do behave as model neighbours, and I can imagine one of them going into the old lady's flat to bring her shopping or whatever, while also hiding stuff in places she couldn't reach. I'll phone Doug now.'

She walked out of the pub, stood in the shelter provided for smokers, and spoke on her phone. She waited for a couple of minutes and spoke again. She returned and sat down.

'Doug looked at the file while I was on the phone. They did speak at length to the old lady but didn't search her flat. Even if they had, I doubt whether they'd have found anything because the

Kemps would've foreseen that possibility and moved any incriminating stuff elsewhere. They're exceptionally good at covering their tracks. Doug says his colleagues are hugely frustrated at not being able to pin anything on them. The Kemps are always one step ahead.'

'Thanks. And please pass my thanks to Doug,' Redstone said. 'I'd like to go back to the flats and visit the old lady. Not today, but on Monday. Will you come with me?'

'What would be the point?'

'Er—' he paused and swallowed. 'Research without a clear goal often produces the most interesting results.'

Smith looked at him closely. 'Ok,' she said. 'I'll come with you. Same meeting arrangements as today.'

'Good.' He raised his glass. 'To you and Doug.'

After Smith left to return to central London, Redstone walked briskly through a park back to his house, feeling the thump of his heels with each step. The rain had stopped, but there was still that chilling wind, and everything looked dull under the overcast sky. Some leaves were blowing about. The only other people in the park were a couple of dog walkers and a man standing still in front of a bench, staring down at his hands.

The weather was not helping his mood. He determined to stop thinking about the murder and concentrate on something else. Who to take to Chequers sprang to mind.

At home, he phoned Sophie, and she answered immediately.

'Hi, Dad. Everything all right?'

'Fine, thanks. How about you?'

'I'm just finishing work. I'm going out tonight with a friend. We're trying a new restaurant.'

'Boyfriend or girlfriend?'

'Oh, Dad, I'm not a child. As it happens it's a boyfriend. His name is Oskar. And you'll never guess – he's Norwegian!'

'Good heavens!' said Redstone. 'Is that just coincidence?'

'Yes, absolutely. We met in a meeting about fisheries. He's based here in Brussels. Before you ask, he doesn't come from Kristiansheim – that would be a coincidence too far. He's from Oslo.'

'And you're getting on well with him?'

'Very well. Extremely well. He's gorgeous – you'd love him. Why don't you come over some time?'

A pang of sorrow twisted in Redstone's gut – Kate would have loved to hear what Sophie was saying and to be able to meet Oskar. He forced himself to sound cheerful. 'That sounds great, but I'm tied up for the next couple of weekends. In fact, that's why I phoned you now. I hope you'll be impressed – the prime minister's invited me to Chequers.'

'Wow! I am impressed. The prime minister's country residence! You're getting quite important!'

'No I'm not. Anyway, I'm invited to take a guest. Would you like to come with me? It's Saturday fortnight.'

Sophie's voice changed. 'Oh, Mum would have loved to have gone with you. Do you honestly want me?'

'Yes, I do. You're right about Mum, but, well, that just can't be, and I guess we have to move on. Though I can't say I'm being fully successful at that myself.'

'Well, it does sound as though you have started to move on, I'm pleased to say. How about your own Norwegian friend?'

'No, it's too soon to invite Christina. Too early.'

'Ok. I'm just looking at my diary – oh, I'm going to a party with Oskar that evening. He particularly wanted me to go. It's at the Norwegian embassy. I don't want to let him down, Dad. And to be honest, I'd feel horribly nervous and out of place going to Chequers.'

'Sophie. I do understand. I'm not sure I won't feel out of place myself. Though I must tell you something else that happened yesterday – the prime minister asked me to serve as his special adviser. I wasn't sure how serious he was, and I'm still not, but you might feel a bit proud of your old man.'

'Wow! I do, Dad. You agree with his politics, don't you? Why don't you take the job? You could do something useful for a change – not just save humanity by inventing awesome drug systems.'

'I can't see myself stuck in Number 10 all the time. It's bad enough for the few weeks I'm working there now. All that political manoeuvring. I long to be back in the lab.'

'I think you'd actually like both roles – running the country and improving everyone's health.'

'You left out making more millions.'

'True. Can't you produce another amazing invention?'

'Ok. I'll do that this evening. Treacle will help me.'

'Give her a kiss from me. I must rush now. Love you!'

'Love you too, Sophie. Take care. Bye!'

Redstone leaned back. He'd nearly told Sophie about the visit to the murder site, but at the last minute decided against it. It would have spoilt her evening. He wanted to protect her.

He turned in his chair and saw Treacle sitting in the doorway, cleaning her black coat. 'Sophie told me to kiss you, but I think that would be a bit unhygienic, seeing where you are putting your tongue at the moment,' he said. The cat ignored him.

He switched on his sound system and listened to a playlist he'd compiled years before. Bill Withers came on, singing *Ain't No Sunshine When She's Gone*. Tears streamed down his face.

MONDAY 24 OCTOBER

Redstone and Smith walked through the empty streets of Winchmore Hill. It was still cold, but not as miserable as the previous week.

'I've just realised that I don't know the name of the woman we're visiting,' said Redstone. 'And, on reflection, do we know if she's still there?'

'She does still live there,' said Smith, 'and her name is Mrs Molly Goodyard.'

They arrived at the flats and climbed the stone steps. As they started along the walkway towards Mrs Goodyard's flat, a small man with thinning ginger hair stepped out of a door and strode towards them.

'What d'you want?' he said, blocking their way, his chin jutting forward.

'Hi,' said Redstone. 'We're just going to visit someone in a flat along there.' He pointed over the man's shoulder.

'Everyone's out,' said the man.

'Are you sure?' said Redstone. 'The person we're visiting has great difficulty in going out.'

'I said everyone's out,' he said loudly. 'We don't want your kind here. Turn around and go home!'

'I'm not sure what you mean by… I really would like to check that she's not there,' said Redstone. He moved to get past the man, who moved sideways to block him. He started jerking his arms about.

'I said, go home!' he shouted. 'I saw you nosing around the other day. You're up to no good. Fuck off! Right now!' Smith put a hand on Redstone's arm.

'Look,' said Redstone, 'all I…'

'Are you stupid!' the man cried. His face flushed and he wiped his nose with his hand. 'Can't you understand plain English?'

Ignoring Smith tugging his arm, Redstone stayed stationary. He didn't see why he should take orders from this man, who seemed a bit deranged. But then the man yanked a large military-looking knife from inside his jacket and pointed it at Redstone, waving it in small circles. Redstone backed away quickly, keeping his eyes on the knife, which was pointed and had two sharp edges, one serrated. 'Ok, ok,' he said, holding his hands out. 'We'll go. No need for…'

The man edged steadily forward, staring at Redstone's face with inhuman, unblinking eyes, still waving the knife at his chest. Shocked, Redstone edged backwards along the walkway to the corner next to the stone staircase, where he found himself trapped. The man kept coming, snot oozing from his nose. The knife looked murderous, and so did the man. Redstone's pulse was racing, and he felt sick. What the hell was happening? What had he done to bring this on? Was this man going to stick that knife into his body? Was Redstone going to die exactly where his wife was murdered? It couldn't be real – yet it was. He looked around desperately. He was sweating heavily, and his legs felt weak.

Suddenly, Smith leapt onto the man's back, grabbed and twisted the wrist holding the knife, and yanked the man round to face the steps. She shoved his back so that he stumbled into a lurching run, hooked her foot behind his ankles and pushed him forward so that he fell headfirst down the steps onto the concrete landing. She jumped down to land with one heel on the back of his neck. The man gave a grunted sigh and lay still, empty and collapsed, face down, still holding the knife.

Smith bent down, looked closely at the man and pressed a finger against the side of his neck. She came back up the stairs, took her phone out of her bag and pressed two digits.

'The younger Kemp brother, Terry, threatened Redstone with a combat knife. He was drugged up and out of control, and I judged Redstone to be in real danger. So I took Kemp out. Yes, he's dead. No, no witnesses that I can see. You know where I am. Ok, we're on our way.'

Redstone stood frozen, his mind in turmoil, unable to think clearly. He felt dissociated from the real world.

Smith pulled his arm. 'Let's go, now.' She led the way past Kemp's body. Redstone couldn't see any blood.

They walked back the way they came. Redstone was drenched in cold sweat, and his arms and knees were weak and shaky. There was nobody around. Everything was still. 'Let's go somewhere where we can talk about what happened,' said Smith calmly. She looked at a map on her phone and led the way into the park through which Redstone had walked the previous Friday.

'You may be in shock,' she said.

'I don't know,' said Redstone. 'I've never seen anything like that.' The sight of Smith landing on Kemp's neck played through his mind again. 'Christ! I don't know what... You were so fast!'

'It's all training. I used to be in... the army. You just use what people call muscle memory, though I hate the term. You don't have time to think. Thinking would slow it all down, anyway.'

'Did you have to kill him? Did you have to jump on his neck?' He suddenly had an overwhelming feeling of guilt.

'If an assailant is better armed than you, but you're temporarily in a better position, you have to consolidate your position. If I hadn't killed him, he would have got up and attacked us.'

'Don't you think he might not have actually knifed me?'

'No. Didn't you see? He'd lost it. He was unstable. He'd been using his own product.'

'Don't you feel bad for taking someone's life? I feel awful about it. I put us in that situation.' He swallowed.

'Let me ask you a question. Is the world a better place with Terry Kemp dead?'

'That isn't your decision to make. Our society's abolished the death penalty.'

'I didn't notice that applying when I was a soldier in the field.'

'I know the "MI" in MI5 stands for Military Intelligence, but that's an anachronism. It's real title now is the Security Service. You're a civilian now.'

'MI5 recruited me for my skills and experience, which are different from those of most of my colleagues. We're supposed to think for ourselves, and I thought for myself. I don't have the slightest regret. He was a venomous evil cockroach who'd caused untold misery and would have continued to. So I stamped on him.'

'Literally and figuratively.' Redstone felt his shock ebbing away. 'Why was he so… why did he need to stop us going further on the walkway?'

'Maybe there was something in Molly Goodyear's flat that he didn't want us to see.'

'Yes. Perhaps it was the same thing that got Kate killed. What happens now?'

'A clean-up squad's been sent. If the body's discovered and reported before they arrive, they'll turn around and go back to base. If not, they'll take the body away and ensure there are no traces of what happened. Not that I think there are any.'

'And what will happen to the body?'

'I don't know. Either it'll be cremated, and nobody will ever know what happened to him, or it might be "discovered" somewhere. Probably that.'

Redstone looked at her. She seemed a bit flushed, otherwise completely normal. 'You don't look terribly shocked by what you've just been through. I was just a spectator, and I'm hugely shaken up.'

'It was nothing compared to… well, I could use a drink.'

'Me too. Shall we go back to the pub we were in last week?'

'Not a good idea. Let's go into town.'

*

Redstone sat in a pub on Whitehall, opposite Downing Street. The saloon was deep and narrow, full of polished dark wood. His table was next to the window, and he watched crowds of tourists drift by while he sipped his drink. He kept replaying the attack in his head.

Smith came in, looked around and walked over to join him.

'For some reason,' he said, 'I fancied a glass of champagne – quite inappropriate in the circumstances, but you did save my life. I got you one too. I hope you like champagne?'

'I do, indeed,' she said, and raised her glass. 'To life!'

'A great toast. To life!' They clinked their glasses and drank.

'It's fortunate that you like champagne,' said Redstone, 'because I bought you a bottle as a thank-you present.' He handed her a bag, and she took out the bottle and looked at it.

'Looks expensive. Not that I know much about champagne,' she said.

'It is good. I hope you and Doug enjoy drinking it together.'

'We will! Thanks a lot.'

'You've been ages on the phone – did you get to speak to Doug?'

'Yes. I've found out a lot. Let me update you on what happened after we left.'

'Go on.'

'The body was discovered before the clean-up team arrived, by Paul Kemp, brother of the deceased.'

'Ah,' said Redstone. 'Him.'

'Yes. He phoned 999 and asked for an ambulance. When the paramedics arrived, they assumed it'd been an accident – Terry Kemp had slipped and fallen down the stairs. There was no knife.

They phoned the police. When the police arrived, they also assumed it had been an accident.'

'What about the phone call you made? Weren't MI5 involved?'

'Yes,' said Smith. 'My colleagues told Scotland Yard that Terry Kemp had been killed by an MI5 operative in the course of duties. Shortly after the local officers arrived on the scene, Scotland Yard told them to treat the death as a probable accident, which, of course, was what they'd been doing anyway. Scotland Yard told them to interview Paul Kemp and any neighbours who were around. They also told them to search Molly Goodyard's flat.'

'Excellent fast thinking.'

'Yes, but it seems that Paul Kemp must have been faster. The police found nothing.'

'Did you learn how Paul Kemp took the news?'

'He pretended to believe that it was a horrible accident.'

'What do you think he'll do now?'

'I don't know. I'll ask Doug this evening, though he isn't close to all this – he currently works on counter-terrorism.'

'Did you tell Doug what really happened?'

'Yes. He was sure I'd acted correctly, and even thought I had a legal duty to protect you in the way I did. He thinks the police will advise the Crown Prosecution Service that there's no evidence of a crime, even if the autopsy shows anything other than injuries consistent with a heavy fall down concrete steps. And I doubt whether anything else will show up.'

'So you're off the hook, not that you seemed worried you were on one.'

'Right and right!' said Smith and raised her glass again. Redstone raised his, and they each took a sip.

'One other thing slightly bothers me,' said Redstone. 'When you phoned your people just after the event, you said, "You know where I am." How did they know?'

'All anyone needs is an appropriate tweak to their phone, and then their position can be monitored by someone who has the right permissions. My phone has that tweak.'

'Ah, yes. I should have known,' said Redstone. 'Do they constantly monitor your whereabouts?'

'No – it's just that they can call up the information if they need to.'

'I suppose they, or should I say you, use similar technology to track people of interest other than your own staff,' said Redstone.

'I couldn't possibly comment,' said Smith with a smile.

'What about me?'

Smith remained silent.

'Did MI5 fiddle with my phone while I was with the PM the first time?'

Smith sighed. 'As I've said before, you're very valuable to the country. Don't worry – we don't use the information for anything personal. In any case, we only use the facility when we need to find out where you are. Indeed, I don't think it's yet been used at all.'

Redstone felt a flash of annoyance, but on reflection decided that there was no harm in Laura and her colleagues being able to find out where he was. He sat quietly for a minute. 'I suppose I can't discuss today's events with anyone except you?'

'No, I'm afraid not,' said Smith.

'Well, I'll tell Treacle anyway.'

'No, you can't tell anyone. Who's Treacle?'

'Treacle is my main confidante. I often tell her difficult stuff, even when she's not present. She's a great help.'

'Is she your imaginary friend, then? I had one of those when I was two.'

'No, far from imaginary. She'll be waiting for me in the hall when I get home, greet me and ask for dinner.'

'You're getting me worried. I thought you lived alone. You positively mustn't talk to a single person about today's events. You never know who else they'll speak to.'

'That's all right then. Even MI5 couldn't get Treacle to talk. Even if you offered her the finest quality cat food.'

Smith burst out laughing. 'I didn't have you marked down as a pet lover. What's she like?'

'She's black and affectionate, and pretty bright for a cat.'

'Quite like Doug, then!'

*

Back in their attic office, Redstone suddenly stood up. 'Good heavens! I think I can do it!'

'Do what?'

'Go into the wavy dimension! I did what Jim said, and I felt a sort of stirring. If I'd continued, I'm sure I would have gone!'

'Great!' said Smith. 'Do you want to try now? Just spend a few seconds there, and then come back. Don't go outside this office till you've got a bit of experience – Jim Clothier said it was pretty awful at first.'

Redstone tensed. He was sweating. And then he did it – he twisted his body mentally, and after a short feeling of pressure in his head, he found himself in just the environment that Clothier had described. He seemed to be in a corridor that was transparent yet lined with mirrors. Whichever way he looked – left, right, up, down, forwards – he could see himself a few feet away. In between, he could see his office and Smith standing looking amazed. He felt intensely nauseous and tried to avoid vomiting, but failed. He threw up in the corner.

'Oh, God,' he groaned. Should he clear it up? The scientist in him took over. Would the vomit stay there forever? There wouldn't be any bacteria in this dimension to help it decay. Ah –

but there were bacteria in his gut. Would the smell get into the normal dimensions? He used his hand to wipe cold sweat from his forehead and used a tissue to wipe his mouth. He carefully put the tissue next to the pool of vomit. The thought of leaving it all there appalled him.

Smith spoke. He could make out most of what she was saying, though her voice was muffled and echoey.

'I hope you can… me. That was astonishing! Even though I've… before, it seems… magic! I suggest you… round the office and then appear somewhere different from… you disappeared.'

Feeling shaky, but less sick, Redstone walked around. If he ignored the view beyond a few metres away, he found it easy to orient and locate himself. He wondered whether Laura would be able to hear him if he spoke.

'Hello, Laura! Raise your arm if you can hear me.'

She didn't move.

He tried again, this time shouting at the top of his voice. She looked up but didn't raise her arm.

He walked in front of her and stared into her eyes. She showed no sign of seeing him. He suddenly felt queasy again, so walked behind Smith and twisted back into the normal world. She whirled round.

'Did you hear me?' she asked.

'More or less,' he said, already feeling much better, 'but I gather you didn't hear me?'

'I certainly didn't hear you say anything, but there was a faint sound at one stage. I can't describe it properly – it was as though lots of musical instruments were tuning up very softly.'

'I did shout to you. I suppose that some of the energy in the sound waves I produced did make its way into the normal world, but with frequencies different from the sounds I made. Good to know.'

He walked round to his chair and sat down heavily. 'It was just as Jim Clothier described,' he said, 'except for the vomiting. I was actually sick. It was like the worst seasickness I've experienced. Can you smell anything?'

Smith sniffed the air. 'No, nothing.'

'That's a relief. I'll just have to fight the need to throw up. I can't let that stop me – the experience was amazing! I've now seen another dimension, and Jim Clothier's the only other person in the world to have seen it, as far as we know. Ever! I've got to go back. I'll give myself a few minutes and then try again, but this time, I'll walk about this building – just to see if doing that raises any problems.'

'Good idea,' said Smith. 'I'll phone Jim to tell him the good news.'

'First, I need to clean up the mess. I'll take some cleaning stuff with me.' Redstone went out to a cleaner's cupboard along the corridor and returned with a bucket of soapy water and a mop. He waved goodbye to Smith, who was talking on the phone, and twisted into the wavy dimension, again feeling a pulse of pressure in his head.

The nausea came back, but he was able to control it this time. Covering his nose to avoid the smell, he cleaned up the mess, left the bucket and mop in the corner and walked to the wall separating his office from the corridor outside. Could he get into that corridor without going through the doorway? Being in another dimension should allow it. He peered at the wall, but it seemed solid and impermeable. He pushed against it, and nothing happened. But then he realised that he could bypass it by twisting in a way which he wasn't going to be able to explain to Laura, or indeed anyone else. He did so, feeling the unpleasant pulse again, and found himself in the corridor outside his office. He was astonished. What an extraordinary ability!

He made his way downstairs, and into the grand rooms used for high-level meetings. Finding his way was like moving in a foggy street because he could see only up to a few feet away – but worse, because of the other confusing images. The strain was starting to give him a headache. He edged into a room containing about a dozen people, some of whom he recognised as cabinet ministers and some as officials. He realised that a cabinet committee meeting was taking place. Looking at the papers in front of one of the seated ministers and decoding what he could understand of what people were saying, he decided the meeting was about education policy. He felt it was wrong to linger, so he stumbled out. As he did so, he noticed a tissue on the floor – not the floor of the normal world, but rather the floor of the wavy dimension.

'Bloody hell!' he exclaimed. He rushed back upstairs, moving carefully but as fast as he could, entered his office, made sure that he was in a place where nobody could see him through the open door, collected the bucket and mop and twisted back into the normal world. Smith started.

'Listen,' Redstone said. 'I've discovered something serious. I found a used tissue in the wavy dimension, by one of the rooms used for cabinet committee meetings. Someone else has been there! This means we aren't the only people with the technology. What's more, someone's been using it to spy on our government!'

Smith stared. 'You're sure of this? It couldn't have got there in some normal way?'

'I'm sure. We need to talk to Jim Clothier. No, Gavin McKay. As soon as possible. Christ! How can we keep state secrets now? How can we defend people against sneak attacks?'

'One thing at a time,' said Smith. 'Let's go downstairs – I'll phone on the way down to arrange for transport and set up the meeting. But first, get rid of that foul-smelling bucket!'

*

Half an hour later, the four of them were sitting in Gavin McKay's office on the second floor of Thames House. The view of the river was mainly obscured by the trees on the other side of Millbank. The pale wooden office furniture and soft seating, which looked as though it came from Ikea, all looked lost in the long, wide room.

'Great news that the procedure's worked,' said McKay. 'But first, have you fully recovered from the confrontation this morning? It's just as well Laura was with you, even though your outing was nothing to do with our task.'

'Yes, thank you,' said Redstone. 'Laura was superb. I wouldn't be here without her quick thinking and… um… skill.'

'She's one of our stars,' said McKay. Smith looked pleased. 'Now, let's get onto why you wanted this meeting.'

Redstone explained what he had found.

'Ah,' said Clothier. 'I can explain how the tissue got there. I must have dropped it!'

'Christ, what a relief,' said Redstone. 'How did it happen?'

'When I found that the procedure had started to work on me, I discussed with Gavin here where I should try it out. We agreed that a good test would be somewhere where security was always extremely high. If I could get in there and out again without being detected, the procedure would have proved its worth.'

'That's right,' said McKay. 'I decided on Number 10, partly because I'm a mischievous bugger.'

'The test did show something we'll need to think about,' said Clothier. 'It was difficult to find somewhere where I could step into the wavy dimension unobserved. And just as hard for re-entering. In the end, I went into the public toilet in St James's Park. Both times.'

'Did you wander around Number 10 at ease, then?' asked Redstone.

'Yes, though as you'll have seen, it's difficult to see more than a few feet. Gavin had told me something about the layout, but it wasn't straightforward to get to anywhere interesting. Eventually, I found myself in a cabinet committee meeting on social security policy. I didn't stay long. I had a bit of a cold and must have dropped the tissue then.'

'I also left a tissue in the wavy dimension,' said Redstone. 'I used it to wipe my mouth after vomiting. But I cleaned up afterwards. You didn't warn me about how horrible it would be.'

'I didn't feel as bad as it seems you did,' said Clothier. 'Maybe it's because my hobby is sailing. Sorry about that.'

'Sailing? I had you down as a fellow nerd.'

'Oh, I am a nerd. You probably have to be a nerd to be able to go into the wavy dimension. A top nerd. But there's nothing in the nerd handbook to say we can't enjoy sailing. You're on your own, thinking about the physics of the various forces…'

'Get on with it,' said McKay. 'Bloody nerds.'

'Sorry,' said Clothier.

'When you were in the wavy dimension, did you make any sounds which people in the normal world heard?' Redstone asked.

'I tried half-heartedly, but I didn't want to risk arousing suspicion. I think a couple of people may have sensed a noise in the background, but they didn't pay much attention to it.'

'Why are you so sure it wasn't a spy from a foreign power who left the tissue?' asked Redstone.

'Scientists can't be sure of anything, as you know,' said Clothier, 'but I'm willing to bet a lot of money on it.'

'What's your reasoning?'

'The technology's amazingly difficult. I suppose there are many people in the world who would be able to travel into the wavy dimension, like you and me, if they were given the treatment, but that would require not only our electronic equipment but also our chemical – the substance I injected into you. I can't tell you how hard it is to synthesise that stuff.'

'Say more. Remember, I'm a chemist.'

'Well, in the end, we got three different labs to make precursors, and we did the final synthesis here, but the number of steps required was enormous and the yield,' he turned to McKay, '– the amount we got in the end – tiny.' He turned back to Redstone. 'I call the chemical "WD41", the WD standing for Wavy Dimension and the 41 for the number of steps involved in the synthesis. We used our full supply on you, and it'll take many weeks to get enough for another batch.'

Redstone smiled at the reference to the well-known lubricant. 'I'd better get on with the spying then, before the WD41 wears off.'

'We use the word "investigating" rather than "spying",' said McKay. 'But yes – now's the time to get the investigation moving fast. And given that you're unique, let's try to keep out of scrapes, shall we?''

'I'll do my best. The ball's now in your court – you have to tell me when you think there will be a meeting worth my attending as an unknown observer.'

'We've been keeping an eye out for such a meeting, and as it happens, the next one is tomorrow morning. Lesage is due to meet his chief engineer, and no one else is scheduled to be present, as far as we know. My bet is they'll discuss the problem, whatever it is, in the screened room. Laura will sort out the details of how you get there and where you disappear and return to our world.' He nodded to Smith.

'That's fine,' she said and stood up. The others rose too.

'I'm exhausted after today's excitement,' said Redstone. 'I'm going home. See you tomorrow in the office, Laura.'

'Not so fast,' said Clothier. 'We need to give you a check-up.'

'Oh. I'd forgotten.'

In the basement, Clothier measured Redstone's blood pressure, asked a few general health questions and took a blood sample. 'Everything seems fine, and I doubt that the blood results will show anything unusual. I'll phone if there's a problem.'

'Before I go, what will you do when a foreign power does develop the technology? It's bound to happen sooner or later.'

'We've got plans,' said Clothier firmly.

So have I, thought Redstone, but not concerning a foreign power.

TUESDAY 25 OCTOBER

'Apart from the horrible nausea, this mission – as I suppose you'd call it – seems straightforward,' said Redstone, 'except for the problem of having to be out of sight when I disappear and reappear. Victoria's a busy area. Any ideas?'

'Can you get into a car without opening the door?' asked Smith, leaning back in her chair in the attic office.

'I expect so. I could get past walls in this building, so I can't see why it should be a problem.'

'Ok. This is my suggestion. We drive you to near France Nucléaire's office, and you do your thing inside the car. And we wait for you, and you get back into the car and return to this world.'

'I can see that the first bit would work,' said Redstone, 'but how can you wait in a parked vehicle for what might be a couple of hours in that part of London?'

'Good point. We could square it with the police, but even so, it might attract attention.'

'How about getting a Portaloo put somewhere?'

'Er… as a matter of fact, we do sometimes deploy them for… well, for other purposes. We put up barriers too, to make it look like the road is being repaired. We'll do just that.' She looked at his clothes. 'You'll have to dress appropriately – you'll need to look like a road repair worker.' She smiled.

'If you were about to say that what I'm wearing now is fine, you've got a point,' said Redstone. 'When I went back into science, it was great not to have to wear a suit anymore. And then I stopped buying new clothes altogether, after Kate died. I must do something about it.'

'Well, what you're wearing now isn't quite appropriate – you can leave the sports jacket here and wear jeans instead of those chinos. I'll get you the jeans and a hard hat. Tell me your sizes. We need to move quickly.'

She phoned Thames House and organised their needs.

'The clothing will be here in fifteen minutes, and at ten thirty a white van will draw up downstairs to take us to the street behind France Nucléaire's office. The Portaloo and barriers are being organised there as we speak.'

Redstone was impressed. 'You people certainly move fast when you have to.'

The clothing arrived, and Redstone went down the corridor into a toilet to change. On returning to the office, he found that Smith had changed too, into jeans and a shapeless grey sweater. They went downstairs, where Lewis was waiting in the white van. He was wearing a heavy woollen jacket with a dull blue and red ethnic pattern, and his brown hair was pulled back into a ponytail.

They quickly arrived at the street behind France Nucléaire's office. Lewis parked next to a section of road cordoned off by red barriers. Inside the barriers were some plastic sacks of rubble, and a plastic cabin, a little bigger than a telephone box. Smith and Redstone got out of the van, and Lewis drove off.

'It's quite awkward, having to hide from Lewis what you're up to,' said Smith. 'I'm going to talk to Gavin McKay about whether we can let him in on the secret.'

They unhooked a length of barrier and stepped into the enclosure.

'You'll see that the door of the loo has a sign showing engaged or free, as you'd expect. You can go in and lock it from the inside, disappear and leave it like that. Then people won't be surprised when you eventually come out.'

'Unless they're standing watching the loo for ages, waiting for someone to emerge.'

'A risk we have to take. Phone me when you've finished. Good luck!'

Redstone entered the toilet and locked the door. He twisted into the wavy dimension, shrugged off the surge of pressure in his head and tried to ignore the bad nausea as he strained to orient himself amongst the multiple images. He moved out into the street, his symptoms calming down a little, walked carefully to the front of the building, into the lobby and through a door to the emergency staircase, and climbed the plain concrete stairs to the top landing.

Suddenly he gasped with shock and clung to the rail. He'd realised that he could twist through the floor and doing so would mean plunging to his death. He had to concentrate. He wiped his forehead.

Following the floor plan MI5 had produced, he made his way to what they suspected was the shielded room. Nobody was around. He entered the room, which was windowless, had padded walls and was set out for meetings. If MI5 had it right, Lesage's meeting was due to start soon – the sooner the better, as he was starting to feel quite ill.

After a few minutes, Lesage came through the door followed by another man, burly and bearded – presumably the UK company's chief engineer. They seated themselves at the meeting table.

They spoke in French. *'Now we can... freely. What progress... made?'* said Lesage. Redstone was relieved to find his French adequate to make sense of the conversation, despite the sound being muffled and echoey.

'Very little. I tried two... dealing with it. Neither of them worked.'

'That's not good enough... running out.'

Beardy looked worried and exasperated. '*As I keep telling you, I've no expertise in... We're not going to make progress unless... expand the group of people who know about the problem.*'

'And as I keep telling you,' snapped Lesage, *'it's impossible to... into the secret. You know very well what would... if the British became aware. Or even our... government, or our Paris management.'*

'But I also know very well... if we fail to solve it soon, there will be a disaster. Our own... insignificant by comparison.' Beardy stared at Lesage belligerently.

'Just get on with it. Do more research. You're... engineer – teach yourself how to...' Lesage replied, staring back. Beardy shrugged his shoulders and said nothing.

'What about the British Nuclear Inspectorate? Are they still... the figures we're sending them?' asked Lesage.

'Yes... they're satisfied with the safety of all the... The figures look good... they're not perfect.'

'Excellent. At least... working well.'

'How did you get on with the prime minister's... came here last week?' asked Beardy.

'Ah, Redstone... doesn't know much about nuclear... He tried to get information... confident that he learned nothing... Fortunately... agreement with Madame Hitchcock... limit to what the British can find out. As you know.'

'So, he's not going to... difficulties?' asked Beardy.

'No. We can't ignore him, but I'm confident... our little secret.'

'Our big secret, or rather your *big secret,'* said Beardy bitterly.

'We're... together. I repeat – get on with it,' said Lesage. *'Is there anything else... discuss in this horrible room? I need to get somewhere with a window and...'*

'Nothing more as far as I'm concerned,' said Beardy. They stood up and left the room.

Redstone also stood up. He felt a wave of sickness, a developing headache and a strong compulsion to get out. He made his way back to the portable toilet, twisted back into the normal world and breathed a sigh of relief that he could once more see clearly for more than a few metres, did not have to process the multiple images and could hear normally. And the urge to throw up was gone. He phoned Smith.

'I'm back.'

'Good. Go out of the loo and walk down the street away from Victoria. We'll pick you up in the van.'

As they drove back towards Parliament Square, Redstone looked out at the tourists and the office workers and felt amazed that everyone was going about their business as if the world were normal. It didn't feel that way to him anymore. He was dying to tell Laura about his experience but knew he couldn't speak about it in front of Lewis.

'I bet you're wishing you could tell me what happened but can't because of Lewis's presence,' said Smith.

'You're a mind reader,' said Redstone. 'Sorry, Lewis.'

'No need to apologise,' said Lewis. 'Just don't disappear into the wavy dimension while I'm driving – I might crash!'

Redstone burst into laughter. 'I take it you've been cleared to know what we're up to!'

'I have. And I tell you I found it difficult to believe. It's the stuff of science fiction! This is the most important and amazing secret I'm ever likely to have to keep!'

'And he will keep it, of course,' said Smith to Redstone. 'But let's do the debriefing properly, in our office. I'll debrief my colleagues later.'

'Ok,' said Redstone. 'But I must tell you both that the whole thing went pretty well. The technique is horrible, but fantastic. I haven't got to the bottom of the nuclear problem, but I learned a lot. It should help us find out what's going on.'

He mused a moment and added, 'We're going to need Alan Cunningham's help. We don't have to tell him how we got the information, of course, but we'll have to tell him what I learned. Can we arrange another meeting with him?'

'Lewis, would you please get onto that,' Smith said.

*

They sat with cups of coffee in their attic office. Smith took out her notebook. 'Tell me all,' she said.

'I found my way to the room we identified on the plan. It was the right room, and Lesage and another man came in on schedule. The second man was big and bearded. I assume he's their chief engineer. He's certainly in on the secret.'

'I'll look into who he is from your description, but I bet you're right,' said Smith. 'Did they speak in English?'

'No, French. I had a bit of trouble understanding them, but not only because my French isn't perfect – more, I think, because of the way sound is distorted in the wavy dimension. I could have done with subtitles! But I'm pretty confident that I got more than just the gist of what they said.

'Carry on.'

'There's bad feeling between Beardy and Lesage. It seems Lesage initiated whatever the problem is, and he's tasked Beardy to sort it out. Presumably Beardy was brought in after his predecessor resigned. But Beardy's not having any success. He said the problem's outside his area of expertise. Lesage won't let him bring more expert engineers in to help because he's terrified information will leak out.'

'That's useful information. When we find out who Beardy is, we'll ascertain his areas of expertise. That'll at least narrow down the nature of the problem.'

'And the problem is serious. Everything I was told at the beginning is backed up by what I heard. They spoke in general terms, but there's no doubt that there's some sort of disaster on the horizon unless they solve it.'

'And was there any clue about the nature of the problem?'

'Nothing more than I've already told you. But there was an exchange which I found odd – Lesage asked Beardy about the figures France Nucléaire submits to the Nuclear Inspectorate, and Beardy confirmed that they were fine.'

'What's odd about that?' asked Smith.

'Why should Lesage raise that issue inside the screened room? He said he hated it in there and was keen to get out.'

'Do you think the figures hold some sort of information about the problem?'

'It looks that way,' said Redstone, 'but I can't see how. The figures relate to the existing power stations, not the new ones, plainly. Maybe Alan Cunningham will have an idea about how the two things could be connected.'

'You must ask him. Did anything else crop up?'

'Yes. I think they said that the French government and France Nucléaire's headquarters don't know about the problem.'

'That's important.'

'Also, Lesage mentioned Hitchcock, sort of approvingly. I think he was referring to the fact that the Inspectorate can't visit the sites, but there was something in his tone…'

Smith's phone rang. She listened. 'Ok, I'll tell him,' she said. She put the phone down.

'Lewis thinks the best place to talk to Alan Cunningham is near his home because that would minimise the chance of Hitchcock learning that he's involved with us. You should phone his mobile and ask to meet him in Welwyn or nearby. It would be helpful if the meeting could be this afternoon. Here's his number.'

*

Redstone sat in the airy restaurant of a big department store in Welwyn Garden City, gazing out at the street. The wide road was shadowed in the twilight, but he could still see the central reservation, planted with varied mature shrubs. It looked attractive and peaceful.

Cunningham arrived with a tray bearing a coffee and a large slice of gateau. ‘Fancy some of my cake?’

Redstone looked at it longingly but declined. ‘We’ve obtained some more information about what France Nucléaire might be up to, but it doesn’t mean much to me, so I hoped you might be able to help.’

‘Happy to do so. What is it?’

‘First, we have confirmation, if we needed it, that the problem is potentially disastrous. Second, we also have a strong suspicion that Valerie can’t be trusted not to tell France Nucléaire what we’re up to, so you must keep our meetings from her, I’m afraid.’

‘Ok. What else?’

‘The main puzzle is about the data which they send your Inspectorate. There’s a strong indication that those figures are somehow linked to the problem.’

‘I don’t immediately see how that could be the case,’ mused Cunningham. ‘The figures relate to the existing power stations, not the new batch. Maybe there’s information buried in them which would throw light on fuel issues with the new reactors, but I can’t see it for the moment.’

‘Do you happen to know their UK chief engineer?’ asked Redstone.

‘I’ve met him a few times. Why?’

‘Is he a burly, bearded man?’

‘Yes, that’s him. Georges Dupont. Why?’

‘We saw him talking to Lesage, and the context made us suspicious. Do you happen to know what his engineering expertise is?’

‘Yes, he’s an IT specialist. He helped design the IT systems which monitor the plants and provide us with all the data.’

‘That’s extremely interesting,’ said Redstone. ‘Is there any way you or your staff can interrogate the data you’ve been receiving over the last couple of years to see if there are any suspicious patterns?'

'Yes, I'll get onto that tomorrow. I can't see what it'll turn up because, of course, we've already looked at the data in depth as it came in, but you never know.'

'Thanks. Enjoy your cake! We'll be in touch.'

Redstone pushed his chair back and started to rise when he noticed Cunningham's expression change. The nuclear inspector looked up at Redstone with a deadpan face. 'Before you go, I need to test how good a scientist you are.' He cleared his throat.

Redstone stared at him. 'Eh? What on earth do you…'

'How do you tell the difference between an Indian, and an African elephant?'

Redstone pondered for a moment. 'It's something to do with the ears…'

Cunningham interrupted triumphantly. 'Typical scientist. It's easy – the African elephant is an elephant!'

Redstone paused, and then saw the joke. He started to laugh and found he couldn't stop. Cunningham leaned back, looking pleased with himself and grinning broadly.

Redstone waved his hand, still laughing. 'I look forward to our next meeting!' he spluttered.

WEDNESDAY 26 OCTOBER

Redstone looked up from his computer. 'I'm going to finish this section of the draft speech and then spend the rest of the day at London Bio,' he said to Smith. 'I phoned Joanne. They seem very keen to see me for some reason.'

The door opened and a slim man in his forties came in.

'Hi. I'm Roger Feast.'

'Hello. You're…'

'The prime minister's principal private secretary.'

'Right.'

'I've just had a message from Brussels. The PM has spoken to the President of France. You know that the French used to be our main enemy, of course, but that's no longer true.' He paused. 'Now, it's the Treasury.'

Redstone laughed. 'Anyway,' Feast continued, 'the result is our Nuclear Inspectorate should examine anything they want to within the West Avon site. Or anywhere else. The president couldn't understand why we'd made the arrangement to keep out, and his staff will squash any objections from France Nucléaire.'

'That's great,' said Redstone. 'Will you be telling the Nuclear Inspectorate?'

'It's being done as we speak.'

'Even greater. And Valerie Hitchcock will need to be told, I suppose?'

'Yes,' said Feast with an almost straight face. 'I'm going to send her a formal memorandum. I'm also going to tell her to ensure that the chief nuclear inspector has all the resources he needs for investigating the security of nuclear fuel.'

Redstone looked at Smith. 'I'd say that this man will go far, except that he already has.'

Feast smiled. 'There's always further to go,' he said. He turned and left the room.

'I imagine that Alan's going to be given a hard time by Hitchcock,' said Smith. 'She'll know that you're behind it, but she can't get at you.'

'Alan's tougher than he first appears,' said Redstone, 'but I'll warn him.'

His phone rang. 'This is Jill, in Sir Dominic Malvern's office. Just a friendly warning – he's on his way to see you, and he's not a happy bunny.'

The door burst open, and Malvern stamped in. His face was red, and his jaw clenched.

'Hello, Dominic. Come slumming?' said Redstone.

'I've just heard of the trick you've pulled. How dare you get the prime minister to talk to the French President without clearing it with me first!'

'Well…'

'What makes you think you don't have to do things in the proper way?'

'But…'

'How can I ensure our policies are coherent if things like this are done behind my back?'

'Does that mean that you'll be handing in your notice, then?'

'Don't be so bloody insulting! Why wasn't I kept in the loop?'

'I think you know…'

Smith interrupted. 'Shut up, Mark,' she said. 'Sir Dominic – we're sorry that you feel that way, but you know that Mark's reporting directly to the prime minister. Perhaps you should take it up with him.'

'Who are you? I'm not going to…'

Smith stood up, moved close to Malvern and looked calmly into his face. He faltered. His face paled, and he seemed to deflate. He turned and walked out, closing the door softly behind him.

'You did it again!' said Redstone.

'Not really. Didn't you see? He suddenly understood why he's being excluded from what's going on. He realised that we know about his liaison with Hitchcock. And he may have deduced that she's the one leaking to Lesage. He's no fool.'

'Oh. Does that affect anything we're doing?'

'I'm not sure. People don't always behave logically. He may just keep on with the relationship but stop telling Hitchcock secrets. Or she might… use her resources to force him to carry on leaking.'

'Are you implying she's got some hold over him? Is she blackmailing him? What's it about? Does he like to dress up in – oh, I don't want to think about it!'

'You evidently just have,' Smith said, smirking.

'We'll just have to see, I suppose. About the leaking, not what he does in private.' He blushed. 'Oh, another thing – is Jill Totteridge one of yours?'

'I haven't a clue what you're talking about,' said Smith.

Her phone rang. She listened and put it down. 'Lesage has set up another meeting with his chief engineer for tomorrow at ten a.m. We can be sure what's going to be on the agenda! It's important that you're there.'

'Agreed,' said Redstone. 'Same arrangements as before?'

*

Redstone walked into his laboratory, panting, as usual, after climbing the stairs. Everyone started clapping. Redstone stood still, astonished.

'I know you think it's surprising that an oldster like me can manage all those stairs, but applause is going a bit far!'

'Fabulous though that achievement is,' said David, 'we're even more impressed by your thinking about the cancer treatment. A lot's happened in the past week. Can Saira and I talk to you about it?'

‘Of course,’ said Redstone. David and Saira followed him into his office.

‘I’ll start,’ said David. ‘We’ve been working flat out on your ideas. Saira worked all weekend. We decided to make up some cream, but Saira realised that if we modified your proposal it would probably work better. Saira?’

She walked up to the whiteboard, pushed up the sleeves of her jumper and drew some chemical formulae. ‘I thought that we could replace this,’ she pointed, ‘with this. The reason is that…’

‘Yes, I can see!’ exclaimed Redstone. ‘Well done! I should have thought of that myself.’

‘As someone said at the meeting, the great advantage of your approach is that all the components of the formulation are already licensed. And they’re easily available. So we decided to make a batch. It took a bit of juggling, but after a few trials we came up with this!’ She reached into the pocket of her lab coat and took out a small glass jar with a metal screw lid. She handed it to Redstone. He unscrewed the lid and sniffed the contents.

‘Typical chemist,’ said David. ‘Always smell things before doing anything else!’

Redstone smiled. He handed the jar back to Saira. ‘Nice to see it, but we need to figure out a testing regime.’

‘We’re ahead of you,’ said David. ‘We’ve already got some mice with the right sort of skin cancers, and we’re treating them with the cream. But we’ve got something else to discuss with you.’

‘Yes,’ said Saira. ‘Have you noticed that Colin has a lesion on his cheek?’

‘Yes,’ said Redstone. ‘It’s a basal cell carcinoma – just the sort of cancer we hope to be able to treat. It’s not dangerous, but it can be unpleasant. He’s due to have surgery in a couple of weeks, and he’s not looking forward to it because of the stitches.’

'That's right. Well, he agreed that I could take a few cells from the lesion. More than agreed – he was keen. So I did, plus a few normal cells from nearby on his cheek. He hardly felt a thing!'

'You're making me nervous,' said Redstone. 'I suppose that's ok.'

'Sure it is. They're his cells – he can donate them to us if he wants! Anyway, I put them in a culture, grew them over a few days and then treated them with our cream. These are the microscope pictures.' She fiddled with a tablet and passed it to him. She leaned over. 'This pair is before the treatment, and this pair is after. You can see that the cancer cells have almost disappeared, but the healthy ones appear to be unaffected!'

'I'm astonished,' said Redstone, swiping the pictures backwards and forwards. 'And Saira, I'm deeply impressed by your skill, growing these cultures. Wow, the results are amazing!' He paused. 'I'm no expert in this area, so tell me – what's the downside? There must be problems. Side effects?'

'We know the side effects of the components,' said David. 'Most of them are trivial. There's a small risk of allergic reactions, but they can be controlled. However, now the components are combined, there may be new side effects. We'll have to do lots of testing to find out. Or get other labs to do it.'

'Anyway,' said Saira, 'that's not the end of the story. I showed these results to Colin, of course. He'd like to be a human guinea pig. He wants to see if the cream will get rid of his carcinoma, so he doesn't have to have surgery. He'll sign any disclaimer we want.'

'Now I'm worried,' said Redstone. 'I have no expertise in clinical ethics. Nor does anyone else in the company, as far as I know. Is that right, David?'

'Yes. Colin and I had this discussion, and we found a firm of lawyers to guide us. They're producing papers for us all to sign.

Then we'll be able to treat him. We're also getting a dermatologist to monitor the carcinoma before and after the treatment. But before we go any further, we need your approval.'

'I'm extremely happy with the way you've been handling this and with what you propose. We'll have to get everyone to sign confidentiality agreements. And we need patent cover as soon as possible.' He got up and paced around the office. 'We need an emergency board meeting to agree to all this. I'll get Joanne to ring the outside directors to see who's available this afternoon. She can ask those who aren't available to speak to me on the phone so that I can seek their proxy votes.' He walked out, spoke to Joanne and came back.

'She's doing it now. Is Colin in today?'

'Yes, he's downstairs in his office,' said Saira.

'I'll pop down to chat to him – not only about his health but also on the financial implications. We're going to need a lot of money. Would you like to come with me, Saira? You can learn a bit about the commercial side of the company.'

'Oh, yes, please.' She stood up, a smile on her face. The two men rose too. 'I ought to shake your hands,' said Redstone. He grasped David's hand and shook it warmly. He turned to Saira and grasped her hand, but she pulled him towards her. 'Don't be so formal!' she said and kissed him on the cheek.

'Quite right,' he said and held her upper arms and returned the kiss. He reflected how pleasant that had been, and realised he'd been missing a woman's touch since Christina had returned to Norway.

*

'Well, the board meeting went very well,' Redstone said to Joanne. 'Thanks for organising it so quickly and efficiently.'

'Pleasure,' said Joanne. 'You should be proud of the way the project's developing. If it works out, our company will save millions of people lots of pain.'

‘And even some lives,’ said Redstone. ‘But it’s early days yet. And now, after all that, I’ve got to switch my attention back to the prime minister’s work.’

‘You’ve got something even more important coming up,’ said Joanne with a smile. ‘Your trip to Norway. Here’s the pack of tickets and travel instructions. Are you excited?’

‘I am,’ admitted Redstone, ‘but it’s more complicated than that. I’m quite nervous. And part of me is irritated that I’m going to be away for a few days when so much is happening here. And so much of the time will be taken up in travel!’

‘Yes, but some of that’ll be on a private jet. Have you been on a private plane before?’

‘No, never,’ said Redstone. ‘I admit I’m looking forward to that bit. It’ll be interesting to see how the other half lives.’

‘You are the other half now,’ said Joanne.

‘I suppose so. Anyway, I’m really looking forward to being with Christina again. You must meet her – I’ll bring her in to see you and the others next time she’s here.’

‘One step at a time,’ said Joanne.

THURSDAY 27 OCTOBER

Redstone sat on the floor of France Nucléaire's screened meeting room. Lesage and Dupont walked in. As soon as the door was shut, Lesage started shouting.

'Those... swine! They know perfectly well that no nuclear material has been diverted to terrorists! It's all a trick! It's that... Redstone!'

'I understand they'll be visiting West Avon next Tuesday. In force,' said Dupont.

'Yes! Will they be able to see anything... give them any clues?'

'What is there to see? My advice is... them politely, let them have access to the whole plant, and indeed show them around. I'd be happy to do that.'

'Well, not the whole *plant,'* said Lesage. *'There's clearly one... which could reveal everything.'*

'Of course, but no visitor would see... ...awkward.'

'I don't share your confidence. That bastard Redstone is... and tricky.'

'Maybe, but you told me that he isn't an expert.'

'He'll be with people who are.' Lesage paced the room. *'It would be... if you weren't there to be questioned. I don't trust you not to give something away. I'm going... for you to be called urgently to Marseille to help with an engineering problem there. Just... and leave. Go... you get the message, which... later today.'*

'Suits me,' said Dupont. *'Who's going to show them around?'*

'I'll go down myself,' said Lesage. *'I like your idea of showing them... I'll make sure that Redstone visits the turbine hall.'*

'It is impressive,' said Dupont. *'It should make him... how good our engineering is.'*

'Of course,' said Lesage. He stood, with his chin on his fist. He smiled. *'Let's get out of here.'*

Redstone made his way back to the portable toilet, phoned Smith, and was picked up as before. At the back of Downing Street, Redstone suggested that they walk in St James's Park before going up to their office.

They strolled along the edge of the lake. A disgruntled-looking pelican was standing on a small island in the lake. Others were in the water, which was rippling and dappled with sunlight. More waterfowl were moving here and there on the lake and standing on the grass. Redstone wished he knew what they were.

'I think it's safe for me to tell you what I overheard, isn't it?' he asked.

'Yes, nobody's taking any notice of us. And if they are, they'll think that it's just another man taking his granddaughter for a walk in the park.'

'I don't think that's a biological possibility, unless you're implying that I look sixty and you look twenty,' Redstone said.

'Well spotted. Now tell me what you heard, Grandpa.'

'I'm not sure you're old enough to know. Anyway, here goes.' He outlined what he had overheard. 'I'll phone Alan Cunningham and tell him all that and see what he makes of it.'

They crossed the footbridge over the lake, Smith stopping them twice to allow tourists to take photos.

'I would have just walked through,' said Redstone. 'Life's too short to waste time waiting for people to take photos of each other.'

'That epitomises the difference between us. I'm kind and caring, and you're a man.' They turned at the end of the bridge and walked back towards Horse Guards. The vaguely foreign-looking domes and turrets of the buildings beyond Whitehall were prominent against the pale blue sky.

'Did I upset you when I called you Grandpa?' said Smith.

'Not at all,' said Redstone. 'I assumed it was just a joke.'

'Of course it was a joke. Glad you weren't upset.'

Back in the office, Redstone browsed through the *Financial Times*, as he did first thing every day. He was surprised to find a short profile of himself, complete with photo. A journalist had interviewed him a few weeks earlier when London Bio's deal with Star Boston Pharmaceuticals was announced, but he'd thought the story had been shelved.

He phoned Cunningham and summarised what Lesage had said in the meeting with Dupont, implying that the information had been obtained by routine MI5 means. 'So, do you have any idea about what place on the West Avon site might reveal something to you or your colleagues if you spent enough time examining it?'

'Not offhand, but I'll give it some thought. Maybe it will strike me when we're there.'

'Ok. I'll see you at the site on Tuesday. Laura will arrange the travel details while I'm away for the next few days. Bye!'

'You heard that, I suppose,' Redstone said to Smith. 'I'm going home now, to get ready for my trip.'

'Have a lovely time, but be careful. Don't underestimate the Norwegians. Don't tell anyone any secrets!'

FRIDAY 28 OCTOBER

Redstone was met at Oslo airport by the pilot of the plane which was waiting to take him to Kristiansheim. They weaved through the bustling terminal to the top of a stairway, where an even-featured man of about Redstone's age, dressed in a smart navy suit, was waiting.

'Here's the other passenger,' said the pilot. They went down to the tarmac and stepped up into a small plane, where a uniformed attendant welcomed them. Everything in the narrow, curved cabin seemed to be cream leather or polished walnut. The pilot disappeared into the cockpit, the attendant ran through safety procedures, and the plane took off.

The other passenger introduced himself as Peter Grieg, one of Christina's friends. 'I'll be at her dinner tomorrow evening.'

'Have you known her long?'

'Ages. I come from Kristiansheim originally. I moved to Oslo when I went to university, and I've stayed there ever since. Christina sometimes stays with me and my wife when she visits Oslo.'

'Isn't your wife coming to the dinner?'

'Unfortunately, she had other commitments. But she urged me to come – not least because she's eager to hear what you're like!'

'Oh,' said Redstone. 'I didn't realise I'm significant to Christina's friends. That makes me quite nervous.'

'Sorry about that. I'm sure you've nothing to worry about. It's just that it's been so long since Christina was involved with a man. And the fact that you're from another country is even more… er… fascinating!'

'Why?'

'She doesn't even like leaving Kristiansheim. It's quite a job to get her to travel to Oslo, though she sometimes has to go for her work. She's happiest when she's at home. Her friends are all from the town.'

'Has she always been like that?'

'Yes – well, perhaps a little less so when she was young and at university. We were all more adventurous then, I suppose. That's when she met her husband.'

'Am I allowed to ask about him?'

'I can tell you he was much more interested in travel and meeting new people. I think this difference between them was what led eventually to their divorce. And I'm confident that you're the first man she's, er, been involved with since then.'

Redstone sat back and considered what Grieg had told him. He wasn't sure what to make of it.

He looked out of the window. All he could see was cloud. 'Would there be interesting scenery below if we could see it?' he asked.

'Yes, we're flying over mountains. Pity about the weather. I hope it's better when we reach Kristiansheim, though I'm not optimistic. We typically get two hundred and fifty millimetres of rain a month at this time of year.'

Redstone was amused that Grieg knew this figure, but supposed he would too if he lived somewhere that wet. He then realised that he knew the average figure for London, and it was only twenty per cent of Grieg's figure.

'Tell me about yourself,' said Redstone. 'What do you do for a living?'

'I'm the Norwegian minister for energy,' said Grieg. 'I think Christina invited me not only because of our old friendship but also because of your work for the British prime minister. She told me you're writing a major policy speech which will include energy policy.'

'I am,' said Redstone. 'That's very thoughtful of her. Could you tell me about Norway's policy on electricity generation?'

'Most of our electricity is generated by hydroelectric power. A few years ago, we did consider building one nuclear power station, to increase diversity of supply. We decided that it wouldn't make sense to do it ourselves, so we'd get a foreign company to do it. France Nucléaire was the obvious choice, given their huge experience.' He looked out of the window, then back at Redstone. 'I know your country use them, of course, but we decided against it.'

'Why is that? Against nuclear power itself, or France Nucléaire?'

'The two were linked. We decided against France Nucléaire and then felt that there was no other company with comparable experience. So our policy has been to top up hydroelectric power with electricity from gas-fired power stations.'

'May I ask why you didn't go with France Nucléaire?'

'It was mainly because we didn't feel fully at ease with their nuclear engineering. After a lot of research, we concluded that it was a touch too – how shall I put it – experimental for our taste. Please keep that to yourself.'

Redstone had a flash of insight. 'Was a certain analyst I know involved in that?'

'Nice try!'

Redstone reflected that Grieg's answer told him nothing. Maybe he should ask Christina. But that would put her in a difficult position. It was years ago and so it now didn't matter one way or the other. He wouldn't bother.

'Our experience with France Nucléaire has been fine,' he said to Grieg. 'The speech I'm working on is for our prime minister to deliver when he opens the first of the new batch of reactors they're building for us.'

'Good. I also know about the remarkable boost to the output of your existing reactors. We found it very interesting.'

'Yes, it's been a great help.'

‘Anyway, Norway stands ready to help our British friends if you need to import more of our gas for generating electricity, as your government knows.’

Redstone considered this. Half the UK’s gas already came from Norway. The Norwegians were shrewd negotiators, and if they knew the UK was desperate for even more gas, they’d strike a hard bargain. The sums of money were potentially huge. It was important that he said nothing about potential problems with the UK’s nuclear electricity generation.

The flight attendant served an excellent cold lunch, which Redstone devoured. He eased his seat back and started to reflect on how enjoyable it was to be flying in a private jet, but then was hit with the familiar pang of anger and sorrow when he realised he couldn’t tell Kate about it. That bastard Kemp had to get what he deserved. His ruminations were interrupted by the attendant announcing that they were coming in to land.

They exited the plane into cold, pouring rain and hurried into a small terminal building. They were greeted by a man who introduced himself as their driver and escorted them outside to a gleaming black Mercedes. They left the airport and entered the compact town, its buildings a mixture of old ochre wooden structures and modern blocks of concrete and glass. They left the town, drove through some countryside and turned off onto a narrow road which Redstone realised was a drive. They curved around pine trees and came to an aged, wide-fronted two-storey stone house. Behind it was an incongruous-looking modern communications mast.

The broad wooden front door opened and Christina came out onto the porch, wearing a thick jumper. Her face lit up as Redstone jumped out of the car and ran up the steps.

‘Welcome to Kristiansheim,’ she said. He grasped both her hands, and they stood smiling at each other for an awkward moment before he kissed her cheek. He inhaled her fragrance and felt the softness of her lips as she kissed his cheek in return and squeezed his arm in a moment of private intimacy. She glanced at the driver and at Grieg and squeezed his arm again.

'Come in, come in! Sorry about the awful weather.'

Grieg was first inside the large stone-flagged entrance hall. She went over and kissed him chastely, exchanged a few words and gestured behind her. A grey-haired woman in a black dress appeared and led Grieg up a grand staircase while Christina escorted Redstone into a cosy room fitted out as a study with a couple of leather armchairs.

'That was Marta. She's the housekeeper and cook. I couldn't live here without her.'

'I suppose I'll have to meet with her approval,' said Redstone.

'Of course,' smiled Christina, 'but you're already ninety-five per cent of the way there because of what I've told her. Anyway, did you have a good journey, and would you like something to eat or drink?'

'The journey was fine, thanks, and we were well fed on the plane. I don't suppose you have any English tea, do you?'

'Yes, I drink a lot of it. You stay here, and I'll go and make some.' She left the room.

Redstone stood up and wandered about the study, looking at the books on the shelves. They were mainly in English and included volumes about energy policy. A group of photos, some quite old, hung on the wall opposite the window. One was of Christina, her daughter, Ingrid – both looking much younger – and a smiling man who Redstone assumed was the ex-husband. It was hanging at a slight angle, and he straightened it. He went to a row of CDs and studied the titles.

Christina entered, carrying a tray with tea and biscuits.

'Either you're a wonderful spy who's thoroughly researched my taste in music, or we're soul mates,' he said.

She smiled. 'I take it that you're a jazz fan? I already guessed you like the blues from when we first met in the tube station.'

'Yes, and I like the same type of jazz as you, apparently. This one…' – he pulled out a CD by the Modern Jazz Quartet – 'has the best piano solo I've ever heard.'

'Let me guess. Do you mean on *Carnival*?'

'Yes! That's amazing!' He looked at her fondly. She beamed.

'Is this where you work?' he asked. 'I can't see a computer.'

'No, I've got a boring modern office at the back.'

She poured the tea. 'I think I've planned this all wrong.'

'I take it you're not talking about the tea.'

'No,' she smiled, 'I mean the weekend. I was so worried that you'd be bored and unimpressed by our little town, out here in the middle of nowhere, that I've overcompensated. We have Peter Grieg with us till Sunday morning and five other people for dinner tomorrow night. Now you're here in the flesh, everything seems different from what was going through my imagination. I now wish we were here alone.'

'Don't worry about it. It'll be fine.'

'Would you like me to show you your room?'

'Please. I need to freshen up.'

They climbed the staircase.

'Will Ingrid be joining us?' asked Redstone.

'No, she's staying in Oslo. I asked her to come, but she declined. I'm afraid that she's got mixed feelings about my relationship with you.'

'Do you think that she might resent me out of loyalty to her father?'

'I doubt it,' said Christina. 'She seems to think of her father as the man who deserted us both. She encouraged me to chat you up, as she put it, in London, but I'm not sure what's going through her head now.'

She showed Redstone a bedroom. 'And mine's next door,' she said.

'Will Peter Grieg be sleeping near these rooms?' asked Redstone.

'No. I've put him down there.' She pointed along the corridor.

'And does Marta sleep on the premises?'

'No, she has a house in the grounds with her husband. You met him – he drove you from the airport. Come with me, and I'll show you my room.'

They walked into Christina's bedroom.

'It's very feminine,' said Redstone, looking at the bottles and jars on the dressing table and the cushions, the elaborate curtains and the pieces of pottery around the room.

'Yes, it's the one room where I've imposed my wishes on the house, rather than the other way round. This place has been in my family for generations, so I feel it owns me rather than the other way round.'

Redstone yawned. 'Sorry – I'm shattered. I've had a very full week, and I got up much earlier than usual in order to get here. Do you mind if I go to my room and have a rest and a shower before dinner?'

'Of course not,' Christina said solicitously. 'And don't get dressed up for dinner – it'll be casual. Just you, me and Peter. The more formal dinner is tomorrow.'

*

Feeling refreshed, Redstone went downstairs and wandered about in search of the dining room. He found Christina and Grieg standing in a panelled room which was adorned with several paintings and illuminated by a complicated chandelier over the table. Places for three were laid at one end of the table. Christina and Grieg were holding drinks. Redstone accepted a glass of wine, they sat down, and Marta served the food.

‘I always enjoy eating here,’ said Grieg. ‘Marta’s an excellent cook.’ Marta smiled.

‘So, you come here often?’ asked Redstone.

‘Not so much nowadays. My job keeps me in Oslo for much of the time. I meet Christina in Oslo more than here, now. You may not know that she plays an important role in our political party, as well as…’

‘Not that important,’ said Christina.

They carried on chatting and eating, and Redstone found that he was thoroughly enjoying the evening. Grieg was interesting and intelligent, but to Redstone’s pleasure, Christina matched him, and came across as more imaginative. The three of them had a lively debate about how societies should help those citizens whose roles were being transformed by advances in technology and by globalisation. Redstone thought that he could use some of the ideas in his speech for the prime minister.

Shortly after ten o’clock, Grieg announced that he was tired and would retire to bed. He wished them good night and went upstairs. Christina smiled at Redstone. ‘It’s just you and me, now,’ she said.

Redstone felt wonderfully comfortable with Christina but anxious about what he should do next. She had prepared a bedroom for him but ensured that it was next to hers. He would love to sleep with her, but what did she want? Actually, did he want to sleep with her – wouldn’t it be unfaithful to Kate?

‘Which bedroom did you like better,’ she asked nervously. ‘The one with the frilly curtains or the one next to it?’ She looked down and blushed.

He didn’t hesitate. He put his finger under her chin, and gently lifted her head so that he could gaze into her eyes. ‘Easy choice’ he said, and kissed her gently and at length.

Still holding the gaze, she smiled, took his hand and led him to the stairs.

*

They lay in one another's arms. Redstone sighed with pleasure. 'That was…' He stroked her back and kissed her gently. 'Oh, Christina, thank you.' He paused, embarrassed. 'I do hope… I mean, it's been a long time since I…'

'Even longer for me,' she said. 'I'd forgotten how… It was marvellous. I feel complete, for the first time for… well, never mind how long!'

'Me too.'

They lay in silence. She lifted her head and looked into his eyes. 'Are you happy?'

'How can you ask? I haven't been happier for years.'

She snuggled up again. 'It's so different from when we were in London. Don't you mind the provincial surroundings and the provincial woman?'

He kissed her. 'I haven't noticed you being provincial.'

'But I am. I get uneasy if I go away from this town. What's more, I'm no good at getting close to others. My only friends are from this area, mainly from my childhood.'

'You seem to have got pretty close to me,' Redstone said. She hugged him.

'Yes, I don't know what went right for once. I've been mulling it over while we've been apart. Maybe it was Ingrid urging me on.' She was silent for a moment. 'Was it you who approached me first or the other way round?'

'You asked me if the tube was going to Russell Square, and it just developed from there. We're equally guilty.'

'I'm enjoying being guilty more than I have being innocent.'

'How did you cope so well with London if you get uneasy about leaving Kristiansheim?'

'I used a psychological trick on myself. I pretended I was an actor playing the part of a woman of the world, one who didn't suffer from agoraphobia and wasn't shy. It was successful, I think, but keeping it up was quite hard work. It took a lot of energy. I was exhausted by the time we got back home.'

'That's brilliant. Anyway, you seem pretty relaxed now. Look, both these, er, muscles are nice and soft.'

SATURDAY 29 OCTOBER

After breakfast, Grieg announced that he needed to spend the day working and excused himself. Christina asked Redstone if he would like to go for a walk, even though the weather was poor.

'I'd love to,' said Redstone, 'but I didn't bring the right clothes or shoes to go walking in these conditions.'

'There's a good outerwear shop in town. May I take you there? We can buy everything you need.'

They went outside to a garage which contained a small Nissan electric car. Christina unplugged it.

'This is the car I use to drive myself in the area,' she said. 'It's very green – it uses hydroelectric energy generated at night.' Redstone wryly reflected that the day before, she'd paid for two people to share a private plane to fly across half of Norway, but said nothing. He slid the passenger seat back after mistakenly going first to the left side of the car.

She drove into the town, and they ran through the rain from the car into a narrow, deep shop. The shopkeeper greeted Christina in Norwegian, but she answered in English.

'This is my English friend. We need to fit him with clothing and boots for walking in the woods today.'

The shopkeeper smiled at Redstone. 'Welcome to Kristiansheim,' he said. He looked Redstone up and down. 'Shouldn't be a problem.'

A half hour later, Redstone and Christina walked out of the shop, Redstone carrying his old clothes in a bag and wearing a warm, waterproof outfit. He felt good.

'Let's go back home, get a hot drink and a sandwich and set off,' said Christina.

*

They walked for two hours through woods which surrounded Christina's house. The rain rattled and hissed on the trees, and water plopped as it hit the ground. The wet leaves smelt of autumn. The terrain was hilly, but the ground was firm, so Redstone found the going easy. Christina said that she would have liked to take Redstone to the coast, but the rain and wind would have made it very unpleasant. For much of the time they had to walk on narrow tracks in single file, which made talking difficult, but when they could walk abreast, they chatted happily. Redstone realised that he was falling in love.

They returned to the house. Redstone was exhilarated by the exercise and the fresh air, and almost enjoyed the ache in his muscles. He went upstairs to shower and get changed, leaving Christina conferring with Marta about the arrangements for the evening's dinner.

*

Redstone stood with Grieg as the other guests arrived. They were all locals who seemed to know all about him and were keen to chat. One was a striking blonde woman wearing a low-cut, light blue dress which matched her eyes. She seemed vaguely familiar, and as he was chatting to her, Redstone realised he'd seen her acting in a TV crime series. She'd been at school with Christina. Redstone joked with her that he liked the dress she was almost wearing, and she grinned and punched him on the arm. Christina, whose wine-coloured velvet dress revealed rather less, came up and pulled him away.

'Your gaze hardly left her breasts!'

'I was just admiring the engineering which kept everything up.'

'Well, you can admire my engineering. Later.'

He was amused to find that Christina placed the actress at the other end of the table from him, next to Grieg.

He noted wryly that everyone seemed better dressed than him. His suit seemed old-fashioned and shabby compared with those worn by the Norwegian men. He needed new clothes. Pity he couldn't take Christina clothes shopping with him in London in the next few days.

Conversation flowed easily during dinner. After the guests left and Grieg said goodnight and went to his room, Redstone and Christina stood in the hall, smiling at each other. He looked at her.

'Nice legs,' he said. 'Are they new?'

She looked down and smoothed her skirt. 'No,' she said. 'I got them on Amazon a while back.'

They stumbled upstairs, clinging to each other and making more silly jokes.

SUNDAY 30 OCTOBER

Christina was still asleep. Redstone got up quietly and went to the bathroom. When he came out, he saw that Christina had woken. She gave him a big smile and sat up.

'I haven't got any medical training,' said Redstone, 'but I think you must be a woman.'

'If you were a competent scientist, you wouldn't jump to conclusions. You'd test your theory by… Oh!'

*

'You'll have to leave by eleven to get to Oslo in time for the London plane. When will you get home?'

'About four thirty London time, if everything goes smoothly,' replied Redstone, his arm under Christina.

She turned onto his chest and hugged him fiercely. 'It's been marvellous,' she said. 'I'm so happy and so unhappy. How can it last?'

'I know,' said Redstone. 'I feel the same. I haven't got any answers. Well, it can last, but not as a normal relationship. It's obvious that you belong here. You'd be desperately unhappy after just a few weeks in London.'

'Oh…'

'And I couldn't live here. I'm a Londoner. I'm used to the big city, the cosmopolitan surroundings, the noise, to say nothing of my work, my friends, my colleagues.'

'So what shall we do?'

'I don't know. Do you want to go to London and spend a few days with me again?'

'Definitely, yes, I'd like to go tomorrow – but I can't. Being practical, I have lots of commitments here. It would have to be a long weekend, like the one you've just spent here.'

'Ok. How about three weeks from now?'

'I can't go then, because I have to be in Bergen all weekend for the annual conference of our political party. How about the following weekend?'

'I won't be free,' said Redstone, 'because that's leading up to when the prime minister gives the big speech I'm working on.'

They settled on the weekend following that of the prime minister's speech.

'That's five weeks away,' said Christina, bleakly. 'What am I supposed to do till then? It's been fantastic. My friends say I'm a different person.'

'Maybe you should think about finding someone who lives here,' said Redstone, hoping she'd say she wouldn't.

'There isn't anyone. Most of the intelligent men of my sort of age are already married, and those that aren't are gay.'

'There must be some who are divorced, like you?'

'I suppose so,' she sighed. 'But that's not what I want.'

*

Redstone opened his front door. Treacle wasn't there to greet him. He unlocked the back door, went outside and called her. There was a rustling at the end of the garden, and the cat bounded very fast down the lawn, stopping gracefully in front of Redstone and raising herself on her hind legs for him to stroke her head.

'I've a lot to tell you,' he said, 'but let's have dinner first. Do you fancy some cat food? Would you mind if I have something different?' She followed him inside and watched closely as he switched off the cat feeder and poured fresh food into her bowl.

Later that evening, Redstone phoned Sophie. He told her about the weekend and asked her advice about what he should do.

'Love will find a way, Dad,' she said. 'Just be patient!'

He phoned his son in California. Graham was having brunch with friends, but was happy to talk.

'I'm going to be blunt, Dad.,' he said. 'I'm sorry if this upsets you, but you've been a bit of a – well, let's say you haven't been all that sensible. All this was predictable. I was in favour of your having a fling with Christina while she was in London, but you should have seen it for what it was – a holiday romance. So should she, especially as she's so rooted in her home town.'

'But…'

'Holiday romances never last. You should have kissed goodbye when she went back to Norway, and called it a day. Now you've got in deeper, but that's still what you must do. It's just more painful than it needed to have been. Sorry if I'm upsetting you, but…'

'That's not what your sister advised,' said Redstone, who was used to his son saying what he thought, and rather admired him for it. 'She said that I should be patient and that love conquers all.'

'Well, she would, wouldn't she? She's an incurable romantic, and anyway, she's got her own agenda with her Norwegian boyfriend. She can hardly tell you not to pursue your relationship while she's enjoying being with him, can she?'

MONDAY 31 OCTOBER

Redstone arrived at the block of flats. He walked openly to the foot of the staircase, climbed the stairs and made his way along the walkway to Kemp's front door. He looked around carefully, saw nobody and twisted into the wavy dimension, feeling the familiar pulse of pressure followed by the sickness, along with tension from what he was about to do. He twisted past Kemp's front door, feeling another pulse, and entered the flat, which seemed empty, as far as he could tell through the distorted scenes his eyes and brain were registering. He checked that there was indeed nobody there and, with huge relief, twisted back into the normal dimension.

He was amazed at what he saw. The flat was beautifully furnished with expensive-looking antiques, oil paintings, tasteful rugs on polished floors, a high-tech kitchen and a luxurious bathroom. There was a study with a modern desk and a professional-looking PC with a large screen. A stack of high-end newspapers and business magazines sat neatly on an occasional table. Only one room was furnished as a bedroom. It was dominated by a large bed on a dark oak frame with polished head and footboards. Redstone examined it carefully and looked underneath. He walked to the foot of the bed and paced out its width. He took out a small notebook and sketched a diagram of it with approximate measurements.

He decided to take a bit of trivial revenge on Kemp, as a kind of warm-up. He donned a pair of rubber gloves, entered the bathroom, locked the door from the inside by sliding the elegant fitted bolt, and twisted into the wavy dimension and out round the closed door into the hallway, wincing at the pressure in his skull.

He left the flat, walked carefully to the stone staircase and twisted back out of the wavy dimension. Nobody was around. He walked out of the grounds and returned home.

After a coffee, he loaded his wallet with cash and drove a few miles to a large DIY store on the other side of Enfield. He parked in the huge ill-kept car park and an hour later returned home with a holdall carrying an assortment of purchases, including a length of heavy chain.

*

Redstone pressed his entrance pass against the reader and climbed the stairs to his lab. He felt at ease for the first time in days. David and Saira were working side by side and greeted him warmly. He went into Joanne's office, kissed her cheek and walked through to his desk.

Joanne came in with a mug of tea. 'Are you ready for the inquisition?' she asked.

'Fire away.'

'Well? How was it? How was the private jet? How did you get on with Christina and her friends? What's her house like? Are you leaving me for her?'

'I certainly couldn't leave you for anyone, Joanne,' he said. 'Dealing with your other questions, the private jet was very convenient. There were only six passenger seats, and they were large and well-spaced. But the plane was small – I couldn't stand up properly – and the toilet at the back where the plane narrows down was almost impossible for me to use.'

'That could have been disastrous!'

'Yes. However, there was no hanging about, which was great. The plane went when the passengers wanted it to, not the other way round. So, if you're thinking of buying one, do, but get a big one.'

'And there I was, just about to order a small one,' smiled Joanne. 'Stop beating about the bush. How did you get on with Mrs Nissen?'

'Call her Christina. We really hit it off. If she lived in London, I think we'd soon be becoming a couple. But she couldn't live here –her whole life revolves round her town. She's got an impressive old house she's inherited, and it owns her rather than the other way round. She seems to be significant in Norwegian politics. Her friends mostly live nearby. It's just impossible. I couldn't live there, and she couldn't live here. We just don't know what to do.'

'I haven't got an answer, I'm afraid. As you'd say to me, what happens next?'

'We've arranged that Christina visits London in five weeks' time, which is the earliest we could fix. I wish it could be sooner, and so does she.' He sighed. 'Ah well, let's change the subject. I've got the visit to Chequers coming up this weekend, and when I was in Norway, I couldn't help noticing how poorly dressed I was compared with the Norwegian men. I need some new clothes. Would you come with me to help me choose?'

'It's no good asking me,' said Joanne. 'I know nothing about men's fashions, or even women's, come to that. Anyway, I'm too old to judge what a youngster like you should be wearing. Why don't you ask Saira?'

'I can't ask her. It's too much of a personal thing – she's a senior scientist, not my confidante, like you. Anyway, she won't want to go shopping with me.'

'I'm sure she'd jump at the chance. Ask her. The worst that can happen is that she says no.'

'And laughs in my face. Oh, ok, I'll ask her. And while I'm on the subject of Chequers, I can't think of anyone to take as a social partner. Any ideas? I don't suppose you'd come with me?'

'No, and no,' said Joanne. 'You'll have to go alone. Unless you invite Saira, of course!'

'Now you're being ridiculous,' said Redstone. 'But I will go and ask her about the clothes-buying.'

He walked out into the lab. Saira and David were still working together.

'Sorry to interrupt,' said Redstone. 'Any progress on the skin cancer work?'

'It's still early days,' said David, 'but nothing's happened to dampen our enthusiasm. The only potential problem is raising the early finance so that we can jump all the regulatory hurdles and get full patent protection. Colin's working hard on that. Meanwhile, the lawyers have come up trumps. They've produced some straightforward documents for Colin to sign to allow the trial of the cream to go ahead, Colin's signed them, so have I, and the trial's started.'

'That's fantastic!'

'Yes,' said Saira. 'So far, Colin's had only one complaint. He says that the cream makes him smell like a bag of fish and chips!'

'I can think of worse smells!' said Redstone. 'That's the acetic acid, of course. Did someone explain it to him?'

'Yes,' she said. 'I told him I could mask the smell but that we'd have to make sure that any perfume I added wouldn't interfere with the operation of the cream, and that would cause a delay. He said I should give him some mushy peas and carry on with the cream as it is.'

'Good. Let me know if you need me to help in any way, including on the finance stuff.' He cleared his throat. 'Saira, could I ask you for a personal favour? You must feel free to say no.'

'Of course,' she said. 'What is it?'

'I've decided I should stop looking like a shabby tramp and get some new clothes, but I need someone to come with me to help me choose them. Someone with good dress and fashion sense. You always look beautifully turned out. Would you come with me?'

She smiled. 'Of course! I'd be delighted! When do you want to go?'

'Ah - thanks. Maybe on Thursday? And well done for not saying, "About time too."'

*

At home, Redstone Skyped Christina.

'My children have completely opposing views about our relationship,' said Redstone. He recounted what Graham and Sophie had each said.

'My daughter sides strongly with Graham,' said Christina sadly. 'Ingrid said it was a holiday romance, with you playing the part of the Greek fisherman, and we should have recognised it for what it was and not let it get out of hand. She strongly disapproves of our continuing the relationship.'

'Maybe we should get Ingrid and Graham together – they seem to have a lot in common!' said Redstone.

They chatted for a little longer before saying goodnight.

TUESDAY 1 NOVEMBER

Redstone sat on the train with Cunningham and three of his staff, all trying not to kick each other under the table. He felt relaxed in the company of these technical experts, and was pleased by Cunningham's friendly efforts to integrate him into the group. The inspectors planned how to deploy themselves once the group arrived at the nuclear site. Redstone reminded Cunningham that there might be one particular place where an expert could spot something which would throw light on the problem.

A minibus was waiting at Bristol Temple Meads station. They were driven out of the city, along a motorway to a huge industrial complex. They passed a chemical plant with thousands of metres of fat pipes, in parallel straight lines and elegant curves, joining cylindrical metal columns, ten storeys high, buried in complex frames of tubes and girders. They passed an oil refinery with an orange-and-yellow gas flare roaring from the top of a high, narrow cylindrical metal chimney. There were also vast windowless industrial sheds, each capable of encasing a whole block of houses.

Ahead was the nuclear power station, looking like an enormous golf ball nestling amongst a collection of giant rectangular blocks dropped by a careless giant child. They drove through two security checks and stopped outside an office block.

The group were escorted into a meeting room, where Lesage greeted them and introduced four of his staff. 'These colleagues will escort you to any part of the plant you wish to visit and ensure you get all the information you want.'

The inspectors explained what they wanted to see, and the group dispersed, leaving Lesage and Redstone in the room.

‘As you know,’ said Redstone, ‘I have no engineering expertise. If it’s acceptable to you, I’d just like to see the reactor, to get a feel for it. And have a look at the control room.’

‘Of course,’ said Lesage. ‘I’ll be happy to escort you myself. And I hope you’ll take the opportunity to visit the turbine hall. It’s a magnificent example of our engineering, and you’ll be able to see much more than is possible in the reactor area – because the reactor shielding stops anyone from seeing much, of course.’

They walked out of the office block to a car which drove them a short distance to the reactor building. After passing through more security checks, they entered the reactor hall. Redstone was struck by how full it was, with pipes, small cranes, lifting gear on rails and other pieces of equipment he could not identify. The only space was in front of him, where most of a large circle on the floor was studded with metal protuberances. The building resounded with a cacophony of droning, chugging and occasional crashes.

‘What you see is mainly the peripheral equipment,’ Lesage said in a raised voice. ‘Much of it is used only for refuelling. The reactor itself is buried under the floor. Most of the noise is from pumps.’

Redstone realised that the metal protuberances must be connected to the ends of the fuel rod clusters.

They walked through the building, Lesage pointing out various pieces of equipment, though it quickly became apparent that his knowledge was superficial.

‘The control room is attached to the reactor building. Follow me,’ he said. They left the noise of the reactor building and entered a windowless high-ceilinged room, quiet except for a background hum. Lesage introduced a man and three women seated at a long desk, on which were keyboards, switches and buttons. In front of the operators were computer monitors, and on the facing wall, a large array of big screens showed the plant in diagrammatic form. Numbers on the diagram were occasionally changing. Most were in green, but some flashed to amber and then back to green.

'You can see how the plant is monitored,' said one of the women. 'Each number represents a measurement of temperature, or pressure, or position of a control rod, or water flow, neutron flux, et cetera. We can adjust some things using our keyboards and the other controls you see in front of us. But we can't adjust the core parameters – that's done by the IT system, for safety reasons.'

'And the big display above the screens shows how much electricity we're sending to the grid!' said another of the women, proudly.

'Can you override the IT systems if there's an emergency?' asked Redstone.

'Indeed,' she replied. 'In a sense, that's our main role, why we're here. However, it's never happened, and we hope it never will!'

Redstone carried on chatting to the operators.

'Let's have some lunch, and then I'll take you to the turbine hall,' said Lesage.

They returned to the office block and sat down to eat from a small but elaborate buffet. Redstone could feel tension between him and Lesage, and conversation was strained. He would rather have been with the inspectors, eating sandwiches out on the plant.

After lunch, Lesage escorted Redstone to the huge turbine building.

'We must get kitted out before going any further,' he said, leading Redstone into a small changing area. Lesage donned a dark blue boiler suit and safety helmet and gave Redstone a bright orange set. 'Forgive the horrible colour. It's to mark you out as a visitor. Before we go into the turbine hall, I'll explain what you're going to see because it'll be impossible for you to hear me once we're inside. You'll need to wear the ear defenders on your helmet.' At a large diagram on the wall, he gave his summary and then conducted Redstone through two sets of doors into the turbine hall.

Redstone was amazed by the scale. The vast concrete floor was packed with massive blue-painted machines, fat pipes with many joints, long platforms carrying other machines, and handrails everywhere. A couple of blue-clad workers were dwarfed by it all. Bright pendant lights hung from the ceiling far above.

The noise was astounding – it was deafening, even through the ear defenders. He could feel the thrilling roar in every part of his body. Lesage gestured, and they walked past the turbines, the generators and the electrical gear, returning through the two sets of doors to what seemed like deep silence. They took off their ear defenders.

'I have a suggestion for you,' said Lesage. 'It's that you climb the stairs to the walkway at the top of the building to see the equipment from above. That's by far the best way to get a clear understanding of the layout and scale of our operation.'

Redstone readily agreed. Lesage pointed him towards the entrance to a metal staircase and excused himself to make a phone call from an office attached to the turbine building.

Redstone climbed the stairs, stopping after a few landings to recover his breath. Reaching the top, he donned his ear defenders and passed through doors back into the turbine hall. The noise was as deafening as before. Ahead of him stretched a walkway with the wall on its right and a metal railing on the left. At the far end was a small box-shaped room attached to the wall.

He stepped along the walkway, stopping to gaze down at the spectacular view. He estimated he was about forty metres above the floor. Directly below him were the huge turbines. As he moved further along the walkway to get a better view of the generators, the door of the room at the end opened, and a man came out, wearing safety goggles and dressed in the same dark blue kit that Lesage had been wearing. He walked towards Redstone. He was a big man, as big as Redstone, who reckoned that it would be a bit of a squeeze for them to pass each other.

The man approached and angled to Redstone's right to pass. Redstone stepped towards the railing. But then the man pushed Redstone, grabbed his boiler suit and started to heave him up and over the railing. Redstone stared in horror at the roaring machinery far below and immediately twisted into the wavy dimension so that, to the man, he seemed to disappear. With Redstone's weight and resistance gone, the man lurched forward to the railing and started to tip over it. Redstone twisted back into the normal dimension and yanked the man back onto the walkway. Whirling around, the man stared at Redstone and then ran towards the staircase.

Redstone fell back against the wall and slumped to the floor, breathing heavily and feeling shocked and weak. He'd just escaped being murdered and had, on reflex, saved the potential killer from death. Lesage must have planned it all. He was amazed that Lesage would go to such lengths. He was now even more determined to pursue the issue to a conclusion.

He calmed down and got his mind to address his present situation. His priority was to get off the walkway and down to ground level and the exit. He still didn't feel safe. The big man had presumably by now told Lesage that the attempted killing had failed. He rapidly descended the staircase.

Lesage was waiting for him. He seemed a different man, sweating and exuding fear. He took a step back and spoke in a cracked voice, clearing his throat repeatedly.

'Er… impressed?'

Redstone drew closer to Lesage, who backed away again. 'Yes, I enjoyed the view. It was indeed impressive. But you must do something about your health and safety. One of your workers passed me on the walkway and seemed to lose his balance. If I hadn't pulled him back, he might have fallen over the guard rail. Of course, I'll have to tell Alan Cunningham about it.'

'Awful!' said Lesage. 'I'm terribly sorry you had that experience. Thank God you weren't hurt. And thank you very much indeed for what you did to help the worker. I'll ensure local management installs safety measures so that nothing like that can happen again.'

They returned to the conference room where the inspectors were waiting. 'We'll talk on the train,' Redstone said to Cunningham, out of Lesage's hearing. 'But out of interest, what were you all wearing while you were doing your inspections?'

'The standard France Nucléaire safety kit, their elegant navy-blue boiler suits,' said Cunningham. 'Why?'

'Tell you later.'

*

In the train, the group huddled together to compare notes. The inspectors said that everything had been fully compliant with safety standards. They'd been given full access to whatever they wanted to examine. They'd seen the fuel assembly area, the rest of the plant and the control room, had spoken to the controllers and had been shown all the records they'd requested.

'Was there any particular place where if you'd stayed longer you might have spotted a problem?' asked Redstone.

'No, I didn't see one,' said Cunningham. 'Perhaps the control room might fit your bill, but the readings we saw were exactly what we would have expected from the material that France Nucléaire send us.'

'Any overall conclusions?'

'My impression was that the engineers on the plant were glad to see us. They were proud of their systems and the way the systems were implemented, and proud of the plant. They enjoyed showing the plant and their systems to people who understood what they were looking at. In truth, they seemed sorry that France Nucléaire had reached the arrangement with the government that we wouldn't make routine visits.'

'Overall, then, you saw nothing of concern?'

'Nothing,' said Cunningham, and the others agreed.

'How was your own visit, Mark?' asked Cunningham.

'I enjoyed it and found the plant interesting and impressive, until the very end.' He described what had happened, without mentioning how he escaped being pushed over the railing or saying that the man had deliberately tried to kill him.

Cunningham and his colleagues expressed astonishment. 'That's extremely serious,' said Cunningham. 'If their staff can act in the turbine hall in as dangerous a way as you describe, they could be even more dangerous in the reactor building.'

'My guess is the local management will deny that the man concerned was a member of staff, and I'd be inclined to believe them,' said Redstone.

'In that case, their security is crap, if an unauthorised person can get into the turbine hall. We'd also want to talk to them about that,' said an inspector. Cunningham agreed.

'Alan, shall we go and get a drink?' asked Redstone with a meaningful look. Cunningham immediately got the message, and they walked down the swaying train to the buffet car. They stood at the end of the counter, out of earshot of other passengers.

'I wasn't completely open about what happened, because I didn't want your colleagues to hear everything,' said Redstone. 'The man deliberately tried to kill me. I suspect he was hired specifically to get rid of me. I think I was given a distinctive orange set of clothing to ensure that he identified the right person. And I'm sure, from his reaction when I got back, that Lesage was the man who hired him.'

'Jesus Christ!' said Cunningham, looking shocked and putting a hand on Redstone's shoulder. 'I did notice that Lesage's demeanour had changed when we all met up at the end, but it seems extraordinary that he would go to such lengths. Why should he regard you as such a threat? We found nothing suspicious at all.'

'But our security people have evidence that Lesage is very worried about something, and presumably, he thinks I'm likely to find out what it is.' Redstone looked out of the window and turned back. 'Since everything you saw today seemed fine, I suppose the lesson is that the threat concerns the new wave of power stations, not the existing ones or the fuel arrangements. In line with what we've suspected from the start.'

'I still don't see what it can be,' mused Cunningham. 'But if you're right, then France Nucléaire will be telling the prime minister's office in the next few days that the grand opening planned for November twenty-ninth has to be postponed. That will be solid evidence.'

'Yes.'

'What am I allowed to tell Valerie about today?'

'Tell her everything you found, or rather didn't find, and also about the incident on the walkway as I described it to your colleagues just now. I expect she'll pass on the news to Lesage, who might be lulled into a false sense of security. If we're lucky, he might let slip a clue about what the problem really is.'

'Ok. I'm terribly sorry you went through that experience. Are you feeling all right now?'

Redstone was touched by his continued concern. 'Yes, I'm fine thanks.'

'Good.' Cunningham's face went deadpan. 'But before I go back to my colleagues, let's test your knowledge of metal corrosion. When a knight in armour was killed in battle, what sign did they put on his grave?'

Redstone grinned. He sighed theatrically. 'Go on, tell me.'

'Rust in peace!'

Redstone groaned. ‘You absolutely should go back! I’ll stay here and phone Laura to bring her up to speed.’

WEDNESDAY 2 NOVEMBER

Redstone returned from his delayed health check-up in Thames House, where Clothier had told him that everything was still normal. He sat in the attic office, working on the draft speech. He realised he would soon have to talk to the secretaries of state responsible for the policies he was thinking about, so he phoned the PM's office to arrange the meetings.

Smith came in. 'Glad to see you're still alive,' she said. 'I might have lost this year's bonus if you'd been killed.'

'I'm quite pleased myself not to have been killed,' said Redstone.

'We've put security measures in place to ensure it doesn't happen again. You probably won't notice them, so don't worry.'

'And they are?'

'We'll have officers keeping an eye on you when you might be vulnerable. We've done a risk assessment to narrow down when that might be.'

'Which is?'

'Let's come back to that. Anyway, we've also been discussing why Lesage would go to such lengths. People in the corporate world don't usually resort to murder to advance the interests of their employer. We assume that he must have some personal motive, which is highly likely to do with money.'

'What about sex?'

'Unlikely in this case. We've told our French opposite numbers that we're concerned about his behaviour and asked them to investigate his financial affairs. Meanwhile, we're doing the same.'

'Good,' said Redstone. 'But couldn't another motive be fear? For example, fear of being found out?'

'Yes, but whatever it is that he doesn't want to be found out was itself the result of another motive, and it probably boils down to money in the end. It normally is money or sex.'

'You are a cynical lot,' said Redstone. 'I'm sure I'm motivated by more than that. What about the urge to find things out, to experiment? Wanting recognition?'

'Would you murder for any of those?'

'Probably not. But I might for revenge.' His face darkened, and Smith looked at him closely.

The door opened, and Roger Feast announced, 'I come bearing a verbal gift, which may or may not be to your liking.'

'If you've come to propose marriage, the answer's no,' said Redstone.

'Damn. In that case, I'll have to resort to plan B, which is to tell you that France Nucléaire has been in touch with full details of the ceremony for the opening of the new nuclear power station at Dymbury on November twenty-ninth.'

'I see what you mean about it being mixed news. We're certain that there's a major problem, but presumably they wouldn't go ahead if they weren't sure it could be sorted by then.'

'Or that if it isn't sorted, it wouldn't interfere with the ceremony.'

'True. Did they say when the new plant would actually start producing electricity?'

'Yes. That very day, though only a token amount. I'm told it takes a long time to get a power station working at full capacity, so the ceremony is just symbolic. The PM is to press a switch, and the electricity will flow, to produce heat, light, sound and motion – they'll have a display with lights, sounds, a small electric tram and electric space heaters.'

'They've missed out cooling and communications. And computing.'

'Good point,' said Feast. 'I'll suggest that they chill some nice French wine for us and that there's a big TV screen showing communications with some French bigwig. Though there will be all sorts of French bigwigs there in person, so it looks as though there's no way they can cancel now. By the way, I've arranged for you to meet the secretaries of state with responsibility for industrial and science policy, but the Secretary of State for Energy's office says that you should meet her permanent secretary instead.'

Redstone sighed. 'I suppose Valerie Hitchcock herself intervened so that she can control what I offer the PM to say. Well, it's not going to happen. Could your staff please tell the energy people that it's their minister or nobody?'

'I hoped you'd say that. My pleasure. In fact, I might phone them myself!' Feast smiled at Smith and walked out.

'He's even more impressive than I'd realised,' said Redstone to Smith.

'Yes. People who get appointed to that job often end up as cabinet secretary.'

'He's a different kettle of fish from Dominic Malvern. But well-run organisations often replace someone with a person who's quite different.'

Smith's phone buzzed on the desk, and she picked it up. 'Fine,' she said and turned to Redstone. 'Urgent news. Dupont is meeting Lesage in just over two hours' time. I think we need a fly on the wall, don't you? Lewis will be here in an hour with the van.'

*

Two hours later, Redstone was seated on the floor in the corner of the screened room, in the wavy dimension, trying not to be sick.

Lesage and Dupont walked in. Dupont's face was flushed, and he spoke first. *'At least the inspectors... happy with what they saw.'*

'Of course. I'm not surprised.'

'And my staff were happy to talk to them. They can't understand... inspectors no longer make regular visits.'

'You know very well,' said Lesage.

'But the incident on the walkway was... totally unforgivable.' Dupont pointed at Lesage. *'The man was certainly not one of my staff. And there's no record in... outsider being logged in, except for the normal contractors. And he wasn't one of them.'*

Lesage said nothing.

'My engineers are considering going on strike to protest against... their name.' Dupont raised his voice. *'They're furious... seem that one of them could be so stupid as to endanger the life... or indeed anyone else.* And so am I!*'* he shouted.

Lesage still said nothing. Dupont carried on.

'...my suspicions. I suspect that you *personally... that man to get onto the site and into the turbine hall. I suspect that* you *told him where to go, and... he knew how the target would be dressed. I suspect that* you *ordered him to push Redstone... We're immensely fortunate that Redstone was so agile.'*

Lesage cleared his throat. *'All that's just guesswork, which I won't dignify...'*

Dupont banged the table with his fist. *'If I find the slightest evidence... I'll resign immediately and tell the authorities what I know.'*

Lesage stood up and walked around the table to stand behind Dupont's chair. He leaned forward and spoke softly in Dupont's ear. Redstone had to strain even harder to hear.

'I bet you won't.'

'If that's a cheap...' said Dupont.

'You seem to forget... I know... visiting the casinos. Just think... happen if you withdrew. I suggest... your energies to finding a solution...'

Dupont sagged in his chair. *'I told you – it's outside my area of expertise!'*

'Then you had better develop... fast,' said Lesage and left.

*

Back in their office in Downing Street, Redstone took some paracetamol for his headache and then briefed Smith on what he had heard.

'Laura,' he added, 'odd though it might seem, I quite like Dupont. I feel he'd help us if he could. I think he's a weak man with big problems, whose heart's in the right place. Is there any scope for your colleagues to get him on our side?'

'We'd call it "turning",' said Smith. 'There might be. We need to find out as much as we can about his financial problems. I'll get onto it.'

While Smith phoned Thames House, Redstone phoned Alan Cunningham, who was unable to add anything to what they already knew. Redstone told him about the arrangements for the Dymbury opening. 'I don't think they'd get the PM to perform the opening ceremony if they expected major problems later. Could it be that the big issue is to do with subsequent reactors in the new wave, while Dymbury's ok?'

'I can't see how that would work,' said Cunningham, 'because all the reactors are of the same design. That's been one of France Nucléaire's strengths – no messing about between one reactor and the next, so little scope for new problems to arise. The harsh truth, Mark, is that we need your MI5 friends to come up with more information. Have a word with the formidable Laura.'

Redstone did so.

'We need to throw some grit in the works,' she said. 'I'd like to feed some false information to Lesage which would make him panic and make a mistake, or at least cause him to blurt something out with you listening. To give us a clue as to where to investigate next. What shall we feed him?'

'Well, the two most promising avenues so far are that it's something to do with the fuel system, and that somehow the data which Alan gets are related to the problem. I'm worried that the fuel angle might have been a red herring deliberately fed us by Lesage, but we might as well try it. I'm more convinced about the data because we've found out that Dupont's expertise lies in that area.'

'Ok,' said Smith. 'You draft a memo to the prime minister, bringing him up to date and telling him that those are the two lines of enquiry which we're following vigorously. It won't actually be for the prime minister, though we'll tell Roger Feast what we are doing. It'll be bogus. We'll make sure its contents get into Lesage's hands.'

'How?'

Smith steepled her fingers. 'We'll give a copy to Jill Totteridge, and she'll tell Malvern that she was slipped it by someone in the PM's office who thought it wrong that Malvern wasn't kept in the loop. Malvern will tell Hitchcock, we hope, and in turn, she'll tell Lesage.'

'So, I was right about Jill Totteridge!' exclaimed Redstone. 'You can undeniably get that part of the chain to work, but the rest of it's pretty dicey, isn't it?'

'Welcome to the Security Service's world,' said Smith. 'This is cast iron compared with other cases I've worked on. It's not the easy stuff you scientists are used to – it's dealing with people. We'll just have to wait and see. If it fails, we'll try something else.'

Redstone smiled. 'You must come to my lab some time and see how easy science is!' He hunched forward. 'But you said Malvern now realises we know about his affair, and he may also have worked out that Hitchcock is the leak. Surely that'll stop him telling her stuff like this? He is the cabinet secretary, after all – used to keeping all sorts of important secrets.'

'But when we talked about this, you guessed that Hitchcock has him under her thumb. You speculated that she's got something on him because of something sexual.'

'I know. I've changed my mind. I just don't think it's plausible. Well, I suppose the sex stuff is plausible, but I don't believe he'd give in to pressure from Hitchcock. It would be unthinkable.'

'People aren't predictable. Unlike chemicals.'

'Ha! I must give you some ethyl azide.'

'What's that?'

'An unpredictably explosive chemical.'

'Ok,' she laughed. 'You win this round. But I stick to my point. Let's see what happens.'

He turned to his PC. 'I'll draft this fake memo. By the way, I won't be in tomorrow morning – I've got to buy some new clothes to look reasonably smart when I go to Chequers this Saturday. A colleague from London Bio has kindly agreed to accompany me and give me some advice.'

'That's good of him.'

'*She's…*' they both smiled, '… always very well turned out. She seemed keen to help.'

'Are you going to take her as your companion when you go to Chequers?'

'Certainly not! She's just a colleague.'

'Sounds more than just a colleague. Then who are you going to take?'

'I've decided to go on my own. I haven't got any unattached female friends except Christina. I wish…' He sighed heavily. 'Kate would have loved the opportunity to bend the prime minister's ear about social work.' He sat with his head bowed before looking up. 'I'll draft that memo to the PM.'

After half an hour, he read his draft to Smith. 'What do you think?'

‘Excellent. I liked the bit about our concerns being confirmed by an event during your visit to West Avon. I suppose you mean the attempted killing of a certain person?’

‘I do. It confirms there is a genuine issue. Lesage will get the allusion. It should help shake him.’

‘I wonder if it’ll spark another attempt on your life. As I was saying before, we’ve done a risk assessment and concluded that Lesage is unlikely to try again soon, because it would be too obvious who was behind it.’

‘Would this memo change things?’

‘Possibly. I’ll discuss it with colleagues. We also think that if there is a next time, it will follow the same pattern, namely that he’ll attempt to make it look like an accident. We’re pleased with the measures you’ve taken to keep your home address out of the public eye, but Lesage could probably find out where you live. However we think it’s very unlikely that he’d try to get at you there, because it would be so hard to make it look accidental. And your lab has good security, as, of course, do we here. So, our conclusion is that what risk there is lies in ordinary situations.’

‘What does that mean?’

‘Like when you cross the road, where you might become the victim of a hit-and-run. Be careful. And we’ll step up our efforts to look after you, which I assure you will be unobtrusive.’

Redstone listened with growing anxiety. It hadn’t properly sunk in that he might be targeted again. ‘Good God, Laura, you know how to make a man feel good, don’t you?’ he said. ‘You’ve made me worried. Though I have been here before, in a way. The reason Kate and I made our address unavailable to the public was that she was considered vulnerable because of her work. Some clients of social workers are mentally ill and can be violent.’ He clenched his jaw. ‘Not that the precautions succeeded in saving her life.’ His thoughts went to Kemp and what he was going to do to him.

Smith nodded. 'Get that memo over to me and I'll arrange for it to get into Jill's hands. I'll also give a copy to Roger Feast and explain what lies behind it. It's up to him whether he tells the prime minister.'

'How long do you think it might take for the contents to get to Lesage?'

'Quickly. It's explosive stuff, and if Malvern decides to tell Hitchcock, he'll do it straight away. And the same for Hitchcock telling Lesage.'

THURSDAY 3 NOVEMBER

As Redstone and Saira walked out of the London Bio building, he asked her how Colin was getting on.

Saira smiled excitedly. 'It's early days, of course, but it's looking good. He's sure the lesion is reducing, and I agree.'

'That's excellent. I'll go and see him when we get back. Now let's face the shops.'

They hunched up against the cold rain. Saira turned up the collar of her soft black leather jacket. 'Before we go any further,' she said, 'let's get one thing clear. Who's in charge of this shopping expedition?'

'Er…'

'Right. Agreed – it's me. Let's start off in Jermyn Street.'

'Ok, and with a bit of luck, we can finish there too,' said Redstone.

'Wrong attitude. This is an outing, not a chore!'

Redstone hailed a taxi, and twenty minutes later, they were walking in and out of specialist menswear shops.

'Some of these places do have good quality clothes, but others just try to make you think their rubbish is good quality,' Saira observed.

At the end of the morning, they were sitting in a recess in a café in Piccadilly, surrounded by bags of clothes. The room was decorated in art nouveau style, with padded seats and faded mirrors.

'I needed this coffee,' Redstone said. 'I'm exhausted. Shopping has never been my favourite occupation. But you look as fresh as a daisy!'

'I genuinely enjoyed it. I like clothes shopping, as you will have noticed.' She looked around. 'I've never been in here before.'

‘I like it,’ said Redstone. ‘It’s partly aimed at tourists, but the staff are pleasant and helpful, and they do excellent coffee. Are you sure you wouldn’t like a cake or a tart or something?’

‘I’m fine, thanks.’

‘Let’s relax here for a bit. No hurry to get back. How about you telling me something about your background, if you don’t mind talking about yourself?’

She told Redstone that she came from Northampton. She was an only child, and her parents had been against her going to university, saying they feared that potential husbands would be deterred if she was too well educated. But she had gone anyway, causing family strain which only got worse when she announced that she was rejecting religion. And then she had married a non-Muslim, which had been the final straw for her parents, who had proceeded to stop all contact with her. They didn’t resume relations even when she divorced a few years later and her ex-husband moved to New Zealand. She now regarded London Bio as a sort of family, and reminded Redstone of the various social activities staff engaged in together. She urged him to join in with them sometimes, but he gave a non-committal reply. He asked if there was anything he could do to make the atmosphere in London Bio even more friendly, but she assured him it was excellent as it was.

They left the café laden with shopping bags, hailed a taxi and settled back as it made its way through heavy traffic up Charing Cross Road. The rain was still pouring down, making pedestrians hunch against the cold and wet. When the cab drew up at the London Bio building, they ran to the shelter of the concrete canopy overhanging the entrance.

Redstone turned to Saira. ‘You’ve been incredibly helpful. And very good company.’

‘Well, I deserve a kiss, then, don’t I?’ Redstone smiled and kissed her cheek.

As he bent down to deposit his bags so he could find his entrance pass, he heard a loud crack and the roar of a motor bike speeding away from the kerb behind him. Saira collapsed in a heap in front of him. He stared at her uncomprehendingly and then, in horror, realised that the crack he'd heard was a gunshot. Blood was seeping through the front of Saira's coat. He felt unable to move and an intense wish that this was not happening, while knowing it was and that he should be doing something. A man rushed over and pushed him aside, shouting for someone to dial 999 as he tended to Saira. Another man was speaking urgently into his phone. Passers-by were taking photos. An ambulance screamed up and a police car arrived a few seconds later. Sirens were wailing. Strong hands bustled him inside the building. Joanne appeared and took him up in the lift to the calm of her office, where he collapsed in a chair. His coat was bloodstained, and he tore it off.

He sat, his mind in a turmoil of shock, horror, guilt and shame that he had not acted to help Saira. Joanne gave him a mug of tea. David came in, weeping openly.

'She's just been pronounced dead,' he said, his voice cracking. Joanne began to cry and was soon sobbing uncontrollably. And Redstone, too, found himself crying hard, his shoulders shaking as he sat and wept. Thoughts jumbled in his head. Another death – but this one was squarely because of him, even though he hadn't pulled the trigger. Laura Smith had assured him that he would be safe from this sort of attack. If MI5 hadn't been complacent, Saira would still be alive. If he hadn't asked her to help him choose clothes, she wouldn't have been put in harm's way. What a trivial cause for this awful tragedy! He wouldn't have had to ask her if he'd had the nous to choose his own clothes. He wouldn't have had to choose his clothes without help if Kate hadn't been killed. Kemp would pay for this.

But he must stop selfishly thinking it was all about himself. A talented scientist with much of her life before her had been brutally murdered. What about her family? Her friends? All this because of Lesage. Redstone was in a position to exact revenge, using the wavy dimension, and he vowed to do that, after he'd taken revenge on Kemp. But it had to be soon, before the ability wore off. And then he'd get out of this new life and return to the quiet existence of a month ago.

He said to Joanne and David that he ought to go and talk to their colleagues. Most of the other staff were crowded together in the lab outside Joanne's office, and many were crying. He spoke to them about what had happened and how wonderful Saira had been as a colleague and a scientist.

His phone rang. It was a police officer, requiring him to go to New Scotland Yard to give a witness interview. The officer told him he would just be asked about what happened at the time of the shooting – they already had relevant background information. He said a police car was waiting outside the London Bio building.

'Can't you do it here?'

'No, sorry, sir. We need to see you away from your colleagues.'

The police driver efficiently weaved through back roads towards the river. Redstone looked out at normal people carrying on normal business, and his eyes filled with tears for Saira, who would never be one of them. He assumed it was Laura Smith who had given the police the 'relevant background information'.

The car drew up outside New Scotland Yard, and Redstone was ushered into a small room furnished with pastel blue soft seating. A plain-clothes officer in a crumpled suit took notes as Redstone described what he had seen and heard.

As the officer left the room, Smith entered, wearing a heavy camel-coloured sweater and jeans. At the sight of her, Redstone jumped up and shouted, 'MI5's incompetence has led to the death of an innocent, talented, lovely woman! You told me Lesage wouldn't attempt anything like that. I want no more dealings with you and your people! That's it! My work with you is finished!'

He strode towards the door, but she stood in his way.

'I understand your feelings,' she said calmly, 'but you've jumped to the wrong conclusion. Please sit down and listen.'

Redstone clenched his fists and remained standing. 'I'll give you five minutes. Then I'm going.'

'We had an MI5 operative monitoring you. He was about to try to help Saira Sharma when another man took over – a paramedic from University College Hospital. Our man had seen the shooter drive off on his motorbike and phoned our headquarters. We liaised with the police immediately.'

'A lot of good that did.'

'Listen. The shooter drove down Euston Road onto the A40, which was stupid because there are hardly any places where he could get off that road. The police pursued him and caught up with him on the elevated section just past Hangar Lane. He shot at them, which was an even bigger mistake because they shot back and killed him.'

'Too bloody late for Saira, though, wasn't it?'

'Listen. It was easy to identify him because he was carrying ID. Anyway, he had a criminal record, and the police have his fingerprints and picture on file.' She leaned forward. 'He was one of Kemp's drug gang. Kemp used him as an enforcer. The shooter had a photo of you in his jacket pocket.'

Redstone gasped and sat down heavily. 'Oh, God, Laura, so sorry I blew up like that. It never occurred to me that two people were out to kill me at the same time!'

'No, it didn't occur to us, either. But I now have an idea of how and why it happened. I remind you that we have the capability to monitor where you've been, using your phone. We've now looked at the record of your movements. Would you care to tell me what you were doing at Kemp's flat on Monday? I could see from the monitoring data that you suddenly disappeared. I assume you entered the wavy dimension and, I guess, went into Kemp's flat.'

Redstone flared up again. 'You've been tracking my movements!'

'Kemp's motive was probably revenge for the killing of his brother,' Smith continued. 'We believe he has a camera monitoring the entrance to his flat. He could have seen you and me when we went together, and assumed that I was the weak and defenceless female and you were the dangerous man.'

'Even if he had seen me, how would he know who I was, and where I worked?'

'Good question,' said Smith, 'but I've a possible answer. I know this might seem a bit far-fetched, but if he reads the *Financial Times* he would have seen the recent article about you, including your picture and a description of your company.'

'Oh, Christ – he did have a load of newspapers and business magazines.'

'That's probably it, then. He knows it was your wife that he killed four years ago, and he simply put two and two together. You were seeking revenge. That's why you killed his brother, he thought. Now he was going to get his own revenge and prevent you from trying to kill him.'

'Oh, God!'

'It's now time for you to tell me why you went into his flat and what you saw there, in as much detail as possible. Did you see the camera?'

Redstone thought back. 'No, but I didn't look.' He told her everything he could remember about the flat.

'And why did you go there?'

'To be honest, Kemp was right. I was scouting out the flat. I had a plan to get rid of him without actually killing him myself.

And I confess, I also played a trick on him, just to rattle him – I bolted his bathroom door from the inside and then left using the wavy dimension.'

'What an idiot!' said Smith. 'You gave away any element of surprise and secrecy just for a childish trick. And what do you mean about getting rid of him without killing him?'

'I was going to go back at night, anaesthetise him with ether from the lab, gag him and chain him to the bed so he couldn't escape and would die of thirst.'

'What on earth were you playing at? Why not just kill him? And what about forensics?'

'I thought about forensics and had stuff prepared to cover my tracks. I do know some chemistry, after all. As to why I didn't plan just to bludgeon him to death or kill him with a knife, frankly, I recognised I haven't got the stomach for it.'

'So, you thought it better to make him die a slow agonising death than to sully your hands by killing him outright?'

'I now realise that I've been a total fool. And my actions caused Saira's death. Oh, I can't… What have I done?'

'You'll have to face that thought, because your actions told Kemp that you had some way of circumventing his security and getting into his flat. But now you have to decide what to do. You have three options, as far as I can see. First, just leave it.'

'I—'

She spoke over him. 'Second, continue with your idea of committing extra-judicial killing yourself in a more efficient way than what you'd planned – but I must make it clear I'm not going to help you, and what's more, I'm warning you that it's very hard to get away with murder, even if you are able to disappear at will.'

'And third?' asked Redstone.

'The third option is the one we hope you'll choose. That you use the wavy dimension to help us and the police nail Kemp. You'd do that by helping us to collect evidence which would enable the police to mount a successful prosecution and put him away for life.'

'Why would MI5 be involved? Surely it's just a criminal matter.'

'MI5 nowadays has a remit to work with the police to fight organised crime. We're officially involved. Anyway, frankly, we need to protect you. You're a valuable asset.'

Redstone thought quickly. He couldn't give up working with MI5 till Kemp had been dealt with. He owed that to Saira and Kate. And he needed MI5's help for his own safety. So he couldn't give up the nuclear project yet.

'Ok,' he said, 'I choose the third option. What exactly do you want me to do?'

'Because of the attack, we'll be able to get warrants to allow you to enter Kemp's flat without breaking the law and to allow us to intercept his communications. We want to do all that without his knowledge. Specifically, we want to monitor what he does on his computer. He's a sophisticated man, and we're sure that he would keep records of his activities, though no doubt encrypted.'

'Can't you just take his computer?'

'No.'

'I could.'

'We want him to carry on using it without realising that we're monitoring what he does.'

'How can you do that?'

'We need to install equipment onto the computer. So we need you to go into the flat and plant a device. While you're there, you could also look for the camera. And, of course, search for any other evidence.'

'Why haven't you done that before? You people don't need to be in the wavy dimension to get into someone's flat.'

'Because we have no way of getting in without him knowing, since he has CCTV.'

'Ok,' he said. 'Of course I'll do it. When?'

'We'll put you in there as soon as we believe he'll be out for some time. And this time, you must become invisible before you enter the flat, not while you're standing outside the front door. And no silly tricks to tell him you've been there!'

'Ok,' said Redstone shamefacedly, 'you've made your point.'

'Meanwhile,' said Smith, 'we have to reassess how we keep you safe. You're now under threat from two sources. We haven't changed our assessment of the risk from Lesage, but the threat from Kemp is more difficult. We need to keep you out of places where you'd be vulnerable. He doesn't know where you live, as far as we know, but it wouldn't be impossible for him to find out. We'll check the physical security of your house, and increase our surveillance. Your normal life shouldn't be too disrupted. It's when you're travelling to and from your lab that there's the greatest risk. Do you agree to let us drive you on those journeys?'

'Of course, of course,' he said. 'I don't want to risk anyone else's life. Can I explain to my staff who we think was responsible and why I'll be driven to and from the lab?'

'Yes, tell them the police suspect that the bullet was meant for you and that they think the person who hired the killer is the man who murdered your wife. Tell them he's a drug dealer who fears you might have found out something that incriminates him. If it gets out and he hears about it, he might realise he'd better back off, at least for a while. And if it doesn't get out, no harm done.'

'Can I assure the staff that they're not under threat and that what happened to Saira was just a terrible accident?'

'Yes – but they should keep an eye open and dial 999 if they suspect something.'

'Thanks. Oh, one last thing. Please do me a favour – would you tell the prime minister's office that I won't be going to Chequers this weekend? I just can't face it, and I'd be lousy company. I'm sure the PM will understand, given the circumstances.'

'Of course,' said Smith. 'One other thing, before you go back. In normal circumstances, you'd be mobbed by the press, as would your staff at London Bio. But the police have warned them off. They've told the press, and that includes all the TV outlets etc, that if they publish information which would help the man behind the killings, they'll be charged with aiding a murderer.'

'Oh, thanks.'

'There will be quite a lot of coverage of the shooting – in fact, it's probably out now. But you shouldn't be badgered. Tell me if you or your staff do get harassed by the press. We've said the same thing to Saira's parents and the rest of her family.'

'Thanks again,' said Redstone. 'I suppose I'd better phone my children and Christina before they learn about this awful… this tragedy through the media.'

A police car took him back to the laboratory building, which was now almost deserted.

'I told everyone they could go home,' said David. 'Most did. I wanted to get on with the skin cancer work, so as not to let Saira down.'

'I understand,' said Redstone. 'Awful though it seems, we'll have to hire a new scientist to work on it with you. You can't do it all yourself. Anyway, your expertise doesn't cover all the skin science Saira knew.'

'I agree. How about calling the post the Saira Sharma Fellowship?'

'Great idea,' said Redstone. 'I'll get Joanne onto it tomorrow.'

He leaned back against a bench and told David about the killer. 'It's all too much. I've decided I'm going to give up the work for the PM when I've finished something I'm in the middle of.'

'Oh, don't make any hasty decisions, Mark! You should at least sleep on it.'

Redstone grunted non-committally and went into his office. Joanne had gone home. He sat at his desk and phoned his children.

Graham was very sympathetic about the shooting and then sought to persuade him to go over to California, until the police had Kemp under lock and key. 'You'd fit in well, as a successful science entrepreneur. Please come! I'd love to show you around, and you'd soon settle in!' Redstone was struck by a sharp pang of sorrow as he thought how much Kate would have loved to have gone to California to see how Graham was getting on. He swallowed. 'You paint a very tempting picture,' he said, 'but I can't leave my colleagues at London Bio after what's just happened.'

'I understand,' said Graham. 'But do be careful. Take all the precautions the police suggest. Hire a bodyguard, if necessary. This isn't a situation where brainpower is enough. It's outside your area of experience. Be humble, for a change!'

Sophie's reaction was quite different. 'Of course it's awful that Saira was killed. Terrible for you and everyone else. But it's not your fault. You didn't shoot her, or even have a clue that she would be in danger. Dad, you're only now coming out of a four-year... a sort of depression, following Mum's murder. Don't give in to those feelings. You need to make the effort to continue with the work for the prime minister. Burying yourself in London Bio is the last thing you need. And it won't keep you safe, evidently.'

'Well, I wasn't going to stop the work immediately, but it's all getting too much.'

'What about Christina? Surely she can help you get through this?'

'She's too far away, Sophie.'

'Oh, Dad, I hope you're not going to give up with her too. You never used to give up on anything, and I thought you were at last getting back that way. Don't make any hasty decisions. I know everything seems awful at the moment, but the bad feelings will recede.'

'Ok, I promise I won't do anything rash.'

He phoned Smith and told her that Graham had suggested he hire a bodyguard.

'It's not necessary, as long as you don't do anything silly,' she said. 'We'll look after you. If truth be told, a private bodyguard would probably get in the way.'

Redstone then made the call he was dreading. He phoned Christina, and her emotional reaction to his news deepened his own feelings still further. She offered to come over to London immediately, but he asked her not to.

'It's not necessary, and anyway, I need to spend time with my London Bio colleagues, possibly even over the weekend.'

'Oh, I see,' she said. Her tone made it obvious that she was hurt by his response.

'I'm ever so sorry, Christina, but you'd be alone for a lot of the time or mixing with people you don't know and who don't know you. I just don't think it's the right time, though I'd love to have you here if…'

'I know, I know, you don't have to explain,' she said in a tone which made him think she was still upset.

They rang off, and he slumped back in his seat. Why did he not want her to come?

FRIDAY 4 NOVEMBER

Redstone sat bent over his desk at London Bio, ploughing through accumulated paperwork and emails. He was touched to find a handwritten letter of condolence to him and his staff from Anne Jones, the prime minister's wife. And he was pleased and surprised to receive an email of condolence from Dominic Malvern.

He got up and wandered around the labs. Staff were working in silence, or huddled in small sombre groups. The subdued, gloomy mood exacerbated his own feelings of guilt and loss. If only he'd not been so stupid – Saira might still be alive. And what had he done to his relationship with Christina?

He walked into Joanne's office and leaned against the wall.

'I suppose David told you I'm going to give up the work for the PM. I hope I'll be able to get back to my normal life very soon.'

'Oh! David did tell me, but we thought it was just an immediate reaction to what happened. You shouldn't dump that work. You'll regret it. At least don't make a decision for the moment. Don't burn your bridges.'

'Well… I haven't told anyone in Number 10 yet, but I don't see the point in waiting.'

'The point is you're still in shock. At least give it a few days…' Joanne's phone rang. 'Excuse me,' she said and took the call.

'That was about Saira's funeral. It's tomorrow, noon, at Basingford Crematorium. In their religion, people must be buried or cremated quickly after death. Though there won't be a religious ceremony, apparently.'

'That would fit with Saira's beliefs. Where's Basingford?'

'Near Northampton. I'll print out details and circulate them to the rest of the staff.'

'Could you please arrange transport at the company's expense for anyone who wants it? I'll drive myself.'

'Of course.'

'I'm dreading this. It'll be the first funeral I've attended since Kate's.'

His mobile phone rang. He walked into his office.

'Hello, Laura. I was just going to phone you. If I can deal with my issue first, I have to go to Saira's funeral tomorrow. Is it ok if I drive myself there?' He told her the venue.

'Yes,' she said, 'that's fine. I'll make sure there's security at the crematorium. It might even be me. If it is, I won't contact you – I'll try to remain at a distance. Now for why I phoned you. Lesage has arranged an urgent meeting with Dupont for Monday morning. Will you be ok to monitor it as before?'

'Yes, that's fine,' said Redstone.

'And more on Lesage and Dupont – we now have the results of the research on their financial backgrounds. As we knew, Dupont's a gambler. He was in serious debt, but in the last two years he's been earning a large salary and has paid off most of his creditors.'

'And Lesage?'

'He leads an expensive lifestyle. He was spending above his income but recently went into the black because he's been earning huge bonuses. Thanks to the excellent performance of the reactors.'

'Interesting,' said Redstone. 'I wonder if he's fiddling the figures on the quantity of electricity they're selling. I would have thought that was virtually impossible, but if Dupont's been helping him, maybe they've found a way. Dupont is a data expert.'

'It would fit what we've learnt,' said Smith, 'apart from the reference to a fuel problem, which might be a red herring anyway.'

'I'll phone Alan Cunningham when we've finished this call. Let's see what he thinks.'

'Good,' said Smith. 'Now, Kemp. A council workman has visited his street to check the state of the trees near the road, and accidentally installed a hidden camera trained on Kemp's front door, linked to MI5 headquarters. We're already starting to build up a picture of his patterns of movement in and out of his flat. It won't be long before we're in a position to put you in there.'

'Excellent. If anything good does come out of Saira's death, it'll be that we nail that murdering shit.'

Redstone phoned Cunningham, who offered his condolences.

'The media are saying that it was a criminal killing aimed at you,' he said. 'Could it be related to our French friend?'

'No,' said Redstone. 'The police are sure they know who's behind it, and it's nothing to do with Lesage.' He explained Kemp's attack. 'But on Lesage, do you think he could have been fiddling the figures for the quantity of electricity they've been selling to the grid? With Dupont's help?'

'No,' said Cunningham. 'That would be impossible. The buyers don't take the sellers' word for how much power is supplied – they monitor it themselves.'

'Oh well, it was worth asking,' said Redstone. 'He's been earning lots of money from the improved performance of the reactors, and we wondered if it was fear of losing that money which was driving him.'

'Clever idea, but it doesn't fly. We need more information! But for goodness sake, take care. You seem to lead a dangerous life.'

SATURDAY 5 NOVEMBER

Redstone got out of his car and looked around. The crematorium comprised a small group of low modern buildings fronted by a paved area at the edge of an expanse of gardens studded with memorials and containing a small lake. The whole complex was surrounded by farmland and wooded hills. He pulled up the collar of his coat against the cold wind and walked towards a group of his colleagues standing outside the chapel. Here and there in the grounds were people in ones or twos, walking through the gardens, or standing by memorials. There was a strange mixture of pleasant calm and deep sadness.

His eye was caught by movement across the lake. Smith, wearing her blue quilted jacket, was jogging towards a man on a rise near the edge of the grounds. He was wearing a canvas gilet with several pockets and holding a big camera with a long lens.

Smith reached the photographer, who started to wave his arms. Then he tumbled to the ground, leaving his camera in Smith's hands. She did something to it and threw a small object into the lake. The man got up and abruptly fell again, this time flat on his face. The camera sailed high into the air and landed on the ground. The man got up again, blood on his face. Smith pulled her jacket open. The man scooped up his camera and ran away.

Redstone took out his phone and called Smith. He saw her take her phone out of her bag.

'Hi,' she said. 'Everything ok?'

'Yes, but what happened over there?'

'Well, I saw the photographer and went over to tell him that the police had an agreement with all the mainstream media outlets that there would be no photography at this funeral. He told me he didn't work for the mainstream media, so he wasn't bound by their rules. I told him I didn't work for the police, so I wasn't bound by their rules. He got aggressive and then fell over. I took the memory card out of the camera and threw it in the lake. He got up and became more aggressive and then fell over again, only harder. The camera fell on the ground and broke. He got up and decided to run away.'

'Christ,' said Redstone, 'I can see why you want me to leave the physical stuff to you. Why did he suddenly run away at the end?'

'I think he noticed that I'm wearing a sidearm under my jacket. Maybe he felt nervous.'

'I'm sure he did. But I'm feeling a lot less nervous about my safety. Many thanks for what you did!'

'Just doing my job.'

'Laura, when you were in the army, were you in the special forces?'

'Nice weather, isn't it?'

Redstone thought he should feel disdain for Laura's recourse to violence, but in fact he was animated and excited. He wished he had her skills. He felt he wasn't in the right mood for a funeral, but then saw the hearse arrive, followed by a big polished black car. People started to drift into the chapel, and he walked over to join them.

In the chapel, he sat amongst his colleagues. He felt distraught, both for Saira and for Kate. Kemp had to pay.

After the short service, he had a quiet word with Saira's parents. He told them that London Bio would create a scientific post honouring Saira's name. They thanked him politely, but he sensed an undercurrent of anger and felt they held him at least partly responsible for Saira's death. And they were right. Some London Bio staff chatted to him, while other mourners glanced at him but did not speak.

They all left the grounds in an assortment of vehicles and drove a couple of miles to a pub, an old brick building which had been extended many times, producing a warren of low-ceilinged rooms at slightly different floor levels. Artistic photos of barrels and pewter mugs adorned the black-panelled walls. A couple of steps led down to an incongruously modern conservatory, where a spread of sandwiches, cakes and non-alcoholic drinks was laid out. The atmosphere seemed too warm and friendly for the occasion.

Redstone felt alone amongst the crowd. He drank a coffee, exchanged polite pleasantries with a few other mourners, said his goodbyes and drove back home, thinking over and over that this was not the way Saira's life should have developed.

MONDAY 7 NOVEMBER

Smith greeted Redstone solicitously as he walked into the attic office.

'I imagine the funeral was awful for you.'

'Yes, it was horrible. Laura, I've decided not to continue with all this. I'm going to make sure my papers are in order and then go back to my old life.'

'It's not as simple as that,' Smith said unemotionally. 'You were given the job personally by the prime minister, so you'll need to discuss your resignation with him. Your head's full of secrets. All sorts of arrangements will have to be made. And decisions on the protection you'll be given, if any.'

'You're just being awkward because you want me to stay.'

'Of course I want you to stay. But I'm quite serious about what you must do if you want to resign. You're not in some benign civilian role.'

'The PM didn't say anything about any problems in resigning when he recruited me.'

'Are you sure? I wasn't there, but I bet that Gavin and the PM made it clear that taking this on was a big deal, even if they didn't spell out the process for resigning.'

'Well, nobody then knew my life would be threatened.'

'Look, what you're feeling is quite natural, given what's happened. But may I give you some advice?'

'Well?'

'Carry on with the work and see how you feel in a few days' time. If you still want to resign, discuss it with the PM and Gavin McKay. Till then, just try to carry on as before. Things like wanting to sort out France Nucléaire's scheming may override the emotions you're feeling right now.'

Redstone sighed heavily. 'Ok,' he said. 'It's Monday. I'd better go and see Jim for the check-up.'

'Yes. And then it's back to Victoria Street…'

*

Once again, he found himself in the wavy dimension, swallowing bile and peering through confusing images in the shielded conference room at France Nucléaire's office. The surge of pressure in his brain had seemed worse than before. Why was he doing this? He reminded himself that he wanted to play his part in averting a national crisis, indeed was proud to be able to. And he wanted to work with MI5 to get Kemp.

Lesage and Dupont sat at the table. Lesage handed Dupont a piece of paper. *'I obtained this from a helpful... It's an extract of... sent by that interfering bastard Redstone to the prime minister. Read it!'*

Dupont studied it carefully. He read it out in accented English. '"When you asked me to work on your speech, you also asked me to… rumours about a problem with the nuclear reactor programme. The purpose of this… bring you up to speed on that investigation. The Nuclear Inspectorate and I have looked into… and are now convinced that there is a real and serious issue. This conclusion was reinforced by our… and an event during our recent visit to the France Nucléaire facility at West Avon. We are following up… lines of enquiry, and currently, the two most promising are that the issue is connected with the nuclear fuel and that the data regularly supplied… by France Nucléaire contain information which will help us… the issue. I am, of course, aware that the details of the opening of the Dymbury plant are now being finalised by France Nucléaire, and we are taking that… in our investigations. I will keep you informed." *It's clear your stupid... on the walkway did nothing but harm!'*

'But if Redstone had suffered a bad accident, you would have much more time to...' said Lesage. *'Anyway, look at the two so-*

called "lines of enquiry" *he describes. They... have worked out something about the problem.'*

'How did they work out... problem concerns the fuel?' asked Dupont. *'They certainly couldn't have seen any problems with the fuel when they visited... It must have been something you said!'*

'Absolutely not. And I haven't said anything about the data you supply. I can't understand why they... it was worth investigating. I assume they didn't enter your office while they were there?'

'No, it was locked, as you suggested. Anyway, even if they had... what would they have seen? It doesn't make sense!'

Redstone suddenly discovered that if he put his finger in one ear, it was easier to distinguish individual words from the confusing echoes and jumbled sounds.

'Are you certain there's nothing suspicious in the data itself?' asked Lesage.

'Yes. It shows normal variations – of course, the readings aren't always ideal – and the data vary from one plant to another, as the... would expect. They've never raised any problems about the data.'

'We must just carry on as before, and you must renew your efforts to solve the problem. I'll see what I can do to reduce the risk of detection before...'

'Does that mean you're going to do something stupid again?' asked Dupont.

'You get on with your job and I'll do mine,' said Lesage and walked out.

*

Back in Downing Street, Redstone sat down heavily, exhausted. He told Smith what he had heard. 'So, you were right that Malvern would carry on telling Hitchcock stuff.'

'Yes. It confirms she has indeed got something on him.'

'You mean some sexual perversion?'

'Not for me to say. But I won't dissuade you from speculating.'

'The mind boggles. But more important, it looks likely that Lesage is going to try to get rid of me again. You've got to stop him!'

'We'll look after you. You'll be ok,' Smith said. 'What about the information regarding the fuel and the data?'

'And Dupont's office. I must phone Alan Cunningham straight away.'

He did so and put Cunningham on speaker so that Laura could hear. 'Did you try to get into the chief engineer's office?'

'No. Why should I? We aren't interested in people's offices. What could I find there that would help me detect a safety issue?'

'Maybe there's something in it besides ordinary office equipment?'

'Ah,' said Cunningham. 'Now you mention it, I did notice something as we walked past. There was more trunking going into the office than for neighbouring offices. So there are extra cables. Maybe he has extra computers in there. After all, he is an IT expert.'

'Could you pick up anything by looking at computers?'

'I doubt it. If they're displaying data, it would be the same stuff we get from them anyway. And we saw all the data on display in the control room.'

'What do you make of Lesage's nervousness about the data they send you?'

'The data are all normal, with the sort of variability we'd expect. I can't see where the problem might lie. But I'll look at it yet again.'

'Can the data throw any light on fuel issues?'

'Yes, but only for the existing reactors, which we know are working well. I don't know what I'm looking for!'

After they hung up, Redstone turned to Laura. 'I wonder if I should go down to West Avon and enter Dupont's office. In the wavy dimension. What do you think?'

'It'd require a lot of preparation, and I can't see it'd be worth the effort. Suppose there are lots of computer displays there. So what?'

'I could take photos and show Alan afterwards.'

'Yes,' Smith said, 'but from what Alan said, it'd be a waste of time. Let's revisit the idea if he comes up with anything after looking at the data again.'

'Hmm. I'm somewhat relieved because it's so horrible in the wavy dimension, but on the other hand, I think you're…' Redstone's phone rang.

'Hello, Christina,' he said. 'Lovely to hear from you. But I'm in my office in Downing Street at the moment with someone else, and it's a bit difficult to talk.'

Smith got up, waved and walked out of the room.

'Oh, she's left. That was very considerate of her. How are you?'

'Mark, I've phoned to apologise. I've been turning our last conversation over and over in my mind, and I realise you were being perfectly reasonable. I tried to put myself in your shoes, and I wouldn't have wanted you here if it'd been one of my colleagues who… who suffered the awful tragedy.'

'It's lovely of you, Christina. I deeply appreciate it.'

'But that's not all,' she said with a break in her voice. 'I've come to the conclusion that Ingrid was right. You and I – it's… it just won't work. I… I'm sorry.' She started to cry quietly.

Redstone felt as though he had been hit in the stomach. He forced himself to speak. 'Oh, Christina!' He cleared his throat, but no more words would come.

'Well, that's it then, I suppose,' she said through her tears. 'Thank you for a wonderful… I'll always remember our time together.'

'Christina, is it because of what I said the other day? I'm so sorry…'

'No, no, don't blame yourself. It's – it's just circumstances.'

'Can't I…' He swallowed, trying to collect himself. 'I'm finding it difficult to speak… Shall we ring off?'

'Yes, ok. Goodbye, darling,' she whispered.

Redstone sat back in his chair, breathing heavily. He stood up and paced around the office. He phoned Smith. 'Laura, that was very tactful of you. You can come back now – I'm going for a walk in the park.'

'Ok. I'll make sure you're covered.'

He left the building and entered St James's Park. It was a dull November day, and leaves were falling from the trees. There were still plenty of tourists, some feeding the birds and the squirrels, others ambling along in large bunches at an infuriatingly slow pace. He thought one group might be Norwegian, but none of the women looked anything like Christina. Would he ever see her again? He crossed in front of Buckingham Palace, where the tourist crowds were even thicker. The people around him were part of another reality, separate from him and his thoughts. His mind was in a grey turmoil.

He went through the ornate gilded gates into Green Park and strode through the trees, crunching the fallen leaves underfoot. He crossed the busy roads at Hyde Park Corner and made his way to the Serpentine, where he tramped along the bank, chilled by the bitter wind blowing off the big open lake in the middle of his city. He needed a drink.

He found an old pub next to the main road at Lancaster Gate and sat in the back bar, nursing a large whisky. The matt-black panelled walls were dotted with assorted cheaply framed photos of the area as it was a few decades earlier. The room was poorly lit by squat glass chandeliers on the cream slatted ceiling. He toyed with the cutlery protruding from a pewter mug on his table and half listened to a couple of casually dressed men sitting at a neighbouring table discussing other pubs. There was a faint booming beat from loudspeakers on the wall. He felt as miserable as sin.

He phoned Smith and told her what had happened and that he felt like going to the lab. She said she'd send Lewis to take him.

Fifteen minutes later, Lewis collected Redstone in a taxi and drove to London Bio. He got out and scanned the area before telling Redstone it was safe.

Redstone told Joanne what Christina had said. Joanne commiserated. 'I'm sure you got a lot out of your time together,' she said. 'Both of you. Maybe you'll be able to find a new partner who lives in this part of the world. And I hope the same applies to her.'

Redstone found the idea of Christina with a new partner upsetting and the thought of looking for one himself utterly unappealing. He swallowed and stared out of the window.

He phoned his children. Sophie was very sympathetic. 'Things aren't going well for you at the moment – Saira and now this. But it'll pass. Why don't you come over to Brussels for a few days? You'll feel better if you get away from London for a bit.'

'As it happens, I was thinking of going over,' said Redstone, 'to see you and to talk to some people about energy policy. I'll fix it up.'

Graham was also sympathetic but repeated his belief that the break-up with Christina was inevitable and told Redstone that it freed him up to meet someone else.

'That's pretty well what Joanne said. I can't see it happening. I'm not sure I want it.'

'Hmm,' said Graham.

TUESDAY 8 NOVEMBER

Redstone walked into his attic office from a meeting with the Secretary of State for Industry. To his relief, the policy work was taking his mind off his personal problems.

'That was most helpful,' he said to Smith. 'I'm now confident about big chunks of the draft speech. But I still haven't been able to get a meeting with the Secretary of State for Energy.'

'Why not?'

'It's down to that bloody woman, Hitchcock, I'm sure. I keep being told that the secretary of state agrees to the meeting, but her diary is chock-a-block.'

'Could it be true?'

'A minister's diary is always a matter of priorities. I'm deducing that Hitchcock has instructed the diary officer that meeting me has zero priority.'

'Just tell your buddy the prime minister, then. That'll unblock the diary, won't it?'

'It's not the sort of problem to take to the PM. I think the time's come to deal with Hitchcock. We're sure that she's leaking stuff to Lesage, aren't we? Can't we get her arrested?'

'We haven't got anything we could use in court, given how we found out – through your journeys into the wavy dimension, which we need to keep secret. We'd need some other evidence.'

'Ok, then let's repeat the trick we used last time. Let's create a memo that ends up in Lesage's hands, one that only she could have put there, and I'll take a photo of him holding it.'

'Can you take a photo while you're in the wavy dimension? I mean, will it work?'

'Since the light can affect my eye, it can affect the sensor of a camera. I suppose the only question is whether the image on the camera would be damaged by the transition from the wavy dimension back to the normal world. Let's do an experiment.'

He twisted into the wavy dimension, ignoring the pulse of pressure. As always, he was disconcerted by the confused view, with nearby things clear but further objects overlapping and seen from what appeared to be impossible angles. He took a photo and returned to the normal dimension, as the urge to vomit was starting to get the better of him.

Smith jumped. 'Oh, Jesus, I'll never get used to that!'

He fiddled with his phone and held it up triumphantly. 'Here you are!'

She looked closely. 'I can see myself and what's in front of me on my desk, but everything beyond that looks a jumbled mess. Is that what it's really like?'

'More or less,' Redstone said. 'My brain seems to be able to make a bit more sense of it than we see in the photo, but when I'm there, the only stuff I can see properly is nearby. Anyway, the point is I can bring back a photo of Lesage holding a memo he shouldn't have, if we can arrange it to happen.'

'Good. But we'd need to arrange for Hitchcock to get a fake memo direct, rather than through Malvern. Because if he had it, she could deny that she was the intermediary who gave it to Lesage.'

'Good point. Any ideas?'

'We could get Jill Totteridge to give it to Hitchcock. She could say that Malvern wanted her to pass it over personally.'

'But mightn't Hitchcock mention it to Malvern next time they were in bed?'

'Would it matter? By then, the damage would have been done.'

'It would make Malvern realise that Jill works for you.'

'Yes, well, she'd have to move jobs. I know she wouldn't find that a big problem. Anyway, Malvern's time must soon be up because of his role in the leaks, so she could go back if she wanted to.'

'Ok,' said Redstone. 'I'll write the memo. It needs to be addressed to the prime minister and classified top secret. We want something that looks serious but in truth says nothing. Won't take a minute.'

Redstone stared thoughtfully at the stain on the carpet and then typed his memo. He gave a copy to Smith to pass to Totteridge and took another copy downstairs to the prime minister's office, where he explained to Feast what he and Smith were doing. Feast smiled and wished Redstone luck.

'Oh, another thing, while you're here,' said Feast. 'The prime minister and Mrs Jones would like to rearrange the visit to Chequers that you had to cancel. Can you make Sunday twentieth November? You'd be joining some other entrepreneurs and their partners.'

Redstone took out his phone, consulted his diary and agreed. He supposed he'd go alone, and instantly felt a wave of deep sorrow that he'd no longer see Christina, hear the precision and lilt of her spoken English, exchange thoughts with her…

'Do you need any other help from me?' asked Feast.

Redstone cleared his throat. 'I'd like to go to Brussels to talk to officials who work on energy policy in the Commission, and to anyone I can find from other member states.'

'Great idea. As it happens, there's a meeting of the Energy Council on…' he looked at his computer, '…sixteenth November. It would be an ideal place to talk to loads of energy policy experts. You might even be able to collar our own secretary of state! Valerie wouldn't go to something like that. I'll arrange it. You could attend as the PM's energy adviser.'

Redstone returned to his office and worked through his emails. He gasped. 'Laura! Look at this! It was in the junk folder of my London Bio account.'

Smith walked round and peered over his shoulder. '*"Attention, Mr Redstone,"*' she read out. '*"You are in danger. Take precautions."* Interesting. Do you know the sender?'

'It's a friend whose email address was hacked in the past. This is his old email address, but he now uses a different one. And the English isn't quite natural – an English speaker wouldn't say "attention". He'd say something like "warning", or "be careful". But a French speaker might. And an IT specialist would know how to make an email appear to come from a false address. I bet it's Dupont. He's clearly genuinely concerned about Lesage's activities.'

'Good for him. I'll get my colleagues to check it out anyway. Can you please forward it to me?'

'Ok. Do you think it means I'm in more danger than we thought?'

'No. Don't worry – we've got your back covered.'

WEDNESDAY 9 NOVEMBER

Redstone spent a restless night, disturbed by jumbled anger, anxiety and misery about the threats to his life, the tragedy of Saira's death and the end of his relationship with Christina. And although going into the wavy dimension was amazing, he also hated it. He longed to get back to an unexciting, calm existence.

He decided that, despite what Laura had said, he'd give up the secret work for the PM and go back to his London Bio life. But then he changed his mind. He owed it to Kate and Saira to get Kemp put behind bars, which meant his working with MI5. And he felt duty-bound to complete the speech and to get the electricity threat sorted before winter set in. And besides, there was the implied threat that Laura had made.

What to do? He'd let a few more days pass before making a final decision.

When he arrived in Downing Street, Smith had news. 'My colleagues have now worked out how Kemp spends his days. He seems to be a creature of habit. He leaves his flat at about eleven a.m., goes to see Molly Goodyard, the neighbour, and then leaves the block.'

'Where does he go?'

'That does vary from day to day. Sometimes on legitimate business connected with his antique furniture trade. For example, he visited his showroom in Westminster for a couple of hours. Far more often, he's conducting his drugs business, though we haven't been able to gather any hard evidence on that.'

'Does he take something with him that he could hide in Molly Goodyard's flat?'

'He certainly isn't taking anything bulky. Anyway, we sent an operative into her flat, on the pretence of being a council officer checking that the cleaners had been doing a good job. He searched the flat as best he could but found no signs of drugs or money.'

'When should I go into his flat to plant the bugging device?'

'We'll probably be ready by the end of the week.'

'Ok.' He paced around the room. 'You know what? I'm going to finish up here and go home. I need a break.'

*

He was washing up after dinner when his phone rang. It was Christina. He answered, his voice croaky because his mouth had gone dry. She sounded business-like.

'Mark, something's been preying on my mind. Something you need to know, but I shouldn't tell you. Anyway, I've decided I will.'

He cleared his throat. 'Go on.'

'I assume you're dealing with Albert Lesage in this project for the prime minister?'

'A bit. Why?'

'I wanted to warn you. Don't trust him. I regard him as very… very tricky. I had some dealings with him… a few years ago.'

'You'll have to tell me more.'

'Well… I'm not supposed to tell people about my work, so please keep this to yourself, but I was involved in assessing whether Norway should get France Nucléaire to build a reactor for us. In the end, I advised against it.'

'So?'

'Er… Lesage was in a different job then. He was in charge of the French team we were dealing with. He was devious and untrustworthy. His priority was his own interests. We couldn't trust anything he said.'

'Can you expand on that?'

'Sorry, I've already told you more than I should. I just wanted you to be wary of him.'

'Did he try to get off with you? Not that I'd blame him.'

'What? Oh, for goodness' sake. I'm trying to tell you how he operates. Just be careful, will you?'

'Thanks. I so appreciate your phoning. It's great to hear from you. I wish… well, anyway, everything ok with you?'

'Oh, you know. Back to my routines. Are you still suffering – stupid, of course you are. The awful killing. You'll just have to let time pass… sorry, I'm not being very helpful.'

'No, it was kind of you to phone. I know it must have been difficult. Er…'

'Well, I hope…'

'Yes. Thanks again.' They rang off.

He sat and turned over the conversation in his mind. What Christina had told him about Lesage didn't really add anything to what he and MI5 already knew, though, of course she wouldn't have been aware of that. He decided not to relay the conversation to Laura, to avoid betraying Christina's confidence. But what did the phone call say about Christina's feelings for him? Probably nothing new, but it was warming that she cared enough to make the call.

But there was also the fact that she'd worked on nuclear reactor policy. Was it just a coincidence that they'd got together just when he was starting the nuclear project? He thought through what he'd told her about the project since they'd first met, and was convinced he hadn't given anything away. Coincidences did happen, of course. As a scientist, he knew they happened in random systems. It would be very odd if *nobody* he met had any role in nuclear energy, given the number of people who did have some role. Especially the sort of people he mixed with. There was that guy at the Royal Society of Chemistry…

And yet… maybe he should tell Laura, or ask her if MI5 had found anything when they'd checked Christina out, as he assumed they had. But he didn't think Christina could be consistently deceitful. Anyway, what would be the point of asking Laura? His relationship with Christina was over. Best to forget his suspicions.

THURSDAY 10 NOVEMBER

Colin walked into Redstone's London Bio office. 'Hi! I must show you this,' he said, pointing to his cheek. 'Look at my lesion!'

Redstone walked around the desk and looked closely at Colin's face. 'There's a deep red mark, but the carcinoma itself seems to have gone!'

'That's right. I've finished the treatment, and I've suffered no real side-effects except for the red mark. I can live with that. The dermatologist was amazed, though she's reserving judgment for the moment. She wants to see if the cure's lasting and what the biopsy says.'

'Fantastic! I'm truly pleased for you.' He paused. 'I don't want to be a wet blanket, but of course, the dermatologist is right. We need to know the biopsy results.'

'Yes, I understand that. But so far so good!'

'This shows that we must do more development work, urgently. We're going to need lots of money, I'm afraid. Much more than we needed for the drug delivery work, because of the different regulatory requirements.'

'Yes, I've been looking into the possibilities. We're going to need more than we could raise from our own resources. It would be easy to get the work paid for by a large pharmaceutical company, but that would mean we'd lose control of London Bio.'

'I don't want to find myself working again as a small cog in a huge organisation. Or even a large cog.'

'My sentiments exactly.'

'So, we need to raise money from investors.'

'Yes. I've started to make enquiries.'

Redstone's phone rang – it was Laura. Colin waved goodbye and walked out.

'Good news,' she said. 'Lesage has called an urgent meeting with Dupont. I'm guessing he received the fake memo. The meeting's in the normal place in a couple of hours. Can I send Lewis to collect you?'

*

Lesage and Dupont sat in the shielded room. Lesage was flushed. He pushed a piece of paper over to Dupont. *'Read this!'*

Dupont read it aloud, in English. "Prime Minister – Further to my last memo, our enquiries have thrown up a startling… information about the nuclear fuel used by France Nucléaire. It is so sensitive that I need to brief you in person. I will be in touch with your office."'

Redstone strode over and took several photos. He grinned with satisfaction when he captured Lesage taking the sheet of paper, with its contents visible, as Dupont handed it back. He put a finger in his left ear again, to aid his comprehension of the muffled echoey words.

'How on earth did you get that?' asked Dupont.

'I have a very good source inside the British... But that's not the point. I certainly haven't given that... Redstone any new information. So, it must have come from you, or from further... by the inspectors. Explain yourself!'

'I've got nothing to explain. I haven't met anyone from the British government, and the inspectors haven't returned to... sites. You need to go back to your source for more... Anyway, I'm getting fed up with this deception. If they find out, I won't care.'

'I'll personally make sure you do care.'

'If that's a threat to harm me in the same... Redstone, I warn you, I've taken a precaution. I've modified the program so that it stops if I haven't input a password after three days.'

Lesage started shouting, but Dupont continued. *'I'm ashamed of the weakness that gave you... over me. I'm now attending a gambling addiction clinic. This whole thing's your doing and your problem. You need to approach your... source and get him to find out what the new information is.'*

Dupont sat back, looking calm, but Lesage stood up and pushed his chair back so violently that it fell over. His face was red and sweaty. He clenched his fists. He shouted, *'I can't go back to the source, you fool!'*

'Why not?'

'...knows that we have a problem, but not what it is. I must avoid giving... any reason to report it to others within the British government.'

'Surely he'll fear losing his job if it gets out... passing information to you? Anyway, you must have some hold over him to get the information... What is it? Blackmail? Are you paying him?'

'I haven't paid anything. I made promises about a high-level job... And there have been expensive, luxurious visits to... in France. Not that this is any concern of yours. You stick to the engineering problem, and I'll deal with the political issues.' Lesage paced round the room. He spoke to Dupont in a calmer voice. *'Can't you figure out what this new information might be? Might one of your staff have realised what is happening?'*

'I suppose it's possible,' said Dupont, *'but I would have expected... come to me in the first instance if there were any suspicions.'* He furrowed his brow. *'I wonder whether there really* is *new information. Do you think it might be a trick of some sort?'*

Redstone smiled in admiration. He couldn't help liking Dupont.

'Interesting idea,' said Lesage grudgingly, *'but my source is so senior that... to feed her false information, and...'*

'Ah!' interrupted Dupont. *'Now I know who it is! I noticed that you carefully avoided mentioning... gender up to now. If she's very senior, it can only be Madame Hitchcock!'*

'As I said, you stick to engineering, and let me deal with the political side.' Lesage walked around the room. *'However, I think I will go back to her. I'll tell her it's impossible that... new information, and anyway, the problem's solved, and she must have been fed false information. I'll see how she reacts. That should provide... as to what we should do next. Meanwhile, any progress on solving the problem?'*

'No,' said Dupont. *'And I don't expect any. As I keep telling you, I've no relevant expertise. I've now read... about the whole area, but what we need is someone with first-hand experience – someone who knows how to solve practical problems of this nature. Someone who's dealt with... problems which occur in real life but don't find their way into textbooks. Someone who knows the tricks of the trade.'*

Lesage sighed. *'Ok. We're running out of time. If you've been unable to find a solution by next week, we'll have to identify... our staff that we think we can trust and let him into the secret.'*

They got up and walked out of the room.

Back in the Downing Street office, Redstone swallowed some paracetamol for a splitting headache and recounted what he had heard.

'I think the time's come to pull the plug on Hitchcock,' said Smith. 'I'll discuss it with Gavin McKay. He might decide to pull the plug on Malvern too. He'll have to discuss it with the PM, of course.' She paused. 'Oh, by the way, we couldn't find out anything about the source of the email which you guessed came from Dupont. And what about this program of Dupont's? What's that all about?'

'I think it's really significant,' said Redstone. 'I must discuss it with Alan, but I guess it's connected with the data that France Nucléaire gives the Inspectorate. And somehow connected with Dupont's office. We should reconsider whether I should go to

Dupont's office to have a sneaky look around. Not that I fancy the thought of spending even longer in the wavy dimension.'

Redstone phoned Cunningham.

'The computer program reference is interesting,' Cunningham said, 'but it's probably about the project management of building the new power station. That would involve many programs. Dupont could simply be blackmailing Lesage by, in effect, threatening to halt the final stages of fuelling or testing the Dymbury plant.'

'If it's to do with the fuelling of the new plant, then everything fits. Except that we have no idea what the fuelling problem might be or why the fuelling should be different from that of the older plants.'

Cunningham agreed. 'I've been looking again at the data they send us, as we discussed, and I looked carefully at the figures relating to nuclear fuel. I haven't found anything which looks remotely suspicious. Or which could throw light on problems with the new plant. But there's something about the data that's nagging at the back of my mind. I just can't drag it out. It's very annoying!'

'Maybe it would help if I had a look,' offered Redstone. 'Sometimes an onlooker can see more of the game. If you could send me some of the data, together with an idiot's guide about the normal safe ranges for the readings, I might be able to spot something.'

*

Back home, he replied to texts from the twins. '*Feeling a bit better now, thanks. Maybe I'll stick it out till the job for the PM is finished.*' They both replied saying he should persevere.

FRIDAY 11 NOVEMBER

Redstone sat at his desk, poring over printouts of the data Cunningham had sent. Each page contained columns of numbers replicating the readings he had seen in the control room at West Avon. There were corresponding pages for the other power stations. Each page contained one day's readings.

He compared the figures on random pages with what the numbers should be if the plant was operating safely. All the numbers fell within the safe ranges, except a couple which were marginally outside for just one hour in the day. He highlighted those figures.

After a couple of hours, he stopped and squared the piles of paper. 'This is the most boring job I've done in years,' he said to Smith.

She looked up. 'You should try sitting in an uncomfortable, cold hiding place doing surveillance on someone who doesn't move for hours,' she said. 'At least you can use the toilet if you need to!'

Redstone smiled. 'Ok, but all these numbers are exactly what I would have expected to see from a well-run system. Nearly all within the expected ranges, with the odd fluctuation for a short time till the operators did something to correct it.'

'Were the fluctuations potentially serious?' asked Smith.

'Not really.' Redstone shuffled through the mound of sheets and drew together those which contained his added highlights. 'None of them is more than one per cent outside the recommended range. For example, this one shows a temperature of a hundred and twenty-three degrees, whereas the maximum should be one hundred and twenty-two, and this one…' he drew another sheet out of the pile, '…shows…' He stopped and looked carefully at the two sheets.

'Good lord, Laura! I've found something! I'm sure of it! These two sheets contain readings from two different power stations, taken on two different dates. The first one was…' he looked at the top of the sheet, '…fifteenth March and the second was… May ninth. And the numbers on the sheets are identical!'

'Could it be a coincidence?' Smith asked.

'Just a minute – I'll need to do some sums to answer that.' He counted the number of figures on the page and scribbled on a blank sheet of paper. 'The probability of two sheets being identical is roughly one in ten billion.'

'That was quick!'

'It's not that hard when you know a bit of statistics. Anyway, it couldn't be a coincidence. Either the sheets were mislabelled or there's something very fishy going on. I'm going to write a short computer program to examine all the data Alan sent, to see if there are any more identical sheets.' He turned to his PC.

After half an hour, he looked up. 'I've found three more examples of identical pairs of sheets of data. Like the first two, they're supposed to come from different power stations and different dates.' He looked at the screen. 'And the dates are quite regularly spaced, whatever that means.'

'You'd better get in touch with Alan straight away,' said Smith. 'I'm quite impressed!'

Redstone grinned and phoned Cunningham, who said he was in a meeting and asked if they could speak later in the day.

'Alan, you definitely won't want to wait to hear what I've found. Can you leave the meeting?'

'Yes. It's with Valerie. Hold on.' Redstone heard him tell Hitchcock that there was an emergency he had to deal with now. He heard a door shut.

'Ok, I'm in another office. You should have seen Valerie's scowl. Tell me what you've found!'

Redstone explained.

'That's it!' shouted Cunningham. 'I told you there was something at the back of my mind! I'd subconsciously noticed that some of the patterns of data were familiar but didn't quite rescue the thought. Well done! How did you do it?'

Redstone explained that he'd printed the data and highlighted some of the figures which were out of range, which had led to his spotting that two sheets were identical.

'That's the advantage of using paper and ink,' Cunningham said ruefully. 'I looked at the data on a screen, and I'm sure my colleagues did too. We never print that stuff out. We'd be swamped with paper. And I bet the people at France Nucléaire only use screens too.'

'Well, what does it mean?' asked Redstone. 'It can't be a coincidence, or rather four different coincidences, as I've explained. Could it have been some sort of clerical error?'

'No. We get the data directly from each of the power stations at the end of each day. I've seen the operators just press a key and the computer at the power station automatically downloads the data to us.'

'In that case, the data must be changed in the computer at the power station before being sent to you.'

'Why on earth would France Nucléaire program its computers to do that? If there were no operators in the control rooms, I could see that a devious person might want to sanitise any dubious figures before we saw them. But the operators would see the un-sanitised figures, and if there were a problem, they'd be the first to act and indeed to report them. It isn't in the operators' interests to work in an unsafe plant!'

'Could there be something wrong with the system which converts actual readings into numbers?'

'I was wondering the same thing,' said Cunningham. 'Readings of temperature, pressure and so on are just electrical signals which are converted to numbers for the displays and the records. The computer program that does all that is the same for each power station. Maybe there's a bug in it.'

'I noticed that the coincidences happen at regular intervals. What do you make of that?' asked Redstone.

'Maybe it's a result of the bug. Maybe something goes wrong every couple of months. It would explain why they haven't sorted it out. Intermittent problems are the worst.'

'Alan, do you regard this as a serious problem?'

'Well, if readings are incorrectly displayed for one day every few months, there is potentially a serious issue, and France Nucléaire certainly should have reported it to the Inspectorate. On the other hand, the reactors have been working away without any incidents. There could be safety implications, but we need to know more.'

'What happens next?'

'I'll call an urgent meeting with my colleagues, and we'll discuss the ramifications. We'll go back over the data and see if there's anything else suspicious. Now you've pointed us in the right direction, it'll be easy to seek patterns. Then we'll sit down with France Nucléaire and talk it through. My guess is that they'll be just as surprised as we are, and certainly more embarrassed.'

'Are you going to tell Hitchcock?'

'Yes, I think so. Is there any reason I shouldn't?'

Redstone thought. If Hitchcock heard of this discovery, she would no doubt tell Lesage very quickly. His instinct told him that it would be better if they could control when Lesage learned what Redstone had spotted. 'Hold on a minute, Alan – I just want to check with Laura.' He covered the mouthpiece and told Laura his thinking. She strongly agreed.

'Alan – please don't tell her till we say it's ok. Trust me – there's a good reason. Tell her your colleagues had found a technical problem, but it turns out not to have been an emergency after all. And don't tell France Nucléaire until I say it's ok to do so. Can you live with that?'

'Yes, of course,' said Cunningham. 'I can do cloaks and daggers with the best of you. And well done again for spotting the repeats!'

They rang off. Redstone felt guilty, as he had with the cancer cream invention. In a way, the repeats hadn't been spotted by the real him. The wavy dimension treatment had enabled his brain to spot the pattern, and he suspected he wouldn't otherwise have noticed it. He didn't deserve as much credit as Smith and Cunningham were giving him.

He discussed with Smith what Cunningham had said.

'This being an intermittent display problem doesn't quite fit the facts,' she said. 'Remember that GCHQ overheard Lesage saying that the problem would cause the worst rift between the UK and France since Napoleon, or words to that effect. And how does all this relate to the fact that nuclear fuel seems to be involved? And isn't the problem supposed to be with the new reactors, not the old ones? And didn't Dupont say that the problem is outside his area of expertise, whereas it sounds as though the computer stuff is exactly in his area of expertise?'

'All those are very good points,' said Redstone. 'I'm now convinced more than ever that I should get down to West Avon as soon as possible, and see what I can learn from Dupont's office.'

'I now agree. Given your difficulties in seeing far while you are in the wavy dimension, we'll need to make careful preparations. Including giving you detailed maps with visual points of reference every few feet, if possible. I'll get my colleagues onto it.'

Her phone rang. She took the call and turned back to Redstone. 'There's other news. The technical staff have prepared the devices to be installed in Kemp's flat. We're going to give you a selection because we don't know exactly what equipment Kemp has. I'll tell you what to do once you're inside the flat. Are you ok to go now? Kemp is out, and my colleagues think he won't be back for a few hours. Lewis is waiting outside.'

In the car, Smith showed Redstone the contents of an aluminium briefcase lined with foam, in which nestled a couple of dozen devices which looked like USB memory sticks. Each one had a number stuck next to it on the grey foam.

'I'll help you decide which one to use,' Smith said. 'I'll be able to communicate with you. I'd like you to wear this earpiece and microphone, and this camera strapped to your forehead.' She handed him the equipment. 'Once you've plugged the device into the computer, we'll have access to the hard drive. The computer will otherwise work exactly as it did before. Kemp won't notice any difference.'

They parked outside the block. Redstone donned the equipment and twisted into the wavy dimension, feeling amused by Lewis's and Smith's expressions of startled astonishment as he disappeared. The pulse of pressure in his skull seemed greater than on previous occasions, but the nausea was the same. He fumbled his way to Kemp's front door and twisted into the flat, enduring another strong pulse. He looked carefully at the frame surrounding the door and immediately saw a thin cable leading to a neatly drilled hole. He assumed this was to Kemp's surveillance camera. He looked through the flat and checked that Kemp wasn't there, nor was there a sign of any other cameras, so he twisted back into the normal dimension and grunted with pleasure at being able to see clearly and feeling the nausea disappear.

'Hello, Laura – can you hear me?' he said softly.

'Yes,' her voice said clearly in his ear. 'And we have a good picture.'

'I'll show you what I think must be the cable to a camera above the front door.'

'Yes, that looks like what we'd expect. When you leave, see if you can spot the lens. Now, the first thing is to show me the back of his computer.'

Redstone went into the study and looked at the computer.

'Ok. Take out the USB stick you see there and look at it closely. Yes, it connects the wireless mouse. You need to replace it with number seventeen in the case.' Redstone did that.

'Now just walk through the flat, so that I can see everything.'

He walked around, under her direction. 'I find it amusing to see things from your height,' she said. 'You tend to look down rather than up, unsurprisingly.'

He walked into the bedroom. 'Open the drawer in the bedside table,' she said. 'Do it slowly and carefully.'

He opened the drawer, and nestling on top of a cloth was a black boxy pistol. He bent down close to it so that Smith got a good view.

'Well, well, well,' she said. 'You are a bad man, Mr Kemp. You certainly haven't got a licence for that. Now, Mark, go into the hall and look under the top of the table against the wall near the front door.'

He went into the hall, knelt by the table and leaned forward to see underneath the tabletop. A knife was secured to the wood by duct tape.

'Predictable. At least we know what we might be facing if we have to come in heavy-handed,' Smith said. 'Ok, I think we're done. You can come back now.'

Redstone twisted back into the wavy dimension, wincing against the pulse of pressure, and left the flat. He looked up above the front door and spotted the glint of a small lens set into the frame.

He made his way back to the car. Smith and Lewis were chatting in the front. He slid into the back and twisted to get back to normality.

Nothing happened. He tried again, but remained in the wavy dimension. Bile rose in his throat. Smith and Lewis chatted on, oblivious to his near presence. Sweat broke out on his brow, and he felt he was going to be sick. He took deep breaths, leant back and closed his eyes. He decided to give it ten minutes and then try again. He looked at his watch. He waited for what seemed like several minutes and looked again, but only two minutes had passed. His heart was beating hard and fast, and he felt panicky. What if he couldn't get back? He would die in a matter of days, presumably of thirst. His life couldn't be over – he had too much to do, to achieve, to finish. He wanted to hold Christina in his arms again. His children would be devastated by the loss of their second parent. Would MI5 find a way of rescuing him? How could they? He *had* to make a huge effort to get back.

He waited for what seemed like a further fifteen minutes and looked at his watch. Eight minutes had passed. He couldn't wait any longer. He took a deep breath, concentrated hard and twisted. The scene around him quivered and pulsed, and he felt terror and intense nausea – and then, to his intense relief, he returned to the normal world.

Smith and Lewis started. 'You took a bit longer than I expected,' said Smith. 'You look ill. Is everything all right?'

'No, it isn't,' said Redstone, trembling and sweating. 'I've been sitting in the back of the car for what seemed like hours, trying to get back into the normal world and failing. I was terrified. I certainly can't use the technique again till Jim Clothier has sorted me out. And even if he can find a way of resurrecting the ability, I can't go back unless I also have some sort of kit to help me in an emergency, or unless MI5 comes up with a way of rescuing me if I do get stuck.'

Smith and Lewis were very solicitous and helped Redstone to calm down.

‘Jim did say at the start that the effects of the treatment would wear off, but I confess, I’d pushed that to the back of my mind,’ Redstone said. ‘I’m cross with myself. It was stupid. What got into me?’ He thought further. ‘But what could we have done differently? I had no warning signs that it was wearing off. And the weekly check-ups have patently been a waste of time, as regards this, anyway.’

He wiped his face. ‘Maybe I should make it clear – I do want to persevere. I want to finish the nuclear investigation. But not at the risk of a horrible, lonely, lingering death!

Smith and Lewis exchanged glances. ‘Our first step must be to tell Jim what’s happened,’ said Smith. She phoned. ‘He’d like to speak to you,’ she said, handing Redstone the phone.

Clothier expressed his regrets. ‘Well,’ said Redstone, ‘at least I’ve got back in one piece. Can I come into your place today for some more irradiation and to discuss how we avoid this happening again?’

‘It’s not as simple as that,’ said Clothier. ‘It’s not the effects of the radiation that have worn off – it’s the effects of the chemical, the WD41. It’s gradually been metabolised by your liver. I wish I could inject more into you, but we used our whole supply last time. We’ve started to make more, but as I explained, it’ll take many weeks before we’ve got some.’

‘Are you sure that’s the explanation?’

‘Yes. We did several experiments with tissue cultures. The radiation effects look very long-lived – maybe permanent – but as you know, you need the WD41 as well for the process to work.’

‘Oh. Well, can I come in anyway?’

‘Yes, I’m sure you should.’

*

Redstone entered Thames House. A young man approached him.

‘The director general would like to see you, Dr Redstone. Would you please come with me?’

Redstone entered McKay's office, and the young man left.

'Please sit down, Mark. You've had an awful week – how are you feeling?'

'I'm pretty shaky, but otherwise ok, thanks.'

'We have access to professional help for our people when they go through bad experiences, and you're welcome to use it. Just let me know. Now we need to discuss our plans in light of what happened to you.'

'Yes,' said Redstone, 'I was expecting to do that with Jim Clothier.'

'I don't mean scientific or operational plans. I'm afraid it's more basic than that. I'll get to the point. Now you're unable to go into the wavy dimension, your ability to help us has become limited. There seems to be no prospect that we can get your ability back for many weeks, which would be too late. The nuclear power issue must be solved imminently, otherwise our electricity supplies this winter… well, you know all that. We have to find another way.'

'I…'

McKay held up a hand. 'I know you've developed a thorough knowledge of the problem, and you've been working effectively with the Chief Nuclear Inspector as well as my people. So I propose you carry on working with us for another week, and then we part company, with our deep thanks for your efforts. I'm sure your colleagues will welcome you back to working full time at London Bio. I understand you want to do that anyway.'

Redstone felt as though McKay had punched him. He had no idea this was coming. He was furious with himself for not thinking it through. He'd concentrated just on the technical issues, as though science and technology could solve everything. So much for his enhanced cognitive abilities! Faced with the reality of being kicked off the investigation, his thoughts about leaving voluntarily had gone out of the window. He now keenly wanted to carry on, to see the task to its conclusion. But he couldn't find any arguments against what McKay had said.

'Can I at least have the weekend to think through if there's any way out of the problem?'

'You can have the whole of the coming week if you like,' said McKay, 'but we'll have to move on. We did wonder how long the effects of the WD41 would last, and we do have a contingency plan. We hoped we wouldn't have to use it before your work with us was complete, but it was no more than that – just a hope.'

'May I ask what your contingency plan is?'

'Obviously, I won't go into detail, but in essence, it's falling back on our usual tools – mainly intercepting communications and using what we call human intelligence.'

Redstone inferred that MI5 had regarded him as dispensable. They'd realised that in the worst scenario, he might have got stuck in the wavy dimension and died there. McKay was more ruthless than he had realised. He supposed he shouldn't be surprised.

'Could I come in anyway, for a chat with Jim Clothier on Monday?'

'Of course. I'll arrange it.'

MONDAY 14 NOVEMBER

Redstone sat in Clothier's office in Thames House, nursing a cup of coffee.

'Have you recovered from your awful experience last Friday?' asked Clothier. 'I remember how I felt when I found the effects were starting to wear off, and my experience was nowhere near as traumatic as yours. Mine was just a momentary pause before I twisted back.'

'I can't say I've had a great weekend. Not only was I nearly stuck in the wavy dimension, but I now realise that MI5 regarded me as dispensable.'

'MI5's a collection of people who all have individual emotions. I don't regard you as dispensable, and I'm certain that the same applies to Laura. I'm terribly sorry about what happened on Friday. I mistakenly assumed that you'd get a warning sign, like I did.'

Redstone noted that Clothier didn't deny that McKay thought of him as dispensable. 'Bizarrely, before Friday's experience, I'd been planning to jack it all in anyway,' he said, 'but Laura persuaded me to defer a decision. And she was right. I strongly hoped that I could help sort out the nuclear power issue as well as bring Kemp to justice.'

'Obviously we hoped so too. It's just a matter of chemistry. We can't make more WD41 in time. There are too many steps in the synthesis, and you know how it is – each one can take many hours, or more, because of slow reactions or the need to dry materials or… I don't know why I'm bothering to say all this to a chemist. You know better than I do.'

'Yes. It makes a bizarre contrast with a new product we're developing in London Bio. We've been able to produce it very quickly because we didn't need to do any synthesis – it was mainly just a matter of blending the right existing materials.'

'Well, this isn't like that.'

'No. But I wondered whether I might be able to spot some way of speeding up the synthesis. Looking at it through different eyes might achieve something.'

'Why not? Can't do any harm.'

'As you explained,' said Redstone, 'the chemical is incredibly complex. How did you work out what was needed?'

'We worked out that we required a molecule which would do three things at once: bind to the relevant parts of the relevant neurones, sensitise them to the magnetic and electric fields, and keep them connected in the right way. We got ideas on each part from the scientific literature and then combined the three. It took a lot of trial and error. If you're thinking that we could design a different molecule, forget it. Even if it could be done, it would take ages.'

'No, I wasn't thinking that. I was wondering how you decided where to split the molecule into three, for the three different labs to make before you combined the pieces to make the final product. But now I understand.'

'So what? How does that help?' asked Clothier.

'I'm not sure it does. Could I have another look at the structure of the final molecule and see if I have any ideas for an alternative way of making it? I recall most of the structure, but not all the details. I have a vague feeling that if we broke down the structure differently, we might find it much easier and faster to synthesise.'

'Of course,' said Clothier.

'And there's another thing that might help,' said Redstone. 'The irradiation, and perhaps the WD41, seem to have enhanced my ability to see patterns and connections.'

'As we mentioned some time ago, that's not surprising,' said Clothier, 'when you consider why we were treating your brain in the way we did.'

'Maybe it will help. Or maybe it won't, now that the WD41 has worn off. Let's see what we can come up with.'

Clothier typed on his PC, and a molecular structure appeared on the screen.

'Ah, yes,' said Redstone. He studied the structure. 'I can see where you naturally joined the three components, but if you look here, I think this bit has a similar structure to a drug we could easily buy. Can I access the internet here, on my phone?'

'No, but you can use this PC.' Clothier shifted over.

Redstone typed for a minute. 'As I thought. Look!'

Clothier studied a formula on the screen. 'Yes, I see!' he said excitedly.

'I need to sit down and think this through in my lab, with my reference books and programs,' said Redstone. 'May I have a printout of the structure?'

Back in London Bio, he sat at his desk and thought about how the substance might be synthesised. Ideas popped into his head, only for him to discard them as flawed. He left the office and went downstairs, walking around the labs and chatting to the staff. Suddenly he had a brainwave. He rushed back into his office and rapidly covered three pages of lined paper with formulae.

'Joanne,' he called out, 'could you please see if you could get me Steve Robbins on the phone? He's professor of organic chemistry at Cambridge.'

A few minutes later, Redstone was telling Robbins that he was engaged in a complex synthesis which had to remain confidential for commercial reasons, but he needed Robbins' advice. He explained the problem he faced and asked for the most up-to-date way to tackle it.

'Interesting,' said Robbins, 'but only mildly so! You can easily carry out the transformation using a method we invented here. I'll send you the references.'

Minutes later, Redstone was reading the details on his PC. He phoned Clothier.

'Hi. I think I can make the molecule in a couple of days, at most! I've got most of the materials I need, but there are two chemicals which you can probably get much more quickly than me. Shall I tell you now what they are?'

'That's fantastic! Yes, please tell me.' Redstone did so. 'Yes, I think we can get those today. I'll have them shipped over to your lab. Good luck!'

Redstone went out to the laboratory and started to set up apparatus on an empty bench. He explained to David that he was working on something confidential for someone he'd met while working at Number 10.

'This is the first time you've done any practical chemistry for… what, a couple of months?' said David.

'Yes, and I now realise how much I miss it. Sorry I'm not allowed to explain more.'

By late afternoon, the bench was full of a jumble of glassware, but at the front were two small, stoppered flasks which Redstone looked at with pride.

'Hey, everyone,' he called. 'Look at these! I've put them through the usual checks, and they're really pure! I didn't know I had it in me!'

A few of the other scientists gathered round and congratulated Redstone, who had a big smile on his face. He wished he could tell Christina.

Joanne came out of her office. 'What's all this merriment about?' she asked.

Redstone showed her his flasks. 'Very clever, Dr Redstone,' she said. 'Now try making a lamb curry!'

Redstone's phone rang – it was Laura. He walked into his office. 'Did Jim Clothier tell you what I was up to?' he said. 'I've had a highly successful day doing real chemistry, and by the end of tomorrow, I should have synthesised the magic compound. I'm feeling utterly chuffed!'

'Great! As soon as you have it ready, we can get it into you, and we can get you back into action. Although I suppose there might be a delay, like there was last time. I'll tell Gavin McKay. He'll be delighted if you can stay on the case.'

'We'll have to wait and see how long the delay is this time. And we'll have to devise a contingency plan in case I get stranded in the wavy dimension. Anyway, what can I do for you?'

'I thought you'd like an update on the Kemp investigation. The device you put into his flat has proved extremely useful. We now have evidence that Kemp printed the photo of you which the police found on the motorcycle killer. And we've also found, on Kemp's hard drive, pictures of me and you outside Kemp's flat. So, the case against Kemp for Saira Sharma's murder is looking stronger, though not quite strong enough yet. We need to do a bit more work, and then we can move in and arrest him.'

'Excellent. Anything else?'

'There may be. I'm hearing whispers. I think you'll be better placed than I am to find out the truth. I suggest you come into Downing Street as soon as you've finished the washing up in your lab!'

'As a matter of fact, you think you're joking, but I have washed up all the apparatus I used. All I've got to do is put it away and then I'll be round.'

An hour later, Redstone was sitting opposite Smith, looking at her expectantly.

'There may be some news about Valerie Hitchcock,' she said. 'I suggest you go downstairs and see if your mate Roger can tell you anything.'

Redstone went down to the PM's offices. As he walked in, Feast was walking out.

'Ah! I was just coming to see you! Come into my office. I've got some news.'

Redstone went into Feast's office. Feast closed the door. 'On the basis of the evidence you managed to gather, Valerie Hitchcock has been suspended pending further enquiries.'

'I don't honestly know how to react,' said Redstone. 'She's been stupid and obstructive, and she's done the country a disservice. But I can't gloat at a colleague's demise.'

'I understand,' said Feast. 'I guess you'll have similar feelings when I tell you that Dominic Malvern has also been suspended.'

'Oh!' exclaimed Redstone. 'I wasn't expecting that, though on reflection it is a logical step, since he was the person supplying information to Valerie.'

'Yes, that's right.'

'But do you think he would have told her those things if he'd known that she was passing it all to Lesage?'

'Possibly not, but that's not the point. One of the prime tenets of maintaining security is not to tell secret information to anyone. He knew that. I'm afraid his cock obscured his brain.'

Redstone laughed. He asked Feast if it was known who would be taking over both jobs.

'At the moment, they've only been suspended, not sacked, so in theory the jobs are not yet vacant. You'll have to wait for that news, I'm afraid.'

'Will the suspensions be announced?'

'No, but no doubt the news will leak out. Our line will be that we won't confirm or deny anything, and we won't comment while investigations are ongoing. If you're wondering about our friend in France Nucléaire, my guess is that he'll find out pretty quickly. Possibly even from Valerie herself. I don't think that relationship has much longer to run!'

Back upstairs, Redstone told Smith what he had learnt.

'Don't feel sorry for them. They betrayed their country,' she said.

'I suppose you're right. I'm going back to the lab to finish the synthesis.'

*

Redstone stood at his bench, admiring the rotary evaporator, a round glass flask which was slowly turning and getting rid of the solvent from his chemical solution.

'David, could you please keep an eye on this and let me know if it explodes and destroys London? I'll be downstairs talking to Colin. I want to find out where he's got to on raising our finance.'

David walked over and looked at the apparatus. 'It's sort of compelling, isn't it? There are some unique pleasures in practical chemistry.'

'I fully agree. I've thoroughly enjoyed doing some real benchwork. Beats all the political intrigues in Whitehall.'

'Maybe, one day, you can tell us everything. Meanwhile, I'll babysit your solution for you.'

Redstone went downstairs.

'Hi, Colin. Everything still ok with your carcinoma? I can't see any change. Any news from the dermatologist?'

'No, I'm still waiting.'

'Well, good luck! It would be a marvellous tribute to Saira if the cream succeeds. I still feel so… well, let's just hope for the best.'

'Thanks.' He pinched his nose. 'I've been working on raising the finance. Or rather, on raising finance while not getting taken over by a big company. But no joy, I'm afraid.'

Redstone sighed. 'If it comes to it, I suppose we'll have to give in and live with a takeover. We'd all do well out of it financially, but the family feel here wouldn't survive.'

'I know. Will you give me to the end of the week before we change our strategy?'

'Of course. As I've said before, do let me know if there is anything I can do.'

Redstone went back upstairs and saw that the evaporation was complete. He disassembled the apparatus and held up the flask, which now contained a white solid.

'One more step,' he said, 'and it's finished.'

An hour later, he trudged into Joanne's office. 'I've just made some brown sludge,' he said despondently. 'The last step didn't work. I've buggered it. I'm not sure what to do now.'

'Why don't you phone your friend Steve Robbins in Cambridge? He helped you last time.'

'Worth a try, I suppose. Could you get him for me?'

Five minutes later, she came into his office. 'He's out for the rest of the day but back first thing tomorrow. Is there anyone else you can try? Or do you want to wait till the morning?'

His shoulders slumped. 'Oh. I suppose I'd better wait. He's the best. Frankly, I'm not optimistic that even he can rescue it.'

'Does it matter that much? Just tell your contact that you tried, and it didn't work out. You've done your best. I'm sure they won't mind. You can't succeed at everything.'

Redstone smiled wanly. He wished he could tell Joanne what it was all about. But maybe there was a point in what she had said. Did it matter? He hated going into the wavy dimension, and being forced to quit all this intrigue might be the best thing that could happen. The authorities would get Kemp without him, eventually. Or maybe they wouldn't, given their record.

He'd try Robbins in the morning.

TUESDAY 15 NOVEMBER

At 9:30 a.m., he was on Skype explaining to Robbins what he'd done.

'Of course that step wouldn't work,' Robbins said. 'If you'd asked me when we spoke last time, I would have told you. Don't you remember steric hindrance? The molecules can't link because the side groups are getting in the way.'

'Oh, I see. But what can I do now?'

'Good question. I suspect your brown sludge is the result of this…' He drew a reaction on a piece of paper and showed it to Redstone. 'Not only did you forget about steric hindrance, but you didn't block off this hydroxyl, so your other molecule has reacted where it shouldn't have done. This is what you've got to try, but I wouldn't be surprised if it doesn't work and you have to start again from scratch.' He sketched out three reactions.

'I'm most grateful, Steve, and I apologise for my poor organic chemistry.'

'That's ok. We all have our strengths and weaknesses. Talking of strengths, I must say I'm intrigued as to what you want this molecule for. I assume it's another earth-shattering pharmaceutical to do with skin, given London Bio's last success, but it doesn't seem to have the right functionality. I know you haven't given me the whole structure, but even so…'

'I wish I could tell you, but I can't. I promise you'll be the first to know if…'

'I understand. I faced a similar problem with my own start-up.'

I bet you didn't, thought Redstone, but said nothing.

*

Redstone stood by the bench, nervously holding a flask of viscous amber liquid. He'd completed the first two steps Robbins had suggested. Nothing obvious had gone wrong, but he couldn't yet tell if the chemistry had been successful. Time was running out – he couldn't miss the train to Brussels. He mustn't let Sophie down. He wiped his brow and set to work on the final step.

Two hours hour later, he triumphantly held up a small bottle containing a clear liquid. He went into Joanne's office and showed her. 'Success! This is what I've made – or rather most of it – I've kept some in our freezer. Just in case.'

'Very impressive,' she said. 'Well done. It was worth persevering.'

'Thanks, Joanne. Even though you told me to give up.' He grinned. 'No, really, your praise means a lot, even when it's based solely on love. Or ignorance.'

She laughed. 'If you want more praise, why don't you put the same effort into finding yourself a new woman?'

'Huh. I'm having dinner with Sophie this evening, and I wouldn't put it past her to bring some beautiful woman along.'

'I would have thought you'd have realised by now that you need someone based here, not abroad.'

'Yes, but Sophie never saw it that way. Anyway, I'll be back tomorrow evening, so there won't be time to achieve much on the love front. Don't worry.'

*

Redstone stood in Clothier's office showing him the WD41. 'I'm fairly sure it's pure enough, but could you just run it through your instruments to check?'

They went along the open corridor to a small area where several instruments stood on a work surface. Clothier used a small syringe to extract a sample of the chemical from the bottle, and injected a drop into one of the instruments.

'It's all automated,' he said. 'By the time we walk back to my office, the results will be ready on my PC.'

They returned to the office. Clothier announced that the purity was excellent. 'Well done!' he said. I need the full details of how you made it, so that I can… well, let's get on with it. Shall we inject you now? We'll need only about a third of this.'

'How long will it take before I'm able to twist into the wavy dimension again?'

'Frankly, I have no idea. We have no experience to draw on. My guess is that it will be considerably faster than the first time because your brain's already organised in broadly the right way, but that's no more than a guess.'

Smith walked into the room.

'Just the person,' said Redstone. 'Laura, I need a survival kit to take with me on future trips into the wavy dimension. It should contain a needle with a dose of WD41 and all the provisions I'd need to last me a couple of weeks. Just in case.'

'Good idea,' she said. 'Water will be your main priority. We'll sort something out. Changing the subject, I've just heard from our computer experts. They say Kemp uses a memory stick to store all his data, and he's taken extraordinary care not to leave anything of real interest on his PC, or even in the cloud. We suppose he does that so he can hide his confidential information away from anyone who might get access to the computer. You didn't see a memory stick when you went through his flat, did you?'

'No. I doubt it's there, anyway. There wouldn't be any point in ensuring that the data wasn't on the PC but then keeping it nearby.'

'No, that's what I thought,' said Smith. 'Damn! We absolutely need to see what's on the stick. I'm sure it'll give the police enough to arrest and charge Kemp. But memory sticks are so small! It could be anywhere! He could even be keeping it in his pocket all the time!'

'I don't think he'd do that because if he were searched, it would be found. I reckon he's got a convenient hiding place.' He tugged his chin. 'And I've got an idea where it is. I bet he hides it in Mary Goodyard's flat. He goes there every day.'

'And I bet you're right!' exclaimed Smith. 'I'll get officers to go and search her flat immediately.' She rushed out.

'I've never seen Laura so excited,' said Clothier. 'This case has got to her. She totally wants to put Kemp away.'

'Excellent,' said Redstone.

'As long as her feelings don't cloud her professional judgement. She's normally such a cool customer.'

'I'm the one whose feelings and unprofessionalism have buggered things up,' said Redstone. 'If it wasn't for me, Saira would still be… I can't see Laura making the same mistakes.' He looked at his watch. 'I'd better get going. I've got a Eurostar to catch.'

*

Redstone settled back in his seat, waiting for the train to depart from the St Pancras terminal. He looked out of the window and marvelled at the engineering which allowed the huge weight of the train to rest on tracks well above the lengthy, bustling mall lined with smart shops and restaurants.

Two hours later, the train eased into Brussels Midi station. He walked along the platform into the noisy, crowded, low-roofed concourse and out to the taxi rank. Twenty minutes later, he checked into a smart hotel in the Avenue Louise, a very wide, multi-lane road with tree-lined grassy areas between the traffic flows. He phoned Sophie to say he'd arrived, and they arranged to meet for dinner.

He was about to shower when his phone rang. It was Smith.

'I thought you'd like to know that the PM has replaced the Secretary of State for Energy,' she said. 'The new one is Ruth

Able. She'll be there tomorrow, and you'll have the chance to meet her.'

'Ah!' said Redstone. 'I know her, vaguely. She used to be the chief economist at Western Energy. Senior staff in the Department of Energy used to go to their offices once a year for a presentation by her and her colleagues on the outlook for oil and gas.'

'How amazing!' said Smith. 'A minister who knows the subject of her Department!'

'So cynical, for such a young woman,' said Redstone. 'But you're right in that she certainly knows a lot about the energy scene. I thought very highly of her. I'm looking forward to meeting her tomorrow. What's the public line about why her predecessor was replaced?'

'A natural move back to the backbenches after years of excellent guff, I mean service,' said Smith. 'Obviously, the real reason is she allowed herself to be too much under Hitchcock's thumb.'

'Yes. We can expect changes, including giving independence to Alan Cunningham and his troops, I'm pleased to say.'

'I don't think he needs troops,' said Smith, 'but if he does, I'm bidding to be in charge!'

Redstone laughed. 'Thanks for letting me know. See you on Thursday.'

'One more thing before I ring off. My GCHQ colleagues have noticed a big increase in phone activity from Lesage. He doesn't say anything incriminating, but what he does say doesn't always make sense or ring true – in other words, we think he's using some sort of pre-arranged code. He speaks to pay-as-you-go phones in France and the UK. We suspect that he's starting to panic as a result of hearing of Hitchcock's suspension. Be careful. We'll be taking extra precautions to look after you. But you still won't notice them.'

After showering, Redstone made his way to the restaurant Sophie had chosen. It had a high ceiling and exposed brick walls, and at the back were big French windows leading to a small courtyard containing artfully lit potted plants. There was a low murmur from other diners, punctuated by the clatter of dishes. He sat at the table Sophie had reserved.

A small group, including a beautiful young woman in a flowery dress, entered the restaurant. The way she held her head, the way she walked, the shape of her face made Redstone's heart surge as he remembered similar occasions in Cambridge all those years ago when he had fallen in love with Kate. He felt tears prickling in his eyes. She called out, 'Dad!' and rushed over. They clung to each other. If only Kate could see her now. If only Sophie could see Kate seeing her now.

'Dad, this is Oskar,' Sophie said, breaking away. 'I've told you about him. And this is Nathalie. You and she have something in common – she's worked for the French Ministry of Energy. She was keen to meet you.'

They sat down to eat. Nathalie was a dark-haired French woman who spoke superb English, and, according to Oskar, Norwegian and other Scandinavian languages. She worked in the Commission as an interpreter. The food was excellent, and the conversation flowed.

Redstone paid the bill, and they all stood. Nathalie said that she was holding a small dinner party in her apartment the following evening and invited him. He apologised, explaining he'd be catching the last train back to London.

He walked back to the hotel, glowing from the after-effects of good food, drink and company and, above all, Sophie's obvious happiness which left him feeling uplifted and even inspired. Oskar seemed a pleasant, intelligent young man, but Redstone wished he could hear Kate's assessment. It would have been so insightful.

Sophie had been very close to Kate but had managed to move on. He should do the same. He smiled at his daughter's attempt to pair him off – he'd enjoyed Nathalie's company, and she was an attractive woman, but he didn't want to get involved with her. He still greatly missed Christina. And what would she have said about Oskar?

WEDNESDAY 16 NOVEMBER

Redstone took a taxi to the UK's Brussels office, which was in an undistinguished building on the edge of a large roundabout.

The Energy first secretary greeted Redstone respectfully and showed him into a small conference room where a few people were standing, drinking coffee. Amongst them, Redstone recognised Ruth Able. He went over to introduce himself, but she remembered him from their previous meetings. She told him that the prime minister had informed her that Redstone would be at the Energy Council meeting.

'Let's chat about energy policy ideas after the meeting finishes,' she said. 'I need to absorb all the briefing I can before the Council meeting starts!'

After the briefing, they walked a short distance to the new, modern Council building. Redstone sat behind the minister and her advisers during the meeting. In the coffee and lunch breaks he spoke to several officials from other countries and from the Commission, absorbing their ideas about future energy policy developments. They all seemed happy to exchange views with him.

At the end of a tiring day he left for the Eurostar terminus.

*

He sat back in the train. His phone rang – it was Laura.

'Good news,' she said. 'One of my colleagues became a social worker for the day. She searched Mary Goodyard's flat and found the memory stick.'

'Where?'

'Under a layer of rice in an old food container on a high shelf in the kitchen. She copied it and put it back. Kemp won't know it was found. Our technical experts are decrypting it as we speak.'

'Excellent. Any guesses for when they'll have extracted the data?'

'I hope they'll have it done by tomorrow. Assuming it contains the information we expect, we'll have plenty of evidence to allow us to arrest Kemp.'

'Great. See you tomorrow.'

He sat back again and tried to sleep but was kept awake by the loud, grating voice of a fair-haired man in his thirties sitting at the other end of the carriage. The man was telling the woman opposite him about his exploits on Wall Street. He talked incessantly. Redstone grew more and more fed up and eventually stopped a passing stewardess, explained he was trying to rest and asked her to ask the man to lower his voice. She went over to the man and spoke softly to him.

'What fucker has been complaining? Tell him to mind his own fucking business!' the man said very loudly, glaring down the carriage. Redstone sighed and got up. Other passengers craned their necks to watch. He walked up the swaying aisle to the man, who stopped talking as Redstone approached.

Redstone leaned over and rested a hand on the man's shoulder. The man's eyes widened. 'What…'

Redstone pressed down with all his weight and gripped hard. The man gasped and grabbed at Redstone's hand but was unable to move it. Redstone bent down and put his face right in front of the man's.

'It's very unpleasant to hear someone continuously shouting,' he said in a clear, quiet voice. The man squirmed under Redstone's grip. 'Why don't you go and find a seat on your own, in another carriage?'

Redstone removed his hand from the man's shoulder, straightened to his full height and stood waiting. The man avoided Redstone's eyes, got up, collected his bag and walked towards the next carriage. The other passengers started clapping. As he approached the door he turned and shouted hoarsely, 'You interfering…,' wrenched open the door and disappeared.

Redstone turned to the woman sitting opposite the vacated seat. 'Thank God,' she said. 'I was praying the other passengers wouldn't think I was with that loudmouth!' He smiled and returned to his seat, receiving taps of approval from other passengers as he walked. The stewardess brought him a glass of champagne and thanked him profusely. He felt exhilarated and rather self-satisfied. He reflected that he wouldn't have behaved like that before he met Laura.

'Mustn't get too pompous and arrogant,' he muttered. He settled back and quickly fell asleep.

He awoke with a start to find that the train was stationary in St Pancras and most of the other passengers had already got off. He collected his bag and coat, stepped down from the train and made his way along the platform, which was now almost deserted. At the end, he turned towards the escalator down to the main concourse, which he could see over the guard rail on his right.

He heard running and looked to his left to see a big man charging at him. *Again! Danger! Can't twist!* flashed through his mind.

He started to brace, but another man kicked the ankles away from the charging man, who fell forward with a thud. A third man flung himself on the sprawled figure, knelt on his spine, yanked his arms back and secured his wrists with a plastic tie.

The kicker pulled out an ID card and showed it to Redstone. 'Laura Smith sends her regards,' he said, grinning.

His colleague got up and stood with one foot on the big man's neck. 'I think you've encountered this fellow before,' he said. 'In West Avon. Recognise him?'

Redstone straightened, wiped his forehead and took a deep breath. He looked closely. 'His face was hidden during the power station attack. But yes, I think it's him.'

'It would be a remarkable coincidence if it wasn't. Same method of attack.'

'Yes,' said Redstone. 'How the hell did he know I'd be here?'

'Laura said that Lesage was bound to have contacts in Brussels who might tell him. Maybe amongst the French contingent there – did you tell any French person your travel plans? Anyway, this was an obvious vulnerability, we thought.'

The man on the ground writhed and shouted incoherently, but the MI5 agent above him pressed harder with his foot, and the man quietened down. 'Let's take you to a nice interrogation room and see what you have to tell us,' the agent said.

Redstone made his way home, feeling scared and excited by the incident and relieved at the efficiency of the MI5 agents and that Lesage's thug was under arrest. Now the incident was over, he had a strange sense of invulnerability, though his common sense told him that he was still in danger from Kemp and probably from Lesage too. He must take care. Which French people had he spoken to while in Brussels? He'd chatted to some French officials in the Council building, but he didn't recall mentioning his travel plans. He had, however, told Nathalie the previous evening. And she'd worked in the French energy ministry, so might well know Lesage. If MI5 discovered it was Nathalie, Sophie might eventually find out she'd caused trouble by bringing Nathalie to the dinner. He wouldn't want that, so he decided to keep quiet.

THURSDAY 17 NOVEMBER

Redstone sat in the Downing Street office, putting the finishing touches to the speech in advance of his visit to Chequers on the coming Sunday. Smith came in.

'How are you after yesterday's excitement?'

'Fine, thanks. I think I'm becoming a bit inured to these violent incidents. Any news about the attacker?'

'Yes. His name is Edouard Marcel. He's a petty criminal from Paris and has a criminal record for assault and theft. He claimed he'd never heard of Lesage and has never been to West Avon. He denied that he was about to attack you at the Eurostar terminal. When we told him that his fingerprints matched some we found in the West Avon turbine hall, he just clammed up and refused to answer any more questions.'

'What happens next, then?'

'Well,' she said, 'we don't have enough for the police to charge him. There were no witnesses at West Avon, and he didn't manage to get to you at St Pancras. Our French opposite numbers think he was recruited by an intermediary, and the only contact with Lesage would have been when Lesage let him into the West Avon plant. Marcel might indeed not know who Lesage is.'

'Are you telling me they're going to get away with it?'

'No, I'm saying that we need to attack the issue from the Lesage end too. If you were able to do your thing with the wavy dimension, it'd be easier to get evidence. Any sign of the ability returning?'

'No, none at all,' said Redstone sadly. 'I keep trying, but zero results.'

'We'll hold Marcel as long as we can. That should get Lesage anxious, and maybe in that state, he'll make a mistake.'

'Changing the subject,' said Redstone, 'have your colleagues decrypted the memory stick data?'

'No, not yet. But it's just a matter of time.'

*

Redstone leaned back and straightened his papers. 'That's it! The speech is finished. I'll send it down to the PM.'

'Are you pleased with it?' asked Smith.

'Yes, but at the moment, my main emotion is… I feel slightly flat. I'm always that way when I've finished something major, like writing a scientific paper at the end of a project. Kate used to get annoyed when I said I'd got post-natal depression.'

'I don't blame her.'

He suddenly felt a wave of bitterness and anger that he couldn't tell Kate about the speech. He was going to get Kemp, one way or another. For Kate and for Saira.

'You ok?' asked Smith. 'Why don't you take the rest of the afternoon off and do something nice to cheer yourself up?'

'Good idea. There's an exhibition of American art at the Royal Academy. They've got some Hoppers – he's one of my favourite artists.' Smith picked up the phone and arranged security for him.

Redstone strode along the edge of St James's Park, enjoying the bright sunshine and cold air on his face. He walked through the quiet back streets of St James's to Piccadilly and entered the courtyard of Burlington House. A large abstract rust-coloured metal structure dominated the centre. He looked at it carefully but decided it did nothing for him. He debated whether to call in on the Royal Society of Chemistry to the right of the Royal Academy, but decided to head straight for the exhibition.

He edged through the crowded gallery and stood in front of one of the Hoppers, a painting of the interior of a cinema with an usherette standing in a corridor on the right of the picture and the screen and backs of seats on the left. As always with Hopper,

Redstone was inspired to devise a story explaining the expression on the usherette's face and that there was just a solitary man watching the film.

He stood in the crowd for some time, looking at the painting. A woman in front of him turned to walk away. 'Sorry I stood there so long, blocking your view,' she said to Redstone.

'Nothing to apologise for,' he replied. 'You didn't block my view at all. I could see over your head.'

'Oh, I can see that now. It must be useful for you both to be so tall, in galleries like this.'

Puzzled, Redstone looked to his left and found himself staring into the face of another woman, with wavy blonde hair. He felt a small shock because he was unused to looking directly into the eyes of women when they were both standing. He glanced down to see if she was wearing high heels, but she wasn't. Looking back at her face, he saw a calm, slightly amused expression. He turned to the woman who hadn't blocked his view.

'Actually,' he said, 'I've never seen this lady before in my life! We're not together.'

The woman was unembarrassed. 'Still useful for you to be tall.' She smiled and walked off.

Redstone turned back to the blonde woman next to him. She was very good-looking. 'Hi,' she said, 'I'm Jenny. But let's not get married straight away!'

He laughed. 'I'm Mark. Er… it's going to be embarrassing if we walk through the rest of the exhibition at the same pace and don't speak. Shall we go together?'

'Good idea.'

They walked around the rest of the pictures, exchanging opinions about them. Redstone found himself enjoying her company, and not looking forward to parting. As they left the exhibition through the shop, he said 'Er, are you in a hurry? If not, could I offer you a cup of tea?'

‘That would be lovely,’ she said.

‘It’s normally very crowded in the tearoom here. Let’s go to the Royal Society of Chemistry, next door. We can get a cup of tea and a biscuit and sit in peace there.’

They went out into the courtyard and into the RSC. Redstone took Jenny up a wide staircase to a grand panelled corridor. They went into a deserted airy book-lined room, furnished with a few chairs and tables. Drinks were set out at the side. They sat and drank tea. Redstone felt at ease, and the conversation flowed.

She looked at her watch. ‘Good lord! I must rush. Hope I’ll see you again sometime.’

‘Me too,’ he said. ‘Many thanks for your company.’ They stood up and shook hands awkwardly. She walked out.

Redstone sat down again and leaned back. ‘Well,’ he muttered, ‘an attractive and interesting woman. Available. Based in London. But…’

He longed to be with Christina. He wanted to see her eyes when she smiled, to smell her hair, to embrace her, to… Should he phone her and try to resurrect the relationship? What if she told him to get lost?

His phone rang. It was Smith.

‘GCHQ has decrypted the data on the memory stick,’ she said. ‘The police are going to mount an operation tomorrow, from Enfield police station. It would be useful if you could be there for the pre-briefing, because of your knowledge of the inside of the flat. Can you meet us there at 5:00 a.m.? I know it’s early, but it’s best to do these things at that sort of hour.’

‘Of course. What was on the memory stick?’

‘Quite a lot. Tell you more tomorrow.’

FRIDAY 18 NOVEMBER

Redstone entered the police station, an ugly rectilinear brick-and-concrete building next to the equally ugly civic centre. It brought back painful memories of visits after Kate's murder. At least he didn't now have to search through files here clandestinely to find out who killed her. He knew, and the bastard would soon be behind bars.

He was shown into a room set out like a classroom, containing several uniformed police officers chatting in groups, and Smith, who was wearing a denim jacket and jeans. She walked over to him.

'Morning. You look a little bleary!'

'You don't,' Redstone said. 'I'm not a natural early riser. I'll soon wake up. What's the order of events?'

'Chief Inspector Hussein will brief the others on how the raid is to be conducted. You're here to answer any questions about the layout of the flat. I've told him that you once went in it, without explaining how. Or why.' Redstone smiled ruefully.

Smith continued. 'The officers will go to draw their weapons, we'll all dress up and we'll go to the block of flats. The police will raid the flat and arrest Kemp.'

'You're sure he's at home?'

'Yes, we have continuous monitoring from the camera outside. He entered the flat last night and hasn't left.'

'Can I come?' asked Redstone.

'I thought you'd ask that,' said Smith. 'I've persuaded Chief Inspector Hussein to allow you to sit with me in my car in the road outside the block. Even I am not going in with the police. They're trained to act as a unit, and I'd just get in the way. But we should both enjoy the spectacle of Kemp being dragged out.'

'Thanks. So, the memory stick had enough on it to justify an arrest?'

'More than enough. It turns out that Kemp is a meticulous record-keeper. I suppose he has to be, as the chief operating officer of a substantial business. He keeps lists of suppliers of the different drugs he's sold, dates of purchase, quantities, prices, and details of his sales to intermediaries. He also keeps a list of associates, which includes the name of the thug who shot Saira Sharma. He's even listed how much he paid each of them.'

'Wow!' said Redstone. 'Sounds like a gold mine!'

'It is. He also lists details of his various overseas bank accounts. The only thing missing is the location of his stashes of drugs and money. We can work out the quantities of drugs and how much cash there must be, but the memory stick contains no clue about location.'

'Maybe you can get that from him after he's arrested. Or from his associates, as you call them. I assume the police are going to arrest them too?'

'Yes, there'll be a series of raids across North London at the same time as ours. But I'm fairly sure Kemp wouldn't have told them such significant information. We'll probably just have to do a lot of careful detective work.'

The chief inspector called the room to order and began the briefing. He displayed on a screen a sketch of the layout of the flat. He introduced Smith, who said a few words about Kemp's history and explained that MI5 had used its resources to ascertain the layout of the flat and the contents of Kemp's computer. She reminded the audience that Kemp had a gun and a knife in the flat.

She mentioned the camera Kemp used to monitor what was happening outside his flat. 'So how will we effect entry without warning him we're going in?' asked one of the police officers.

'Good question,' said Hussein. 'One of us will go up to the flat entrance, keeping close to the wall, and put a sticky patch over the camera lens. Here it is.' He showed them a metal rod with a large black cloth patch attached to a frame at the end of the stick. 'We've tried it, and it works well. Once it's in place, the sticking officer…' people chuckled, '…will withdraw quietly and then the entry group will assemble at the door, ready for my command.'

He continued with the briefing. There were a few more questions, but none requiring Redstone's input. Hussein ended the briefing and the room emptied. Redstone followed Smith to her car.

The convoy of two police cars, a police van and Smith's car drove quietly through the streets to Kemp's block of flats. They parked in a side road. There were several people about, despite the hour, and those passing looked curiously at the police vehicles.

The officers left their vehicles and crowded together at the foot of the staircase leading up to the walkway. Redstone could just see them and Kemp's front door from Smith's parked car. Smith turned up the volume on her communications radio. They heard Hussein whisper to the 'sticking officer', a tall man, who then walked slowly up the stairs and edged along the wall to Kemp's flat. He raised the metal rod and placed the black patch over the camera lens. Immediately, a loud alarm went off inside the flat.

'Fucking hell!' shouted Hussein. 'Go! Go! Go!'

'He must have an alarm which goes off if the lens is obscured,' said Smith, clearly both annoyed and grudgingly admiring.

The officers rushed up the staircase to Kemp's door. One shouted, 'Armed police! Open the door!' He waited two seconds and then used a ram to burst the door open. The officers ran into the flat. The radio announced, 'Clear!' three times, and then a voice said, 'Boss! He's gone out the back window!'

Two officers ran down the stairs. Smith got out of her car, and Redstone followed. The officers ran down a narrow alley at the side of the block to a solid wooden gate which led to the block's gardens. One climbed over and opened it from the inside.

Smith turned to Redstone. 'You must get back inside the car!' she said. 'Kemp will be armed and extremely dangerous.' Redstone realised that she was right and reluctantly did as she said. Smith walked cautiously down the alley and disappeared through the gate, holding a pistol in front of her.

Other officers came down the stairs and went down the alley. A voice said on the radio, 'No sign of him in the gardens.'

Another voice said, 'His car's still here, so he must be on foot.'

Hussein's voice said, 'Search the surrounding streets!'

Smith came back up the alley to the car. She sat heavily in the driver's seat and shook her head.

'The bathroom window was open, and a rope was tied to the radiator and was hanging out of the window. Kemp must have had it there just in case, because he didn't have time to secure it when the police burst in. He must have been getting nervous.'

She sat there thinking. 'There's something wrong,' she said. 'He didn't have time to disappear from the garden like that. And I couldn't see any signs that he'd landed off the rope. No footprints, no indentations in the grass.'

'But the police couldn't have made a mistake about whether he was still in the flat,' said Redstone. 'It's not that big. Surely they would have searched thoroughly?'

'Yes. But I'm still uneasy. I'll wait till they find Kemp in the area or till Chief Inspector Hussein gives up, and then decide what to do.'

They sat in the car, listening to the desultory chatter on the police radio. Smith took out a Thermos flask and poured herself and Redstone a coffee. She offered him a chocolate biscuit. 'Always be prepared,' she smiled.

Eventually, Hussein came over to Smith's car. 'I'm calling it off,' he said. 'Kemp must be long gone by now. I'm sure we'll find him soon. I've put out a general alert, including all ports and airports.'

The police officers straggled back to their vehicles and drove off. Smith and Redstone were left alone.

'You said yesterday you felt flat after completing a project,' Smith said. 'I feel worse than that. I'm going into Kemp's apartment to see if I can figure out how he got away.'

'Be careful,' said Redstone. 'If he is still there, he'll be dangerous. And you're not wearing the body armour the police were dressed in.'

'No, I'm not,' admitted Smith. 'I thought I'd just be a bystander, though I did bring my sidearm, as you saw. Don't worry – I'll be cautious.'

Redstone watched her walk to the staircase, wishing he could accompany her. He hated the thought of Kemp escaping. He tried twisting into the wavy dimension, and to his astonishment he succeeded instantly.

He got out of the car and made his into the flat through its broken door, slowly and carefully negotiating the confusing images of the wavy dimension. Smith was in front of him, pointing her gun ahead. She went into the living room, looked around carefully and went out again, Redstone following, and then she entered the bathroom, where she examined the rope dangling out of the open window. She moved on to check Kemp's office, not knowing that Redstone was still close behind her in the wavy dimension. Finally, she stepped into the bedroom.

A loud bang made Redstone's ears sing. Smith collapsed to the floor. Kemp jumped down from a ceiling hatch onto the bed, holding a gun, leaped off, and ran past Redstone out of the flat. Redstone ran after him but banged into a wall whose position he hadn't judged correctly, confused by the multiple images of the wavy dimension. He twisted back, feeling the familiar relief that came with returning to the normal world. He sprinted to the entrance of the flat, but Kemp was gone. He rushed back into the flat and knelt beside Smith, who was conscious and gripping her arm, which was bleeding heavily. A red pool was spreading on the floor. He tugged out his phone and dialled 999, tossed the phone on the bed and shouted that he needed an ambulance and the police as he looked for something to tie around Smith's arm. He tugged a sheet off the bed, ripped a strip off it, and tied it tightly above the wound. The bleeding slowed. Smith's face was deathly white, and she passed out.

A police car arrived outside, siren wailing. Two officers rushed into the flat. They checked that Smith was being adequately looked after and ran out, one of them talking rapidly on his radio. An ambulance arrived, and two paramedics took over. One told Redstone that he had done the right thing. He sighed with relief and walked out of the flat as the ambulance sped off with its siren blaring and lights flashing.

Other police cars had arrived back at the scene from which they had departed only fifteen minutes earlier. One took Redstone back to Enfield police station, where he spoke to Hussein, but there was no news of Kemp. Smith had been taken to University College Hospital, where there was expertise in treating gunshot wounds, and it looked as though she would quickly make a full recovery.

Redstone sat in his car. He was shocked at the shooting but guiltily relieved that he hadn't been the target this time and concerned that Laura had been wounded while doing something he'd got her into. At least she wasn't badly hurt. The main problem was that Kemp had got away. The police seemed confident that he'd soon be captured, but Redstone wondered whether they were underestimating Kemp, who'd outwitted them continuously over the years and had now done it again.

He started the engine and drove home.

SATURDAY 19 NOVEMBER

Redstone was woken by a sharp pain jabbing above his right eye, which was swollen and watering. The side of his head felt as though it was being squashed by a heavy weight. The patter of rain on the window was unbearably loud. He winced against the brightness of the bedside clock, which showed 1:30 a.m. The smell of soap from the bathroom made him want to vomit, and his stomach felt bloated. His heart sank – it had been ages since his last migraine attack. He stumbled to the bathroom and tore open the packaging of his migraine medication without checking if it was past its use-by date.

Twenty minutes later, the symptoms had hardly diminished. He wiped cold sweat from his forehead and cursed. The medication should have kicked in by now. He turned over and tried to get back to sleep.

Waking at 8:30, he was relieved to find that the migraine had gone but annoyed that it was so late.

Two hours later, he walked into a bright side ward at University College Hospital. There was a faint smell of lilies. He was greeted by a large, good-looking man with a shaved head.

'I'm Doug Smith. Laura's told me all about you. We owe you a huge thanks for saving her life!'

'I don't think you should thank me for anything,' said Redstone. 'Quite the reverse. If it wasn't for me, Laura wouldn't have got involved in the Kemp case, and she wouldn't be here now.'

'You're being too complicated,' said Doug. 'When she was shot, you took swift action to stem the bleeding, and you dialled 999. If you hadn't followed her into the flat, God knows what would have happened. It was Kemp who got involved with you, not the other way round.'

Redstone turned to Laura, who was propped up against the pillows, looking pale but cheerful. 'How are you feeling?' he asked.

'Wiped out, and my arm hurts like hell, but basically, I'm fine,' she said. 'I should be back on duty in a few days. And I echo Doug's thanks.'

'I feel bad that you got hurt hunting that bastard. Has he been caught yet?'

'No,' said Doug. 'He drove off in his car in the direction of Central London. We haven't yet located it, but it won't be long. He'll have passed several ANPR cameras... sorry, that's automatic number plate recognition.'

Redstone nodded. 'I've been thinking about what happened. Why did he shoot Laura? He'd have been better off remaining hidden in the loft and then leaving the flat when everyone had given up.'

'My guess is he recognised Laura from the CCTV pictures he got when you both encountered his brother. He'd been hunting you for revenge, but when he saw she was carrying a gun he realised she was a professional. I reckon he put two and two together and realised she was the one who killed his brother. So he took his revenge on her. He must have thought she'd have other officers nearby, which is why he rushed out in such a hurry.'

'Makes sense,' said Redstone. 'But how come he was up there in there first place? Surely he didn't have time to climb up between when the camera was covered and when the police burst in?'

'Interesting. Officers did look in the loft when they searched the flat, but they didn't spot the hole he'd made in the wall shared with the loft next door – the one over his brother's flat. The hole was hidden behind a pile of boxes. He'd set up the neighbouring loft so he could stay up there for a long time. There was a folding bed, food and drink and even a camping toilet.'

'That's a lot of forward planning.'

'Yes. I think he realised we'd be closing in on him after his thug murdered Dr Sharma. He knew we'd most likely mount a raid while we thought he was asleep. So he's probably been hanging the rope out of the bathroom window every night lately, and sleeping in the loft.'

'He'd thought it all through.'

'Right. He's a very bright man as well as being ruthless scum. Maybe not as well as – he needs to be talented to be such a successful criminal.'

'Even more important,' said Laura to Redstone, 'are you going to give that bunch of flowers to someone else? They look as though they need water.'

'Oh, sorry!' said Redstone. 'They're for you, of course!' He handed them to her, and she immediately handed them to Doug.

'I'll go and get something to put them in. I think you two need to talk without my being here, anyway.' Doug left the room.

'Quickly,' said Laura. 'I assume you went back into the wavy dimension yesterday?'

'Yes, I suddenly found I'd regained the ability.'

'Excellent. Thanks so much for risking it without a survival kit. Don't do that again!'

'To be honest, I did it without thinking it through, but you're right, of course.'

'Anyway, since the ability has returned, you should get down to West Avon on Monday. My colleagues have prepared the maps and diagrams you'll need to help you find your way to Dupont's office. And a survival kit. Liaise with Lewis while I'm out of action. He'll phone you later today to make arrangements.'

'Great,' said Redstone, straightening the chart hanging at the foot of the bed. 'I'm sort of looking forward to it – to what I might find there. More than I'm looking forward to tomorrow, frankly.'

'What's happening tomorrow?'

'I'm going to Chequers.'

'Oh, of course,' said Laura. 'Sorry – I've had other things on my mind. I'm sure it'll be interesting. I look forward to hearing all about it. Why aren't you keen?'

'It's just not my sort of scene.'

'But you must want to see what the place looks like. And most people would give their right arm to spend a day relaxing with the prime minister and his wife.' She looked at her wounded left arm. 'Except me, of course – I need my right arm at the moment.'

Doug came back into the room carrying a vase containing the flowers.

'We've just been discussing Mark's worries about going to Chequers tomorrow to spend the day with the PM and his wife,' said Laura. 'He'd rather spend the day mowing the lawn and stroking his cat. Or was it the other way round?'

'Ho, ho,' said Doug. 'Frankly, I'd feel the same in his shoes.' He turned to Redstone, 'Laura told me you'd been invited. Just tell the PM that police and MI5 officers deserve much higher salaries and then relax and enjoy yourself!'

SUNDAY 20 NOVEMBER

Redstone drove through manicured villages and rolling farmland. The green Chiltern Hills were crystal clear and deeply shadowed in the low morning sunlight. The lovely weather and surroundings lifted his mood. He turned off the road down a single-track lane which ended at imposing gates with a small gatehouse on each side. The gates were open, but posts in the road prevented vehicular access. An armed police officer checked Redstone's details and spoke into his radio. The posts sank into the ground, and Redstone drove up the long, curving drive to the front of the building, which looked like an English version of a French chateau.

As he left his car a man greeted him and led the way up the steps into a spacious panelled hall with a lofty ceiling and an ornate carved wooden gallery. It did not feel homely. There was a buzz of conversation and the clink of glasses from a room off the hall, accompanied by a smell of alcohol and coffee. He followed his ears and found himself in a cheerful room, also panelled, furnished with brightly upholstered armchairs and a sofa. There were a couple of dozen other guests, men and women, chatting animatedly in small groups, one containing the PM.

Redstone felt like an inferior outsider. He knew none of the other guests, who he assumed probably all knew each other, and he had no partner to help him make small talk. He hated this sort of occasion and now wished he hadn't come. He took a drink and stood to one side, deciding which group to try to jostle into, so that at least he would look as though he was socialising, even if he stood and said nothing.

'Hello, Mark.' Redstone turned to see Anne Jones. 'You look like a lost sheep. Let's have a little chat and then I'll introduce you to some of the others.'

He looked at her gratefully. She was wearing a tailored floral-patterned suit with a plain silver necklace. 'How nice to see you. And you look very smart!'

'And so do you,' she said with a smile. 'New suit?'

His face fell. 'Yes, but it's an awfully bad story. How I got it. One of my colleagues helped me with some clothes shopping and then – oh, you know, of course. I was very touched to get your note.'

'Yes, the awful… I wanted to commiserate with you now in person before anything else, and so does – ah, here he is.'

'Welcome,' said the PM. 'Yes, I heard what Anne was saying. It's dreadful. You have our sincere condolences.' Redstone thanked them and told them of the progress of the police inquiry.

'I hope you can regard today as a time to unwind a bit,' said Anne. 'You seem quite tense, if I may say so. Not surprisingly, after what you've been through recently.'

'I suppose I am a bit stressed,' said Redstone. 'But it's not just what's happened recently. It's also that I'm a bit out of my comfort zone. You must be used to guests being nervous when invited to lunch with the prime minister and his wife?'

'Oh, Mark,' she said. 'Look at it from our viewpoint. You're a highly successful scientific entrepreneur with a tremendous knowledge of your subject – much deeper than anything I can match, let alone Michael, who's just a politician who got lucky.' The PM smiled. 'We're rather in awe of *you*,' she continued. 'Anyway, we're just people, the same as everyone else in most respects. Especially Michael. And so are the other guests.'

Redstone laughed. 'That reminds me of something my Norwegian friend said a few weeks ago when I told her I was nervous about meeting Michael for the first time. Only she was much coarser.'

'She sounds just my sort of woman,' said Anne. 'I was sorry to hear that you were coming alone – why didn't you bring her today?'

'I'm afraid we've… we're no longer together. My fault. And now I'm deeply regretting it.'

'Well, do something about it, then!' said the PM. He looked to Anne for confirmation.

'He's right, you know,' she said. 'You've only got one life. Don't waste it.'

The prime minister looked around. 'Some of us are going for a walk, and then we'll have a late lunch. Coming, Mark? After lunch, when the other guests have gone, I need to have a chat with you about work.'

He led the way onto the large terrace at the back of the house. They descended to the grounds.

On the walk, Anne asked Redstone about his recent work at London Bio. He told them about the cream and the good result when Colin had tried it. He mentioned the difficulties in raising enough money to continue the development without giving up control of the company.

'I work on this sort of problem,' said Anne. 'I'd very much like to try to help you raise the finance you need.' Redstone accepted her offer enthusiastically.

On their return from the walk, they took assigned places at a long table in a dining room overlooking the terrace. He found himself seated between two wives of businessmen invitees. As the lunch progressed, the woman on his right spoke only to the man on her right, so he made conversation with the woman on his left. She talked at length about the species of flowers she'd planted in her huge garden in the South Downs. She spoke without turning her head to face him, and he strained to hear against the background chatter, which got louder as more alcohol was consumed. He made what he hoped were appropriate comments.

After lunch, he slipped out to the terrace while the other guests dispersed, absorbing with relief the quiet, and the view of the sunken garden, the meadows and hills beyond. A red kite circled over a field. He wondered whether he should move to a house with such a view but quickly dismissed the thought.

The PM collected him and led the way to a study. 'Let's talk about the speech,' he said. 'I was very pleased with it. Let's go through it together.'

When they had finished, the PM turned to the threat to the power stations. 'I've had briefing on your progress, of course, but is there anything else you can tell me? The issue must be resolved before I give the speech. And obviously before winter sets in. Time's running out.'

'I know. We're getting closer but still haven't pinpointed it. I'm going on a fact-finding trip tomorrow.'

'I take it you're speaking in code,' said the PM. 'Are you going to be dimension-hopping?'

'Yes, that's the plan.'

'I hope you won't think it intrusive or inappropriate, but I'd love to see it!'

'I'm sorry,' said Redstone, 'I would happily demonstrate it for you, but I can't risk doing it without a survival kit. In case I get stuck there. It might be a couple of weeks before I could get back, and that's assuming I have everything I need, including the injection needed to help me recover the capability. Without it, I'd die there, probably of thirst. I nearly did get stuck once, and it was awful.'

The PM stared at Redstone. 'That's terrible! I had no idea. You're very brave to help us, and you have my sincere thanks. And the nation's, if they knew.'

'Thanks. I appreciate that.'

'What's it like? Going into the wavy dimension.'

'I both hate it and love it.'

The PM raised an eyebrow.

'Er… I suppose you want more than that. Let's start with how I get there. I think of it as twisting. I sort of twist in my brain and there I am – in a positively bizarre scene.' He described what it was like.

'Sounds confusing but fascinating!'

'It is. I feel lucky and privileged. I'm almost addicted to it – I marvel at it every time. One particularly amazing thing is being able to twist around obstacles – for example, if I'm confronted with a solid wall, I can twist round it to the other side.'

'I don't understand.'

'It's a result of the geometry of being in another dimension. Er… I'll give you a silly analogy. Suppose you're confronted with the leader of the opposition, standing blocking your path. You decide to walk round him, so as a result, your brain automatically activates your muscles to do that. It's the same for me in the wavy dimension, more or less.'

The PM laughed. 'I wish… but carry on.'

'Well… I get a weird pleasure, a thrill, from doing it.'

'What do you mean?'

'I find twisting round obstacles even more amazing than going into the wavy dimension in the first place. Irrational of me, but that's how I feel. And I might well be the only person in the world able to do it! How amazing is that? And then there's the scientist's perspective – I'm seeing with my own eyes the existence of other dimensions. Up to now, other dimensions have just been a concept.'

'Yes, that must be extraordinary for someone like you.'

'Not only that, but I can actually see the validation of string theory. It explains how everything is formed. It's a massive advance.'

'Do you think there'll be any economic spin-offs from string theory?'

‘It’s a mug’s game trying to predict what new inventions might come from basic scientific theories, and when they do come, they’re often quite unexpected. It can take decades, anyway. Sorry.’

‘Ok. Carry on.’

‘Well, if I can get a bit philosophical, the experience has renewed my awe. The way incredibly complex things and experiences emerge from simple fundamental laws and particles.’

‘Are you religious, may I ask?’

‘No, but I see where you’re coming from.’

‘You said you hate it, as well as loving it. Why the hate? Is it because of the possibility of being stuck there?’

‘There is that, but it’s incredibly stressful trying to make out what I’m seeing and hearing. And there are side effects. Nausea, headaches, migraines.’

‘Are MI5 checking your health regularly?’

‘Yes, they are.’

‘Good. Well, you’re doing the country a great service, as I said.’

‘Thanks, but I’m the one who should be saying thanks. I’m most grateful to you, Prime… Michael, for choosing me and persuading me to do this…’

‘Let’s not get into a gratitude competition!’

‘Sorry.’

‘Not at all. It’s been fascinating. As you said, your experience is probably unique, and hardly anyone else would have the chance to hear what you’ve been telling me.’

‘It’s been good to be able to talk to someone about it.’

‘Excellent. Before we wrap up, one further thing. I find your thinking refreshing and interesting, and your advice has been sensible and valuable. I mentioned it before, but would you consider becoming one of my special advisers?’

Redstone was taken aback. 'Er… I'm greatly flattered, and thanks for the offer but sorry, I'm not keen. I'm happy in London Bio.'

'I'm not asking you to take up a full-time position. I'm sure we could work out some arrangement which allowed you to carry on at London Bio and help me too. I need advice from people outside politics.'

Redstone wasn't tempted. His personal politics were quite close to those of the PM, he'd enjoyed policy work when a civil servant, and now he'd been enjoying developing ideas for the PM's speech. It was the sacking six years ago which had switched him back into science. But being free from the internal politics had been so refreshing that he was determined to escape back to London Bio as soon as he could.

'Sorry,' he said. 'It's not for me. I'm not temperamentally suited to the hothouse atmosphere that Number 10 advisers work in.'

'Pity. Well, I may still call on you for your thoughts if something relevant crops up.'

They talked further, and then the PM stood up. 'It's later than I'd realised,' he said, 'and I'm afraid I've got a lot more work to get through.'

Redstone said his goodbyes, left the house and walked to his car.

*

At home, emboldened and inspired by what Anne and Michael Jones had said, he phoned Christina, but the call went straight to voicemail. He hung up, feeling it inappropriate to leave a message.

He phoned each of the twins, telling them about his day. Like visiting a sewage treatment plant, he said – interesting but with unpleasant elements. Graham sympathised. Sophie accused him of deciding on the weak joke and then tailoring his view of the day to fit it. They both urged him to accept the PM's offer to become a special adviser, but failed to change his mind. And once again he was hit by a flood of sorrow and a sense of great unfairness – Kate would have so enjoyed the experience of accompanying him and would have loved discussing it afterwards.

MONDAY 21 NOVEMBER

Redstone walked through the busy underground area at Bristol Temple Meads station and climbed the stairs, thinking of the task ahead. Lewis was waiting for him in the car park, in a white van bearing the logo of Avon Water. 'I've got your survival kit in the back,' he said. 'I'll show you when we get to West Avon.' He gave Redstone a folder. 'I suggest you look at these maps while I drive us. I'll drop you at sheet number one, and you just need to follow the red line all the way to the chief engineer's office. When you've finished, retrace your steps, and I'll be waiting in the same place.'

Redstone studied the maps. 'This is excellent,' he said. 'I see that some of the landmarks are small signs that conveniently have numbers on them in the right sequence!'

'Yes, you'll see that the signs look old, but of course they aren't. A couple of my colleagues put them in place on Friday. Nobody took any notice of them – of my colleagues, I mean. Or of the signs, probably.'

They drove down urban motorways to the West Avon complex, passing through cuttings, past high-rise developments and alongside industrial parks. Lewis stopped in a large parking lot, amongst other vans and lorries. He pointed to a large rucksack, with a rolled sleeping bag strapped to the top, in the back of the van. 'This is your survival kit,' he said. 'There are instructions in this pocket, telling you how to use everything. There's a needle and a bottle of WD41 in that pocket. And these are your water containers.' He pointed to two large plastic jerry cans. 'Each contains twenty litres, which should be enough in this climate for a man of your size for a couple of weeks, though you'd be rather smelly by the end of it.'

Redstone found these preparations scary. They brought home the reality of the risk that he might get stuck.

'Ready when you are,' said Lewis. Redstone heaved the rucksack onto his back, picked up a can of water in each hand and twisted into the wavy dimension, relieved to find that the pulse of pressure in his head seemed no greater than before. He dumped the kit and the water on the ground behind the van, looked around and managed to make out a small sign, fixed to a post, bearing the number 1. He opened his sheaf of maps and followed the marked route. At sign 9 he had to twist round the security gate. By sign 20 he was at the entrance to the France Nucléaire office block, and six landmarks later he was outside Dupont's office, feeling exhausted and ill.

He twisted round the door, enduring another pressure surge in his skull, and entered the office. Dupont was sitting at a desk, working on a PC. Above him on the wall were two large screens, each displaying data in the same format as Redstone had seen in the control room three weeks earlier. The left-hand screen showed occasional changes in the numbers, just as Redstone remembered seeing in the control room. The right-hand screen looked similar, but every minute there was a change in all the numbers. He noticed that each time there was a change, a two-letter code at the top of the screen also changed. As with the left-hand screen, nearly all the numbers were green, indicating that there were no problems. Occasionally some numbers changed to amber, and then back to green after a few seconds.

Redstone took photos of the screens. Looking around the office, he saw a bank of computer units in a rack the size of a small filing cabinet, but nothing else noteworthy. He wondered what to do next. Was there any point in staying further? He was longing to get out of the wavy dimension.

Dupont went to the door, turned the key in the lock and pulled a bolt across. He returned to his computer and typed for a few seconds. The displays on the screens changed. Both screens now had many more numbers in amber and some in red. Redstone waited for the colours to go back to green, but they didn't. What the hell was going on? What did these screens show? He took more photos. Dupont scrutinised the screens and made some notes on an A4 pad. Redstone took a photo of the notes. Dupont hung his head in his hands and then typed a few words on his keyboard, whereupon the screens changed back to their original displays. He went to the door and unlocked it.

Redstone thought he had all the useful information he was likely to get, since the office was now open to anyone walking in. He was keen to get the photos to Alan Cunningham, who he was sure could explain what they meant. He laboriously made his way back to Lewis's van.

'Well, how did you get on?'

'The map and landmarks worked very well,' said Redstone. 'I took photos, and I'm now going to send them to Alan Cunningham. I'm exhausted. Can I travel with you back to London?'

*

Four hours later, refreshed from sleeping on the journey back, Redstone was shown into Cunningham's office.

'Well, what do you make of the pictures?'

'I won't ask you how you got them,' said Cunningham with a smile, 'but they're fascinating. Shall I take you through them?'

'Yes, please. First, I assume that the left-hand screen in the first batch of photos just duplicates the main display in the control room. Is that right?'

'Yes. I checked the numbers, and they're completely in line with what I would have expected.'

'What about the right-hand screen?'

'The same, but for all the other power stations in the UK operated by France Nucléaire. Each time the screen changed, it showed a different power station. The two-letter code at the top shows which station it is. Again, I checked, and the figures are just what we'd expect to see for each of the reactors. Nothing surprising for a display in the office of the chief engineer.'

'But what about the second batch of displays, the ones with all the red figures?'

'That's more difficult,' confessed Cunningham. 'You told me on the phone that Dupont locked the door before displaying them, and I sort of understand why he'd do that. They show unduly high pressures and temperatures, excessive neutron fluxes and strange configurations of the control rods. If they were real, the company would be facing serious difficulties. But of course, we know they can't be real because the first screens were what the real control rooms display.'

'So what do you think they are?'

'My guess is that Dupont has a program that simulates the new wave of reactors.'

'Then why have they got the same codes as the current reactors?'

'Each new reactor is being built adjacent to an existing reactor. It's normal practice because it makes getting planning permission much easier, and it uses the existing infrastructure – the transmission lines and so on.'

'Ok. Carry on.'

'I imagine he's fed into his simulation program the details of each new reactor, and for some reason I can't understand, they don't operate within the expected tolerances. In a nutshell, they're unsafe. They haven't been completed yet, of course, so the only real problem immediately ahead is the new reactor at Dymbury.'

He turned the printed pictures over until he came to the two displays headed '*DM*', one without the red numbers and one with.

'Compare these two. It's very strange. The model of the new reactor shows great similarities to the real performance of the existing one, except for these figures here.' He pointed. 'It seems there's something odd with the simulated fuel arrays. They're getting too hot, and probably the materials are receiving too much radiation from damaging neutrons. If this were a real reactor, we'd shut it down immediately.'

'It all fits!' exclaimed Redstone. 'We thought it was a fuel problem and to do with computer modelling. And a serious problem concerning the new wave of reactors!' His face fell. 'But it doesn't fit with all our information. It doesn't explain why we found identical sheets of data from different reactors. Shit!'

'You're right,' said Cunningham sadly.

'What about the note Dupont wrote?'

'That's just a summary of the problematic issues, basically saying what I outlined a moment ago. It doesn't add anything.'

Redstone stood up and paced around the office. 'We'll have to ask Dupont. We'll have to put enough pressure on him that he tells all. I'll go to MI5 and tell them what you said and get them to arrange for Monsieur Dupont to be arrested. I'll ask them to bring him to London for interrogation. We'll need you to sit in, or at least observe, so that you can guide the questioning. Do you have any problems with that?'

'Not at all,' said Cunningham. 'I'm very keen to find out the truth, both personally and professionally.' He paused. 'The police have powers to arrest him under the Nuclear Security Act if there's a reasonable suspicion that nuclear safety might be compromised, and I'm willing to testify that I have that suspicion.'

'Excellent. I'll phone to tell them I'm coming.'

Cunningham donned his impassive face.

'Oh God, I can see one of your jokes coming,' said Redstone.

'Nonsense. But before you go, did I tell you that I come from a long line of engineers? In fact my grandfather invented the cold air balloon.' He paused. 'But it never really took off.'

Redstone groaned and grinned. He shook Cunningham's hand and left.

Half an hour later, he was sitting opposite Gavin McKay in the big corner office in Thames House. The windows were at the level of the trees on the other side of Millbank, but the leaves had dropped, allowing a clear view of the Thames. A tug was pulling a line of three large barges downstream.

Redstone told McKay about the meeting with Cunningham.

'The way ahead seems pretty straightforward,' said McKay. 'As you suggested, we'll get Dupont arrested and brought to London. We'll keep him in a police cell overnight, which will soften him up, and then bring him here to an interrogation room.' He leaned back. 'We also need to arrest Lesage. We can use the same charge. He'll be a harder nut to crack, so we'll leave him to stew while we question Dupont.'

'What about the fact that Lesage tried twice to have me murdered?'

'Unfortunately, I don't see how we can use that. On the second occasion, the thug – Marcel, wasn't it? – was prevented by my men from getting to you, and on the first occasion, it would be just Marcel's word against yours. And we don't want any hint of the dimension-hopping to get out. But don't worry – the crime of conspiring to compromise nuclear safety carries very severe penalties.'

'Changing the subject, do you know if there's any news of Kemp?'

'No, the police haven't yet found him. But I'm sure it's just a matter of time.'

Redstone went down to the basement for his Monday check-up and brought Clothier up to speed on the investigation.

'I'm so pleased it's working out well,' Clothier said. 'I'm quite proud. And your health indicators are fine. Any problems?'

'Well, I've had a bad migraine. As it happens, I can feel another one coming on now. But I used to suffer from them quite a lot when I was younger, so you shouldn't read anything into it. It's probably just the stress of everything that's been going on. Anyway, I've got medication which sorts it out. Eventually.'

'Hmm. Let me know if you get more. We might need to do a scan to check everything's ok.'

*

Back home, Redstone tried to phone Christina again, but once more, it went straight through to voicemail. He hung up.

'I wonder if she's choosing not to pick up, Treacle,' he said. He wouldn't blame her. He redialled, and this time left a message saying that he very much wanted to talk to her and asking her to phone him.

TUESDAY 22 NOVEMBER

Redstone and Cunningham sat in a small observation room on the fourth floor of Thames House, looking at a large wall-mounted TV screen which was showing an empty room elsewhere in the building. Lewis sat behind them.

Redstone straightened a microphone on the table in front of him and took a sip of coffee. The door behind him opened, and Smith entered, her arm in a sling.

'Laura!' Redstone embraced her, being careful to avoid her arm. 'Lovely to see you! You look surprisingly well, I must say.'

'I feel fine, apart from the nuisance of having my arm in a sling. I hear you've managed rather well without me!'

'Lewis's been a great help. As have your other colleagues.'

'People are going into the interrogation room,' said Cunningham. 'What happened to you, Laura?'

'Oh, a little accident on an operation. Nothing to do with the nuclear issue.' She sat down next to Redstone.

'Well, the good news is that the police arrested Dupont,' she said, 'and you're about to see him being interviewed. But the bad news is that Lesage has disappeared. He must have realised the game was up. We're working with the French authorities to try to trace him, but no luck so far.'

'Oh,' said Redstone, feeling flat. 'I wonder how far we're going to get without Lesage. Let's see.' The screen now showed Dupont seated opposite a chubby grey-haired man across a plain table. A smartly dressed woman, who Redstone guessed was a solicitor, was seated next to Dupont. Background sounds of the interrogation room came from the TV's speakers.

The chubby man announced the names of those present, and then spoke to Dupont.

‘As you know, you’re potentially in a lot of trouble. The penalties under the Nuclear Security Act are severe. But we know that the leader of your plot was Lesage. If you can help us understand the details of the plot, we can swiftly sort out its consequences. You know we will work it all out, so you might as well save everyone time by helping us now. Please start at the beginning. When did Lesage ask you to get involved?’

Dupont said nothing. His solicitor announced that Dupont had decided not to answer any questions.

‘Bugger!’ exclaimed Redstone.

‘If you’re afraid of reprisals by Lesage, you needn’t worry,’ said the interrogator. ‘He’s on the run, and his days of power within France Nucléaire are over.’ Dupont shifted uneasily but remained silent.

‘If you persist in being unhelpful,’ said the interrogator, ‘that fact will be taken into account by the court.’ Dupont remained silent.

‘I’ll leave you to discuss this with your solicitor,’ said the interrogator and left the room. The screen went blank.

A couple of minutes later, McKay walked into the observation room. ‘I’ve been watching in my office,’ he said. ‘I must admit I’m surprised. I’d thought Dupont would welcome an excuse to get everything off his chest.’

‘Me too,’ said Redstone. ‘My guess is he’s terrified of reprisals. He knows what Lesage has tried in the past.’

‘Yes,’ said McKay. ‘Any ideas on how to proceed?’

‘I wonder if I could speak to Dupont off the record?’ asked Cunningham. ‘I know him a bit, and I could speak to him informally, as one engineer to another. I could appeal to his conscience.’

‘I doubt it’d work unless he could see we know what the problem is. And we don’t, do we?’

‘No,’ said Cunningham glumly.

Redstone slumped in his chair. He'd put his life in danger to try to figure this out, but they'd still not solved it. He hated giving up, but what else could they do?

Laura sighed. 'I tell you what, let's all take a break, have a think and reconvene in a couple of hours, see if anyone's come up with anything. Worth trying?'

'Why not,' said Redstone. 'I'll go for a walk and turn it over in my mind. Sometimes that helps me solve problems. But don't hold your breath.'

He left Thames House and walked over Lambeth Bridge. The weather was heavily overcast, and windows in buildings on both sides of the Thames shone from the thousands of lights inside. The gloom matched his mood, which worsened as he suddenly thought of Christina. He should have resisted when she'd said they should part company. What a fool he'd been.

He looked over his left shoulder at the splendid view of the Palace of Westminster, its lights reflected in the dark, calm water of the river. It was so important to maintain electricity supplies throughout the winter. He thought back about the computer screen figures, stopped, fumbled for his phone and called Cunningham.

'Hi, Alan. As a matter of interest, would the fictional reactors in Dupont's computer simulations be producing electricity, despite all the red numbers?'

'Yes,' said Cunningham. 'The main problems would come when the fuel became exhausted, and so the reactors needed refuelling. The conditions indicated by the red numbers would probably have distorted the fuel assemblies and cause everything to jam. That would make refuelling incredibly expensive and time-consuming. If it wasn't a simulation, of course.'

'But it must be, mustn't it?'

'No!' Cunningham shouted. 'That's it!'

'What do you mean?'

‘One set of figures is a simulation, and the other isn’t – right?’ said Cunningham excitedly.

‘Yes.’

‘Which is which?’

Redstone paused. ‘Ah! I see!’ he cried. ‘I’m coming back now. Could you please tell Laura? And I’d like to compare ideas with you first.’

An hour later, Redstone and Cunningham joined McKay, Lewis and Smith in McKay’s office.

‘Go ahead, Alan,’ said Redstone.

‘This is what Mark and I think has been happening,’ said Cunningham. ‘Some time ago, Lesage realises that France Nucléaire could make a lot more money if they could increase their output of electricity in the UK by a few per cent. And that would mean huge bonuses for him.’

‘In spades,’ said Smith. ‘He got about five million euros extra a year.’

‘Bloody hell,’ said Lewis.

Cunningham continued, ‘So Lesage asks his then chief engineer what will happen if they increase the quantity of fuel in each of the UK reactors. The engineer does the calculations and confirms that the fuel assemblies can be reconfigured as Lesage has asked, and more electricity would be produced, but it would be risky. Damage to the components from the increased radiation and the higher temperature could lead to distortions of the fuel assemblies. If that happened, the control rods might jam and so might the fuel assemblies.’

‘But we know that the reactors are fine, so the risk was worth taking. Don’t we?’ said Lewis.

‘Don’t spoil my story,’ said Cunningham with a smile. ‘So, if it went wrong, refuelling the reactors would become extremely difficult. If everything seized up, it would take years to remove the jammed components and restart the reactors. Working with components emitting high-level radioactivity is incredibly demanding and time-consuming.'

'How often are the reactors refuelled?' asked McKay.

'The French designed their system so that the fuel lasts for three years before a new batch has to be loaded. That's considerably longer than other models of nuclear reactor. It helps their profits a lot, because a reactor isn't earning money while it's being refuelled. Their normal refuelling process takes a couple of weeks. That's remarkably quick, but even so, during that time the plant can't generate electricity, of course. Usually, companies aim to refuel in the summer when there isn't so much demand for electricity. But the timing got out of kilter when France Nucléaire put in the new fuel assemblies.'

'Would there be a risk of an explosion?' asked Smith.

'No,' said Cunningham. 'The operators would have noticed things going wrong long before that, from the displays in the control room, and done something about it. If it wasn't for that, the difficulties would become apparent only when it was time to refuel.'

'Carry on!' said McKay. 'I think I can see where this is heading!'

'We guess that Lesage decides to go ahead anyway. To take the risk. In all the UK reactors. At first, everything goes well, more electricity is produced, and the money comes pouring in. But then the chief engineer sees indications that trouble is brewing, and tells Lesage that the new fuel configuration must be abandoned. Lesage refuses so the chief engineer resigns. And his deputy goes on extended sick leave.'

'Wouldn't your inspectors have noticed the indications of trouble?'

'They would, though probably not as quickly as the in-house engineers. But if I'm right, Lesage foresaw that problem and did two things. First, he arranged with Valerie Hitchcock that we no longer had access to the sites. And second, he got Dupont to fiddle the figures we were sent.'

'But I thought that the figures you saw were the same as the figures the operators at the power stations were seeing every day!' said Smith.

'They were,' confirmed Cunningham. 'Those figures were fiddled too. You need to understand that the displays in the control rooms around the country aren't the actual outputs of the various sensors in the reactors. The sensors produce electrical impulses which have to be converted by a computer into numbers for humans to read. France Nucléaire is a very centralised company, like so many French institutions. All the data from around the UK are transmitted to West Avon, where they're processed. By computers in Dupont's office, as it happens. Those computers then send the information back to the sites, in the form that the company has decided is most useful for the local operators.'

'Ah! Now *I* can see where this is going!' exclaimed Smith.

'Yes. Lesage forced Dupont to write a program to modify the actual data so that what was displayed was within normal tolerances instead of the truth. The real, worrying readings were hidden. That's why Dupont had two sets of data – the true ones, which he kept secret, and the false ones, which he sent out.'

'Wouldn't the operators at a site smell a rat if they adjusted something but the reactor didn't seem to respond?' asked McKay.

'I'm sure the program was sophisticated enough to make it look as though the reactor did respond.'

'Tell them about the random number generator,' said Redstone.

'Ah, that's what gave us a valuable clue. Dupont realised that his program had to produce variations in the synthetic numbers it displayed, such that they sometimes went a little out of the correct range before returning. Otherwise, the operators would have become suspicious because such variations happen in real life. So he used a simple random number generator in his computer program, to produce the variations in the fake data.'

Redstone took over, 'But producing truly random numbers is surprisingly difficult. The simple program he used produced numbers which looked as though they were random, but in fact, they repeated every now and then. We spotted those repeats!'

'He means *he* spotted them,' said Cunningham.

'Well… I suppose so,' said Redstone. Cunningham looked at him quizzically.

'When's the first refuelling due?' asked McKay.

'In a month's time. That's the West Avon plant, as it happens. Then a series of other plants are due to be refuelled, one after another.'

'So, if your scenario is correct,' said McKay, 'we're due to start losing power stations at the start of the winter and then continue losing them, month by month, for a long time. And their power wouldn't be restored for years. And by the end of the process, the UK would have lost most of its electricity supply?'

'That's right,' said Cunningham. 'We might be able to produce a bit more electricity from gas-fired power stations if we could import more gas to fuel them, but that would be nowhere near enough to make up the difference. Nowhere near.'

'It would be a total disaster for the country,' said Redstone. 'Much worse than we originally feared, when we thought it was just the new reactors which were under threat. No modern economy can operate with most of its electricity gone. Businesses would close. Transport would be disrupted. People would die in droves in their freezing, dark homes. No wonder Lesage moved his family back to France. And no wonder he was desperate to get the problem resolved.'

'Let me get this clear,' said McKay. 'Most of what you've said is speculation, isn't it? Certainly, it fits all the facts, but couldn't there be some other explanation for what we know?'

'Maybe,' said Cunningham, 'but we can't think of one. Can you?'

'No,' said McKay. 'Do you think Dupont would admit it's true? If we put it to him?'

'I do,' said Cunningham, 'especially since I can tell him how to solve the problem, assuming it's not too far gone. But that's a big assumption. I'm desperately worried that it might have gone too far by now – that the jamming can't be undone. It might be too late, and if it is…'

'The country's in the shit,' said Redstone. 'Dupont seems a decent man at heart, and I think that as a professional engineer he'd leap at the chance to help us sort it out. We need to ask him, urgently.'

McKay looked sceptical. 'Look, let's try,' said Redstone. 'Let's see if Dupont will confirm we've got it right. If he does, let's make him an offer – he works with us to unjam the fuel assemblies using Alan's technique, if it's not too late.'

'Are you saying you want me to release Dupont if he plays ball?'

'Yes. Only temporarily. We know he'll have to face charges. But we'd hope that his co-operation would be taken into consideration by the court.'

'We'll have to ensure he doesn't do a bunk,' said McKay. 'And protect him against any remaining threat from Lesage. But yes, I agree.'

'Good,' said Cunningham. 'I'd now like to talk to Dupont in a normal room, alone, with no surveillance.'

'Ok,' said McKay. 'Lewis – would you please arrange that? Let's meet back here when your chat with Dupont is finished. Meanwhile, anyone fancy one of these sandwiches? If you've got any appetite after what we've heard.'

*

Two hours later, they reassembled in McKay's office.

'It worked like a dream,' said Cunningham. 'Initially he wouldn't talk, but when I outlined our deductions it was as though a dam had broken. He was obviously hugely relieved. I think he felt that he'd stuck to the bargain he'd made with Lesage, keeping his mouth shut, but since we'd got to the heart of it anyway, he was now free to talk. He confirmed everything we'd worked out, and he's eager to help. If you'll now release him, I'll go back to my office and email him a list of the equipment we need and some tests we need him to do to find out whether we do still have a chance. It'll all take a few days. We'll start with West Avon since it's the most urgent.'

'You seem pretty confident your cure will work if there is still time,' said McKay.

'It's one of the tricks we devised ages ago when scenario-planning for this type of problem. We've only tested it on dummy systems, but yes, I am confident. But first, I need Dupont's team to analyse the resonant frequencies of the fuel rod assemblies. If they work out as I hope, we should be able to fix it.'

'I haven't a clue what any of that means,' said Smith.

'I think he means tapping the tops with a hammer and listening to the sounds they make,' said Redstone.

'We'll make an engineer of you yet,' said Cunningham.

'I'll tell the PM,' said McKay, 'and ensure the Civil Contingencies Unit swings into action. There'll be a huge amount to do to prepare for the worst.'

Arrangements were finalised, and Cunningham left.

'Before I go too,' said Redstone, 'any news about Kemp?'

'No, he's still missing,' said McKay. 'So is his car. We think it must be in Central London somewhere, because the police picked it up on a number of cameras, and there's been no sign of it leaving London.'

'Might he have changed the number plates?'

'Yes, but the police checked all cars of his model and colour, and they all had the right number plates. He's probably driven it into a lock-up under a railway arch somewhere. He's likely holed up in some seedy flat. It may take some time to get him. Normally, it's an informant who tells us the whereabouts of criminals like him.'

'How annoying,' said Redstone.

'I feel more than annoyed,' said Smith. 'I nearly got him.'

'And he nearly got you,' said Lewis.

WEDNESDAY 23 NOVEMBER

Redstone sat eating breakfast. Although he felt relieved that the nuclear puzzle was solved, his mind was full of fears about what the loss of the power stations would mean for the country. Alan had been seriously concerned that it was too late to fix the problem. Was he showing an engineer's caution, or an engineer's judgment?

Smith phoned. 'There's been a development on the Kemp front. We think you might like to hear about it. Are you able to meet in Gavin McKay's office at 10 o'clock?'

'Yes, of course,' Redstone said. 'Have you found him?'

'It's complicated. We'll explain when you get here.'

*

An hour later, Redstone was escorted up to McKay's impressive office. McKay was working at his desk while Smith was looking out of the window at the river. She turned and smiled as Redstone entered, and McKay rose to greet him.

'Before we start on the Kemp story,' said McKay, 'some news on the nuclear power issue.'

'Is it about the prospects for unjamming the fuel?'

'No, not yet, I'm afraid. We're all on tenterhooks, but we just have to wait while the testing is done. Alan Cunningham has been given all the extra resources he wants, and the PM's chaired an emergency Cabinet meeting to get preparations going in case the worst… anyway, I'm sure Alan will tell you the test findings as soon as he can. Still all top secret, of course.'

'You said you had other news.'

'Yes. Our French opposite numbers have investigated Lesage's relationship with Hitchcock. He'd been making her promises about her future – a big job with a big salary in France

Nucléaire. She's been arrested and will be charged with breaches of the Official Secrets Act.'

'Basically, she's a traitor,' said Smith. 'And a blackmailer and a fraudster.'

McKay continued, 'And we now have firm evidence that Malvern gave Hitchcock the confidential material she passed onto Lesage. So Malvern has been sacked. It was decided that it wouldn't be in the public interest to prosecute him.'

'Any news on who will be replacing Dominic Malvern?' asked Redstone.

'Yes – it'll be Sir Roger Feast. I guess you know him.'

'I do indeed. Very impressive man. Excellent news.'

'Now to Kemp. The police have found his car.'

'Where?'

'In the underground car park in the block where he has his showroom, here in Westminster. They searched the building, which contains a couple of other shops and some flats above them, but there was no trace of him. They then examined the car park and found a door leading to a tunnel.'

'Why on earth would there be a tunnel under a block of flats and shops?'

'It's a matter of history. The block's about twenty years old and was built on the site of a pre-war government office. You may not know it, but there's a vast network of tunnels in the Whitehall area.'

'Why?'

'They were built in the war so that people could move around during air raids. And people worked and slept in them. Bunkers, I suppose you'd call them. And they were expanded afterwards, during the Cold War, when there was a real fear of a nuclear attack on London.'

'I suppose Churchill's war rooms are part of the network,' said Redstone. 'I often passed them when I was walking to and from our horrible office in Downing Street.'

'That's right. About the war rooms, I mean, not the quality of your Downing Street office!' McKay looked wryly at his own office and smiled. 'Rather embarrassingly, the entrance Kemp used had been forgotten by all of us. Otherwise, it would have been sealed off.'

'Are all the other entrances sealed off?'

'No, but they're in secure government buildings.'

'Ok. Carry on.'

'So, the police went into the tunnel and found clothes, food and other stuff not far from the entrance. And traces which suggest Kemp kept his money and drugs there.'

'Ah,' said Redstone. 'But what about Kemp himself?'

'That's the thing. It's like a deserted town down there. He could be anywhere.'

'I don't know you very well, Gavin, but from the look on your face, I suspect you're going to tell me of some ingenious plan to find him. And it's going to need someone who can go into the wavy dimension.'

'It would be outside my powers to appoint you to help arrest Kemp. You don't have the legal authority. But… you might like to know how we plan to get him, given your strong personal interest. And your good relationship with Jim Clothier.'

'Very thoughtful. So what's the plan?'

'The difficulty is it would take hundreds of police officers to search the tunnels to find Kemp. What's more, he's armed. It would be a nightmare having to search for a man with a gun, willing to kill, in a maze full of hiding places.'

Smith nodded.

'You have a solution?' asked Redstone.

‘Nobody else uses the tunnel complex, so all human traces come from Kemp. We’re going to use a machine normally employed for hunting terrorists hiding in caves and the like. As we speak, Jim Clothier and his colleagues are setting it up. It’s a remotely controlled device which detects gases and sounds emitted by people. Like a dog does.’

‘Why not use a dog?’

‘He’d shoot any dog that came near him. But the main reason is dogs can’t report back – their handler must be with them, which would be dangerous. Our machine’s fully armoured, and above all, it can signal back.’

‘Ingenious.’

‘It has proved extremely useful in recent… well, never mind. Once Kemp’s been located, our plan is that armed police will move in. Unfortunately, it’ll still be very risky for them. I’m extremely worried about casualties, but… well, he’s got to be caught. Anyway, Jim’s keen to show you his contraption. If you’re ok with that, Laura will take you down to his den.’

‘Before that, tell me again why MI5 is so involved in getting Kemp, rather than leaving it to the police?’

‘You know that we have a remit to work with the police to fight organised crime. Kemp’s a criminal organiser par excellence.’

Redstone reflected that Laura had told him MI5 wanted to protect him from Kemp because his ability to go into the wavy dimension made him a valuable asset. He wondered whether this was still true, given that the nuclear puzzle was now solved. Maybe they wanted to use him on other operations in the future. They’d be lucky – except for this operation, where he’d do what McKay was clearly hinting at but unable to say officially. Get Kemp.

Downstairs, Clothier greeted Redstone warmly. He led the way to a room near the back of the long workspace which Redstone had visited before.

'Meet our machine!' he said. 'I call her TT, short for Terrorist Tracker. She's not clothed at the moment because I've been adjusting her innards.' He gestured to a device the size of a large washing machine on its side. Pipes, wires, circuit boards and small metal boxes were crammed together behind a large battery. The whole device stood on two caterpillar treads, like a very small tank or bulldozer.

'We now have to replace her armour plating.'

'What does she do?'

'She has vision in the visible and infra-red regions, so she can see objects and pick out warm things – in particular, people. She has radar. She has gas chromatography, so she can, in effect, smell. And she also has sensitive directional microphones.'

'Impressive,' said Redstone.

'Furthermore, she's got great software. I've loaded a map of the tunnel system, as far as we know it. But we're fairly sure that there are gaps in our knowledge, so she'll improve the map as she goes. In other words, she can learn.'

He handed Redstone a large tablet. 'All the data are synthesised and then displayed on this screen. You'll see a green arrow and a red patch superimposed on the map. The green arrow shows TT's position, and the patch shows where TT thinks there's a human. It can only be Kemp in this case, since there should be nobody else in the tunnels. It'll be shaded according to the probability that he's in that location: deep red for most probable, shading to light red for just possible. When TT's certain, there'll be a red flashing arrow.'

'Why the caterpillar treads?'

'To climb steps,' said Clothier. 'There are some stairs in the tunnels.' He turned to Smith. 'Let's have a demonstration. Laura, will you be the target?'

'Ok. I'll hide somewhere on this floor,' said Smith. 'Go into Jim's office while I disappear. Don't cheat.'

Redstone and Clothier went into Clothier's office, waited a few minutes and returned to TT. Clothier touched the tablet screen a few times. 'I'm telling it to ignore you and me,' he said.

TT turned and rolled back down the open corridor. Clothier handed Redstone the tablet. It showed a plan of the basement floor, with a red patch near the instrument where Redstone had been irradiated. TT continued to roll towards the irradiation equipment's bay, and the red patch shrank and deepened in colour. TT turned into the bay, and the red patch changed to a flashing red arrow pointing at the irradiation machine itself. Clothier and Redstone walked into the bay and found Smith lying inside the huge magnet.

'I thought the magnetic field might confuse TT, but clearly it didn't,' she said.

Clothier smiled. 'Your experiment might have been better if the magnet had been switched on, but anyway, TT would still have found you!'

Smith got up awkwardly, her arm still in the sling, and shrugged. 'Not exactly the sort of problem I encountered in Afghanistan,' she said. 'Well done!'

'I echo that,' said Redstone. 'A remarkable piece of kit.'

'We're going to take it to the basement of the Ministry of Defence when it's ready, in preparation for the police operation. There's an entrance to the tunnel system there, and of course, there are no security problems. Er… we hope you'll come along to see it there, on Friday.'

'Yes, I'd very much like to. But let's be clear – you're telling me all this because… you like me?'

'Of course. What other, er... legitimate reason could there be?'

*

Redstone sat in his armchair, worrying about the plans to get Kemp. MI5 were dumping a great responsibility on his shoulders, and furthermore he was scared of Kemp and his gun, and hated the prospect of entering the wavy dimension again. Treacle jumped onto his lap, and he stroked her. He was being offered the opportunity he'd wanted, but now, faced with the reality...

His phone rang. He glanced at the caller ID. 'Oh my God, it's Christina!' he said. 'Wish me luck, Treacle.' The cat jumped down.

'Hello, Christina! Thank you, thank you for phoning back. I assume you got my message? Are you ok?'

'Fine, thanks. Yes, I did get your message. How are you?'

'I'm ok. Christina, I... I need to talk to you. I want to apologise.'

'What for?'

'I know this sounds stupid, but I owe you an apology for agreeing with you when you said we ought to end it. I've missed you dreadfully. I made a huge mistake – I shouldn't have gone along with ... I want... I really hope we can get back together. I've got an idea for how we could maintain our relationship. I honestly believe it could work out. Are you—'

She interrupted him. 'Mark, it can't work. I wish it could, but it can't. I'm so, so sorry. Anyway, I've... I've now started a new relationship.'

Redstone felt as though he had been slapped in the face. 'Oh,' he said. He swallowed. 'That's a real shock. I... I wish you well.' He stopped, lost for words. He took a deep breath. 'I suppose I was living in a dream world...'

'Oh, Mark, no. I feel awful about hurting you. I wish... it's just... the problem isn't only our different lives, there's also... oh,

I just can't talk about it. I'm so sorry that I messed you about. I've been awful. You deserve better. If only… but things are what they are.' She started to cry.

'Don't cry, Christina. I'm sure you'll be happy with your new partner. I… oh…' And then he choked up. 'Goodbye, then.'

'Goodbye, my darling,' she said and hung up.

He sat there, stunned. It hadn't occurred to him that she might get involved with another man. But as he mulled over the conversation, he started to wonder whether her new relationship was serious. Or even existed. He sensed that she loved him. Or was he thinking like a stalker? How could he resolve this? Perhaps he shouldn't give up, at least not yet. It was worth another try – he yearned to be with her. The obstacles could be overcome. Or was that just wishful thinking? Yes, it was – he was being ridiculous, putting more weight on his desires and dreams than on the unpleasant truth. He was a scientist – he had to face facts, however unwelcome.

He drank a stiff whisky and went to bed.

THURSDAY 24 NOVEMBER

Redstone walked into Joanne's office at London Bio to find her, David, Colin and Anne Jones sitting and talking animatedly.

'What's going on?' he asked. Joanne looked at him searchingly.

'Shall I start off?' asked Colin. 'The first thing is we have patent cover for the skin cancer cream.'

'That's great news,' he said, mustering as much enthusiasm as he could.

'And also I've got a possible financing package,' said Anne, 'but…'

'That "but" sounds ominous.'

'I could get only one offer which doesn't involve your company being taken over. It's conditional on you personally taking a big financial stake in the development of the cream. In other words, you have to invest a lot of money yourself. Specifically, virtually all the money you've made so far.'

'Why?'

'The people making the offer want to see firm evidence that you personally, as the head of the company, believe in the product. And are fully committed to making it a success.'

'Colin and I tried to get them to accept contributions from the rest of us, but they weren't interested,' said David.

'Yes,' said Colin. 'I thought this stipulation was unusual, but apparently, it isn't.'

'I'm afraid that's right,' said Anne. 'Alternatively, you could sell the development rights. Of course, you'd get less than if London Bio itself succeeded in developing the cream.'

'I feel that selling the rights would be a betrayal of Saira's work,' said Redstone.

‘I agree,’ said David. ‘Ideally, we should keep it in-house. But…’ Colin and Joanne nodded.

‘Ok, so it’s back to whether you want to invest what you’ve made so far, Mark,’ said Anne. ‘You should take time to think about it, but what’s your first reaction?’

Redstone felt weighed down. ‘I’ll have to discuss it with my children, but I say easy come, easy go. I’m sure they’ll back me. So let’s look at the details, on the basis that we’ll probably go ahead. It’s not as if the money has brought me loads of happiness.’

The others looked embarrassed. ‘Don’t make a hasty decision,’ said Joanne. ‘The alternative would be for all of us to remain wealthy but work for another company, the one that would take us over. Or retire. It wouldn’t exactly be a terrible outcome!’

‘I know, but I don’t want to see London Bio disappear into a giant multinational. It means a lot to me. It’s a sort of anchor in my life.’

‘I know. Go through the papers with Anne. But don’t rush to a conclusion. You might feel differently when… when whatever you’re thinking about now has passed.’

*

Back home, Redstone phoned the twins. Sophie agreed he should invest his wealth in the skin cancer project, enthusing about the possibilities of helping reduce suffering. Graham also agreed, saying it was just the sort of thing a serial entrepreneur would do. Redstone knew that Kate would have been proud of them both.

He then phoned Cunningham.

‘Any news on the tests?’

‘It’s looking promising, thank God, but we’re not out of the woods yet,’ said Cunningham. ‘Still a few more tests to do before I’ll be confident that my solution will work. I’ll keep you informed.’

*

Lesage descended the steps from the plane, shielding his eyes against the fierce glare of the sun. He joined the straggly line of passengers making their way slowly across the baking tarmac to the small terminal. He removed his cream linen jacket and slung it over his shoulder, looking forward to getting into the chauffeured air-conditioned Mercedes awaiting him once he was through immigration.

He entered the terminal building. A uniformed man said, 'Señor Lesage?' He instinctively looked over but then said, 'Sorry – you've made a mistake.' He felt someone grasp his arm and looked round to see another uniformed man behind him. Lesage confidently took his jacket off his shoulder and reached into its inside pocket.

'Don't bother to produce your false documents,' said a third man, barely visible at the side, in a Manchester accent. 'You'll need them for toilet paper in the holding cell. While you're waiting to be extradited.'

FRIDAY 25 NOVEMBER

Redstone, Smith and Clothier walked up Whitehall and turned into Horse Guards Avenue. On their right was the huge Ministry of Defence Main Building, a stone neoclassical structure which Redstone thought would look appropriate in Russia. 'My colleagues brought TT here last night,' said Clothier.

They entered the building. An escort took them along lengthy corridors, passing men with short hair, smart suits, and straight backs – a contrast with the way people looked in 10 Downing Street. They descended into a huge basement, with a low ceiling and large insulated pipes stretching from one end to the other. There was a loud hum.

'This is the entrance to the tunnels,' said the escort. He unlocked an inconspicuous metal door behind an array of pipes.

They descended two flights of bare concrete steps, leaving the escort at the top. 'And here's TT,' said Clothier. 'I'm pleased she was able to come down the steps. She weighs about 200 kilos.'

The machine sat on its treads at the bottom of the staircase. Redstone thought that, with its armour, it looked even more like a large washing machine on its side, albeit somewhat menacing with its treads and grey paint. He noticed some grilles and some small lenses, but otherwise could see no openings.

'And here's the command module, or what normal people would call a tablet,' said Clothier. 'We swipe left or right to change between two displays. One is the map, which I showed you yesterday. The other contains the controls – start, steering, and so on. It's all labelled. We can even get TT to return here, automatically, by pressing here.' He showed Redstone the controls. 'Let's see if TT can sense any trace of Kemp.'

They studied the map screen. Some motors whirred softly inside TT. A faint red patch appeared, covering most of the bottom right quadrant.

'Excellent,' said Clothier. 'That's where he entered the tunnel system. Aren't you impressed?'

'Yes, I am. When will the police operation take place?'

'Probably tomorrow afternoon. It takes time to organise and brief so many armed officers for such a dangerous and difficult operation.' He switched off the machine and left the tablet on top of it. 'I can't over-emphasise the risk our colleagues would, I mean will, face.'

'Seen enough?' asked Smith.

'Yes,' said Redstone, looking into her eyes. 'And just to confirm – he'll get life, won't he?'

'He'll rot in gaol for the rest of his days.'

'And MI5 would welcome anything anyone could do to eliminate the danger to the police?'

'Certainly. Though I don't know what you could possibly have in mind.'

*

Back home, Redstone surveyed the equipment he had collected from around the house and loft. He packed it into a rucksack, a folding shopping trolley and a long holdall, and took everything out to his car. Back inside, he started up the stairs. 'Treacle, I'm going to have a rest,' he said. 'Coming up?'

*

At midnight, he exited the London Bio building and drove down to Westminster, passing the theatre district where the roads and pavements were still busy. He parked in a deserted side road off Millbank, put up the hood on his coat, donned the rucksack and picked up the holdall. Laden with this kit he pulled the shopping trolley, holding containers of drinking water, back through Parliament Square towards the Ministry of Defence. As he turned the corner into Horse Guards Avenue, he twisted into the wavy dimension, ignoring the pulse of pressure and the nausea. He entered the building and retraced the morning's route down to the tunnel entrance. He took the kit down the steps, edged past TT, and walked forward till he found a niche. He checked that the spare WD41 – which he had retrieved from the freezer at London Bio – was still safely tucked in a pocket of the rucksack, along with the other survival gear he had assembled, and then stowed the rucksack and the water in the niche, while keeping the holdall.

He left the wavy dimension with a sigh of relief, returned to TT, picked up the tablet and started the machine, which began trundling forward.

The spacious tunnel's walls were concrete, and its cross-section was rectangular. Fluorescent lights were attached to the ceiling every few metres. It felt more like a corridor than a tunnel.

Redstone followed the machine as it rolled forward. The displayed map did not change, except for slight movement of the green arrow which showed TT's position. Redstone saw that he was moving south. After a few minutes, the machine stopped at a junction where other tunnels went off to the left and the right. The red patch on the map, indicating Kemp's likely position, had moved and darkened. It was still at the south but had moved east.

TT carried on south. The tunnel was still of the concrete construction it had been at the Ministry of Defence, but the side tunnels, which had become much more frequent, were darker, smaller and mostly made of brick. Some had curved roofs. They seemed of varying ages.

After another few minutes, Redstone heard a loud rumble and realised that it was a tube train passing somewhere nearby. Shortly after that, the machine halted at another junction, and this time turned left into a brick-lined tunnel which looked very old and smelled damp. It was dimly illuminated by light from occasional vertical shafts in the roof. The red patch on the screen had narrowed dramatically, showing that TT had picked up some significant traces. The patch was deep red but not yet flashing. Redstone reckoned he must be under the Houses of Parliament – Kemp must have decided to hide there. According to the display – which, as Clothier had predicted, was adding detail to the map all the time – the tunnel system was a warren. He paused the machine and unzipped his holdall.

He started TT again and cautiously moved forward, several feet behind it. The tunnel branched, and TT turned right. After a few moments, TT turned into another tunnel and then yet another. Redstone lost his sense of direction. His mouth was dry. The dim, damp tunnel felt oppressive. The red patch on the map was now very small and deep in colour, and near the green arrow.

There was a loud bang, instantly followed by a whine. Redstone realised that Kemp had shot at TT, and the bullet had ricocheted off. He twisted into the wavy dimension. The map showed that Kemp was ahead and to the left. Redstone sidled past TT, and there was Kemp, in another gloomy tunnel, crouched down, pointing a pistol ahead and peering at TT. Of course Redstone was invisible to him.

Redstone edged behind Kemp, opened his holdall, removed a cricket bat and held it with both hands, ready to strike.

He twisted back into the normal dimension. Kemp must have heard something because he spun round. Redstone whacked him on the side of the head, the bat jarring his wrists. Kemp collapsed on the dusty stone floor, dropping his gun. He immediately scrabbled for it, blood seeping from his head. Redstone hit him on the upper arm with all his strength, using the edge of the bat. A bone cracked. Kemp shouted incoherently and moved his other hand towards the gun. Redstone whirled the bat into that arm. Kemp collapsed and lay there, groaning.

Dropping the bat, Redstone heaved Kemp over his shoulder, twisted into the wavy dimension and dropped him on the stone floor. Kemp cried out, looked around wildly, whimpered and vomited.

'The world will be a better place without you, you murderous, parasitic shit,' said Redstone, breathing heavily. He twisted back, retrieved the bat and the tablet and pressed the control which made TT return to the Ministry of Defence. As he followed the machine he made chalk marks on the wall at each junction.

In his car, Redstone leaned back against the seat. He wiped away the tears filling his eyes. A huge and painful journey had come to an end. He sat there, his mind churning. Eventually he pulled himself together and drove home.

*

He slumped in his armchair, replaying in his mind's eye the beating and Kemp's reaction to being dumped in the wavy dimension. The violence was counter to his liberal values, and yet he was certain that Kemp deserved it. Anyway, it had been the only option open to him, given that Kemp had the gun. And it wasn't as if he'd actually killed the murderous bastard.

The world was now safer. Redstone was certainly much safer, as were the people around him. He didn't believe that Kate would be resting in any more peace than she already was – her feelings had gone when she died – but her presence in his mind was now at rest.

He could and must now pursue his relationship with Christina. He decided to write to her – write a full, heartfelt letter, laying open his feelings. He knew he could say things in writing which he wouldn't be able to say on the phone. He'd write that if she truly was in a solid new relationship, he wouldn't bother her again, but if she wasn't, he'd do his best to persuade her to resume with him. He got an A4 pad, moved to the kitchen table and wrote rapidly and at length.

SATURDAY 26 NOVEMBER

Redstone sat at his table, rereading the draft letter. He decided to go for a walk to clear his head which, despite the medication he'd taken, felt dull and pressured after an intense migraine during the night. He was heading for the door when the phone rang. It was Christina.

'I… is everything all right?' he asked cautiously.

'I don't know. My mind's in a turmoil. I've got loads of conflicting thoughts and emotions.' She cleared her throat. 'I think you said you had a plan for how our relationship might work.'

'Yes, I do. I… would you like to hear it?'

'Yes please.'

'Well, our previous thoughts were about how to fit our relationship into the lives we already lead. But I now realise that's the wrong way round. For me, anyway. My relationship with you is top priority. I need to alter the rest of my life so I can be with you.'

'What do you mean?'

He explained that he would divide his time between Kristiansheim and London. He understood her difficulty in being away from home, but he wondered if she'd feel able also to spend at least some time in London if they found a new house there together.

There was silence, and then she said, 'I need to think about it.'

'How much time you'd spend here would be up to you.'

'I still need to think about it.'

'Is it your new relationship?'

'Well, not… anyway, that's… only just started…'

'I've just written you a long letter saying… well, how much I love you and setting out the plan. I was going to post it when the

Post Office opens on Monday because I haven't got the right stamp. I didn't think an email would be appropriate.'

'How sweet! But perhaps you could read it to me instead?'

'Of course – just a minute.' He tore open the envelope and read out the letter.

After he had finished, there was a long silence. Redstone panicked – had he gone too far? Had he made a total fool of himself and embarrassed Christina? But finally, he heard her sniff and say, 'Oh, Mark, that's fabulous! You must have spent ages writing it. And you say such lovely things. If only…' She paused. 'Er, while I'm thinking, how's your project going? Is Lesage still involved?'

'No, it's pretty well completed, and Lesage is certainly finished. He's in a jail in central America somewhere, waiting to be extradited.'

Her voice perked up. 'Oh, what marvellous news! Well done!'

'But what about you and me?'

'Yes! Let's give it a try.'

'Fantastic! Any chance of your coming over to London in the next day or two? I'll be away from London on Monday, but I've got a big event on Tuesday, and I'd love you to accompany me. The prime minister will be delivering the speech I wrote.'

'Er…'

'When I was in Kristiansheim, you said you were free this weekend, and I stupidly put you off. I don't know what I was thinking.'

He heard her gulp. 'Yes, I will. I'm… nervous about being away from here, but… I want to go. I'll organise it immediately. I should be able to get to London by tomorrow evening.'

'That's fantastic! Will you be ok here while I go to the Bristol area on Monday?'

'Yes, I can walk about and see where you live. That's fine. Oh – can you please keep that letter for me?'

*

Later that day, looking at his phone, he found a text from Cunningham from the day before: '*Tests ok! See you Monday.*' He breathed a huge sigh of relief. Everything seemed to be falling into place. He had an uneasy feeling that it was all too good to be true, but brushed it aside.

He managed to get both twins in a group Skype session and told them about Christina. Sophie was delighted, and Graham was cautiously optimistic.

'And I've got something else to tell you,' Redstone said. 'This job I've been doing for the PM – it's been rather bigger than I was allowed to let on.'

'I don't know why I'm not surprised,' said Graham, 'but tell us more.'

'Well, I am surprised,' said Sophie. 'Are you a spy or something?'

'I… it's about a threat to the UK's electricity supply. A huge threat. If it had got out, there would have been chaos, because if our power supply had collapsed the country would have collapsed too.'

'Christ,' said Graham. 'I can see that. Tell us more.'

'And why you?' asked Sophie. 'I know you once worked on that stuff, but it was years ago. Surely there are better qualified people in the government? I mean I love you, and I know you're wonderful, but…'

He outlined the issue, and told them that he'd been asked to work on it because someone within the government had been colluding with France Nucléaire. He described what he and his colleagues had discovered. The problem was now more or less resolved, so he'd decided to tell Sophie and Graham, even though he probably shouldn't.

Both twins were impressed, and asked lots of questions.

SUNDAY 27 NOVEMBER

Smith rang while he was eating breakfast.

'I thought I'd bring you up to speed on Kemp. TT showed no signs of him in the tunnels at all. It's as though he'd left the normal dimensions!'

'Amazing,' he said. 'How long do you think a man could last in an utterly strange and disorienting environment without water or food?'

'Would that man be injured?'

'Let's speculate that he's got a couple of broken bones and concussion.'

'If the man was injured and – disoriented – on, say, Friday night, it would probably be best if he could be – how shall I put it – brought back pretty soon. I wonder if you'd like a lift from your home to Whitehall, right now. There happens to be a car outside your house as we speak.'

*

Christina emerged from the customs hall wearing a maroon jacket with a high collar, pushing a trolley bearing two large suitcases. Redstone, waiting amongst a group of drivers holding signs bearing people's names, thought she looked better dressed than every other passenger. He admired her for a second, waving and trying to catch her eye while she looked around nervously, and then strode towards her. She broke into a big smile and pushed the trolley towards him. He sidestepped it, pulled her into his arms and held her tight.

'Let's go to the car,' he said. He pushed the trolley out of the terminal and over the covered road into the car park, Christina holding his arm tightly all the way.

They left the airport in the afternoon sunshine. Christina leant back.

'Lovely car,' she said. 'I like the wood and the leather upholstery. Very English!'

'Yes, I treated myself. It drives beautifully. Probably the last expensive thing I'll be able to buy for some time, though – I'll explain later. How's your life been since we spoke just after Saira was killed, and I was so awful to you?'

'It seems like a long time ago, doesn't it? But it's only three weeks. Anyway, I wouldn't say that you were awful. As I said at the time, I could put myself in your position. But I was very upset.'

'I'm so sorry.'

'My friends could see that something had gone wrong, so I told them about it. They were kind and caring.'

Redstone waited for her to say more, but when she didn't, he said, 'Was one of these a man friend? The one you mentioned on the phone?'

'Yes. You know him – Peter Grieg.'

'I thought he was married?'

'He is, but only in name. He and his wife have been living separate lives for a couple of years now. They stay together only for the sake of Peter's public appearances as a minister.'

'I genuinely liked him when I met him,' said Redstone. 'I suppose I shouldn't, now.'

'No need,' she said and touched his shoulder. 'He's a kind and thoughtful man, but it's you I… I just couldn't get you out of my mind.'

He glanced at her happily. 'How's Ingrid reacted to your coming here?'

She paused. 'Mark, I need to tell you something. I would have… there was a reason why I kept away, despite… Well, what happened was that Lesage phoned me and threatened Ingrid, if I didn't…'

Redstone felt a flood of anger. 'What! The vicious bastard. What did he want? Was it… sex?'

'No, no. He wanted me to feed him information about what you were doing in your work for the prime minister. I assume you were doing something a bit more than just writing a speech. He'd found out that you and I had… become involved. I told him we'd broken it off, so he was out of luck. He said he didn't believe me and had ways of checking whether I was telling the truth. So I had to keep away from you. I'm deeply sorry.'

'God, how evil can a man get? Did you tell the police?'

'No. His threats were too subtle – just implied. He was careful. Anyway, I had no evidence. And what could they have done? Maybe I should have, but frankly, I was too scared that he'd get to Ingrid somehow.'

'That's how these awful criminals work, isn't it? Anyway, as I said, he's behind bars now, and I've been assured he'll rot in gaol for a long, long time.'

'So now I'm free to follow my feelings,' she said.

'Marvellous! And, back to feelings, how has Ingrid reacted to your coming here?'

'Well, pleased for me, but still a bit worried. I think the fact that I wanted to come has shown her it wasn't just a holiday romance, after all. And you're not a Greek fisherman!'

'Both my kids were pleased when I spoke to them last night. I don't think I told you – Sophie's got a Norwegian boyfriend, so she sees some symmetry there.'

'Oh! Where does he come from?'

'Oslo, I think. Anyway, Sophie can tell you more herself.' He paused while he changed lanes on the motorway. 'And Joanne, my PA, was very happy for me when I phoned her.'

'She's important to you, isn't she? I think she genuinely cares for you.' He nodded. 'That's good. I look forward to meeting her sometime, if… if this works out. Now, tell me what you've been up to.'

'Well, I've actually been doing two jobs for the prime minister, as you guessed. I told you about the speech, and it's great that you can come with me to Dymbury on Tuesday when he delivers it. But there was also a project which was highly confidential. To cut a long story short, there was an awful threat to the UK's electricity supply, and I was helping to sort it out.'

She nodded. 'Tell me more.'

'You were right about Lesage. He'd got his engineers to pack more fuel into the reactors than was safe, so that the power stations would generate more electricity, which gave him huge bonuses. And he got someone to fiddle the figures which were used to monitor the health of the reactors, so that nobody knew what was happening.'

'Ah! So that's it! I wondered how they managed to produce so much more electricity without damaging the core.'

'They didn't. The fuel assemblies would eventually have got so badly jammed that the reactors would have been out of action for years before they could be refuelled. We would have run out of electricity. It would have been catastrophic.'

'So, you discovered it in time?'

'My colleagues did. Fortunately, the problem can be fixed. I'm going to West Avon tomorrow to see the fix working on the first of the reactors. At least, that's what I've been promised!'

*

He ushered her through his front door. The cat stood in the hall and gave a meow.

'Allow me to introduce you. Christina – Treacle, Treacle – Christina.'

'Hello, darling,' said Christina, and squatted to stroke the cat, who started to purr.

*

Redstone Skyped the twins. A sunlit palm tree was visible through a window behind Graham, while Sophie was sitting in an untidy bedroom. He introduced Christina.

'Lovely to meet you at last,' said Sophie enthusiastically. 'How are you finding London?'

'Yes, good to see you,' added Graham. 'I hope... well, London must be vastly different from what you're used to. Let alone having to put up with Dad!'

'Oh, he's not so bad,' smiled Christina. 'Wonderful to meet both of you. I've only just arrived, but I'm sure Mark will help me grow to love this amazing city. And so will Treacle.'

The three of them chatted for a few minutes, and then Redstone took over from Christina.

'I've got something to tell you about Mum's killer.' He paused and swallowed. 'He's been arrested at last, and the police are confident they've got enough evidence to put him in jail for life.'

Sophie started crying, and Graham choked back tears. Redstone found himself on the verge of crying, telling himself that it was because he felt fragile after the migraine he'd experienced a few hours earlier and the emotion of seeing Christina again.

Christina took over, saying comforting words about the end of a saga. 'Let's close this session, and Skype again tomorrow after you've had time to digest what's happened. I'd like it if you could tell me stories about your mum.'

MONDAY 28 NOVEMBER

The control room at West Avon was crowded. McKay and Redstone stood next to Smith, whose arm was no longer in a sling. Dupont sat in a corner with an MI5 minder. France Nucléaire's new UK chief executive, an engineer with a Northern Irish accent, stood next to Cunningham at the front under a big screen. Some France Nucléaire staff sat at the control desks while others stood at the back of the room. Everyone present now knew about the fraudulent readings and the jammed fuel assemblies.

Redstone's thoughts went to Christina. It had been wonderful to spend the evening, night and breakfast with her. Christina's tactful and open recognition that Kate had a residual presence in the house had dispelled his remaining feelings of disloyalty to Kate. He knew Christina was struggling with her phobia of being away from home, and hoped she was ok on her own. She'd seemed to be coping when he'd spoken to her from the train.

But at the back of his mind… he pushed the destructive thought away.

He turned his attention to the big screen. It showed a video display of the floor of the reactor hall, which Redstone had visited four weeks previously. On that occasion, the central part of the floor had been empty, apart from a number of metal protuberances connected to the fuel assemblies under the floor. Now, the floor was dotted with large, squat, black metal cylinders, which were clamped to the protuberances. A web of thick cables led from the cylinders to a cabinet at the edge of the hall.

Cunningham wiped his brow, and clapped his hands to get everyone's attention.

'What you see here, ladies and gentlemen, is an array of what are essentially industrial loudspeakers. They're clamped to the tops of the fuel assemblies, which are jammed, as you know.'

People turned to look at Dupont, who stared straight ahead.

Cunningham continued. 'My plan is to produce a set of vibrations which will shake the fuel assemblies until everything is unjammed. This will happen only if we get the right resonant frequencies, which is why I chose my set of vibrations very carefully. It's all controlled from my laptop, here.'

He paused and pressed a few keys on the laptop.

'You now see on the big screen a set of numbers showing the positions of the control rods. The *real* positions.'

People studiously avoided looking at Dupont.

'You'll have noticed that they're all red. The motors connected to the control rods are pulling on the tops of the rods, but the resistance is too strong because of the jamming, and so nothing's happening. Of course, the reactor's still generating power, though the quantity's now declining because the fuel's becoming exhausted.' He looked around, and people nodded. 'The company needs to refuel the reactor, but it can't because of the jamming. Unless we can unjam everything, the company will be faced with dismantling a highly radioactive nuclear core, which is a hugely expensive and time-consuming operation. It'll take years, and during that period, we won't be getting any electricity from West Avon. And the same story will be repeated around the country. And you all know what that will mean for millions of people's livelihoods and indeed lives.'

Dupont bowed his head and covered his face with his hands. The CEO cleared his throat and asked Cunningham to continue.

'So, we all hope this will work. If it does, the other power stations will carry out the same procedure.' Some of the company staff nodded. 'I must tell you now that I'm not one hundred per cent sure it'll succeed. We've done tests, but there's still a possibility that the jamming has gone too far. I'm afraid there's only one way to find out.'

'When I start the procedure, I'll gradually increase the amplitude of the specially chosen vibrations. The sound will become so loud that you'll hear it clearly in here. It'll get very loud. There are ear defenders in that box being passed around – please use them before it becomes unbearable. Now the important bit. If it works, you'll see those numbers decreasing, and as they do, they'll change from red to amber and then green. Any questions?'

Nobody spoke.

'Ok. I'll start.' He sat in front of his laptop and pressed a few keys. 'I've started. Everything seems to be working, so I'll now gradually increase the amplitude of the vibrations.'

Nothing changed on the screen. Someone said, 'I can hear a faint sound.'

Smith whispered to Redstone, 'I can hear something too. It's bizarre. It sounds like music.'

'Yes, I can hear it now,' whispered Redstone. 'It is music. But I can't quite make out the tune.'

Suddenly, the volume passed a threshold, and everyone could hear it. Someone started laughing.

'It's *Jerusalem*!' said Redstone. He looked at Cunningham, who was clasping his hands tightly but also grinning.

'Keep listening!' he called to Redstone.

The music got louder and louder. They heard some recorded cheering, and then the music changed to *Land of Hope and Glory*.

'It's the last night of the Proms!' someone called out.

'Look!' said Smith. 'The numbers are changing!' Some of the numbers on the screen started to decrease. Their colour changed from red to amber. A cheer went around the room. Cunningham mopped his face with a red handkerchief.

The music got louder and louder. Other numbers started to decrease. People started putting on their ear defenders. The tune ended, and as the recorded cheering died away, the orchestra started playing *Rule Britannia*, and then a strong female voice led the recorded audience singing the words. The music and the atmosphere in the room released something inside Redstone, who found himself choking with emotion, tears running down his face. He reluctantly donned ear defenders, as did the others who hadn't already done so. He could feel the vibrations in his body. All the numbers were now green. Redstone cheered, but he couldn't even hear himself.

The numbers stopped changing, and the music ended. Everyone in the room took off their ear defenders and clapped Cunningham for minutes, shouting and cheering. Cunningham smiled, waved and walked over to McKay, Redstone and Smith.

'What a relief!' he said.

'Altogether inspired!' said Redstone. 'You're a genius! Even Laura was cheering!'

'Why shouldn't I have cheered?' demanded Smith. 'Alan deserved every cheer he got. It's one thing solving the problem, but to do it with such style – wow!'

'You can see that the technicians and engineers have already started work,' said Cunningham, gesturing to the seats in front of the control panels. 'It won't be long before France Nucléaire has come up with a plan to phase the refuelling over the country while the new reactors come on stream, so that overall, we continue to get all the electricity we need.' He stretched. 'To be honest, France Nucléaire has several engineers who would have come up with the solution you've just seen – though they probably would have used white noise generators rather than the Prom! If Lesage hadn't been the haughty secretive idiot he manifestly was, he could have used his own staff to solve the problem.'

'Haughty secretive vicious criminal idiot,' said Redstone. 'We scientists like accuracy.'

Dupont and his minder came up to them.

'I just wanted to congratulate you, thank you, and say how sorry I am to have misled you and to have helped that evil Lesage,' Dupont said, with a good accent. 'I know I'll face trial, and I'm going to plead guilty. I deserve whatever I get, but may I shake your hand?'

'Of course,' said Cunningham. 'None of us knows what we'd do if life took us in a different direction. I wish you the best of luck.'

'Me too,' said Redstone, 'though I don't suppose you know who I am. I'm the guy Lesage tried to get killed. I know you weren't involved in that. Anyway, good luck! And thanks for the warning email.'

Dupont looked shocked and bowed his head. He recovered, apologised again and was led away.

'Are you going to the Dymbury opening and the PM's speech tomorrow?' Redstone asked the other three.

'Of course,' said Cunningham.

'Looking forward to it.' McKay nodded.

'Laura?'

'Yes, I'll be there,' she said. 'I've spent far too much time watching you put the speech together to miss its delivery.'

'Excellent,' said Redstone. 'Before you go, can I have a private word?' He took her aside. 'This is a bit embarrassing, but I feel I've got to ask you something – er – awkward.'

'Go on.'

'It's about Christina. We're together again, and she's currently staying with me. But something's been nagging at me, and I can't get it out of my mind.'

'I can't offer you relationship guidance, if that's what you're asking. Not my scene.'

He smiled. 'No, nothing like that. It's that she knows a lot about our nuclear programme and had some dealings with Lesage a few years ago. In connection with Norway's energy policy. And… more contact recently. Is it just a coincidence? Is she…?'

'Are you asking me if we've checked her out? If she's kosher?'

'Er… well…. In fact… yes.'

'I can't tell you.'

His shoulders slumped. She put her hand on his arm. 'I mean we don't know,' she said. 'Counter-espionage isn't an exact science. It might be just a matter of definition – what's the difference between an analyst and an agent?'

'Well…'

'She might be just what she says she is. Coincidences happen. Or she might not. But why should you care?'

'Because I want to know if I can trust her, of course. If she's got secrets.'

'Those are two different things. You're keeping a huge secret from her, I hope – the dimension-hopping stuff. Your biggest secret ever.'

He nodded.

'There you are. We all have secrets. Nobody reveals everything, even to their closest loved ones. Doesn't mean we can't trust each other.'

'I suppose you're right.'

'Anyway, you've finished doing sensitive stuff for Her Majesty's Government, so it doesn't matter. Just relax and enjoy.'

'Ok. I'll try. Oh, and how's Kemp? Last time I saw him, he was raving about a distorted world.'

'I gather he's been convinced he had an unusual form of concussion. Anyway, who cares?'

*

Redstone walked into the hall of his house and embraced Christina. They clung to each other for a minute, and he felt his tension drain away. The cat rubbed herself against his legs.

'How have you been settling in?' he asked.

'I had a bad patch here without you. It's so different from Kristiansheim. I was longing for home. Anyway, I got a grip on myself. It's extremely comfortable here and so convenient. I went up the road, only a few hundred metres, and I could buy everything I needed in the grocery and the chemist's shop. And I had my hair done.'

'Oh, I'm so sorry – I should have noticed. It looks great.'

Christina gave the cat an amused glance and turned back to Redstone. 'And how was your day?'

TUESDAY 29 NOVEMBER

As the applause died down, a group of reporters crowded around the prime minister in the huge marquee which had been erected next to Dymbury power station. The inside of the vast tented structure was festooned with strings of Tricolores and Union Jacks, interspersed with France Nucléaire's logo. McKay and Smith stood to one side, engaged in deep discussion. Cunningham was among a large group of engineers. Redstone stood with Christina at the back of the marquee.

Sir Roger Feast approached them and greeted Christina politely. He turned to Redstone. 'Well done, Mark – superb speech. The prime minister would like you and your friend to join him and his wife, if you would.'

They made their way through the chattering knots of people to the front of the marquee.

'Hello, Mark,' said Anne Jones. 'Excellent speech, and he,' – she nodded at her husband – 'didn't do a bad job of delivering it!'

The PM smiled. 'Please introduce us!'

Redstone made the introductions and explained that Christina was the friend he'd mentioned at Chequers.

'Pity you couldn't have come too,' said the PM. 'But there's an obvious solution to that – I'll get my office to give Mark another invitation, addressed to you both.'

'Oh,' said Christina, looking nervous and flustered, 'that's truly kind, but we're only… I won't be spending a lot of time in the UK.'

'I'm sure we can work something out,' said Anne.

A waiter came up, and the PM took a couple of canapés. 'Have you tried these?' he asked. 'They're absolutely delicious. Trust the French!'

Redstone raised an eyebrow. 'That's not exactly what I was thinking last time I was in a nuclear power station,' he said.

'Ah. Good point. Sorry. While we've got a moment, thanks again for what you've done. Pity the full story can never be told.' An aide approached, and the prime minister and Anne were ushered away to meet other people.

Smith came over, and Redstone introduced her to Christina. The two women launched into a friendly conversation and soon started discussing Redstone.

He interrupted them. 'I am here, you know.'

'Oh, go and talk to Treacle,' said Smith.

AUTHOR'S NOTE

This book is fiction. The main nuclear technical plot element cannot happen, and none of the characters exists.

ACKNOWLEDGEMENTS

While writing and developing this novel, I benefited tremendously from comments and suggestions given by relatives (especially Viv, Susan and Ruth), friends, acquaintances and friends of friends. They kindly read drafts and gave me many ideas and much encouragement. Some went much further than I could reasonably have expected, giving me detailed, insightful advice.

Many thanks to you all.

Thanks also to Scott Pack, whose professional advice was invaluable, and to Miranda Summers-Pritchard, whose creative editing resulted in the professionally presented work I hope you have just enjoyed.

EGF
May 2020

ABOUT THE AUTHOR

Elliot Finer's career has included scientific research in industry, policy work in the Department of Energy, and a spell in the Cabinet Office. He has published many scientific articles. His only previous fiction is (unpublished) stories for his sons and their friends when they were young.

Elliot and his wife live in London.

Printed in Great Britain
by Amazon

44042093R00199